CROSS FIRE

FONDA LEE

FIRE

SCHOLASTIC INC.

ISBN 978-1-338-30011-6

10 9 8 7 6 5 4 3 2 1   18 19 20 21 22

Printed in the U.S.A.   40
First printing 2018

Book design by Phil Falco & Mary Claire Cruz

Still for my parents

The face was one that Donovan would recognize anywhere. Curly black hair, stubbled jaw, dark eyes emanating a feral shrewdness. Surrounded by his fellow soldiers-in-erze, Donovan managed not to flinch, but even in the safety of the well-lit briefing room, his chest tightened in remembered pain, and his gut jerked in a spasm of loathing.

"Kevin Warde, one of West America's most notorious Sapience operatives," Commander Tate said, jabbing one arm of her wire-framed reading glasses toward the photograph on the wall screen with nearly as much hostility as Donovan felt. "Taking out Warde is tonight's primary mission objective. Intel is citing an eighty-five percent chance that he's inside the Sapience safe house we've pin-pointed in suburban Denver."

Donovan sensed Jet's quick glance in his direction, but he didn't turn; he kept his eyes on Commander Tate and the screen at the front of the room, maintaining an outward appearance of pro-fessional calm befitting an officer of the Global Security and Pacification Forces. Everyone on the mission's eight-person strike team knew that Donovan had a personal score to settle by bring-ing Kevin Warde to justice, and that he had specifically requested Commander Tate allow him to be part of tonight's raid. After his instances of out-of-erze behavior last year, he was fortunate to have been returned to active duty at all; he needed his fellow stripes to know that they could count on him to remain cool at all times.

"Ma'am, is this a kill mission?" Leonides Hsu's quiet, perfectly untroubled voice was at striking odds with the grim nature of his question.

"Your objective is to eliminate Warde as a threat to public safety and the peace of the Accord," Tate answered. "If he walks out the front door unarmed with his hands over his head, you will detain him. Based on everything we know about the man, I'd say that's not likely."

"In other words, don't strain yourself thinking about it too hard when the time comes." Cassidy Spencer grinned and nudged her partner with an elbow. The protective sleeve covering her right arm was decorated with pink skulls and crossbones. If Leon was an ice cube, Cass was hot sauce.

Thaddeus Lowell, their team leader, was studying aerial photographs of the terrorist safe house on a smaller screen, rotating the image and zooming in on it from numerous directions, no doubt going over every detail of the operation in his mind. The property they would be storming was far too close to other residences for SecPac to simply bomb it. Sapience operatives were good at hiding among sympathizers in the general population. There were three buildings in the photograph, labeled A, B, and C: one large main residence, a guest house, and a small outbuilding—perhaps a shed or a garage. Thad tapped Building B thoughtfully. "Commander, are we expecting noncombatants to be a factor?"

According to city records, the property was listed as a bed-and-breakfast. Months of SecPac surveillance had concluded that the people who frequented the Jefferson Chalet were guests of the criminal insurgent variety. Commander Tate said, "We're having the local police clear the area minutes before we arrive, so there won't be time for sympathetic neighbors to tip off the sapes in the compound. It's possible there will be civilians in the area, but we're doing our best to make sure that's not the case. Assume the people you encounter on the property are armed, fanatical, and dangerous." Tate swiped the wall screen. "Here are a few reminders of that fact."

The scruffy image of Kevin Warde was replaced with a photograph of a clean-shaven, smiling man in his thirties, wearing a basketball jersey and holding a beer. He appeared to be at a barbecue or social gathering of some sort. "Jeremiah Cole," Tate said. "An exo builder-in-erze. Abducted on his way home two months ago. His remains were discovered in a warehouse in Boulder a week later; the sapes had harvested his corpse for panotin." Another picture replaced Cole's; this one depicted a professional-looking, middle-aged man in a polo shirt. "Alexander Reveno, a married, forty-five-year-old engineer-in-erze with two children. Snatched from a parking lot in Spokane. A video began circulating on the Sapience network three days later, showing Reveno reading from a script 'confessing' his treason and blaming the government for Hardening him into an exo. He was executed on screen. His body still hasn't been found."

The mood in the briefing room had been confident and eager, but Commander Tate's grim words sobered everyone quickly. The faces of the innocent victims on the screen were reminders that the extremists hated exos as much as they hated the zhree, that they viewed anyone with exocellular biotechnology in their bodies as part of the cooperationist government and a despised symbol of alien rule over Earth. Donovan sat straight and tried to swallow, but a vivid image—a dilating circle of black, the muzzle of a gun filling his vision in an elongating moment of terror—crept into his mind and stole the moisture from his mouth.

It could have been me. It nearly had been. He would've been murdered as one of Kevin Warde's publicity stunts, his body stripped of panotin—the material that made up his exocel—so it could be sewn into combat vests worn by the terrorists. The only reason he'd survived capture last year was because he was the son of the Prime Liaison and had had special worth as a hostage.

Donovan glanced around the briefing room. It was next to Commander Tate's office in the main Comm Hub building of SecPac Central Command and was much smaller than the hall where she usually addressed larger gatherings of officers. The eight exos present—Donovan and Jet, Cass and Leon, Thad and Vic, Tennyson and Lucius—barely fit around the narrow table. The small space felt suddenly claustrophobic to Donovan; he clenched his hands. Maybe Jet was right. Maybe he should be sitting this one out.

On the skimmercar drive over, Jet had drummed his fingers on the dashboard, staring pensively out the window but glancing sideways at Donovan every couple of minutes.

"If you've got something to say, just say it," Donovan said at last.

Jet let out a harsh breath and faced him. "I still don't think this is a good idea. We could've asked Commander Tate for some other assignment." He averted his gaze again. "Look. To be fair, you seem like you're . . . doing better. Still, it's only been seven months. Why risk running into those same sapes? Why put yourself through that?"

Donovan was silent. Jet's concern was reasonable, but defensiveness rose anyway, warming Donovan's face and sending his armor crawling over his shoulders. This past winter, his partner had seen him on some bad days, sunk into apathy or despair or self-loathing, agitated or irritable or simply numb, managing remarkably to always keep it together when on duty but sometimes collapsing, barely functional, at the end of shifts. More than once Jet had shaken him awake from nightmares, or driven him to see Nurse Therrid, or preemptively done all their usual SecPac report writing and paperwork so Donovan didn't have to.

"Besides," Jet went on, filling the uncomfortable quiet, "don't you have to prepare for your meeting in a couple of days? You're an acting adviser to the zhree zun. Isn't that a more important thing for you to be doing right now? Let the rest of us handle these sapes."

Donovan chewed the inside of his cheek but didn't look at his best friend. Commander Tate had already given him the option of an extended leave of absence months ago, but he'd refused. The explanation he'd wanted to give Jet in the car was the same one he gave himself now, staring at the tragic photographs of Sapience's recent victims. He wanted to make it up to his partner and his fellow stripes and put his lapses behind him. He wanted—*needed*—to feel normal again, to believe that even after everything that had happened last year—his capture and imprisonment by rebels, his mother's execution, his father's assassination—he could still do his job, could still accomplish some good in his life as a soldier-in-erze. Putting away a serial murderer like Kevin Warde would certainly be doing the world a favor.

Donovan hadn't felt like discussing his psychological health in the car shortly before a critical mission. "I don't want any free

passes, Jet. This raid is a SecPac priority. We ought to be on it."
More quietly, "Besides, it's too late to change our minds now."

Commander Tate swiped the screen again, bringing up a further set of six photographs. "Warde may be the most wanted man in West America, but he's not acting alone. These are some of the other Sapience operatives we suspect might be in the compound tonight."

Donovan recognized two of the faces on screen right away. Javid, with dark skin and startlingly light, hate-filled eyes, had tried to kill him—twice. Donovan wasn't familiar with the next four sapes, but the final photograph was of a man he had met before. The memory of that encounter made him cringe. Dr. Nakada was younger in this picture, with a full head of black hair and softer features.

"Eugene Nakada," Commander Tate said after she'd briefed them on each of the other suspects and had reached the last photograph. "Nakada is a former scientist-in-erze who turned traitor four years ago and is now working for the enemy. Sapience takes extra pains to keep his whereabouts well guarded; there's only a thirty percent chance he's in the Denver compound, but if you get a visual on him tonight, capturing or killing Nakada is the second-highest priority after Warde himself."

"Why are we so interested in this one scientist?" Vic asked.

"Nakada may have sensitive information and expertise that would make him more of a potential threat than all those other sapes put together." Tate scrolled around on the screen and brought up yet another photograph, this time of a man in a buttoned-down navy-blue shirt and white lab coat, sporting bristly gray eyebrows over warm brown eyes. "Six weeks ago, a prominent scientist-in-erze was assassinated: Dr. Vincent Ghosh, one of the world's foremost experts on exo physiology. Ghosh was one of the few humans to work closely with zhree Scientists and Nurses to conduct important multigenerational studies on how exocellular technology affects human biology—aging, digestion, reproduction, all of that. He was shot dead on his way out of his office in San Mateo. The murderers ransacked his lab and stole his medical research."

Donovan studied Ghosh's photo. He'd been trained to pay attention to and remember faces, and he thought he might have encountered the unfortunate scientist before. At some event with his father, maybe? The Prime Liaison met all sorts of important people.

"Why would the sapes want to steal medical research?" Tennyson's large frame was slouched in his chair; he looked impatient to get going already.

"Isn't it obvious?" Jet growled. "They want to figure out how to better kill us."

"The terrorists who stole Dr. Ghosh's research may have handed it over to Nakada. As Officer Mathews pointed out, they'll want him to develop a way of defeating exocels." Tate smacked her folded glasses against her palm. "Even the *possibility* of that danger means Nakada has to be eliminated."

All the exos in the room were solemn now. Commander Tate leaned stiff arms against the table. Donovan noticed her armor layering across tense fingers, the pattern of broken black stripes—the same Soldier erze markings all of them wore—stretched taut across the backs of her brown hands. The past year had taken a toll on the commander. She still possessed the toned build and sharply authoritative energy Donovan had always known her for, but there were lines worn between her nose and mouth and the dense curls of her short hair had gone almost completely gray. She fixed the younger exos with a grave stare. "Make no mistake, stripes—these are bad people, as bad as they come. Warde and those like him are part of a growing faction of Sapience that advocates even more extreme tactics and violence to achieve their aims." She straightened back up to her full impressive height. "Any final questions?"

Donovan let out a silent breath of relief. The mission briefing was over, and Anya's face had not made an appearance on the wall screen. That meant she wasn't with Kevin right now. She wouldn't be in danger from SecPac, at least not tonight. Some of Donovan's anxiety evaporated, loosening the tension in his back; he felt suddenly lighter, eager to get to work.

Tennyson too was impatient, jiggling one of his knees up and down. His partner, Lucius, was munching on a protein bar—the briefing had cut into dinnertime—but he looked nearly as nonchalant as Leon; at the age of twenty-six, he was the oldest one on the team and had seen plenty of combat before. Jet, who would normally be upbeat and ready to go, was still a little subdued; Cass flicked a paper clip at him, trying to perk him up. Vic was studying the faces of the terrorists on the screen behind Tate, the fingers of one hand combing distractedly through her colorless short blond hair. She glanced at Jet, then Donovan, and a shadow of worry passed over her face, as if she'd guessed at the conversation that the two of them had had in the car.

Had she sensed Donovan's relief at the end of the briefing? What if Anya's face *had* been on the screen? Donovan tried to ignore the doubts that squirmed into his brain, but they persisted, draining some of the strength from his renewed confidence. Could he remain one-hundred-percent dependable to his erze mates if he might have to hurt Anya? Could he still do his job then? Thank erze he wasn't facing that choice today, but what if he did another day?

Donovan firmed his jaw and forced the unhelpful thoughts from his mind.

Thad looked up and down the table at his assembled strike team and answered Commander Tate with his usual confident, laid-back drawl. "We're ready to go, ma'am."

"You leave at twenty-two hundred."

2

They had three hours to get ready—enough time to grab a meal in the cafeteria of the officers' common hall, take a short nap if needed, gather equipment, and perform weapons checks. There wasn't a lot of talk at dinner. Everyone concentrated on eating, no matter if they were hungry or not; they knew they'd need the energy. Afterward, in the locker room, Donovan changed out of his patrol uniform and shrugged on a SecPac tactical vest. Lightweight and snug, it had plenty of pockets to carry gear and extra magazines but left his arms uncovered so he could use his battle armor freely.

Jet pulled his E201 electripulse rifle onto his shoulder, checking the laser sight. "It's too bad Saul Strong Winter's face wasn't on the screen today." Jet seated a round, inspected the chamber, and made sure the coil charger was safely disengaged before setting it down and doing the same with his 9mm sidearm. "If we could nab him tonight too, we'd get most of the sapes we missed last year." Back in October, a hostage standoff at the algae farm had been resolved without bloodshed, thanks to Donovan, but several Sapience insurgents had walked free. Anya had been one of them. So had Saul Strong Winter, the most prominent Sapience leader in West America and the man Donovan held responsible for his father's death. Besides himself.

"Saul wouldn't be with Kevin," Donovan muttered. "That's not his style." Kevin was a maverick and a committed killer; Saul was a calculating rebel commander. "We're not likely to get to him now that he's holed away somewhere and turned himself into a radio personality." Since his escape, the Sapience leader had been broadcasting popular speeches aimed at rousing support for the pro-human independence cause and stirring opposition against the government, the zhree, SecPac, and all Hardened people.

Donovan finished his own equipment checks, attached his SecPac comm unit, and fastened his night vision goggles onto his forehead. On a whim, he took the portable screen from the top shelf of his locker and sat down on one of the room's long metal benches. After a few minutes of tapping and scrolling around on the display, he said, "I knew I'd seen him before."

"Seen who?" Jet asked.

"Dr. Ghosh, the guy who was murdered by sapes." Donovan turned the screen around and held it up to show his partner a news article: "Scientist-in-Erze Honored for Medical Research on the Human Exocellular System." The photograph showed the scientist in a suit and tie, shaking hands with then Prime Liaison Dominick Reyes. "He won a government award of some sort a couple years ago," Donovan said. "My dad hosted him for dinner at our house."

Donovan turned the screen back around. Despite their mutual interest and commitment to human Hardening, neither of the men in the photograph had had a protective exocel of his own. A single bullet had ended each of their lives. In the picture, Donovan's father wore a small, polite smile as he gazed into the camera. His face carried the same serious expression that Donovan remembered so well—a senior statesman projecting competence and authority—but he looked a little more relaxed, less careworn than he'd been shortly before his death.

Donovan shut the screen back inside his locker. At least it was easy to find photos of his father. His mother, on the other hand . . . he had no pictures of her.

When he and Jet were back in the hallway, a voice called out to them from behind. "Officer Reyes." Donovan turned. It took him a few seconds to recognize the approaching man. He took a stunned step backward, his exocel layering involuntarily. "*Brett*?"

Brett—Kevin Warde's sycophantic sidekick, the Sapience lackey who'd filmed Donovan's torture and driven him to the Warren in the Black Hills where he'd been held captive—was *here*. On SecPac property.

Donovan's hand jerked toward his holstered sidearm. Brett came to an abrupt halt, as if realizing it had been a mistake to approach Donovan while he was heavily armed. Startled by his partner's sudden reaction, Jet took two steps forward, exocel bristling defensively.

Brett raised his open hands; they shook slightly. "Please . . . someone told me I could find you here. I know about the mission tonight. I was on the intelligence team that made the call."

Only then did Donovan remember that "Brett" wasn't real. The sape he knew had been a cover identity. This man was an undercover SecPac agent, responsible for last year's destruction of the Warren and for Donovan being rescued in one piece. Now that Donovan studied the person in front of him more closely, it seemed plain that he was not Brett the terrorist stooge. His hair was cut shorter and he had a slight growth of beard, but those were not the changes that made Donovan stare. Gone was the Sapience recruit with the dimly worshipful grin, the bland expression, the quick, slightly twitchy subservience. In his place was an unsmiling, nondescript man with dark civilian clothes and vaguely haunted eyes.

With effort, Donovan dropped his hand from his pistol grip and forced his armor down to a more trusting level. It was still hard to shake his visceral distrust. "Why are you here, Brett?"

The man flinched at Donovan's tone. "My name's not really Brett. There was a person named Brett Sullivan who died years ago. They gave me his identity when I went undercover. My real name is Jonathan Resnick." Even his voice sounded different; slower. He cleared his throat hesitantly. "I . . . wanted to wish you good luck tonight."

Jet's gaze flicked between the two men. "You're the agent who was passing us intel from inside Sapience last year." Jet straightened as comprehension dawned on his face. He brought his armor down and stepped forward, extending his hand. "Thank you for saving my partner's life."

Brett/Jonathan looked taken aback by Jet's gesture. He shook the proffered hand wordlessly. Donovan, no less stunned, saw that the backs of the agent's hands were banded with markings, dark as wet ink. Erze almighty, Brett really was a fellow stripe.

Donovan couldn't quite bring himself to follow his partner's lead. His mind kept flicking between his memory of Brett and the not-Brett in front of him. It was like looking at one of those picture puzzles of two images with small dissimilarities. *Can You Spot the 5 Differences*?

"Could I . . ." Jonathan said, turning to Donovan, "talk to you alone for a minute?"

When Donovan failed to answer right away, Jet said, "You can talk to both of us, if you want to talk." His armor stayed at a friendly level, but his tone brooked no argument.

Jonathan's throat moved in a swallow and he nodded. "I realize it's been a while, and you probably don't want to see me. But I finally got the papers retiring me from undercover work. SecPac's moving me to a new identity. I'll have proper erze status and a nice, quiet desk job, I hope." The agent rubbed the back of one of his hands nervously, as if he was still unused to the markings. "I spent two years of my life being someone else, and now I'm not that person anymore. I wake up in the morning and I'm not sure who the hell I am."

The man's bitterly glum tone gave Donovan pause. Self-doubt was something he understood. "At least you're done with all that now," he said, his voice softening a fraction.

Jonathan raised his eyes to Donovan in sudden pleading. "Please, you have to understand: My mission was to infiltrate Sapience's main base of operations and get to their senior leadership. SecPac was committed to cracking the cell; my orders were to not compromise my position for anything, not even to save lives. My cover identity had to be airtight. I couldn't make one misstep anywhere, or they'd kill me. Kevin would kill me."

Sweat began breaking out on Jonathan's brow as his words came faster. "Kevin was a paranoid bastard. He was also a damn good operative, and he was . . . noble in a way, generous to anyone who needed help. But he made me do things, to prove that I was really one of them. He made me film those videos. And I did it, I did whatever he told me to. We—"

Jet cut him off. "That's enough."

"Why are you telling us this?" Donovan demanded, his voice abnormally high and coarse.

Jonathan looked frantic. "I want you to know that I'm not him. I'm not that person." He took a halting step toward Donovan, who backed up involuntarily. "SecPac still needs unmarked operatives, you know. People who can blend in, who can do what exos can't. But I'm *not* Brett."

Jet took a firm step toward the man. "I'll always be grateful to you. But you should go."

Though his exocel was thickening uneasily up his arms, Donovan put a hand on Jet's shoulder and drew his partner back. "Look . . . Jonathan . . . I get what you had to do. I don't think I can accept it, but I get it. You had orders and you had to follow them. No matter how terrible they were or how much you didn't want to." Tamping down his screaming discomfort, he stepped past his partner and offered his hand. "I know you deserve your stripes— probably more than I do. You saved my life. And a lot of other lives, with what you did."

Jonathan's face loosened a little, not all the way down to Brett's usual slackness, but to something less tormented. Weakly, "You're the only one I could say this to. The only one who could understand. I can't escape the ghosts I've created, but maybe I can quiet them." He clasped Donovan's hand tightly and shook it. "Please . . . catch him for me tonight."

3

A biting springtime wind was racing across the fully dark sky as Jet and Donovan jogged toward the T15 stealthcopter waiting on the tarmac across the road from SecPac's main buildings and campus training fields.

"There's something seriously messed up about that guy." Jet still sounded agitated. "He had some nerve coming up to you. Erze almighty, that was the *last* thing you needed right now."

Donovan slowed, then stopped, causing his partner to do the same. "After the things he's been through, you can't blame him for needing closure. Jonathan Resnick's been working to bring down Warde longer than we have. I get why he felt like he had to be here tonight."

Jet blew out a resigned breath and came back toward his partner. "You made your point back in the car. I trust you, all right? We're doing it. We're going to end this." He gave Donovan a firm clap on the back, his usual grin only partly forced.

Donovan nodded, and they ran together the rest of the way. Support crew were making final checks on the stealthcopter. "Load up!" Thad shouted over the wind and the rising whine of the spooling micro-fission engines. "Where's Vic?" he asked, shooting Jet a teasing smirk.

"Not with me." Jet spread his hands in a gesture of innocence. "She's your partner, Lowell."

"She's over there," Donovan said, as Vic hurried up and joined them at the T15. Cass, Leon, Lucius, and Tennyson were already taking their places inside.

"No hanky-panky in there, you two." Thad smacked Jet on the shoulder. "I know it'll be dark and cozy inside, but just remember we've all got state-of-the-art night vision tech."

Jet flipped Thad the middle finger as he climbed through the cabin doors of the T15. Vic adjusted the hold on her rifle and paused before following, pursing her full lips in an expression of mock thoughtfulness. "I suppose it would be a breach of protocol if I pushed the mission leader out of a moving stealthcopter?"

"Tate might be pissed—extra paperwork and all," Donovan agreed, though he shot Thad a grin. Jet and Vic always acted entirely soldierly with each other when on the job, never betraying their off-duty relationship. They really ought not to be surprised that their friends took to teasing them mercilessly about their out-of-uniform activities.

Donovan and Thad leapt in after their partners, wedging into the dark, cramped space. As soon as everyone was inside and seated, the doors slammed shut and the stealthcopter rose straight into the air with a deep vibrating thrum, ascending so quickly that Donovan felt, as usual, as if he'd left his stomach on the tarmac. A few seconds later, the T15 slowed its rise and began speeding south. Donovan couldn't see anything in the pitch-black of the cabin, but he knew they were flying out of Round Three and racing, nearly silent, over the sprawling lights of the densely inhabited Ring Belt, which stretched for miles outside the walls of the circular city.

It took less than thirty minutes to reach Denver. Not enough time to zone out or sleep, but just enough time to start feeling overly warm and restless in the tight quarters. Donovan kept his armor at a low, resting state to save energy and concentrated on taking deep, steadying breaths. The encounter with Brett—*dammit*, Jonathan—had shaken him up more than he'd let on with Jet. He was grateful the immediacy of the mission wouldn't give him time to mull. At times like these, when he was forced to focus on impending danger, he felt capable and normal, deeply and reassuringly connected to his fellow stripes. In erze.

"Three minutes." The message from the cockpit piped up in their comm unit earbuds. There was a rustle of tight movement as people shifted, readying themselves. Donovan made sure his E201 was securely attached to the front of his body before opening the stealthcopter door and sliding the fast-roping bar into place. He checked to make sure the ropes were secure, then leaned out slightly. The airstream blasted his face as the streets and buildings of Denver passed underneath the T15. In the distance, the Rocky Mountains loomed, a long stretch of jagged dark mass on the nearly invisible horizon. Much closer, but still appearing like a small model in a diorama, Donovan could see the magnificently lit Capitol Building, surrounded by the artificially lush green lawns of Restoration Park.

Donovan had visited Denver several times. His father had maintained an office in the Capitol and had traveled between it and the Round frequently. Much of this city, the Prime Liaison had explained to him, had been destroyed in the War Era, but after the establishment of the Accord of Peace and Governance, the closest major human city to Round Three had been rebuilt as the capital of West America. There had been disagreement about how much the Capitol Building ought to reflect human versus zhree architectural styles. The final structure was a hybrid—the wings of the building were long and low and fronted with straight white columns, but the central structure rose in a cluster of connected spires like the Towers in the Round. The largest, central one was topped incongruously with a golden dome: a historic relic, hundreds of years old, salvaged from the rubble of the war.

Donovan pulled his gaze away from the cityscape and focused on the tracts of suburb below: houses with yards and fences, shopping centers, office buildings, parking lots, stretches of green space and sparse woodland. On the surface, the capital city was a burgeoning metropolis, a shining testament to human resilience and the proud result of more than a hundred years of peace and partnership. But an ongoing war simmered underneath, as it did everywhere else. Donovan caught sight of their target: a two-story redbrick house behind a high, wrought iron fence. None of the lights were on.

The vibrations of the T15's engines changed as it came to a hover over the property. Donovan tossed one rope down; Vic threw the other. "Go, go, go!" Thad's shout rang double—in the confines of the cabin and in Donovan's earbud. He went to full armor instantly, his exocel knitting the near-impenetrable microscopic lattices that raced from node to node over his body like a second skin. Jet slapped his shoulder, and Donovan grabbed the rope and dropped toward the ground below. The rope whipped between his hands as he descended in a controlled plummet. He caught a whiff of the distinctive smell of scorched panotin—the friction from the rope burning the surface layer of his armored hands. It didn't hurt him, but it didn't smell good.

He hit the lawn almost at full speed, bending his knees as he connected with the ground, his exocel shuddering up his legs and spine in a wave as it absorbed and dissipated the force of the impact.

Donovan flipped his night vision goggles down over his eyes, hefted his E201, and sprinted toward the house, knowing that Jet would be dropping right behind him and on his heels. As he ran, a harsh spotlight beam fell onto the building from the hovering stealthcopter, bathing the roof and curtained windows with stark white light. "This is SecPac!" an amplified voice called down from the T15. "Come out of the house with your hands up!"

Donovan took the three steps up to the front entrance and pressed himself against the wall next to the doorframe. Jet and Cass stacked up next to him. Leon performed a quick check for explosives, then pounded on the door with his armored fist. "SecPac!" Leon's command was loud and harsh, bearing no resemblance to his usual soft voice and calm demeanor. "Open the door and surrender peacefully. No one will get hurt. This is your final warning." No sound or movement from within.

Leon tried the door handle while Cass covered him. It was locked and dead-bolted. Leon clasped a hand over his fist, thickening his armor, then swung his arms down like a sledgehammer. He left a battered knob, but the solid-metal door didn't budge. "Going explosive," he announced, pulling a palm-sized breaching charge from his vest pocket and peeling the backing off the adhesive strip. Leon slapped it to the door, pushed the detonator into place, and retreated to the wall next to Cass. Donovan and Jet backed up several feet. Donovan counted five slow seconds in his head.

The explosion blew the door off its hinges and sprayed shards of wood and metal everywhere. Donovan didn't wait for the debris to clear; bits of shrapnel glanced off his arms and shoulders as he plowed through the smoke-filled opening, breaking right and taking first position in the corner of the room. He felt no fear or anxiety—just a single-minded desire to get the job done. It was a good feeling, easier to handle than a lot of other ones.

He expected to be greeted by enemy gunfire and was mildly surprised when nothing happened. He was in a large sitting room adjoining the entryway. The gritty, monochromatic vision of his night goggles showed him the shapes of furniture and a staircase, and the figures of Jet, Cass, and Leon, who'd flowed into their places right after him and were sweeping field of fire through their rifle sights. No one else moved. No sapes. "A1 breached," Donovan said into his comm unit. "No contact, no shots fired."

"B1 breached," came Vic's voice, sounding slightly concerned. The other four team members were handling the guesthouse and the outbuilding. "No contact here either."

"C building is secure," Lucius said. "Storage. Plenty of supplies."

"So where the hell are the sapes?" Tennyson growled. Donovan wondered the same thing. Were they all hiding? It wasn't like Sapience to give up without a fight. While talk was going on over the comms, he and Jet kept moving, clearing the ground floor room by room. Cass and Leon took the stairs to the second level carefully, wary of ambush. "Hey, Kevin Warde, come out!" Cass called. "How about you, Javid? You cowering up there?"

"Coffee machine still running," Jet murmured as they swept through the kitchen. Donovan checked over a small bedroom. The sheets were unmade; there were clothes strewn at the foot of the bed. People were living here, all right.

"Keep searching," Thad ordered. "B building is now secure. We're headed your way." Donovan heard the low bass thrum of the T15 landing outside the gates of the property.

Cass and Leon met Donovan and Jet back in the foyer. "Basement," Donovan said, and began to descend the stairs to the one area of the house that hadn't been cleared yet. He took a few steps before Leon reached out and grabbed him by the vest, yanking him back so sharply that Donovan nearly fell onto his teammate. Leon's eyes were wide with alarm; he pointed down to the foot of the stairwell. At first Donovan didn't see it. Then he did: strands of nearly invisible fishing line strung across the final stair, attached to wires running along the baseboards and up the walls, connected to bundles of explosives lashed to the basement's support beams.

A cold sweat broke out on Donovan's neck. Leon had saved his life, maybe all their lives. If Donovan's boot had snagged the trip wire, it would have blown up the entire house and caved the basement in on them. Anyone not killed in the explosion would be buried in the rubble. The sapes had been clever: killing exos one at a time was hard. Better to trap them all in a narrow stairwell and drop the entire building on them. With that brutal realization came another: *They knew we were coming.*

"Erze almighty," Jet said, shaken. They retreated up the stairs.

"I could use Lucius over here," Leon said into his comm. Leon and Lucius were the best on the team when it came to explosives. A minute later, the two of them were crouched on the stairs, examining the deadly setup and discussing. After some nodded agreement between them, Lucius calmly bladed his thumb and forefinger and pinched one of the wires, severing it. He cut another wire, snipped the trip line, and stood back up. Raising their rifles again, he and Leon descended into the basement, stepping slowly and staying alert for more booby traps. Cassidy and Tennyson watched their partners anxiously from the top of the stairs.

The lights went on in the basement. Donovan flipped up his night vision goggles to cut the oversaturated glare. "All clear." Leon paused. "We found something. Something bad."

Donovan followed Cass and Tennyson cautiously into the basement. A wave of nauseating déjà vu rolled over him as soon as he entered. They were in a cramped makeshift laboratory, and he knew immediately who it had belonged to. Much like Dr. Eugene Nakada's previous hideout in Rapid City, the walls of this room were lined with mobile cabinets and shelving units. Except for a few murky specimen jars and trays, the shelves were empty, as if they'd been cleared off in a hurry.

In the center of the room was a metal table occupied by a motionless human form. A man, naked, clearly dead.

Jet breathed out in a hiss. "It's that guy—Reveno."

Alexander Reveno—one of the victims Tate had mentioned in the briefing, the one whose body hadn't been found. Until now. Reluctantly, Donovan approached the table. The line-and-dot engineer-in-erze markings on the corpse's hands stood out against ashen skin. Donovan's eyes drifted upward and his guts lurched. Reveno was missing the top of his head. An entire section of his scalp and skull had been removed like a cap, exposing the gelatinous pale pink folds of his brain. A map of wires and what appeared to be metal probes were attached to the cerebral tissue like a circuit board; they snaked to a machine with a display screen and control panel.

"Sweet erze. What were they doing to him?" Jet reached out and touched a control knob on the machine's panel. Reveno's exocel rippled sluggishly to life down the left side of his body, like a dead limb flopping under electrical stimulation. Jet jerked back at the sight.

Lucius and Tennyson were already handling the situation like professionals. Lucius had the camera attachment on his goggles flipped down and was taking photographs of the secret lab and the victim's body from multiple angles while Tennyson went through the cabinets and shelves, gathering anything that might be useful evidence. Cass and Leon had gone back up the stairs. Donovan could hear them on the floor above, going through the house once more for anything worth seizing. Donovan knew he ought to get moving as well, ought to start doing something productive to help salvage the mission—but he felt uncertain and paralyzed, unable to stop staring at the mutilated body on the table.

Thad and Vic came down the stairs. "It's not pretty," Jet warned them. Vic's eyes went wide and she turned away quickly, stifling a gag. Donovan felt a bit like throwing up himself. Soldiers-in-erze were hardly strangers to violence, but this dead exo was different— grisly and clinical.

"Hey." Jet put a hand on Donovan's shoulder and turned him aside forcibly. Donovan gazed into the grim set of his partner's face; this whole thing brought up painful memories for Jet too.

Even Thad took a second to get his bearings back. When he spoke, there was restrained anger and frustration in his normally imperturbable voice. "Gather intelligence and be back at the bird in ten." It was clear that the sapes they'd been tasked to apprehend tonight were nowhere on the premises. Kevin Warde had slipped free—again. Thad toggled his transmitter, reporting directly to Commander Tate as he stomped heavily back up the stairs. "Command, we've got bad news."

4

"The mission was compromised," Thad declared. "The sapes were definitely there—hours, maybe minutes, before we arrived. Someone tipped them off."

In the darkness of the T15's cabin, Donovan felt rather than saw the round of shadowy nods. The mood on the short trip back to the Round was the opposite of the focused, anticipatory optimism on the flight out. Everyone was palpably deflated by the failure. Heads and shoulders were slouched; anger and unease warmed the stuffy confines of the stealthcopter.

"Sympathizers in the Denver PD?" Vic suggested. Local police forces were supposed to cooperate with SecPac, but it was common knowledge that the relationship between soldiers-in-erze and civilian law enforcement was often less than friendly. Cops usually weren't Hardened. Some were corrupt, helping Sapience by overlooking their activities or tipping them off about SecPac operations.

"It can't have been the DPD," Thad insisted. "We gave them minimal notice of the raid, and no specifics. The sapes knew exactly where we were going to be, and they had enough time to wire a basement full of explosives just for us. We're lucky to all be alive right now." Thad's eyes were no doubt on Donovan; he'd be dead for sure if Leon hadn't acted so quickly. "The only people who knew the details of the mission in advance were stripes."

There was a prolonged, uncomfortable silence. "You're saying someone in SecPac gave information to the sapes?" Jet's voice was sharp with disbelief. "Who would do that?"

"Someone in Equipment Control? Or Mission Ops?" suggested Lucius. "They have advance knowledge of planned raids and personnel assignments."

"Or Dispatch," Cass said. "They know where we are at all times."

"My sister-in-law works in Dispatch," Tennyson said defensively. "The background checks and erze evaluations there are as strict as anything."

"They're strict everywhere, but that doesn't mean mistakes don't get made," Cass said. "Look at Nakada. He was in erze before he turned traitor."

"So was my mom," Donovan said quietly.

"Yeah, but . . . a *stripe* going over to Sapience?" Jet exclaimed.

The tone of his friend's voice made Donovan glad it was too dark for him to see the accompanying expression of revolted skepticism. He kept silent, fighting a woozy sensation in his stomach that had nothing to do with the motion of the stealthcopter. Jet had asked what kind of soldier-in-erze would betray information to the enemy. That had been him. Last year, Donovan had tried to help Sapience save his mother from execution. It hadn't worked.

Thad cut off the escalating conversation. "Look, we all want to believe that every person in the erze is trustworthy, even the ones who aren't Hardened, but sometimes it turns out that's not the case. It's not up to us to speculate about who the snitch might be. We should leave that to Commander Tate."

For several minutes, the only sound was the low background

hum of the stealthcopter's engines. "This stinks," Cass declared loudly and bitterly.

A grumble of agreement traveled through the cabin. Donovan leaned his head back against the bulkhead and closed his eyes. His erze mates were understandably upset, but for Donovan it was much worse than that. He'd hoped to finish something tonight. Seeing Kevin and Dr. Nakada in SecPac custody wouldn't change the past, but at least it would've stitched up a part of him that still felt like an open wound. The mission's failure had dashed salt on him instead. He was certain he would soon be visited by nightmares of exos with heads sawed open. And Jonathan Resnick, anxiously waiting back in the Round for news that would bring him some measure of peace or reassurance—he wouldn't be sleeping tonight either.

— — —

There was more work to be done after landing back in Round Three: transferring all the photographs and evidence they'd carried back with them to SecPac Intelligence, unloading the body of Alexander Reveno, stripping off and storing their gear, and debriefing with Commander Tate. The commander was clearly as frustrated as any of them by how the night had transpired.

"What you found tonight is entirely classified," Tate told them. "Any evidence that Sapience has a scientist actively researching exocels with the aim of developing a weapon cannot become public knowledge. And it certainly can't be shared with our zhree allies, not even Soldier Werth."

The already dispirited mission team of exos shifted uneasily.

"I'm not telling you to lie to our erze master," Tate clarified, lowering her voice, "but I *am* telling you that *I* won't be mentioning it to him, and neither will you or anyone else in SecPac. Nakada's work is a threat to exos, and I want to be sure that *we* are the ones to put an end to it—not the zhree. The last thing we need right now is to give the leaders of the Mur Erzen Commonwealth any more reason to renege on their commitments to humanity."

It took them a moment to gather Commander Tate's meaning. The zhree colonists on Earth relied greatly on Hardened humans, but the High Speaker back on the zhree homeworld held a dim view of that partnership; it was one reason relations between Earth and Kreet were strained. Any weapon that could disable exocellular armor might be used as justification to put an end to the exo experiment altogether. The idea that all of them in the room—indeed, all exos alive today—might be the last of their kind, an anomalous, ill-conceived blip in history . . . it was so horrible to contemplate that armor rose on everyone's skin and the silence grew even gloomier.

Thad spoke for all of them. "Understood, ma'am."

"Nor do I want the slightest word of a security breach leaving anyone's lips," Tate ordered. "If there's a mole in SecPac, rumors will spook him before we can ferret out who it is."

It was nearly dawn by the time Jet, Donovan, Cass, and Leon got back to the house they shared. Cass went upstairs to try to get some sleep—she and Leon were scheduled to be on patrol later that evening—but Jet and Donovan were working day shifts this month and decided it'd be better to try to stay awake and crash early. Jet started a large pot of coffee brewing and put bread in the toaster before setting to scrambling eggs. Leon came into the kitchen and sat down at the table with his sketch pad and pencil.

"You're not going to try to get some shut-eye too?" Jet asked him.

Leon shrugged. "Can't sleep yet. Too amped."

The other two exos nodded. The mission had been over too quickly; their bodies had been primed to expect a fight, but the tension hadn't been given release. Donovan poured milk over granola, mixed in a tablespoon of nutritional supplement formulated for exos (with four of them in the house there was always a gallon-sized container of the stuff on the kitchen counter), and took it to the table, pausing to look over Leon's shoulder and watch him methodically pencil-shade the ample cleavage of a nude pinup girl with the head of a cat.

"Nice," he said, and sat down with his breakfast.

It was hard for Donovan to believe he'd lived here for five months already. Shortly after his father's death, Jet and Leon had searched out this house—conveniently only ten minutes away from SecPac Central Command—and taken the initiative to move the four of them in together. It was about time anyway; exos in their late teens and early twenties typically lived in common erze residences of four to eight people. According to Nurse Therrid, reinforcing erze bonds was the best way to bolster one's mental health. Donovan had been an urgent case, but Cass had needed support too after her combat injury and difficult recovery last year.

The small house wasn't much to look at compared to the state residence of the Prime Liaison, where Donovan had lived most of his life. Yet despite its modest size and the random clutter, the place held a sense of family and a feeling of home for Donovan that his father's house—stiff and formal as it was, overly large for two people, and frequented by political staffers whom Donovan didn't know—had never possessed. He grieved and ached for his parents, but he didn't miss the house at all.

Jet brought eggs and toast over to the table, and the three of them ate in companionable silence. Jet scrolled through the news. Taking a swallow of coffee from his oversized mug, he set his screen down on the table and nudged it toward Donovan.

Donovan glanced at the article Jet had brought up. "Who Will Be the Next Prime Liaison?" In smaller type under the main head-line: "Amid Protests and Delays, Zhree Leaders Prepare to Choose Country's Next Human Ambassador." A photograph showed three people standing together on the broad steps of the Capitol Building in Denver, which Donovan had seen from a distance mere hours ago. A tall, stately man in a blue suit and a smiling, middle-aged woman in a beige jacket, both with the bold, interlocking rings of the Administrator erze on the backs of their hands, and a younger, bearded man in a denim shirt, his hands conspicuously unmarked.

"So you know who you're going to pick tomorrow?" Jet asked.

Donovan pushed the screen back toward his partner. He felt strange looking at the people vying to take his father's place. One of them would soon be sitting in his father's office, living in his house. "I don't get to pick," he reminded Jet. "The zhree zun will make the decision. They'll want me to speak for my dad, to say what I think his opinion would've been."

"So you're going to say Schiller, right?" Leon said, deadpan in his sarcasm. Marcus Schiller, the unmarked man in the photo-graph, was clearly a protest candidate, backed by the increasingly vocal and popular Human Action Party. Schiller denounced the entire process of choosing a Prime Liaison. He decried the lack of a general vote from the human population and the absence of strict restrictions on length of term. The only thing he promised he would do as Prime Liaison was eliminate the role of Prime Liaison.

Jet snorted. "Well, I trust you to pick a new Prime Liaison more than I trust most of those politicians in Denver, and a hell of a lot more than the masses of squishies who don't know a word of Mur or have never even met a zhree. You know exactly what it takes to be a Prime Liaison; they don't." He shook hot sauce over his scrambled eggs. "After tomorrow, you're done with doing double duty as a special adviser, right? No more meetings in the Towers?"

"Are you going to miss it?" Leon asked, switching to a finer pencil. He'd abandoned work on the cat-headed temptress in favor of an equally buxom centaur. "Being in on the important political decisions? Ever wish you were marked with rings instead of stripes?"

Donovan shook his head at once. "Hell no. The country needs a real Prime Liaison." The assassination of Dominick Reyes had left a vital role empty at a difficult time. Despite Donovan's protests, Administrator Seir had made him an interim adviser to the zhree zun, a position that should've lasted only two or three months but, given the political gridlock in Denver, had stretched into over six— more than enough time for Donovan to appreciate how enormous his father's job had been and how deeply he was in over his head.

An alert flashed onto Jet's screen just as Donovan's comm unit went off as well, vibrating on the kitchen counter. Leon tucked his pencil behind his ear and looked down at his own comm; they'd all received the same message. "What's an erze inspection?" Leon wondered aloud. "Because apparently, we have one next Friday afternoon."

Jet's eyes narrowed as he read through the entirety of the communication. "This didn't come from Commander Tate. It came straight from Soldier Werth. 'All active-duty, Hardened soldiers-in-erze in Round Three are to present themselves for ceremonial inspection by visiting Mur Erzen Commonwealth dignitaries.'" Jet handed the screen to Donovan, who'd leaned over to read it over his partner's shoulder. "Sounds an awful lot like the High Speaker's visit."

"We all remember how well that went," Leon said dryly.

Donovan frowned. "That was only last year. And they're sending someone again?" Usually, decades went by between visits from Mur Commonwealth leaders. Earth was too remote and unimportant a colony for the zhree homeworld of Kreet to pay much attention to. Granted, the High Speaker had had his visit to Earth unexpectedly cut short, but if he or one of his representatives was returning to complete the aborted tour, then why return to Round Three?

Jet muttered the thought aloud for all three of them. "This can't be a good thing."

— — —

After Cass and Leon departed on patrol early that evening, Donovan settled on the sofa with his screen, intending to review his notes before the next day's meeting in the Towers. Jet said, "I was planning to go over to Vic's for a while."

"Okay," Donovan said. "Or she could come over here, if you want."

"It's our Hardening anniversary this week. A tough time for her parents, you know. I should go over there and bring some flowers or something."

"Right." Donovan's voice fell a little. "I forgot that was this week." Ordinarily, a Hardening anniversary was a minor celebration warranting a get-together with friends, perhaps a barbecue or a night out, but it had never been a happy occasion for Vic or her family. Vic's twin brother, Skye, had died at the age of five in the procedure that had made them exos.

Jet paused at the front door and glanced back. "You good?"

Donovan pulled off the headphones he'd just put on and looked up from his spot on the sofa. "I'm fine," he said. This was not the first time Jet had seemed torn between wanting to spend time with his girlfriend and being fearful about leaving Donovan alone. To be fair, there had been a couple of instances last year when Donovan had said things—about not deserving to be a stripe, about how he should've died instead of his father—that had freaked Jet out. With everything that had happened in the last twenty-four hours, it wasn't surprising that Jet was looking at him with trepidation, but there were times Donovan resented his friend's concern.

Jet remained standing by the door for another second, then came back and sat down on the edge of the armchair across from Donovan. "I can't stop thinking about the mission last night," he admitted. "About how the sapes knew we were coming. Wiring that basement to explode—it wasn't just about killing us. They wanted to destroy the evidence that Nakada was there, dissecting exo bodies."

Donovan set the screen down on his lap. Eugene Nakada's daughter had died in Hardening; since then, the scientist had become obsessed with how exocels worked. "Digging inside an exo's brain would be exactly his sort of research," Donovan agreed.

"We've been hunting Nakada for months, but he's managed to stay one step ahead of us. We assume Warde's protecting him, but maybe it's more than that. I feel like we're missing something." Jet stood up and started pacing. "Cass said something in the stealth-copter this morning: Dr. Nakada was in erze before he turned traitor. Out of all the sapes in that house, he's the only one who ever lived in the Round, who might still have friends here. Whoever the informer is, I think Nakada's the connection." Jet stopped. "We should interview his ex-wife again."

"We questioned her twice," Donovan reminded him. "She says she hasn't had any contact with him for years. She's an exo, her file's clean as a whistle, and she's engaged to be remarried to some-one in her same erze."

"Yeah, I know," Jet said doubtfully. "But she and Nakada had a kid and went through a tragedy together. That's got to stay with her. There's a good chance she still cares about him and is secretly helping him to evade capture."

"She's an administrator-in-erze," Donovan pointed out. "How would she have access to information about SecPac operations to tip him off?"

"Maybe someone in SecPac is helping her."

"So now we're looking for two traitors, from two differ-ent erze?"

"I don't know yet, all right?" Jet replied, frustrated. "I just think we haven't dug into Nakada's connections enough. He used to be marked and he had a life in the Round. People don't just leave their past behind that easily."

That was true. Donovan got up and stretched, giving up on his reading for the night. "You're right. We should bring it up with Commander Tate. She's probably already—"

There was a knock on the front door. Jet and Donovan both

looked at it in surprise. Jet shrugged. When Donovan went to the entrance and opened it, he found a stout woman in a tan blazer, black skirt, and Administrator erze markings standing on the front step.

"Donovan Reyes?" she said.

"Yeah," Donovan replied.

"I'm here regarding the execution of a will in which you are the named beneficiary."

Donovan frowned in confusion. "My father's will was executed months ago. Someone came and walked me through it already."

"This isn't in regard to your father's will," the woman replied. "You're the legal recipient of certain possessions that belonged to the late Dr. Vincent Ghosh."

Dr. Ghosh? The scientist-in-erze who'd recently been gunned down? The one in the photograph with his father, whose award-winning research had been stolen by Sapience? "I never knew Dr. Ghosh," Donovan said, utterly perplexed now. "There has to be a mistake."

"I'll explain the circumstances," said the woman. "May I come in?"

Donovan held the door open and the woman entered. She walked into the kitchen with Donovan and Jet following, set a handbag down on the table, and drew a sealed, padded envelope from the inside of her bag, along with a screen, which she tapped while speaking to Donovan. "Dr. Ghosh specified that in the event of his death, the contents of his personal safe box were to be removed and delivered directly to Prime Liaison Dominick Reyes. Unfortunately, his instructions were not updated to reflect the fact that the original named beneficiary is also now deceased. As you are the legal heir to Dominick Reyes, the item in question now belongs to you." She handed the screen to Donovan. "Please sign here."

Curious as well as bewildered, Donovan signed, and the woman handed him the envelope. It was not large—about the size of a deck of cards, sealed with packing tape and unmarked. "Have a nice evening," said the administrator-in-erze. Jet opened the door for her to leave as Donovan turned the object over in his hands. Digging under the packing tape with a bladed index finger, he sliced the envelope open. Inside was a small box containing several data storage discs.

"What are they?" Jet asked.

"Beats me." The discs were labeled *Data Set 1, Data Set 2, Data Set 3, Models, Summary of Results*. Donovan went back to the living room and found his screen stashed under the coffee table. He inserted one of the discs—*Data Set 1*—into the device's read slot. A long list of file icons filled his screen. Opening one at random, he saw dozens more icons, which, when opened, turned out to be black-and-white medical images. "I think these are brains," Donovan said. "Lots of brains."

Jet came and looked over his shoulder. The images had labels and notes, all of it indecipherable medical gobbledygook. "Seems like the doctor saved a copy of his work," Jet said. "Maybe he wanted to be sure his research wasn't lost if Sapience got to him."

"But why send this to my dad?" Donovan wondered. "You'd think it ought to go to his colleagues in the Scientist erze."

"It could be that he wanted your dad to know exactly what the sapes were after." Jet squinted at the screen. "I wonder if there's information in here that Sapience gave to Nakada to help him make the weapon they want. Could give us clues as to what he's up to now."

"Good point." Donovan kept scrolling.

Jet glanced at the clock on the wall. "Vic's going to wonder what on earth happened to me." He shifted from foot to foot, reluctant yet anxious to leave. "I'll be back in a couple hours."

Donovan nodded and waved his partner off distractedly. When Jet left the house, Donovan sat back down on the sofa, still perusing Ghosh's files. He found the stark images weirdly mesmerizing; it was strange to think that there was a real person behind each black-and-white walnut shape on the screen. Several minutes later, he'd managed to figure out from the tiny labels that most of the brain scans were from exos of varying age and gender. HRD M 39. A thirty-nine-year-old male exo. Another was labeled NHRD F 26. A non-Hardened twenty-six-year-old female. He couldn't figure out much more. The scans had light and dark spots that appeared to indicate brain activity under certain stimuli, but a person would need a medical degree to know what any of it meant. The images and words began to blur in his vision. Maybe he'd be able to make more sense of them if he hadn't had such a long, stressful day and wasn't already exhausted.

Donovan ejected the disc, thinking to go up to bed, but then slid in *Summary of Results* and browsed through the list of files. This disc was filled with written reports, so dense with medical jargon that Donovan closed them after trying to read the first paragraph. One final file caught his attention, though: *Letter to PL D. Reyes.* Donovan opened it and text filled his screen.

Mr. Prime Liaison,

Per your request to provide periodic status updates on the confidential project we discussed, I'm pleased to say I've found what you're looking for. The exocel inhibition reflex is controlled by specific nuclei connections in the amygdala, which are formed during the Hardening process. I've confirmed through clinical studies that the neural circuit is triggered by physical aggression toward any zhree. Theoretically, the connection could be surgically disabled, but as I said in our last conversation, that is mere speculation, as no such procedures have ever been attempted, and data on brain surgeries performed on Hardened patients by zhree Nurses is not available to us. Contact me if you would like to discuss this further.

Sincerely,
Vincent Ghosh, MD, PhD, SciE

Donovan read the letter again. The exocel inhibition reflex that Ghosh referred to could only be one thing. Twice in Donovan's life, he'd tried to hurt a zhree. The first time, he'd been goaded by none other than the High Speaker of the Mur Commonwealth; the second time, he'd punched Nurse Therrid in the eye to escape medical confinement. Both times, his armor had fallen involuntarily. Even remembering the instances made Donovan queasy;

losing conscious control of one's exocel was a terrifying, shameful sensation.

If he was understanding this letter correctly, his father, during his time as Prime Liaison, had instructed Dr. Ghosh, the leading expert on exo physiology, to study the neural fail-safe that the Mur colonists had engineered into every Hardened human to ensure that they could not use their exocels to harm zhree. His father had wanted to know if and how the reflex could be removed or overridden.

Donovan searched through the rest of the files for more correspondence but didn't find any. He removed the memory disc and turned the small object in his hands. Dominick Reyes had been the country's most stalwart supporter of cooperationism. He'd believed unequivocally in human Hardening and in the erze system that he oversaw. The zhree zun had respected and trusted him more than any other human. So why had he been secretly directing a scientist to figure out how to undermine zhree biotechnology?

Donovan slid the disc safely back in the envelope. His throat felt suddenly thick and tight with confusion and resentment. If only his father could answer his questions, could explain the inscrutable decisions he'd made. If only his father were here, *period*. Alive.

He'd never really known his mother—Donovan had reconciled himself to that painful reality already. Now it seemed he hadn't really known his father either. He swiped his tired eyes with the back of his striped hands and went up to bed.

5

Sunrise had not yet fully lit the cloudless sky the next morning when Donovan took an electricycle from the garage and drove the long, straight spoke road to the center of the Round, where the Towers that marked the hub of the city rose high over the surrounding landscape in a grand cluster of interconnected alien spires. Although the Towers of Round Three were the seat of zhree government for half the continent, they were also feats of alien architecture so breathtaking that Donovan sometimes found it hard to remember that they were not unique, that there were eighteen Rounds across the world, each anchored by their own set of equally impressive Towers. When he arrived, Donovan parked the e-cycle near one of the arched entrances and hurried to the assembly chamber almost at a run. It wouldn't do to be late.

Despite the early hour, there was no less activity in the curving hallways and cavernous chambers of the Towers than at any other time of day; the zhree did not maintain the same sleep patterns as humans. Donovan swerved around groups of domed hulls and flashing fins, avoided being accidentally smacked by the limbs of a Merchant gesturing animatedly in conversation, nodded in hasty greeting at the other humans he passed, and slowed to a walk as he reached his destination. He stopped just inside the room, dropping his armor respectfully and waiting until Soldier Werth noticed him and motioned curtly for him to join.

The zhree zun were arranging themselves into their usual circle around Administrator Seir, who always led these meetings. Donovan brought his armor up slightly higher than halfway—the Towers were still cold in the mornings, too cold for human comfort. He took his place next to his erze master. "Zun Werth," Donovan said. Soldier Werth regarded Donovan with one of his six large yellow eyes. One fin gave a shallow dip of acknowledgment.

Donovan lowered himself into the metal chair that the zhree had at least been considerate enough to have brought in for him. The six-legged attendees of the meeting didn't tire of standing, but Donovan certainly did. The mental discomfort he couldn't do much about. He still found it disconcerting to be included in a zhree speaking circle, sitting almost as if he were an equal next to Soldier Werth, who had authority over Commander Tate and all soldiers-in-erze.

"You've all had time to consult within your erze and to contemplate the candidates the human government has presented us for the role of Prime Liaison." Administrator Seir began without preamble, his trilling musical voice ringing in the assembly chamber. "We will make the final determination today. Builder Dor, who is the choice of your erze?"

"Campton." In the Mur language, it did not sound like *Campton* but like two whistled syllables and a flashing fin pattern that Donovan understood to be the closest translation of the human name. Builder Dor added, in a decisive strumming tone, "The Builder erze has confidence he would be effective in continuing the work of Dominick Reyes."

Administrator Seir dipped a fin in acknowledgment. "Merchant Hess?"

"DeGarmo," said the Merchant. "She is more visionary in her views of improved cooperation between the species and will inspire the support of more humans."

"Scientist Laah?"

And so it went, around the circle. The preference was split between Peter Campton and Angela DeGarmo, with Campton leading. Donovan shifted in his seat. He'd studied all three candidates, had heard their responses to tough questions posed by Congress and by the zhree zun, and weighed the merits of each, even Marcus Schiller. Administrator Seir would come around to Donovan soon, wanting his assessment on what his father's choice would've been.

"Soldier Werth?" asked Administrator Seir.

"Campton." Werth left it at that. It was something that Donovan appreciated about the zhree—compared to humans, they had very little personal ego. They rarely felt the need to repeat what had already been said, and it was always understood that the zun spoke unequivocally for the entire erze.

Suddenly, Donovan was uncertain about what that meant for him. He was a soldier-in-erze; technically, Werth had just spoken for everyone who bore his stripes—zhree and human alike. Of course, Werth hadn't consulted with each of them individually, but Donovan was sure he would have at least considered input from Commander Tate and other senior humans in SecPac. Did that mean he should defer to Werth and answer the same as his erze master?

But he wasn't in this circle as a SecPac officer. If the zhree needed a representative of SecPac they ought to have Commander Tate here. Donovan's pulse rose as his mind spun in indecision. Campton was, indeed, the candidate who seemed the most qualified; it was no surprise that he was Soldier Werth's choice. Campton had years of experience working in the Liaison Office. He was forthright, pragmatic, highly intelligent, and had a zero tolerance policy toward terrorism. Campton had helped Donovan's father establish important erze expansion programs that would qualify hundreds of thousands more humans for markings and erze status, and gradually increase the number of exos Hardened each year. *Progress.* That's what Donovan's father had always stood for; what Peter Campton appeared to stand for too.

The other candidate, Angela DeGarmo, was the governor of Cascadia, the region of West America stretching from Vancouver to San Francisco, which contained some of the highest populations of marked humans beyond the vicinity of Round Three. DeGarmo was a strong proponent of technology transfer, improved living conditions and modernization of human cities, more equitable integration between human and zhree political processes, and something the former Prime Liaison would never have approved of: peace negotiations with Sapience.

"Donovan?" Administrator Seir prompted.

Donovan hesitated. "DeGarmo," he said.

He hoped the Administrator would move on to Scholar Ean next to him but Seir paused, four of his eyes shutting, the other two focusing fully on the lone human in the group. "Are you speaking based on what you believe your father's decision would be?"

Donovan caught the sharp twitch of Soldier Werth's fin next to him. He swallowed. His father would choose Campton. But his father had done unexpected things before. The envelope lying in Donovan's drawer was evidence of that. "I . . . I'm not sure what my father would decide," he admitted.

"If you're not speaking as the offspring of Dominick Reyes, are you speaking as a soldier-in-erze? Or stating your own individual leanings?"

It was a trick question; his erze master was right there, so the first option wasn't a possibility, and what need did the zhree have for the personal opinion of one teenage human? *This is why I didn't want this job*, Donovan thought miserably. "Neither." He hoped he didn't sound as unsure as he felt. "I guess I'm speaking as . . . a human. As an exo. I think DeGarmo is who we need right now to . . . to change some of the things that need changing." He closed his mouth, feeling awkward and impotent at expressing himself in this forum. His exocel crawled up in anxiety across his chest and back, making him suddenly too hot.

Adminstrator Seir regarded him for a silent moment, then slowly opened his other eyes and moved on. "Scholar Ean?"

After Seir had heard from everyone, he fell silent. Donovan had been so anxiously wrapped up in his own thoughts about what he was going to say that he hadn't counted how many zhree had spoken in favor of each candidate, but it didn't really matter—this wasn't a vote. Administrator Seir would take into account the preferences of the different erze, consider all the opinions he'd heard, weigh them with his own judgment, and make a final determination.

A solid five minutes of silence descended over the assembly room; to Donovan it was a painfully long wait. He fought the urge to shift or fidget. None of the zhree spoke or moved. Donovan's father had once explained to him that compared to humans, whose organizations tended to have many levels of authority, zhree social hierarchy was flat but rigid; thousands of individuals in an erze answered to one leader. Seir was currently the highest-ranked

Administrator in the colony; his decisions prevailed not only in Round Three, but ultimately across Earth. Donovan supposed that meant Round Three was the closest thing there was to a planetary capital. And that meant the Prime Liaison of West America might have more influence than any other world leader.

At last, Administrator Seir straightened his fins and said, "I will inform the human government of West America that Angela DeGarmo will be the next Prime Liaison to Round Three. She will assume the role immediately."

There was no agreement or dissent or further discussion; that was the way it was with zhree. However, as Donovan released the slow breath he'd been holding, he imagined that Soldier Werth was glaring at him. It made him start sweating again.

"Donovan," Administrator Seir said, startling him. "You've done well, considering the unusual demands we've placed on you. Your obligations here will end after today."

"Yes, zun," Donovan said, very much wishing DeGarmo a swift confirmation and speedy journey to the Round. "Thank you."

"Soldier Werth," Seir said, "it was good of you to allow us to temporarily take your human-in-erze away from his other duties. I trust he'll be able to fully resume his normal role in the Soldier erze without delay."

"That would be best," Soldier Werth agreed, rather dryly, Donovan suspected, though it was not easy to tell for certain given the cadence of the Mur language.

Administrator Seir moved immediately to the next topic of discussion, one of greater global concern. "As you've heard, a representative of the Homeworld Council is on his way to Earth and will be arriving in Round Three in ten days."

Though his nerves were still on edge, Donovan sat up and paid attention; this must be related to the alert about an erze inspection that had been sent to the Hardened SecPac officers yesterday morning. Seir paused, and from the slight riffle of fins through the circle, Donovan got the sense that the zhree zun were as ambivalent about the news as he, Jet, and Leon had been.

"What is the purpose of this visit?" Builder Dor asked, a wary note in his voice.

Soldier Werth answered. "The High Speaker has sent one of his most trusted advisers to conduct a military assessment of the colony. I expect the Homeworld Council intends to evaluate whether the current level of defense spending on Earth is warranted."

"We know the High Speaker is inclined to reduce investment in the frontier regions of the galaxy. This visit will be an opportunity for us to explain how we plan to maintain and defend Earth as a colony of the Mur Erzen Commonwealth with the resources we currently have," Seir declared. "In our last discussion, we identified the highest-priority issues for each erze. Now we must propose solutions that the High Speaker and the Homeworld Council will understand and find acceptable. Nurse Thet will begin with how we can improve hatch rates and brood nutrition."

Nurse Thet took a step into the circle and began talking at length about incubation challenges and brooding cycles. After several minutes, Donovan started to zone out. He couldn't help it; it was hard to stay focused on long conversations about things he didn't understand, sometimes involving words he didn't even know, and it didn't seem as if the discussion was going to shed any further light on the message from yesterday. Even with a fluent understanding of the Mur language, Donovan found that these sessions taxed him to the maximum of his ability. When the zhree spoke directly to humans, they usually spoke slowly, moving their fins deliberately, so the translation machines they trailed around with them could accurately relay messages. In here, there were no translation machines. The zhree colonists discussed and debated rapidly, the fins on the tops of their domed bodies flashing light and dark patterns like whipping signal flags, their many eyes instantly capturing the back-and-forth exchanges from opposite sides of the circle. Even on a good day, Donovan could only do his best to keep up.

Today was not one of those good days. His mind had been too full of troubling images and nagging questions for him to sleep well last night. The chair seemed especially hard and cold this morning, and the animated zhree voices ringing off the walls reinforced how out of place he was. There wasn't always much for him to do in these meetings; sometimes the zhree zun asked him questions or solicited his human viewpoint, and he always answered as best he could, but for the most part, it seemed ridiculously naive and delusional that he'd ever imagined he could make any real difference. He wasn't his father. He didn't have visionary ideas about how to improve life on Earth or relations between the species, and he clearly didn't have any special insight into what his father's plans had been. He could barely stay awake in this conversation about . . . about . . . Donovan blinked and paid sudden attention again. Soldier Werth had stepped forward and was speaking.

"We have scarcely enough Soldiers to defend the planet, and Kreet has already declared it will not bolster our forces. Improved hatch rates won't help us in the short term. Our highest priority when it comes to planetary security must be increasing the number of Hardened soldiers-in-erze." Soldier Werth's multi-directional gaze was determined; his short, thick fins stiffened in a weighty pause before continuing. "We need to combat the upswing of violence on the planet's surface *and* start bringing humans into more substantive support roles alongside Soldiers. There's no reason why a human can't be taught how to pilot a transport ship or operate an ion cannon."

"What if all newly Hardened humans were marked by the Soldier erze?" Administrator Seir asked.

There was a protesting wave of flaring fins around the circle. "Preferential selection of Hardened humans is already given to the Soldier erze!" Builder Dor said, his fins snapping resentfully. "The Builder erze is *always* lacking enough exos."

"There's need for exos in areas besides the military," Engineer Phee agreed. "Non-Hardened humans are vulnerable to pressure changes and radiation. We could use human engineering support on ships and orbital platforms, but there are simply not enough exos."

"I agree that assigning all Hardened humans to the Soldier erze isn't the answer," Soldier Werth said to Seir. "A human has to have the right qualities to successfully wear Soldier markings. Judging which ones are suitable is both an art and a science; I select each exo for my erze personally."

Even though his erze master appeared to be caught up in the discussion and ignoring him completely, Donovan felt his spine straighten with pride.

"The only way to meet our colony's needs in the long run is to aggressively increase the overall number of humans Hardened," Werth declared.

"We all know the High Speaker is reluctant to place so much reliance on human allies," hummed Administrator Seir. "But assuming for a moment that the homeworld doesn't object, what's preventing us from doubling or tripling Hardening rates?"

Nurse Thet responded. "Most of the Rounds have already expanded Hardening facilities and medical care capacity for exos. Hardening rates can be quickly accelerated, but we are limited by how many healthy and qualified human hatchlings are volunteered by the adults."

The zhree zun pondered this for a minute. "Can we incentivize more humans to accept Hardening?" Administrator Seir asked. "There's no reason why it can't become a natural rite for their species as it is for ours."

"The incentives are already strong: automatic erze status, better living conditions, greater opportunities, resistance to injury and disease, lifespans nearly double that of humans lacking exocels," said Scholar Ean. "Unfortunately, many humans still fear Hardening as something foreign to their kind, and even the current three percent mortality rate is unacceptable to many humans who might have broods of only one or two offspring throughout their lives."

Soldier Werth struck one of his limbs on the ground for emphasis. "Given the urgency of this colony's military needs, conscription ought to be considered. One healthy human youngster out of each mating pair of two erze-marked adults."

It took Donovan a second to understand. Then he shot to his feet. "You can't do that!"

Dozens of hard amber eyes focused on him as all the fins around the circle abruptly stilled. Donovan flinched back from his own outburst as soon as it escaped his mouth. He'd rudely contradicted his own erze master, and for a second he couldn't put two words together. Heart pounding, he found his voice again. "With respect, zun, no matter how much we need more exos, it would be wrong to force humans to offer up their kids to be Hardened. It should be a choice. It can't be something you make people do. It *can't*."

None of the zhree said anything in response, and in the uncomfortable silence, more words spilled from Donovan before he could figure out how best to phrase them. "Right now, humans are marked because they want to be. They *won't* want to be if you do this. You'll make people hate and fear exos even more." Panotin crawled involuntarily across his taut knuckles. "Sapience already spreads lies telling people that exos are brainwashed slaves and that the zhree plan to Harden all humans and control our whole species. If you play straight into what they're saying, you'll only make Sapience stronger. You'll turn more people against the whole idea of cooperation. We could lose the erze system, maybe even the peace of the Accord."

With genuine bafflement, Scientist Laah said, "But Hardening is the morally responsible thing to do. Aren't humans clearly better off with exocels?"

"You didn't make the choice for yourself when you were a small hatchling, Donovan." Soldier Werth's slow tone of remonstration made Donovan wonder if he hadn't put himself on the wrong side of his erze master permanently. "Are you not grateful to be an exo?"

Donovan opened his mouth and closed it again. Of course he would rather be an exo than a squishy. But that didn't make the idea of conscription right. "I'm glad I'm Hardened," he said slowly, "but I wouldn't ask anyone else to Harden their kids if they didn't want to." He glanced nervously but resolutely around the circle of unblinking alien eyes. "It has to be a choice," he repeated. "Or else . . . or else you're no better than what the sapes say."

A tense silence followed. Donovan wondered if he would be sent from the room. He refrained from looking at Soldier Werth. Hadn't his erze master just said that he chose his exos carefully? Donovan was sure Werth didn't choose them so they could undermine him in front of the other zhree zun. An erze handled disputes and disagreements internally but was always united behind the zun when dealing with others; Donovan had never heard two zhree with the same markings disagree with each other in public.

But what else could he have done? That was why he was here, wasn't it, to advise the zhree? They'd put him in this position, so how could they blame him for offending erze decorum?

"The plan we propose to Kreet should include scenarios for both a moderate and aggressive rate of increase in the exo population," Administrator Seir declared at last. "We won't rule out any options at this point."

Soldier Werth's six large eyes took in the entire circle, but one opaque yellow orb stared directly at Donovan. "Human self-determination is a noble principle," he said, "but one we may need to sacrifice if it means convincing Kreet to support our plan instead of the alternative."

Administrator Seir gave voice to the thought in a resigned strum. "Abandoning Earth."

6

It was nearly noon by the time Administrator Seir adjourned the meeting and Donovan got out of the Towers. Soldier Werth left without acknowledging him further, striding out of the assembly room in a brisk tripedal gait, his expression, such as it was, inscrutable.

Donovan walked back to his parked e-cycle and sat in the spring sunshine for several minutes without starting up the engine. Was his erze master right? Was it better for the zhree to impose mandatory Hardenings if the alternative was Kreet withdrawing support and leaving Earth defenseless? Or even, as Commander Tate feared, deciding to put an end to the Hardening of humans altogether? Were those really the grim possibilities that lay ahead?

Donovan's father had always argued that the survival and progress of humankind depended on being part of the galactic community and eventually rising to the level of the zhree. His mother insisted that nothing the aliens could offer or impose was worth sacrificing human freedom. What would they have thought of the discussion in the assembly chamber today?

Donovan shook his head; he was neither his father nor his mother, thank erze. He would never have to make the kinds of decisions they'd made. He gripped the e-cycle's handlebars; the machine verified his exocellular body signature and pulled forward under his guidance.

He had the rest of the day off duty. Leon and Cass were no doubt asleep after their patrol shift, and Jet was probably with Vic. Donovan slowed indecisively as he reached the next intersection. Making up his mind guiltily, he turned left onto the main spoke road and, with the wind flying pleasantly at his back, took the straight path all the way to the wall of the Round. The guard at Gate 5 waved him through, and Donovan sped the e-cycle from the clean, wide streets of Round Three into the narrower, more crowded concrete landscape of the Ring Belt. Twenty minutes later, he slowed as he entered an old, neglected part of the city that few people considered to have any redeeming qualities: the Transitional Habitation grids.

Jet wouldn't be pleased to know that he had come here. The TransHabs were not the sort of place an erze-marked person normally visited, and certainly not alone. SecPac officers on patrol in this area kept a hand near their weapon and their armor raised. The low-income apartment buildings that crowded the neighborhood had been built after the War Era to house refugees; in a way, they still served that purpose. Even though all the streets here looked the same, Donovan didn't need the e-cycle's navigation. His destination was familiar to him now.

Coming here had become an addiction, a habit that Donovan couldn't break even though he knew he should. The e-cycle's quiet hum died as Donovan pulled it to a stop in front of an unremarkable five-story building, no different from any of the others. Once a week, sometimes twice, he found himself parked here on the corner, even though what he saw hadn't changed in over two months: a wooden post plastered with old flyers and staples, two Xs spray-painted side by side. One X still bright white because Donovan had put it there himself a week ago, the other old and fading away to nothing.

Last year, when Anya had escaped the algae farm and returned to her sister's apartment, she and Donovan had begun exchanging a simple message: an X on the post, every couple of weeks. It was their way of saying "I'm still here" and "I'm okay," and maybe even "I miss you." For the first several months, every time Donovan saw Anya's freshly painted X on the post, he would get out of the skimmercar, sometimes with Jet's worried and disapproving gaze following him, and apply a new coat of paint to his own X. He would gaze up at the blocky, concrete building behind the post and imagine Anya inside and feel nearly sick with the urge to go in and find her—to see her again, to talk to her, to be near her—even for a few minutes.

"Come on, D," Jet would call, his voice curt. "Let's go."

He always left. In those early months when his spirits had been at their lowest, he would remember that he'd promised Anya's sister he wouldn't ever darken their apartment door again. He and Anya were from different worlds, on different sides of a conflict that had been going on for a hundred years. The two of them together could only be dangerous and dysfunctional, the way Donovan's parents had been. If there was one thing Donovan didn't want, it was to risk becoming like his parents. No, he convinced himself, again and again, it was enough—it *had* to be enough—just for him to know Anya was okay. That was, until she stopped responding.

Donovan took out the spray-paint can he kept in the e-cycle's storage compartment and walked up to the post. He repainted his X, as he had before, though it felt like a futile gesture now. Anya had surely tired of their little game. What was the point? Why leave messages for someone you never saw, never spoke to, could never have a real relationship with? He couldn't blame her for no longer acknowledging him, though he kept hoping she would.

Donovan stowed the spray-paint can and swung his leg back over the seat of the e-cycle. He wrapped his hands around the grips of the handlebars but didn't pull the vehicle forward. Instead, he sat, still staring up at the building. He remembered his relief at the mission briefing, when Anya's face had not been among the pictures on the wall screen behind Commander Tate. He was thankful she wasn't with Kevin, but where was she? Had something happened to her?

Donovan got off his e-cycle. Perhaps it had been the failed raid in Denver, or Brett's reappearance as Jonathan, or asserting himself on his final day as adviser to the zhree zun—but something made him feel different today, bolder and more anxious at the same time. Or maybe it was simply that Jet wasn't here to stop him. Donovan let his feet carry him across the sidewalk, into the building, and up the short flight of narrow concrete stairs to the door he'd promised he wouldn't visit again. He stood in the hall, breathing a little too loudly.

Why are you doing this? If Jet were here, that's what he would be angrily demanding right now. Donovan set his jaw, replying with the truth: *I still care about her.* He rapped on the door. Immediately, he heard a scurry of movement from inside, but no one came to the entrance. He knocked again, more loudly. An unfamiliar man's voice shouted, "What do you want?"

Taken aback, Donovan answered automatically. "This is SecPac. Open the door." Immediately, he kicked himself. That was the exact *wrong* thing to say. He was alone in a hostile neighborhood with his erze markings visible, and none of his erze mates knew where he was right now. He had no idea who the man behind the door was and whether he was armed or dangerous. Also, he was not here on any sort of official SecPac investigation or search; he had no legal reason to demand that whoever was inside allow him entry.

"I'm not opening the door for no stripes!" came the angry reply.

Taking a deep breath, Donovan put on his calmest, most convincing public-officer voice. "Sir, I'm not here to search the apartment or arrest anyone. I need to speak with Ms. Dodson." That could apply to either Anya or her sister. "I have reason to be concerned for her safety. Can you tell me if she's here?"

A scuffling erupted behind the door and then the dead bolt was drawn back and the door opened only to the width permitted by the latched chain. A man's pinched face appeared in the crack between the door and the frame. His red-rimmed nostrils twitched and his watery, shifty eyes darted over Donovan. "I've done nothing wrong, and I'm not letting in a *shroom pet*!" The cheeks of his thin face were sweaty.

"Is Ms. Dodson there?" Donovan demanded.

"If you're talking about the broad who used to live here, she's long gone. Moved away. Your SecPac info's way out of date, man!" He chuckled as if this was hilarious.

"She had a younger sister, a teenager," Donovan pressed.

"They're both gone, all right? They haven't been back and I don't know anything." The door slammed shut and the dead bolt clicked loudly into place. Donovan heard the man moving and cursing inside.

Anger and frustration welled in Donovan's chest. He was used to dealing with uncooperative people, but being called an alien tool was always hard to take. The guy was clearly hiding something; Donovan was sure that if he broke the chain on the door and went inside the single room that lay beyond, he'd find stolen goods or weapons or drugs.

That was a job for the police, though, not soldiers-in-erze, and despite the rude reception, Donovan's instincts told him the man was telling the truth. Anya and her sister hadn't lived here for months.

Donovan went outside, got onto the e-cycle, and gunned it back toward the Round without looking back. With Anya no longer there, the TransHabs seemed every bit the nasty, squalid place that it truly was. He couldn't wait to get away from it and return home.

So that was that. Anya was gone and not coming back. He'd probably never see her again.

He wasn't sure if the pressure building inside him was misery or relief. Anya hadn't even bothered to let him know she was leaving. She'd put him firmly in her rearview mirror and moved on with her life. He ought to do the same—quit stopping by the street corner to spray-paint that stupid, childish X on the post and stare up at that ugly building like some idiot knight at the bottom of a forbidden tower. Maybe, just maybe, Anya had left more than him behind. Maybe she'd left Sapience behind too and gone in search of a new life, a fresh start.

He could hope.

— — —

When Donovan got home, he parked the electricycle and was about to enter the front door when he heard Vic's voice though the open kitchen window. "What about Donovan?"

"What about him?" Jet's voice, wary. Donovan stopped, his hand on the door.

"Don't you think he still needs you around right now?" Vic asked.

Donovan couldn't see either of his erze mates, but he could hear them clearly enough that the brief pause that followed seemed deafening. Jet said, with a hint of defensiveness, "I'd still see him practically every day. You know I'd do anything for D, but he doesn't want help. He works through stuff on his own. I didn't think it was a good idea for him to go on the raid, but he insisted. There're things he's still not talking to me about, but he's doing a lot better."

"Survivor guilt doesn't go away that quickly, Jet. I would know." Vic sighed loudly. "All I'm saying is, you haven't been in *this* house long. It just doesn't feel like the right time. We have to be sure it's what we want."

"*I'm* sure." Footsteps moved near the front of the house, and when Jet spoke again, his voice was much closer. "Moving in together doesn't feel like rushing to me. If you don't think it's a good time, fine, but if it's because *you're* not sure, you should say—"

The front door opened. Jet startled to see his partner standing on the other side.

"Hey," Donovan said lightly, stepping in as if he'd just arrived and hadn't heard a thing. "You guys headed out?" He looked from Jet to Vic. They blinked at him with suspicious guilt.

"We were going to grab a bite to eat," Jet said.

"Come with us," Vic added quickly. "We're going to the pita place down the street. I'm obsessed with their shawarma wrap." Donovan thought maybe he ought to decline and let the two of them continue their serious conversation without his inadvertent eavesdropping, but Vic maneuvered him back out the door while Jet shut it after them.

Donovan tried to walk a little behind his friends; he felt awkward for having overheard them and unsure of how to feel about what he'd heard. He supposed it was only natural for Jet to want to move out and live with Vic. Still, he couldn't help feeling wounded. Anya had abandoned him already. This wouldn't be the same as that, but still . . .

Don't be a jerk. He let himself trail even farther behind, bothered by the idea that he might be a burden on his partner—a frustrating, secretive one at that. The truth was, there were things he still felt he couldn't talk about to anyone, not even Jet. Maybe least of all Jet.

His friends noticed him lagging and slowed deliberately to walk alongside him. "So, how'd it go?" Vic asked. "In the Towers."

Donovan forced aside his melancholy and latched onto the conversation opener. "Angela DeGarmo's been named the new Prime Liaison."

"Administrator Seir approved a moderate who says she's going to negotiate with Sapience?" Jet raised his eyebrows crookedly, giving Donovan a curious look.

They entered the small, blue-tiled Mediterranean café on the corner and stood in line to order at the counter. Donovan said carefully, "I was surprised at the decision too. But the zhree zun are on thin ice with Kreet after the High Speaker's visit last year. I think they realize they need the support of humans—*all* humans—to prove to the Homeworld Council that Earth is still worthwhile."

The bridge of Jet's nose wrinkled doubtfully. "They're never going to get the support of all humans. The sapes aren't exactly the reasonable sort. We saw proof enough of that in a basement the other night."

Donovan stared at the menu board without really reading it. "I don't know, Jet. We're stripes, so we're used to dealing with the most bloodthirsty terrorists. But not all sapes are the same. And they don't all agree, or want the same things either."

"Well, that's why there's no lasting peace, isn't it?" Jet pointed out. "Sapience isn't an erze; it can't make a binding decision. As soon as a new leader pops up, or a vocal faction disagrees, they just toss out any old decisions and we're back to square one. That's how it is with squishies."

"Boys, are we talking politics now or getting pita wraps?" Vic prompted, gesturing to the waiting cashier. Donovan was glad for the necessary break in conversation as they placed their orders and found seats around a nearby table. "The important thing," Vic said to Donovan, "is that you're finally off the hook as temporary special adviser. It was an awful lot for them to ask of you."

Jet nodded in agreement and popped the tab on his soda can. "I would've hated to be in your shoes. I imagine it'd be really awkward, to be the only human in front of Soldier Werth and a room full of zhree, all staring at you. I wouldn't even know what to say."

Donovan grimaced. "Tell me about it. It didn't end on a good note either. I think I might've seriously pissed off Soldier Werth." He told them about the discussion that had occurred over Werth's proposal to mandate Hardening one child from every erze-marked family.

"Forced Hardenings? That's . . ." Vic shook her head sharply, eyes narrowing. "How could Soldier Werth suggest that? It's *wrong*. People would never stand for it."

"That's pretty much what I blurted out loud, right in front of the erze master and all the zhree zun." Donovan rubbed a hand over his face. "Thus ends my short-lived political career."

Jet sat back in his chair and took a large swallow of soda. "I don't know. I mean, of course Hardening should be a choice, but then again, long ago countries used to have a military draft when they needed more soldiers. If Earth needs more exos, across every erze, it doesn't seem that unreasonable to expect people to step up. I mean, when you think about it, the mortality rate for Hardening is a lot better than the fatality rate for squishies."

"Seems to me if you'd been the adviser, you would've had plenty to say," Donovan grumbled.

Jet shrugged and stretched out his legs under the small table. "Nah. There's never any right answer to these things. That's why it's better to be a stripe. Just hand me an E201 and point out the bad guys." He grinned to show he was only half-serious. Maybe more than half.

"Well, *I* think you did the right thing," Vic said to Donovan. "Calling that out as being wrong. There's already too much pressure on people to Harden their kids; there doesn't need to be more." She slid a narrow-eyed sideways glare at her boyfriend. "And a three percent mortality rate doesn't mean much when you're part of the three percent."

The smile fell slowly off Jet's face. Apparently, he'd forgotten that their Hardening anniversary was still bound to be on Vic's mind. "You know I didn't mean . . ." He faltered, glanced at Donovan helplessly, then faced Vic with contrition. "I wasn't making light of the risks of Hardening; I was only trying to point out that sometimes risks are taken for the greater good." A worried pause at Vic's pointed silence. "But that was insensitive and badly timed. I'm sorry. Are you really horribly mad at me?"

Vic maintained her glare for another few seconds, then rolled her eyes at Jet's earnest expression. "No. It's too damn hard to stay really mad at you. I do like seeing you grovel and squirm, though."

The server behind the counter shouted out their order number and Jet got up, with some obvious relief, to fetch their meals. Vic watched him go. She blew a sharp upward breath that ruffled her long eyelashes, then ran a hand over her head, tousling her pale hair. "It's a good thing you challenge him," she said to Donovan, motioning toward Jet with a tilt of her chin. "Otherwise, he'd always think he's right. I mean it, though; I think it was brave of you to speak up in front of the zhree."

Jet returned, sliding into his seat with a tray containing their food. Vic looked at her boyfriend, and the small, wry smile on her face rose, reaching her eyes. Tamaravick Kohl was so carelessly attractive that sometimes Donovan had to make an effort not to stare; he knew how much Vic disliked being noteworthy for her looks. Beauty wasn't exactly an asset for a SecPac officer.

As they dug into their meals, Jet tapped the table in front of Donovan, as if remembering he ought to mention something. "I went back to interview Dr. Nakada's ex-wife again this morning. And I got permission from Commander Tate to conduct a SecPac review of all her communications in the last year." He took a bite of his pita, then shook his head at Donovan's expectant look. "You were right: dead end. If she's helping him, she's a pro at hiding it."

"How about all his former coworkers?" Donovan asked.

"So far, nothing, but I'm still digging. Nakada was a workaholic without a lot of friends, but he must've had other connections we haven't found yet."

"Maybe Nakada's not the link," Donovan said as a disturbing thought occurred to him. "What if the traitor *is* a stripe? What if it's Jonathan Resnick?"

"The agent?"

"He'd have access to classified SecPac information. He spent two *years* in Sapience. If there's anyone in SecPac who'd be a sympathizer, it's him." Donovan felt bad for voicing suspicions about the man, but what if it was true? Could Jonathan be a double agent? Or, Donovan wondered, was this simply his distrust of "Brett" coming out?

"I don't know," Jet said. "He seemed awfully sincere that night, about wanting us to bring down Warde. Unless it was all an act."

Donovan chewed and swallowed. "Even if it's not him, maybe it's someone in SecPac like him. Someone in an undercover position with connections to the sapes."

"Those guys must be so strictly background-checked and monitored, though," Jet mused. He paused and gave Vic a nudge. "Hey, you got the shawarma, right? I thought it was your favorite."

Jet and Donovan were almost done eating, but Vic had barely touched her food. "I'm not that hungry," she said, slowly shredding a napkin between her fingers.

"What's wrong?" Donovan asked.

Vic shook her head. "Nothing."

"Come on, you know you're a terrible liar," Jet said. "What's going on?"

Vic's cheeks colored and she pressed her lips together before speaking in a bit of a rush. "I'm worried about my mom. The new medications she's taking have side effects, and . . . it's been a rough month for all of us." She dropped the torn napkin, not meeting either of their concerned gazes. "I don't really feel like talking about it right now. Sorry to be a downer."

Vic's mom had a chronic immune system disorder that prevented her from being erze-marked, something unusual among residents of the Round. Vic's parents had made the fateful decision to Harden their twin children, ostensibly to give them the same opportunities, but also because having at least one exo in the family was a way to gain residency in the Round and access to the superior health care it offered. It had turned out to be a tragic gamble.

Jet put a comforting hand between his girlfriend's shoulder blades, rubbing her back. "Hey," he said, in an upbeat tone that was clearly meant to cheer her up, "have you shown D?"

An oddly roguish smile crept onto Vic's face. She pulled up her sleeve and drew down her armor to reveal a tattoo partly encircling her upper arm: three small chain links, woven between her nodes. "It's not done," she explained. "Localized exocel suppressant only lasts for an hour, so that's as much as I could get in one session."

"Wow," Donovan said. "That's . . . daring."

"It's so freaky," Jet declared. "Suppressing your exocel is all sorts of wrong. And needles in your skin, under your armor?" He gave a dramatic, all-body shudder. "You scare me."

Vic snorted. "You're such a chicken," she said. "A big, armored chicken."

Jet leaned over to plant a kiss on Vic's temple and she smiled, rubbing a hand along his thigh with a casual affection that made Donovan lower his eyes. He crumpled the foil wrapper on his plate into a small aluminium ball. No wonder Jet, like Anya, was eager to move on.

7

An unseasonably hot sun beat down on Donovan's head the following Friday as he stood at attention on the largest training field on SecPac campus. On his left, Jet let out a soft, impatient breath; across an aisle gap to his right, Cass shifted her weight.

They were standing third row back from the front of the formation, which was arranged according to a baffling logic Donovan had never seen employed in inspection before: men on one side, women on the other, in reverse seniority with the youngest officers in the front rows, extending all the way back to the most senior stripes. With the exception of a reduced force patrolling the Ring Belt, every exo soldier-in-erze based out of Round Three appeared to be present. They'd been standing and waiting for nearly ten minutes. Right this moment, Donovan thought wryly, would be a really opportune time for Sapience to bomb something.

Commander Tate paced in front of the formation. Earlier, she'd addressed them briefly. "Hopefully, this won't take long," she'd said. "As you know, a high-ranking Commonwealth representative from Kreet has arrived, and Soldier Werth has asked us to present ourselves for ceremonial inspection, so look sharp. With any luck, we'll be out of this sun and on our way soon."

That possibility was looking less and less likely. In Donovan's experience, Soldier Werth was never late, so there must be something else going on, some delay in the visitor's schedule.

Commander Tate's glower was steadily deepening; she seemed more nervous than he'd ever seen her before. He was sure that she had not shared her suspicions about this whole affair with the rest of them.

Donovan's nerves stretched thin with the passing minutes. During the High Speaker's unpleasant visit last year, he'd been singled out and humiliated in front of the zhree zun and dozens of people. *Just stare straight ahead and keep your mouth shut*, he ordered himself now. *Don't draw any attention to yourself this time.*

A skimmercar arrived, gliding around the traffic circle and parking out of Donovan's sight. A few minutes later, a handful of zhree figures approached from the road. Commander Tate went to meet them, and unable to contain his curiosity, Donovan craned his head slightly into the aisle to better see what was going on.

A wave of sudden disquiet traveled through the assembled ranks of exo officers. It started at the front and rippled back—no sound or motion, just a feeling, a collective cascade of nervously rising armor. Soldier Werth was coming toward them. Walking next to him was a Soldier whose striped body pattern was different from any Donovan had seen before. Behind the two of them followed three other Soldiers with the same foreign erze markings.

The small group paused as Commander Tate reached them. Words were exchanged, and then the party continued toward the assembled soldiers-in-erze. In a powerful voice that needed no amplification even on a large field, Commander Tate called, "Atten*tion*!" and as one, the exos straightened and dropped armor smartly.

The visiting Soldier surveyed the ranks of humans for a moment, then walked along the first row silently. Soldier Werth accompanied him. Through the aisle gap, Donovan caught a better glimpse of the stranger. His eyes were small for a zhree, his legs stout, and his gait a little slow and deliberate as if nursing a stiff old injury; he favored walking on three limbs, with a fourth supporting his stride occasionally, like a cane. The dense stripes on his hull were thin and jagged. He held the fins on top of his body unnervingly still, betraying no expression that might usually be read in subtle gestures. When at last the stranger spoke, it was with a distinct homeworld accent, but his voice was so firm and precise that Donovan understood it easily.

"This is all of them, then?"

"Nearly all of them, zun," Soldier Werth replied. "Some remain on duty, protecting the Round and its surrounding human habitations." Soldier Werth's voice sounded unusually tense. Donovan realized that Werth had addressed the other zhree as a superior. This new Soldier outranked his erze master.

The stranger began walking up the empty aisle between the ranks of men on one side and women on the other. He motioned for his trio of subordinates to stay behind, and at a gesture from Soldier Werth, Commander Tate remained waiting at the front of the field as well. The corners of her eyes crinkled as she watched the two zhree continue alone. As the Soldier passed directly beside him, Donovan kept his eyes fixed straight ahead but felt the homeworlder's scrutinizing gaze passing over him before moving on to the next row.

"Are they capable of reproducing off planet?"

The question was so unexpected that even Soldier Werth seemed a little thrown off; there was a pause before he replied, "There have not been enough cases to know for certain. The

Nurses say they require gravity and radiation protection similar to that of their native environment, but there's no reason to believe they couldn't reproduce on a planet such as Rygur or a colony station such as Murtis 3."

"How long do they live after Hardening?"

"We estimate a hundred and forty Earth years on average," Soldier Werth replied. "The younger ones at the front, perhaps twenty or thirty years longer than that. Human exocellular technology continues to improve, as does medical care."

Donovan strained to keep listening, but the two Soldiers passed out of his hearing range as they continued their conversation down the aisle. Several minutes passed. Jet nudged Donovan's foot with his own; the two of them exchanged a sideways glance. Jet's creased eyebrows asked: *What the . . . ?*

Donovan's shoulders rose in reply: *Hell if I know.*

They faced sharply forward again as the two zhree returned down the center, the visiting Soldier still asking questions. "How do you compare their intelligence to other Class Two species such as the vosnumi, or the delkrans of Sirye?"

"I have limited prior experience working with delkrans and even less with vosnumi." The tone of Soldier Werth's answers was growing increasingly terse. "But by all accounts, and my own observations, humans compare favorably. More aggressive than the vosnumi, perhaps, and shorter-lived than the delkrans, but just as intelligent, arguably more so." Soldier Werth came to a sudden hard stop a few rows from the end of the aisle, less than ten feet from where Donovan stood. "If you'll indulge me for asking, Soldier Gur, what is the purpose of these questions? The communication from Kreet left me under the impression that you were here to assess troop levels. Yet you haven't been to the orbital defense platforms or our surface military facilities. Instead, the first thing you ask to see are the Hardened humans. Why?"

With his purposeful but slightly off-kilter gait, Soldier Gur took a few steps back toward Werth. "I understand your confusion." Four of Gur's eyes slid shut as he focused the nearer two on the other Soldier. "The High Speaker sent me here not merely to evaluate military assets on Earth, but to develop a drawdown schedule."

Soldier Werth went still. "Then the Council has already decided."

"The High Speaker is communicating the specifics to Administrator Seir as we speak," Soldier Gur said. "After a considerable amount of deliberation, the Homeworld Council has decided that the Commonwealth shall begin withdrawing its presence from Earth."

When Soldier Werth finally spoke again, his voice sounded oddly off-key. "The Council cannot possibly have yet fully evaluated our proposal to maintain the colony with reduced investment."

"It is the opinion of the High Speaker and the Homeworld Council that the colonial proposal relies too heavily on human involvement, and as such is an unreliable long-term solution. Given our vulnerability to the Rii in this sector, withdrawal is the most strategically sound option. The reduction in force will be gradual, but will commence as soon as possible. The High Speaker has appointed me to oversee the process."

Donovan forgot his earlier instructions to himself and turned his head to stare aghast at the two Soldiers. The only reason he knew he hadn't misunderstood was the fact that Soldier Werth also appeared to be having a difficult time taking in the news. Werth's fins began to move in response, then stopped, then moved again as he spoke in a single, flat, heavy note. "I see."

"You're disappointed," Soldier Gur observed matter-of-factly. "That's understandable. You've devoted the work of your erze to this faraway colony and it will be difficult to transition away from it." Gur raised a limb to stave off response and his voice took on an encouraging tone. "However, don't fear that your time and experience here were a waste. I've led my erze on deployments to twelve different star systems and twenty-five different planets, and I can assure you: The Mur Commonwealth will have need of you and your Soldiers elsewhere. I even doubt that being hatched out here will be much of a disadvantage to you in the long run."

"You haven't yet answered my question, zun," Soldier Werth said, his fins moving barely enough to be understood, "regarding your interest in humans."

"Humans are the most problematic factor in determining a drawdown schedule," said Gur. "As a sentient Class Two species on a Mur colonial holding, they're technically entitled to Commonwealth protection. Theoretically, once the Council reneges claim on the planet, as it presumably will after the withdrawal is complete, then that obligation would cease." Gur tapped pincer fingers thoughtfully against a leg as he peered at the humans around them. "But humans are not found anywhere else and there's something about the Hardened ones that makes them seem . . . almost zhree. Considering the Rii threat in this part of the galaxy, failure to make arrangements for the preservation of a fellow exocel-enabled species would be politically frowned upon on Kreet and, I warrant, unacceptable to Earth-hatched colonists."

Soldier Gur was certainly a homeworlder, but he was unlike the High Speaker. Donovan remembered how skeptical and disdainful the High Speaker had been of humans; Gur seemed too worldly and seasoned a Soldier to view them with any particular scorn or esteem. Humans were an operational challenge to be accounted for, as simple as that.

"When the time comes, we will need to evacuate a population of humans with us. The question is how many, and which ones." Soldier Gur gestured down the field at the surrounding exos. "Fortunately, I can commend you colonials for having established a selection process already. You've already screened for intelligent, healthy, skilled humans to bring into your erze, and the Hardened ones are robust enough for interstellar travel. That is an excellent starting point. It will still be complicated—we will have to consult each erze and optimize across multiple factors to ensure a genetically viable and socially functional population. Your expertise in humans will be invaluable in this regard, Soldier Werth." Gur's eyes were still fixed on Werth, and now his fins snapped in firm expectation. "As will your leadership in maintaining erze morale and aiding me in all aspects of the drawdown process."

Donovan had always associated three figures in his life with total authority: his father, Soldier Werth, and Commander Tate. He goggled in disbelief now to see both his commander and his erze master struck dumb. Commander Tate's face was a gathering storm cloud over her clenched jaw. At first, Soldier Werth was like a statue; then his fins cut sharply through the air. "You will have whatever assistance you require, zun. We may be a frontier colony, but we understand erze duty as well as any Soldiers of the Commonwealth."

"I expect no less," said Soldier Gur, dipping his fins in acknowledgment. He began to walk again, all six eyes sliding open once more. "Now I would like to address these humans. Do they understand our language?"

"Some of them, to varying extents." For a second, Donovan thought two of Soldier Werth's eyes rested on him, noticing him standing nearby and realizing that the human had heard and understood all that had been said. Werth followed Soldier Gur. "I'll have a translation machine brought out."

Sweat trickled down Donovan's neck; he felt it sticking his uniform shirt to his back. His heart was galloping as if he'd run for miles. Was this really happening? Had he just heard the conversation that sealed the fate of Earth and the entire human species? A couple more minutes passed in sweltering silence. It was unbearable. Donovan wanted to move, to look around, to see who else realized the truth. He bit his tongue and held his place silently.

At last, a portable platform and a translation machine were brought out from the nearest building by a non-Hardened staff member who gaped openly at the foreign zhree and retreated with haste. Soldier Gur ascended the two steps of the platform so that he stood visibly overlooking the entire assembly of exos. "Soldiers-in-erze." The translation machine relayed Gur's words in a magnified baritone human voice. "Changes are forthcoming. Do not be anxious about them. Your erze master will explain everything you need to know at such time as you need to know them. What has not changed are your duties; you will continue to perform them as you always have." Soldier Gur spoke even slower and more deliberately than usual, as if doing so would aid in the humans' understanding. "The one change you must be aware of now is this: I will be remaining on Earth along with three hundred of my Soldiers." He gestured in example to the three standing behind him. "They are of equal authority to the Soldiers you are already accustomed to. Any orders given by myself or by them are to be considered erze orders. Obey them as you would obey instruction from your erze master." Gur stepped off the platform.

Visible discontent pervaded the exo ranks now. The officers shifted, expressions of stifled incredulity on every face. Soldier Werth's fins were flattening in even more severe displeasure. Donovan imagined it was already hard enough for Werth to accept that this homeworlder was taking over; it was a deeper cut still for Gur to claim all the exos wearing Werth's markings were now under his authority.

Donovan doubted the foreigner could read unhappy human facial expressions, but if Gur noticed Werth's simmering anger, he didn't react to it. "There's more to discuss regarding the humans, but it can wait until I've assessed the other variables." Gur began striding away toward the skimmercar, expecting the other Soldier to follow. "What percentage of your Soldiers were hatched on Earth?"

Soldier Werth delayed a beat, just long enough to exchange a wordless glance with Commander Tate. Five of his eyes blinked so that for an instant, only one was staring directly at his highest-ranking exo. One of his fins made a short slash in the air. The line of Commander Tate's jaw flexed as she jammed her lips together and nodded.

"Sixty-three percent," Werth said in answer to his interrogative guest as he strode after Gur. The musical zhree voices faded as they drew away, Gur's retinue following behind. Commander Tate waited until all the zhree had returned to the skimmercar. Then she turned back to the now excruciatingly stiff and disgruntled exos. "At ease," she said.

They broke into motion and shouting at once. "So that homeworld shroom is in charge now?" "Are the zhree really going to *leave*?" "Can someone tell those of us who were in the back what they were talking about? We couldn't hear a thing!"

Tate raised both of her hands, and when that didn't result in the usual silence she commanded, she bellowed, "Get a grip, stripes!" They quieted sufficiently for her to continue. "We don't know nearly enough to go bursting our nodes yet. I'll talk to Soldier Werth and get more clarity around what's really going on and what we can expect." Tate had her sharp, energetic authority back but still wore the expression of a person who'd been hit by a bus and was dazedly trying to pick up scattered belongings and remember where she'd been going before the accident. "When I find out more, you'll hear it. *In the meantime*, don't go spreading panic. Keep this to yourselves."

"Commander," Katerina called out, raising a hand. "Is it true, what the homeworlder said? That from now on, he and his Soldiers are the ones in charge, and orders from them are erze orders?"

Commander Tate's eyes lit with a cold blaze. "I don't want any of you disrespecting the foreign Soldiers or giving them the slightest reason to pay attention to us. But you *don't* answer to anyone with different stripes." She looked around. "Let's get out of this scorching heat already. And back to work, before Sapience realizes we've all gone on extended lunch break."

They were dismissed, but no one seemed to be leaving. They milled about on the field, speculating anxiously. Before Donovan could take two steps, he was surrounded. Everyone knew how well he understood the Mur language, and they'd seen that he'd been standing near enough to hear most of the conversation between Gur and Werth. "What did they say?" Claudius demanded. "It sounded like they were talking about *evacuating*. That can't be right, can it?"

Cass and Jet were moderately fluent in Mur and had also heard much of what had transpired. They exchanged worried and uncertain glances with each other, then looked to Donovan. "What does this mean?" Cass asked in a near whisper.

Donovan met the disbelieving gazes of his erze mates. He barely heard the words come out of his own mouth. "The end of the world as we know it."

8

Six days after Soldier Gur's pronouncement, Donovan and Jet crowded in next to Tennyson and Lucius along a side wall of the packed Comm Hub briefing hall. People were talking in small groups, their voices strained. Tennyson said, "You guys seen the news? The sapes are celebrating. A crowd of them attacked that big protest march in Denver."

"Everything's going to hell," Lucius muttered.

The strange thing was, at first glance the world didn't seem all that different. When Donovan looked out his bedroom window in the mornings, he still saw the sun rising in the east behind the spires of the Towers, which stood as firm and solid as ever. Ships still appeared in the sky over the landing fields, skimmercars sped along the roads, people walked down the streets and went about their daily lives. Yet an unbelievable new reality was rapidly unfolding.

Administrator Seir and the zhree zun had communicated the Homeworld Council's decision within each of their erze. People had friends and family outside the Round, so rumors had begun to fly even before the Prime Liaison was informed and the human government and the media became involved. By now the entire world had learned that the seemingly impossible was happening: The Mur Erzen Commonwealth would be withdrawing support from Earth, and the zhree colonists had been ordered to begin evacuation preparations.

To Donovan, the only real evidence that this wasn't all a giant hallucination could be found in the streets of the Ring Belt. Earlier that day, he and Jet had responded to reports of a Sapience-related disturbance and found two straw-stuffed zhree effigies burning in a parking lot, along with a nude mannequin with exocel nodes and Soldier's stripes drawn onto it with black permanent marker. A dozen or so people were cavorting in the street, hollering. When they caught sight of the SecPac skimmercar, they threw bottles and bricks and fled. Jet dealt with the fire while Donovan caught the slowest perpetrator and handcuffed him.

"Once the shrooms are gone for good, we're going to deal with you pets and traitors," the man shouted, twisting on the asphalt. "Earth for proper humans again!"

Judging by the worried chatter in the briefing hall, that incident had hardly been the only one. Commander Tate came into the room and took the podium. She did not look as if she'd been sleeping well. "I know you have a lot of questions, and I'm not going to be able to answer all of them. But here's what you need to remember: We're *stripes*. It's our job to project calm out there. If you're approached by the media or civilians, the one line you should be repeating is that *nothing's changing right now*. The drawdown schedule is still being developed and it's going to be *gradual*. We're looking at a five- to ten-year transition plan. Take a page out of DeGarmo's playbook and stick to the same message that the Liaison Office has been delivering over and over again. No public speculation. Clear?"

Donovan had seen the new Prime Liaison on the news fielding anxious questions, her reassuring manner strained to the utmost. "The government of West America, along with other nations around the world, will work closely with the representatives of the Mur Commonwealth to ensure a gradual and orderly transition process." Donovan felt sorry for DeGarmo; she'd barely taken office as Prime Liaison and *this* was what happened in the first month? Even Donovan's father had never had to deal with a crisis of such magnitude.

"Commander," Sebastian called out from the third row. "What about the Rii? Will they attack Earth once the Mur colonists leave?"

Murmurs rose from the assembled officers. The nomadic Rii were enemies of the Mur Commonwealth, and Earth was in a strategic location on the frontier of Commonwealth space. Last year, the appearance of Rii scouting ships in the solar system had prompted fears of possible invasion. Tate scowled at the question. "Do I look like a fortune-teller to you? A Rii attack could happen in a year, or a hundred years, or never. We don't know what planetary defense is going to look like without Soldiers—obviously, that's going to have to be a big part of the transition plan that will be jointly developed by the zhree zun and human governments. Until we hear further information, we have more immediate problems to deal with."

The commander shoved her glasses onto the bridge of her nose and consulted her screen. "Sapience activity is up. By a lot. We're seeing major breakouts near Rounds Four, Seven, Eight, Thirteen, and Fifteen, and additional reports coming in from cities all over the country and the world."

"The sapes are going to get what they wanted, aren't they? The zhree gone, squishies in charge," Tennyson said angrily. "What do they have to fight for anymore?"

Commander Tate looked up from the podium. "Some of them think they've won and they're celebrating the way sapes do, with high-grade explosives and plenty of ammunition. The more strategic ones know that this is just the beginning, and they see the opportunity to finally topple the government and set themselves up to call the shots. And on top of that, you've got some latecomers rushing to join up with Sapience; they figure that once the zhree leave, they'd better be cozy with the people who have the survival skills and the guns."

People like Kevin. Where was Anya in all this? With a stab of worry, Donovan imagined her out there somewhere amid the dangerous restiveness. Was she celebrating too? Was she joining in the surge of violence, or trying to steer clear of it?

"The Prime Liaison has declared that transition talks with the zhree colonists will begin as soon as possible," Tate told them. "The Round is the only place deemed secure enough to hold those discussions. There are going to be a lot of political leaders in here over the next several weeks, including the President of West America and members of Congress. Which means increased security at all the gates and rotating protection details. Patrol schedules are going to change; you'll get specifics in the next day or two. SecPac's primary objectives right now are to quell the surge of Sapience uprisings and ensure the complete security of the transition talks."

Tate swept a low gaze over the room. When no one raised any further questions, she said, "It's not the end of the world. And if it is, we still have jobs to do. Dismissed."

People dispersed to attend to duties while others lingered in the room, conversing in low voices. Small crowds gathered around wall screens broadcasting news from around the world. In East America, riots had broken out in New York, Boston, and Philadelphia. In South-East Africa, Round Seventeen had deployed air strikes against Sapience-held territories in Sudan.

Jet was looking at his comm unit display. "Soldier Gur's in Round Seventeen right now. Kamo posted to the cadre message board. Sounds like they had the same 'erze inspection' as we did." Soldier Gur had departed Round Three, leaving a couple dozen of his Soldiers posted in and around the Towers, where they stalked about, inspecting things and making people nervous. Gur had taken the rest of his contingent with him as he traveled to other Rounds across Earth, evaluating zhree military and civilian assets and setting evacuation plans into motion. Donovan and Jet were getting day-by-day updates and reactions from the fellow soldiers-in-erze in their cadre, the international cohort of peers that they'd gotten to know well during their years of SecPac training.

"Any word from Amrita?" Donovan asked. Yesterday, one of their cadre mates in Round Ten had shared the worrisome news that her partner, Mustafah, had been called into a disciplinary hearing for failing to drop his armor to one of Gur's Soldiers.

"Two weeks' suspension for insubordination. Gur's Soldier wanted him stripped of his markings. Can you believe that?" Jet made a noise of angry disgust and scrolled through his accumulated messages. "Fernando says that the fighting in the Ring Belt around Round Twelve has gotten so bad that some of the exos are paying to get their families out of the country to safer Rounds."

Donovan's own comm unit went off, beeping insistently and flashing a high-priority alert. Donovan looked down at the display. An order from Tate. *IN MY OFFICE NOW.*

"You didn't get this, did you?" he said, showing Jet the message. When his partner shook his head, Donovan stowed his comm unit and hurried toward the commander's office in the center of the Comm Hub building. Was he in some sort of trouble?

When he knocked on Tate's closed office door, she barked, "Come in, Reyes." Donovan entered the room and stopped in surprise. A woman in a burgundy suit was sitting in the chair in front of the commander's desk. Her hands, one resting on top of the other over one of the chair's armrests, were patterned with the bold, interlocking rings of the Administrator erze. Prime Liaison DeGarmo turned slightly upon Donovan's entrance and gave him a thin, curious smile.

"The famous Donovan Reyes," DeGarmo said.

"Madam Prime Liaison." Belatedly, Donovan dropped his armor and stood attentively, but his eyes flicked questioningly to Commander Tate.

Despite having summoned him here, the commander paid Donovan's arrival little heed; her attention was entirely on her important visitor. Donovan was taken aback to see her face locked in a stiff mask of displeasure. The armor rose thick over the backs of her striped hands as she gripped the edge of her desk, leaning over it. "With all due respect, Madam Prime Liaison, I feel the need to reiterate my strong opposition to this plan." Tate's voice was forcibly level. "The Human Action Party is a thinly veiled political arm of the terrorist organization Sapience, which the Global Security and Pacification Forces are staunchly committed to defeating. We've seen this before in other parts of the world: Sapience taking on political trappings to advance their agenda. The Nueva Libertad party, the Groupe de L'humanité . . . twenty years ago, it was the Earth Renewal movement. The Human Action Party has terrorist underpinnings, and allowing *any* of their members to enter the Round would be an unacceptable security violation."

"Commander Tate, I appreciate your concerns, but these transition talks between the zhree colonists and humankind are going to set the tone for the country, possibly the world, for the foreseeable future." The Prime Liaison's voice was equally calm and insistent. "The Human Action Party has gained wide popular support for its pro-human independence agenda. It represents a far broader swath of the population than the extreme and militant Sapience faction."

Commander Tate's lips twitched as if she was struggling to prevent them from curling in derision. "It's obvious that Sapience still forms the core of the HAP and sets its direction. Why else would they appoint Saul Strong Winter—a known terrorist leader—as their spokesperson?"

"Strong Winter has gained an enormous following with his public broadcasts and speeches. He may be one of the hard-liners, but I believe that many of his views appeal to moderates as well." The Prime Liaison shifted sideways in her chair and motioned to Donovan. "But that's why we've asked Officer Reyes here, isn't it? Officer, you've dealt directly with Strong Winter before—successfully negotiated with him, in fact. Perhaps you can shed some light on whether it would be reasonable to include him in the transition talks."

Both gazes shifted to Donovan expectantly. Donovan didn't move farther into the room. He'd been asked in here as a character witness for Saul? He had no idea what to say, other than the truth. "Saul Strong Winter is the reason my father's dead."

Tate's chin dipped in fierce satisfaction. "There's your answer, Madam Prime Liaison. Your own safety would be in question. That's something SecPac cannot tolerate."

Angela DeGarmo's shoulders rose and fell in a considered breath. "The Guerras were found to have acted alone. Strong Winter wasn't implicated in that horrible crime."

Yes, he was. Donovan could hardly explain that *he* had given Saul the information that had ultimately allowed Sapience to murder his father. "Sapience planned the assassination. Saul was the cell leader. He would've made the call." He thought of Saul's gruff authority, the hardness of the man's deep-set eyes. "He'd do anything for the cause he believes in."

DeGarmo paused significantly. "Even lay down arms and negotiate?"

Donovan stared straight back at the woman he'd helped to put into office. DeGarmo was younger than Donovan's father had been; her hair had subtle streaks of gray and there were wrinkles around her eyes, but her face was otherwise unlined and Donovan had seen an attentively friendly, down-to-earth manner in the way she spoke and nodded at people. She seemed energetically populist in a way that Donovan suspected his father would not have approved of. Yet behind the mild eyes, there was a polite but determined tenacity, the look of someone accustomed to getting what she wanted—and in that alone, Donovan was reminded of his father.

"Yes," Donovan said. "Even negotiate. Saul has strong views, but he's calculating as well. He'll balance what he can accomplish with what it'll cost him."

The Prime Liaison pulled a small screen from the pocket of her dark blazer. She unfolded it, tapped it twice, and leaned forward to set it down in the center of Commander Tate's desk. Tate straightened up and glared at the device as Saul's rough voice began speaking, filling the confines of the office and rumbling over the faint background sounds of the dispatch room outside.

"We don't want to be 'in erze.' We don't want our hands tattooed with alien symbols or our children's bodies mutilated by alien technology. We don't want to be part of a galactic empire that places us at the bottom." Saul's voice was even, deep, and reasonable. Donovan's feet clenched in his boots; for a second, he felt as if he were facing Saul back in the Warren. The underground bunker had been destroyed, but Donovan could easily picture the Sapience commander's wide face and hooded eyes as he spoke into the microphone in whatever secret location he now occupied. There was a pause, a soft exhalation in the recording: Saul no doubt blowing out a long stream of cigarette smoke before continuing. *"Exos are the blunt tool that the shrooms use to maintain control over us. Is there any more effective way to keep humans downtrodden and divided than to give a few of them power and privilege over the others? Hardening is a violent act of colonial oppression."*

Commander Tate jabbed the screen with a finger, turning it off. "These bigoted rantings are an insult to erze-marked and Hardened people everywhere," she growled. "Extremists like Saul Strong Winter would roll back a century of progress to satisfy their romantic vision of human freedom and purity from the time before the Landing. If they didn't have zhree and exos to hate, they'd find other reasons for people to kill one another." The dark weave of Tate's exocel crawled over the cords of her taut neck. "And you want to welcome them to the table."

"You may disagree vehemently with everything Strong Winter says," the Prime Liaison said, rising from her seat and straightening her sleeves. "But you can't deny that there are millions of people in this country and around the world who share his views. People who feel like third-class citizens on their own planet and see this dramatic moment in history as a chance to change that. If we exclude the Human Action Party from the transition talks, those people will believe they've been ignored and dismissed, and they'll flock to the hard-liners who encourage violence. The Prime Liaisons in the other Rounds are all facing this same challenge. What happens here in West America next week will set an example for the rest of the planet."

"If the Liaison Office *insists* on this inadvisable course of action," Tate ground out through a tight jaw, "then hold the talks elsewhere. In Denver. Inviting Sapience members with criminal records into the Round would send the unacceptable message that we're forgiving terrorism."

"It would send the message that we've turned a corner into a new era of human history, one in which the old rules might have to change. That's true, Commander, whether we like it or not." The Prime Liaison picked up and pocketed her screen, then turned toward Donovan. "I can appreciate your personal feelings on this, Officer Reyes. I'm sorry for what you've been through, though I hope you understand what's at stake now."

Donovan hadn't moved an inch from his stiff-backed position near the door. Hearing Saul's voice telling him *again* that he and his fellow exos were less-than-human abominations made his stomach curdle. And the idea of sapes walking free in the Round under the auspices of political immunity made him nearly as angry as Commander Tate. But wasn't this exactly why he'd supported Angela DeGarmo in the first place? Because he'd hoped that maybe a negotiation with Sapience was possible? A curl of shame stirred uncomfortably in Donovan's gut; his father would be turning over in his grave.

"I understand what's at stake, ma'am," he said coolly, meeting and holding DeGarmo's steady gaze. "You need to strike an alliance with the moderates in Sapience. Otherwise, once the zhree colonists leave, your government will collapse or be overthrown. Those of us with marks on our hands will be the first to be targeted and strung up in the anarchy."

"Well," said the Prime Liaison, smiling uncomfortably, "you certainly are a Reyes, in perceptiveness and pessimism. I mean that as a compliment." Speaking to Commander Tate, she said, "The transition talks will begin in the Round as scheduled; with Human Action Party representatives in attendance. I have full confidence in SecPac's ability to see to the safety and security of everyone involved." DeGarmo stretched her close-lipped smile in a deceptively amiable parting, then left the office.

Commander Tate stared at the closed door for a motionless second, then dropped heavily into her chair. She massaged her brow slowly, one hand over her eyes.

Donovan waited, uncertain, expecting to be dismissed. Without looking up, Tate spoke, her normally strong voice unusually muted. "Tell me, Reyes: Do you believe peace can be achieved through diplomacy? That common ground can be found among humans on Earth?"

Donovan lowered his gaze to the floor in front of the commander's desk. His father and mother were proof that people would rather die than compromise their strongest beliefs. But if he believed there was no hope of reaching an understanding between enemies, he wouldn't have walked into the middle of a hostage standoff last year. He wouldn't have said Angela DeGarmo's name when called upon last month. And he wouldn't still be thinking about Anya with the warm, crazy notion that maybe someday . . .

"Yes," Donovan answered at last. "I . . . I think it's possible, ma'am."

"I don't," Tate said. "In all my years as a stripe—and I've had a lot of them—I've seen peace attempts come and go. Periods of heavy insurgency, then cease fires and negotiations that hold for a while before breaking down. One step forward, another two back. These talks never go anywhere in the end. Saul Strong Winter and his supporters are the latest in a long line of terrorist sons of bitches that can only be defeated by force. Even the withdrawal of the Mur Commonwealth isn't going to change that."

"What are we going to do, ma'am?" Donovan asked.

Tate snorted and rose from her chair, all hard edges again. "Orders are orders, Reyes, and we're stripes. We're going to give these talks the best possible chance of success so that no one can find fault with SecPac's commitment to the transition efforts. And when these talks fail—because they will—we're going to do what we've always done best: Fight like hell."

9

"Stay calm, stripes." Thad was fifty meters away, but his voice was firm in Donovan's comm unit earbud. "The sight of battle armor isn't going to help things right now."

Donovan forced himself to take a calming breath and draw his exocel down. It itched to crawl back up. The crowd outside Gate 2 had started gathering yesterday evening before the official start of what the press was calling the West America Future Summit. It was midmorning now and the throngs of competing protestors had swollen to several thousand. Heavy SecPac cordons kept them roped off from the road and three hundred meters away from the security checkpoint area, but as the hours wore on and their agitation rose, they grew increasingly less inhibited about shouting abuse at one another and the soldiers-in-erze on duty.

It was getting difficult for Donovan to discern who in the mass of people was angry about what. A large percentage of the crowd seemed to consist of Human Action Party supporters, chanting, "I say freedom, you say now! Freedom! NOW! Freedom! NOW!" but there was a solid cooperationist block on the other side of the street, including a group of hundreds of exos, of all different erze markings, silently holding hands with placards hanging around their necks: HARDENING IS A HUMAN RIGHT and WE ARE NOT PETS and EARTH IS BIG ENOUGH FOR US ALL. Donovan kept the most vigilant watch on one cluster of demonstrators pushing aggressively close to the barricade with signs that read: **TRUE** SAPIENCE! NEVER NEGOTIATE, NEVER SURRENDER. SAUL ~~STRONG~~ WEAK WINTER. Apparently, Saul had made enemies among the most militant Sapience rebels for consenting to come to the Round and talk to the government at all.

Overhead, a cloud passed in front of the sun, plunging them all briefly into shadow before clearing again. "First Soldier Gur orders the zhree to withdraw from Earth, and now Strong Winter and the sapes are being allowed into the Round. The world's gone completely scorching sideways," Jet muttered in disgust, off comm so only Donovan could hear him. "Are you regretting picking DeGarmo for Prime Liaison yet?"

Donovan stiffened. "I didn't know this would happen."

"No one did," Vic said, raising a hand to shield her eyes from the sun. Donovan caught a glimpse of three new chain links added to the tattoo on her arm. "It's obvious even the sapes weren't expecting this, not so suddenly. Maybe it *is* a good time to get them to talk."

"D's old man wouldn't have stood for this," Jet said. "He'd have a better option."

"Maybe," Donovan said, but his teeth were gritted as he said it. He didn't appreciate his best friend reminding him of his dead father's stone-cold virtues, and even though he couldn't refute Jet's pessimism about the whole Future Summit, he still wanted the transition talks to succeed. Including bringing in Saul. Because what was the alternative? Civil war?

A violent scuffle was breaking out between the True Sapience supporters and the cooperationists; several people were on the ground. The nearest SecPac officers armored up and moved in to

90

control the outbreak, causing other demonstrators to shout and throw rocks at them. Donovan's exocel rose and he took a step forward, instinctively wanting to go to the aid of fellow stripes, but at that moment, three muddy green petroleum-burning SUVs came into sight, rolling up the boulevard through the Ring Belt toward the gate of the Round.

Donovan made his hands unclench as he stepped back, keeping his attention on the approaching vehicles. The President and other government officials attending the summit were flying directly into the small private airport inside the Round, but Saul and the delegates from the Human Action Party insisted on arriving in their own vehicles. Though he had no desire to see Saul again, Donovan was the one SecPac officer who'd met and spent time with the infamous Sapience commander personally and could identify him with certainty. He'd had no choice about being assigned to SecPac's welcoming party for the sapes.

The appearance of the SUVs was met by loud cheering from some parts of the gathered masses and deep boos from others. "Clear the gate," Thad ordered. One by one, the vehicles pulled into the inspection area and the heavy outer barricade closed behind them with a solid clang. Donovan took a deep breath, then strode forward ahead of the other officers.

The passenger-side door of the lead vehicle opened and a thick, booted leg stepped down. Saul got out. He looked much the same as Donovan remembered him; his wide, stiff-jawed face had perhaps a few more furrows in it than before, and the smooth center of his shaved head had grown a bit larger. He was wearing scuffed fatigues and a military vest, and looked as if he might have come straight from a Sapience training camp or a bunker in the woods.

The only thing missing from the picture was an assault rifle over his shoulder.

"Reyes, confirm?" Thad said.

"That's Strong Winter, all right," Donovan said into his comm unit transmitter. He kept his feet moving forward. Surprisingly, seeing the terrorist leader didn't arouse the surge of vengeful hatred Donovan had imagined it would. Instead, he thought: *Saul looks tired.*

"Turn around and face the gate," Donovan ordered, and was relieved that his voice came out as strong, flat, and professional as anyone could expect of a SecPac officer. "Hold your arms straight out from your sides and keep them there until told otherwise. Everyone in your party will be searched and your vehicles inspected before you proceed into the Round."

Saul's square jaw dipped fractionally. His combat boots clomped on the pavement as he complied, the rising motion of his thick shoulders scrunching up the vest around his neck. Donovan ran a scanner over him, then patted him down with brisk but thorough efficiency. He felt around the man's waistband, inside the tops of his boots, checked his lighter, and looked inside his box of cigarettes. None of the Human Action Party delegates would be allowed to carry so much as a nail file into the Round; on that point, Tate had been adamant.

Saul's eyes were impassive, but the corners of his thick lips pressed together as he stood in stoic acceptance of the ordeal. The last two times they'd met, Donovan had been at Saul's mercy; this time he was armed and in uniform and surrounded by erze mates who were watching closely for the sapes to make any wrong move. Perhaps Saul too felt the irony of their reversed roles because he grumbled, in a low voice that only Donovan could hear, "We've come a long way from the Warren, haven't we, zebrahands?"

"You can put your arms down," Donovan said. "Once the rest of your delegation has been cleared, two SecPac vehicles will escort you through the Round to the hotel where you and your people will be staying." As Commander Tate had said, orders were orders. He was determined to handle this uncomfortable situation by the rule book, as if he were a SecPac officer with no personal history or connection to any of these people. A stripe doing his job.

The other half dozen soldiers-in-erze in the inspection area had been scanning the SUVs from a wary distance, in case the whole thing turned out to be a ruse and the Sapience vehicles were laden with explosives intended to blow the checkpoint to smithereens. Upon seeing Donovan's all-clear signal to Thad, they moved in and motioned for the people inside the cars to exit and present themselves for inspection. The Human Action Party had sent about a dozen delegates in total. A few of the people who lined up facing the gate appeared to be lawyer types, but the rest looked like Saul—militant revolutionaries fresh from some Sapience hideout, who'd recently swapped out submachine guns for Human Action Party credentials. With an unpleasant jolt, Donovan recognized one of the men and a woman; they'd been at the hostage standoff last year and tried to drown him in an algae tank.

He began to move toward the line of people, but at that moment, the rear passenger door of the lead vehicle opened and a thin teenage girl stepped out. Donovan's heart seized in his chest and he stopped as if he'd run into a wall. "Anya." The name left him softly and involuntarily, like a released breath.

Anya wore a baggy black nylon jacket and the bottoms of her

jeans were tucked into the tops of her mud-stained boots. She saw Donovan at once. Her large eyes grew even larger in her fine-featured face as her lips parted in a small intake of breath. For the longest second that Donovan had ever experienced, they stared at each other. Donovan stood immobilized. She was like a bright floodlight dimming everything else; all the people and surroundings seemed to recede into the periphery of his awareness.

Anya turned and joined the rest of Saul's people, facing the wall at one end of the line, arms outstretched.

Donovan felt something inside him crumbling, the detached resolve he'd been determined to carry with him falling apart in her presence. He moved in behind her and patted her down with the same careful, professional efficiency he'd used on Saul, as if she were a stranger, but he felt as if every nerve ending in the surface of his hands was raw. He ran his palms over her arms and down her sides. His fingertips brushed along the skin around the top of her waistband and he drew his hands briskly down each of her legs. He felt abruptly ashamed that he was doing this—that he had to treat her in such a perfunctory and humiliating way, as if she were nothing to him, just a nameless criminal suspect, not someone he'd spent so many months yearning to see again. He remembered, too, late, and with a deeply embarrassed jolt, that under the circumstances, she could've requested to be searched by a female officer, but he wasn't sure she knew that, and in the shock of the moment he had forgotten to tell her. He swallowed his mounting discomfort and managed to say, in an undertone, "What are you doing here?"

"What does it look like?" she whispered back. Amused defiance.

The Human Action Party delegates were climbing back into

94

their vehicles. Thad gave the signal for the inner gate of the Round to be opened to allow them through. Donovan stepped back. Anya dropped her outstretched arms and moved her chin, briefly following him with her eyes. Then she turned and walked back to Saul and the SUV. She got in and closed the door.

Two SecPac patrol vehicles stood ready to escort the visitors to their destination. As Donovan watched the convoy of five vehicles pull away from the checkpoint, he felt Jet and Vic come up behind him. When Jet spoke, there was a warning note in his voice. "That was her, wasn't it?"

Donovan let out a held breath that was all the answer needed.

— — —

They got off duty at eighteen hundred, after the opening session of the Future Summit had already concluded. Throughout the day, Donovan had caught snatches of news in which journalists and political analysts speculated about what was being discussed behind closed doors. The biggest questions on the table, the experts said, concerned the speed and extent to which humankind could be expected to take responsibility for things that the zhree had always controlled, such as erze selection, and Hardening, and planetary defense.

When they got home, Donovan went upstairs and into his room, exchanging the bare minimum of words with his erze mate, who looked at him strangely but let him go. He closed the door and sat heavily on his bed, desperately wishing he could go back in time to the few minutes he'd had with Anya at the checkpoint that morning. He'd do things differently, say something better.

He heard Jet go into his room next door. His partner's voice was muffled through the wall but it sounded as if he was talking to Vic over his comm.

A minute later, a message flashed onto Donovan's comm display. It was from Vic. *We'll be talking for a while . . . Now's your chance.*

Donovan stared at the message for a long, stupefied moment, not sure whether to be shocked at Vic's presumption or mortified by how his feelings for Anya must've been blatantly transparent that morning. He got to his feet and sent a reply. *I owe you big time.*

Just be careful.

Thanks.

With a degree of stealth that made him feel embarrassingly dishonest, Donovan eased his bedroom door open, then snuck back down the stairs and out of the house.

The Future Summit was being held in the Towerside Hotel, a modern, expansive building only two miles from the Towers themselves. The initial plan to hold the meetings in the seat of zhree governance itself had been rejected; the Towers weren't equipped to provide lodgings to that many human visitors at once, and Commander Tate insisted on minimizing the amount of travel by the delegates so SecPac could keep a better eye on the proceedings.

There were plenty of SecPac vehicles already nearby so Donovan was confident his skimmercar's arrival would go unnoticed. The hotel's three wings were connected by zhree-style walkways and the walls were inlaid with different shades of metal forming artful designs resembling abstracted erze patterns. Donovan parked nearby and went in the main entrance.

There were a handful of SecPac officers posted on the main

level, Donovan went straight up to Nicodemus in the lobby and asked to see a list of the delegates and their room assignments.

There was another SecPac officer on guard in the lobby of the ninth floor, a middle-aged non-Hardened reservist, one of those people who did the less dangerous and less interesting noncombat jobs in the erze. The man nodded as Donovan exited the elevator, deferring to his rank and armor without question. His heart climbing steadily into his throat, Donovan walked down the hall and stopped in front of room 912. He hesitated for a long moment outside the closed door, but every protest he expected to hear in his own head had died to an acquiescent silence.

He knocked. The door opened so quickly it seemed Anya must've been waiting for him on the other side. For what might have been five seconds or thirty, they faced each other through the open doorway as if caught on opposite sides of a transparent glass barrier that allowed them to gaze through but held them invisibly apart.

She'd changed and yet she was the same. He recalled perfectly her eyes, the slight pout of her lips, the set of her shoulders, and the way she stood, perched slightly forward on the balls of her feet like some alert forest creature. She'd dyed her hair again; it was a deep chestnut brown with lighter highlights and fell barely past her softly framed chin. She was still skinny, but he thought she looked better fed than when he'd last seen her, or perhaps that was because he was encountering her here, in a bright, five-star hotel room and not in the damp concrete surroundings of an underground bunker. The incongruity, the oddness of it, of them being together again, of *her*, as seemingly out of place here as a deer on a space station, dried the words in Donovan's mouth.

Anya stepped aside wordlessly and Donovan walked in. She closed the door and he turned to face her. He cleared his throat. "How're you—"

She took two quick steps forward and suddenly the space between them was gone, snapped like the release of a stretched elastic band, and they were kissing—she was kissing him, and he was kissing her back, and then his hands were on her waist and her arms were around his neck, and it was every bit as good, no, even *better* than he remembered.

He couldn't get enough of her; she was like a bubbling spring of cold, fresh water, the most delicious thing he'd ever known. When they came apart at last, they were both breathing hard and Donovan's heart was pumping wildly against the hand she left pressed against his chest.

"That wasn't exactly how I thought it would go," Anya said weakly.

10

They sat on the bed together, close enough that their knees touched. He could smell the faint scents of pine soap and cigarette smoke on Anya's clothes. Her very presence next to him made Donovan's chest radiate with warmth. "I'm glad to see you," he said.

"Me too. I've thought about you a lot, you know." She gave him a small smile that seemed uncharacteristically bashful. "Sometimes I'd worry about you doing stupid stripe things that might get you killed."

"I worried about you too," he said. "After you left your apartment, I wondered where you'd gone, what you were doing. I don't understand; I thought you were with your sister."

Anya bit her bottom lip and scuffed the toe of her boot against the hotel room carpet. "I didn't want to go with her to Kansas City. We ended up having a big fight and I took off. I thought about leaving you a message or something, but it happened kind of suddenly, and I didn't want you to try and find me. You know, reasons." She glanced at him apologetically.

"Yeah." The way she'd left without telling him still rankled fiercely, but he couldn't really blame her. They were who they were, after all. A Sapience operative advertising her movements and location to him would make about as much sense as him informing her of his mission plans. Logic, however, did not blunt the stab of hurt and deep disappointment. She had no idea what kind of anxiety she'd caused him, how much time he'd spent staring at that wooden post and wondering why she hadn't responded, how upset and relieved he'd been when he'd finally mustered up the courage to find out she'd moved away. Seeing her today at the gate had dashed the hope that he'd clung to so perniciously: that she'd stayed with her sister and left her terrorist ties behind, had started a new life in a new place. She'd done none of those things.

He made his voice nonchalant. "So where did you go?"

Anya pulled her legs up onto the bedspread, picking at a loose thread and not answering at first. "Kevin wanted to go see Saul, so I went with him." Donovan stiffened instantly at Kevin's name. Anya noticed and said defensively, "Kevin's the best there is at getting around and not getting caught. He knows the Sapience network better than anyone. So when he gave me the chance to go along with him again, I took it."

It was difficult enough to accept that Anya was still in Sapience. The thought of her still attached to Kevin Warde made Donovan feel mildly sick. "So you can overlook him torturing and killing innocent people."

Anya leaned away from him. A note of anger and possibly shame colored her sharp retort. "I can't stop him from doing some of the awful things he does. But I'm not a part of it." To Donovan's surprise, she tugged at his hand, as if she desperately wanted him to understand. "Kevin's the one friend who's always been there for me when I needed him. And I needed him to take me to Saul. I was listening to Saul's speeches and wanted to join in what he was doing."

The defiant lift of Anya's chin drifted. "But when we got there, Kevin and Saul had an argument—a bad one. Kevin said some harsh things; he said that losing Max had taken the fight out of Saul and he'd lost his edge and been manipulated by you at the algae farm. And Saul said that Kevin was in love with his own ego and his brutal way of doing things would drive people away from any hope of real change."

Donovan stared at her in surprise. So it was true. Sapience really was divided.

"Kevin said we were leaving, but I said I didn't want to go. So he said, fine, if that's the way you're going to be after everything I've done for you, and he . . . he left me there." Anya blinked and turned her face away; she sounded truly sad about losing Kevin, possibly for good.

Donovan refrained from voicing his hope that her break from Kevin was permanent this time. Instead, he asked, "So how did you end up coming to the Future Summit?"

Anya's shoulders loosened a little, and she settled back in beside him. "I've been helping Saul with his broadcasts. I'm kind of like his technical assistant now. I do the recording and sound editing and try to get the episodes out on a sort of regular schedule to as many people as I can. It's . . ." She shrugged, her expression brightening with a satisfaction that Donovan had never seen in her before. "Great, actually."

"So you're a producer," Donovan said, unable to help smiling in return.

Anya snorted. "Yeah, can you believe it? I was never into computers or technical stuff. But what I'm doing now is making a big difference. Saul's speeches have brought a lot of new people into the Human Action Party."

Donovan thought about the clip of Saul's broadcast that the

Prime Liaison had played in Commander Tate's office. He remembered in an almost physically uncomfortable way how disgusted and angry it had made him feel. Those offensive words against exos . . . Anya had helped to put them out there, to millions of people, and she was proud of having done it.

The strangeness, the wrongness, of the situation hit him then, and for a second, Donovan felt as if his insides were being yanked apart. He could feel his face turning wooden, his armor rising up his spine. How could he sit happily next to this girl, wanting more than anything in the world to lean in and kiss her again? How could *she* kiss *him*, when she was doing everything she could to sow hatred and resentment against people like him? How did it make any sense?

Anya went on, oblivious to Donovan's internal distress. "Not everyone loves the speeches, though. They've caused problems because there are folks in Sapience who agree with Kevin; they think Saul's not going far enough, that he's softening his position to get more followers. After the news came out that the shrooms are planning to leave Earth, some people were upset that Saul agreed to come here and talk instead of calling for an uprising against the government right away."

"Why do you think Saul even agreed to come, then?"

Anya pursed her lips. "Saul wants to change the world, not watch it burn. I think that . . . after Max, he started thinking about the price we've paid, and . . ." She picked at her uneven nails. "He says it's time we fought for the future that we can get instead of the past we lost."

She paused and looked up at him, noticing his reticence. "You're asking me an awful lot of questions," she said slowly.

"What about you? You haven't said much." She sat back slightly and seemed to take him in fully for the first time—his uniform, his markings and exocel nodes, everything about him that identified him as one of the enemy. Anya's expression turned uncertain; Donovan could almost hear her mind grinding through the same doubts he'd struggled with a minute ago. Perhaps she too felt that awful tearing inside, because her shoulders curled forward slightly and she crossed her arms over her chest, guarded.

Last year, he'd been an injured and vulnerable prisoner and Anya had been a new Sapience recruit tasked to watch over him. Now she was Saul's assistant, a delegate for the Human Action Party and firmly entrenched in the Sapience cause. He was an armored and uniformed SecPac officer on home turf in the alien-constructed city he'd lived in all his life. There was no one and nothing forcing them to be together right now; they were here by choice. And they were further apart than they had ever been. Whatever connection they clung to now was thin and fragile, the gulf between them enormous. The lust and joy in their first rush of greeting felt strange, maybe even silly.

Donovan stood up and held out a hand to her. "Come on."

Anya got to her feet cautiously and put her hand in his, her eyebrows drawing together in confusion. He led her to the door of the hotel room and opened it, tugging her out into the hallway.

She stopped. "Where are we going?"

"Out."

"I'm not allowed to leave the hotel."

"Not without a SecPac escort," he corrected her. "You've never been in the Round before; don't you want to see what it's like? It might be your only chance."

She hesitated, but he knew curiosity would win out; Anya had always been fascinated by the very things she fought against. She glanced down the empty hallway, then turned toward Donovan and followed him to the elevator. The reservist guard seemed a little puzzled, but Donovan nodded at him in an unconcerned, cordial greeting, as if he were doing something entirely normal, and the man nodded back and didn't say a word as they got into the elevator.

The full-rank SecPac officers in the lobby required a little more convincing. "I'm taking this delegate to the store. She says she forgot some of her luggage," he explained to Demetrius. "Shouldn't take too long."

"Technically, they're not supposed to leave the hotel. What does she need? We can send someone to fetch toiletries," Demetrius said helpfully.

"Clothes," Donovan said. "In her size. It'll be quicker if I just escort her."

Demetrius didn't argue. As they exited the hotel and crossed the street, Anya whispered, "That was a *lot* easier than I thought it'd be." She kept glancing over her shoulder, surprised that Demetrius hadn't seemed suspicious or concerned. It simply wasn't in the nature of exos to distrust their erze mates. Nor to deceive them. Donovan quelled a sharp spasm of guilt, reassuring himself that what he was doing would cause no harm. He took Anya's hand and led her to his patrol skimmercar. "Have you ever ridden in a SecPac skimmercar before?" he asked her. She shook her head, her eyes wide, and he grinned. "Well, let's hope this is the only time it happens." He opened the door and gestured her in.

Anya stared at the unfamiliar dashboard, the steering column, and the comm unit display, then nervously eyed the partitioned part of the vehicle where suspects were usually contained. She made a small noise of surprise as the vehicle shot sideways away from the hotel on nearly silent micro-fission engines. Donovan reversed the skimmercar into traffic and it rotated automatically, moving with the seamless multi-directionality of all zhree-designed vehicles. Anya clutched the armrests of the passenger seat and laughed in nervous delight. Donovan's smile broadened; it was fantastic how the simplest things that he took for granted were new and exciting to her.

On a whim, he decided to take the skimmercar on a circuit around one of the major concentric boulevards. After setting the navigation, he leaned across next to Anya and pointed out the window. "That's where I used to live." From a distance, only the upper half of the Prime Liaison's residence was visible—the tops of the white columns and the flags on the roof flapping in the wind. Donovan pointed in another direction. "I live over there now, with some friends of mine. You can't see it from here, though." Anya nodded distractedly; her attention seemed to be in a dozen places at once. She pressed a hand excitedly to the window, craning to watch a cluster of zhree hatchlings running along the street to the park, two Nurses corralling them to stay together.

"Are those baby shrooms?" she exclaimed. "And their parents?"

"Hatchlings," Donovan corrected. "That's a brood cell, and its Nurses. Zhree don't have families like we do; they're cared for by Nurses until they're old enough to join their erze." He slowed the skimmercar and directed her gaze over to the left. "That blue building over there was my elementary school, before I was marked." Despite the late hour, a few children were still playing in the schoolyard. Anya let out a short gasp as a little girl jumped off the roof of the building and landed in the bushes, rolling end over end in the brambles. "She's fine," Donovan reassured her. Sure enough, the girl scrambled to her feet and ran back to the climbing tree next to the wall. Jumping off the roof of the school was a favorite pastime of every seven-year-old exo that ever lived.

Donovan took control of the skimmercar again and guided it to the eastern entrance of the Towers. He parked and got out of the car, but Anya remained sitting in the vehicle for several seconds, as if unsure whether to follow. She tilted her head back to stare at the alien spires stretching high into the evening sky, then back at Donovan. "Come on," he coaxed her. "Trust me."

As always, a couple of Soldiers were guarding the entrance, standing motionless and fearsomely battle-armored with all six large yellow eyes staring out watchfully in every direction. Anya's step slowed and her hand, suddenly warm and sweaty, tightened in Donovan's grip. "Don't be scared," he whispered. He strode forward, keeping her alongside. When they reached the guards, he dropped his armor respectfully and made to walk past them into the Towers.

"Wait," called one of the Soldiers. "Is that human . . . unmarked?"

Donovan paused and faced the Soldier, armor still lowered. "Zun, this is one of the dignitaries from outside the Round who's participating in the meetings with the human government this week. I'm taking her on a tour of the Towers."

"I've never seen an unmarked human in the Round before," exclaimed the Soldier, drawing closer and peering at Anya with great curiosity. Guard rotation at the Towers was a dull, ceremonial duty; there was little chance of threat in the Round, so any distraction was welcome.

"Careful, Wiest," said the other Soldier, who hadn't moved from his place. "Humans from outside the Round can carry diseases."

"Wiv, you soft-hulled idiot, have you ever heard of anyone catching a disease from a non-Hardened human?" Wiest exclaimed in an irritated trill.

"It can happen," insisted Soldier Wiv. "What about fin rot?"

Wiest's fins spread in exasperation. "That's bacterial, and you can only get it from bad algae that's been contaminated by human sewage."

"Um, zun," Donovan interjected. "May I?" He gestured forward.

Wiest stepped out of the way to let them pass, then shot a limb out and caught Donovan by the arm. In a low, confidential strum, he said, "I don't know if the erze master has mentioned this to you humans-in-erze, but stay out of the way of the homeworld Soldiers."

Donovan nodded. "I will, zun." He tugged Anya along through the entrance. Once inside, she let go of his hand and wiped her damp palms on her jeans. "What were those shrooms saying?"

"Nothing important," Donovan assured her. "Soldiers get bored and tease each other about random stuff all the time, same as us." He led her more slowly through the main entry chamber and up one of the curving ramps.

"Where are you taking me?" She didn't sound scared, but there was an anxious edge to her voice, despite the way she lingered and ran her fingers with obvious fascination across the metallic weave of the rounded walls.

"Up to the—" Donovan grabbed Anya by the arm and pulled her aside, ducking into a private eating room as one of Gur's Soldiers passed by. Fortunately, the unlit room was unoccupied or he would have greatly offended its occupant; the only thing inside was a meal stand with an empty food vessel and tube. Donovan waited until the domed body with its foreign stripes had passed out of sight down to the lower level, then said, "Okay, let's go."

"I don't understand," Anya hissed, almost accusingly. "Why are you afraid of that shroom if you weren't afraid of the other ones?"

"I'm not afraid," Donovan said. "I'd just rather not run into a homeworlder. Some of my friends in other Rounds have had bad experiences."

"Those shrooms aren't the same? They all have stripes."

Donovan suppressed a snort of incredulity that anyone could confuse Werth's and Gur's erze markings. "The one that just passed has different stripes. It means he's from a different Soldier erze than mine, and he's not from Earth."

"None of the shrooms are *from* Earth," Anya pointed out. "That's why they're leaving."

Donovan frowned. "Soldier Wiest and Soldier Wiv back there were hatched in Round Three. They're *from Earth* and wouldn't be leaving if they had a choice. The High Speaker and Soldier Gur are ordering the withdrawal, even though the zhree zun have—" Donovan stopped, realizing the explanation was not something he needed to go into with Anya right now. "In short, no, they aren't all the same."

"What about those ones up ahead?" Anya whispered.

"Those two? They're fine."

As they passed the two conversing Scholars, Anya glanced over her shoulder. "Why didn't you make your armor go down the way you did before?"

"I only need to drop armor to Soldiers of my own erze, and to erze zun—those are the highest leaders of each erze. Or if I'm requesting something from a zhree and really want to be polite. It's not necessary if I'm just passing someone in the hallway." He glanced upward; they were almost there.

"It's so complicated," Anya murmured. She was breathing harder as she climbed after him but didn't complain. "Different types of shrooms. A whole world I don't understand."

"We're here," he said, and took a branching corridor through a wide entrance with doors that opened silently at their approach. Donovan stepped out onto the open-air causeway. It was sheltered, but this high up, the wind was often strong enough to tear one's breath away. Tonight, there was only a gentle breeze that tousled his hair as he walked out onto the bridge that connected the main spire with one of the secondary towers. He turned around and motioned for Anya to follow him. She did so, moving slowly not out of fear but wonder, gazing around, lips slightly parted, a hand lightly gripping one of the structural support beams.

"The view is better a little farther ahead," Donovan said.

"Is this the very top?" Anya asked.

"Not quite." He pointed up to the highest point of the spire behind them. "The top levels hold the sanctuary and the main communications center, but we can't go in there without permission. This is the best view, though, because you can see in all directions."

"It's incredible," she breathed. The whole of the Round was spread out underneath them, and they could see past the white walls, to the sprawl of the Ring Belt and the vast wide horizon. Donovan led her to the apex of the gently arched walkway. The sun set late in June and the evening light was still making its prolonged departure from the sky, tinting the clouds a rosy hue as the city crept into bluish shadow. Streetlights had come on; looking at them from this height, it was easy to see where the Round ended and the Ring Belt began. Outside the wall, the lights were a blanket of dense bright pinpricks; inside, the illuminated streets gave off one soft glow, thickest and brightest along the spoke roads and the outermost boulevard, so that from above, the entire Round appeared as one perfect, luminescent wheel drawn in white neon on the prairie landscape.

Donovan swung a leg over the waist-high barricade and sat, straddling the ledge, resting his back against one of the support beams, one foot dangling into free space. If he dropped his boot, it would fall a long way before it hit the ground. Anya sidled up next to him, hugging herself against the growing chill as she continued to take in the scene stretched below them. Moving slowly, so Anya could pull free if she wanted to, Donovan put an arm around her shoulders. She leaned gently against him, and Donovan closed his eyes briefly, relaxing around Anya for the first time since he'd seen her at the checkpoint this morning. It had been a good idea to come here.

They watched together as darkness fell completely and the stars came out. Anya edged even closer to him; he felt her breath brushing his cheek. The wisp of hot touch shivered over Donovan's skin, drawing the thinnest layer of panotin trembling to the surface. He turned his head with agonizing slowness, as if trying not to frighten away a beautiful rare bird that had landed on his shoulder. Anya's eyes loomed near his. He had never been able to say exactly what color they were; when lit, they had the hue of a mossy stream or a sunbathed rock, but now they were simply large and luminous with the reflected glow of the city. Months of longing shrank to the space of a heartbeat that hung between them. He leaned in and kissed her.

Their mouths came together with less frantic exuberance than before, but if anything, the intensity was greater, more insistent and questing. Anya leaned slightly over him, tilting his head back against the beam behind them, her lips and tongue burning his, her face and hair filling his vision. Heat coursed through Donovan's body in a dizzying wave. He gripped the solid ledge beneath him with his legs, afraid for a second that overwhelming sensation would sway him off his perch and send him tumbling off the Towers. Anya clutched the front of his shirt; his hands slipped under hers and pressed against the small of her back, pulling her closer.

When they drew apart, he held her against his chest for a few breathless seconds, then kissed her again, more gently and for longer. He had no idea how much time passed, but he could stay up here for hours, enjoying the nighttime view over the Round and kissing Anya.

"When this summit is over, I don't want us to disappear into our own lives again," he whispered when at last they paused to gather themselves. "Maybe Xs on a post wasn't the cleverest idea, but there has to be a different way we could stay in touch. Could we do that?" If they could be friends—*real* friends, maybe more, and not just . . . whatever *this* was—maybe they could have more moments like this, moments that brought them closer together instead of further apart.

Anya hesitated. She licked her lips, her face still inches from his. "You're a stripe; you know how good Sapience operatives stay off the radar. We change locations a lot and never keep permanent addresses or contact information." Donovan was disappointed, if unsurprised, by her answer, but then Anya rummaged in her pocket and pulled out a slightly bent business card. "The Human Action Party has an office—a legit, real working office in the Ring Belt. They don't collect or give out personal information about members, but unofficially, they'll pass messages. It's not perfect, but if you're serious about wanting to get in touch with me . . ." She looked down at the card in her hand for a minute, then handed it to him with an almost embarassed expression.

He slipped the card into his back pocket and smiled. "Took me long enough to get your number, didn't it?" He craned in again and kissed the corner of her mouth. "To be fair, this is the first time we've been together and neither of us is in mortal danger."

Anya's lips fought a smile. She rested a hand on the back of his neck and stretched her fingers up into his hair, her touch sending a pleasant electric feeling tingling into his nodes and up his scalp. A few miles away, a bright light shot silently into the sky like a launched firework.

Anya drew in a breath. "What's that?"

"Looks like it came from the commercial landing fields," he said. "Probably a cargo vessel. They bring in supplies and goods from other planets and carry out seeds and wood and algae and other stuff we export." He pointed elsewhere. "Over there are the military shipyards. When I was a kid I used to imagine piloting a fighter craft. Humans can't fly them yet, but there's talk about changing that, redesigning the controls so that maybe in a few years . . ." He trailed off. For a short while, he'd blissfully forgotten that no one knew what would happen in a few years, not anymore. The planned withdrawal of the zhree from Earth meant things he'd counted on all his life were no longer true.

He shook his head as if he could dislodge unwelcome reality from his mind for the time being and turned his attention back to the view. "You see all those funny-shaped buildings that look like globs stuck together? That's typical zhree housing. That forest is part of the city park. And that's SecPac Central Command over there."

Anya was quiet for a long time. "Do you ever feel guilty?"

He turned his face toward her. "About what?"

"About living here, in this place. About being an exo." She spoke softly, as if asking in mere curiosity, but he could sense the undercurrent of bitterness. "Do you ever think about how many people aren't like you, how everything you enjoy comes at a price for all the people who don't have what you do?" Her voice fell to a whisper. "Does it ever bother you?"

For a moment, Donovan didn't know how to answer. Somewhere inside him, it seemed as if a window cracked open onto winter. The warmth began seeping out of him and a cold foreboding drifted in to take its place. Slowly, he said, "I patrol the Ring Belt nearly every day, protecting people whether they live in the Round or not. I've been to places all over the country and more than a few around the world. I know there are all sorts of people out there, marked *and* unmarked. Yes, I feel fortunate. But that's different from feeling guilty."

"Can't you see?" Anya's throat moved in a swallow as she stared out at the Round. "This is an amazing place, but most people will never see it. The shrooms built it for themselves, and for people like you. Not for the rest of us." She drew in a breath that seemed to be pulled from deep inside her chest. She stepped away from him, opening a handsbreadth of space that felt like an arctic mile. "The world is *wrong*. Unfair, and wrong."

Tension climbed up Donovan's neck and into his jaw. "I know there are lots of ways the world ought to be better. But the way to solve those problems is by going forward, not backward." Donovan's father had used the exact same words on many occasions, but even the oddness of hearing them come from his own mouth didn't stop him. "The world was unfair long before the Landing. I suppose you and your fellow sapes think that after the zhree leave, we should tear down all of this." He gestured expansively, angrily, at the Round—his *home*, everything he'd grown up with and valued. "Do away with erze markings, and Hardening, and interstellar trade, and everything else gained in the last hundred years."

"Maybe that's the only way for us to be truly free."

"Through anarchy and chaos and cleansings?"

"It's the fault of the shrooms that we are the way we are." Anya's eyes blazed. "If we can't manage without them when they're gone—then that's their fault too."

Donovan sat still for a long moment; then he swung his leg back over the ledge and stood up. He'd brought Anya out here hoping to show her the wondrous things about the Round, to bring her into his life a little bit, to weave a few more threads into the strangely powerful but shaky connection between them. But all

Anya saw was inequity and alien oppression and more evidence in support of the Sapience cause. "Why do you like me?"

Anya looked up, her mouth slightly open in confusion.

"You've no reason to care about me." Donovan heard his voice come out stony with hurt. "If I stand for everything you oppose, why do you like me? Why *kiss* me if you don't want my kind to exist?"

"I . . . I never said I don't want you to exist." She still sounded angry, but also uncertain. "I don't know. You're . . . you're always decent to me." She hesitated, reminding Donovan darkly that her basis of comparison for guys started with Kevin Warde. "I've seen you risk your life to save people. My brain keeps pointing out that you've got that armor and that uniform . . . but my heart says you're different. You're a good person, someone who wants to help those who need it. You're not like other stripes."

Instead of reassuring him, Anya's words made Donovan feel empty inside. He shook his head, slowly and heavily. "You're wrong. There's nothing special about me. I'm an exo and a stripe like any other. The reason you think I'm different is because I'm the only exo you've actually met." Jet, Vic, Thad, Cass, Leon . . . they were all as brave and decent as he was. More so. Even her good opinion of him was based on Sapience prejudice.

Donovan sighed. "We should get you back to the hotel."

A slightly stricken expression swept across Anya's eyes. She opened her mouth as if to say something more; if she had, if she'd voiced anything remotely conciliatory, told him she wanted to stay longer, anything, really, he would've reached out to her again, taken her hand back into his, tried to return them to the warm place they'd been in together a few minutes ago.

She didn't. She closed her mouth and nodded.

They made their way back through the Towers in near silence. There was a heaviness between them now. Donovan felt as if he'd been through such a gamut of emotions in one evening that he no longer trusted even his own confusion and disappointment. He drove directly back to the hotel. Fortunately, there had been a SecPac shift change during their absence so he didn't have to explain to Demetrius why they hadn't returned with any new clothes.

He escorted Anya back up to her hotel room door. He didn't try to kiss her again. Instead, he squeezed her hand, and trying hard to think of what to say, he began, "Anya, I still . . ."

"Thanks for taking me around. It was nice of you, and the view was really pretty." She gave him a polite, distancing half-smile, then let herself into the room and closed the door.

— — —

He was not surprised to find Jet waiting in the living room when he returned.

"Where've you been? Never mind, don't answer that." Jet muted the wall screen, which was broadcasting live, around-the-clock coverage and commentary of the Future Summit. He sat forward and fixed Donovan with an accusing glare. "So how was she? Your sape girlfriend."

Anger rose so quickly into Donovan's face that he felt as if he'd put his head into an oven. If he looked at his partner, he might punch him in the mouth. Jet had no idea what had happened tonight and how unhappy he was right now. Donovan dropped into the chair nearest the door and unlaced his boots with ferocious jerks. "That was out of line, Officer Mathews," he growled.

"You're the one who's out of line, and skirting pretty close to out of erze again too." Jet's grimace was fierce as he stood. "I never liked you skulking around that apartment in the TransHabs. And now she shows up *here*. In the Round! She's a squishy, and she's a *sape*. You can't trust her, Lesser D. Seeing her is not only a terrible idea, it's a SecPac security concern."

Considering the way his time with Anya this evening had ended, Jet's words struck home with painful validity, but it only made Donovan angrier. "This isn't any of your business, Jet."

Jet stared at him. "Whose is it, then?" He slowed each word. "I'm your erze mate. We've known each other since we were four. You think I'm saying all this to be a jerk? I'm trying to—"

"*Scorch off.*" Donovan was on his feet as well. "It didn't go well, all right? Are you happy? I like her and I don't think I can stop liking her, but when I saw her tonight . . . at first it was great, but then it was . . . weird . . . and we said some things that . . ." He burned in a humiliating loss for words. "It wasn't the same."

Jet appeared to also be at a loss for words. For a long moment, they stood at an awkward stalemate. "I'm not happy," Jet said at last. "I wouldn't be like that. Relieved, maybe." He rubbed his face. "Look, I just don't want to go through anything like last year again. It'd be better if you could put all that behind you. Things are bad enough now without—"

He was cut off by Donovan's strangled noise of astonishment. In an effort to avoid eye contact, Donovan had turned his face toward the silent wall screen. What he saw there now made his blood turn to ice and the panotin pour to the surface of his body in a flood of rising armor. He stumbled forward and jabbed the control to take the screen off mute.

"—rupt this news segment to make a special announcement." Kevin Warde spoke seriously into the camera. He was standing in front of a plain wall in what appeared to be an empty room with no furniture, no windows, and no distinguishing features at all. Donovan stepped toward the impossible image in disbelief, hands curling as if he could somehow reach out and seize Kevin through the screen. How had Warde hijacked a live news broadcast?

Jet's mouth dropped open in disbelief. His exocel rose into sharp ridges up his arms. "What in all erze . . . ?"

Kevin's arms were crossed over a black T-shirt and camo-pattern vest. The dark, piercing eyes that Donovan remembered so well gazed out intently at his invisible audience from under the curved brim of his ball cap. "My fellow patriots," Kevin declared. "A century of tireless resistance has paid off. The day will soon come when Earth will finally be free of alien occupation." He paused to emphasize the significance of his statement. "This may seem like a time of victory, but the truth is that the fight has only begun. The lapdog government of West America is meeting with alien forces *as we speak* to determine how to maintain their grip on power. They would continue to keep us down, with the help of traitors among us like this one."

The camera view shifted to the right. Brett—no, not Brett, *Jonathan*, was kneeling on the floor, his striped hands bound in front of him. Dull, hopeless resignation showed in every shadow of his horrifically bruised face. His blackened eyes were distant and unfocused as he recited, in a voice devoid of any inflection or emotion, "My name is Jonathan Resnick. I'm a soldier-in-erze and an undercover agent of the Global Security and Pacification Forces. Last year, I infiltrated and betrayed a Sapience cell. My actions resulted in the death or capture of more than a hundred rebels."

The camera pulled back to include Kevin, who nodded in approval, then spoke with rousing conviction. "People who betray their own species deserve to be punished for their crimes. True patriots, *True Sapience*, will never compromise or negotiate with oppressors and traitors. We've fought for more than a hundred years. We're on the cusp of taking back our planet. We refuse to settle for anything less than the freedom and justice we deserve."

Kevin set the barrel of his gun against Jonathan's temple and pulled the trigger.

11

Donovan was eleven years old when he first stood alone in front of Soldier Werth. His future erze master asked him only one question: "Why do you wish to be a soldier-in-erze?"

For the previous two weeks, Donovan and his exo classmates had been put through a battery of physical and mental aptitude testing as part of the erze selection process. Each evening, Donovan's father quizzed him. Which tests had he been given today? How did he think he performed? Did he feel prepared for tomorrow's evaluations? It was important that he get enough sleep and eat a good breakfast each morning. *Yes, Father.*

Why did he want to be a soldier-in-erze? Donovan stood with his armor politely lowered, pretending to listen to the translation machine repeat Soldier Werth's words. He was nervous about giving the right answer. All day long, students had been called out of class for individual interviews. A declared personal preference was taken into account when it came to erze assignments, but it was certainly not the determining factor. Donovan swallowed; Soldier Werth's large, unblinking eyes were even more intimidating than his long, armored limbs and fearsome-looking stripes. Some children, even exos, were too frightened to speak in his presence.

"Answer honestly," his father had advised.

"I want to be in the same erze as my best friend." Jet had wanted to be a stripe since they were five years old. When Soldier

Werth did not indicate any approval or disapproval of his response, Donovan became more nervous and kept talking. "Being in SecPac is dangerous and Jet's going to need someone to back him up. No one else would do as good a job as me because I've been his friend the longest." He wasn't sure what else to say, and Soldier Werth still hadn't reacted. Desperately, "I can be a good stripe, zun."

After what seemed an interminable pause, Soldier Werth dipped one fin. "You may go."

At the time, Donovan had been certain that his answer had not been sufficient, and he was honestly more relieved than overjoyed when he found out he was to receive Soldier's markings. Surely his scores in other areas had compensated for his lackluster interview. Only four years later, on a sunny, wind-blasted ridge of the Altai Mountains, did Donovan come to understand what the Soldier erze expected in its human members.

On that day, he'd labored his way up a rocky embankment with a rifle over his back, wearing only shorts, a T-shirt, and boots against a cold so brutal that it seemed to freeze the moisture in his mouth and the sweat against his armored skin. His lungs and legs were screaming in protest and he wasn't sure if he felt light-headed from the thin air up here or sheer accumulated fatigue. The other thirty-five members of SecPac Cadre 198 Alpha panted up the ridge along with him, managing, somehow, to keep their rough formation together as loose stones slid under their feet, tumbling down the slope and over the edge of the precipice.

Donovan spared a glance behind and instantly regretted it. A misplaced step here would result in a painful and humiliating trip back down the cliff at speeds much higher than he'd experienced on the way up, and he'd likely take out a few teammates behind him as part of the descent. *Only two more weeks of this*, he told himself. *I can survive two more weeks.* Then he could look forward to six months back in Round Three, free from the torment of biannual Combat Readiness Preparation—CRP for short, or as trainees called it, "crap sessions."

"Hurry, please." Amrita, from Round Ten in Indo Tibet, was Donovan's partner today. She was no stranger to high altitudes and blistering cold. Clambering just ahead of him, she latched armored fingers around a jutting stone and shoved her boot into a foothold, testing it with her full weight. The back of her sweat-drenched tank top was frozen as stiff as cardboard. Amrita was incredibly tough and hilariously polite. Many of the female soldiers-in-erze kept up with their male peers in terms of banter and ribaldry, but Amrita never tried. She could do push-ups for as long as anyone, but would say, in her slightly lilting voice, "Please pass me the E720 plain-tip cartridges," as if she were asking for lemon wedges at tea.

Amrita looked back at him. "This part's less steep. Follow my path. And hurry, please." A hint of urgency had crept into her voice. "We're at twenty-five minutes."

They were expected to cover the prescribed four-mile distance in under thirty minutes. A perfectly reasonable expectation for young, fit exos—unless they were practically unclothed at five degrees below zero Fahrenheit and the last quarter of a mile involved scrambling up a frozen mountainside. To stay warm, they had to keep their exocels fully raised, but that slowed their pace and wore a person out fast. The key was to get your core temperature up quickly, bring your armor down partway, and make up time like hell on the flat sections, then armor up again when the cold and wind caught up to you as you crawled the steep segments.

Donovan watched Amrita's foot placements, following her lead. She was nimbler at this part than he was, but though she urged him on, she didn't get ahead of him. That wasn't allowed.

Amrita reached the top of the embankment and Donovan hurried to clamber up beside her, squinting against the glare of the stark Mongolian sunlight, lungs and muscles burning even as his teeth chattered. Flat ground lay ahead of them at last; Donovan repositioned his rifle, gripping it in proper carry position as he pushed his numb legs into a run. Amrita might be quicker than him on the climb, but Donovan was faster in a straight sprint. He passed her, falling to a brisk but controlled pace directly in front of his partner and taking the brunt of the wind resistance as they headed into the final stretch. Less than thirty paces ahead of them ran the two South Americans from Round Twelve, Fernando and Matias, then Jet and his current partner, long-legged Kamogelo from Round Seventeen. At the very front of the group, two zhree Soldiers—the group's pacers—led the way with their rapid, six-limbed scuttle. Donovan heard Amrita closing at his heels; he rebalanced his overworked exocel and lengthened his stride, pushing them both harder toward the finish point.

Thaddeus Lowell jogged down the line in the opposite direction, fresh-faced and shouting at the top of his lungs. As one of the three cadre counselors, Thad was enthusiastic in fulfilling his responsibility to encourage the younger exos. "Come on, move your fat asses, you lead-footed slackers! A little cold never hurt a stripe. Be glad you're not doing your crap session at Round Fifteen!" That's where Vic was now, with Cadre 198 Foxtrot in a desert in North-West Africa.

"Round Three represent!" Thad gave Donovan a high five as

they passed each other. Donovan was too exhausted to reply, and his lips were too cold to form words anyway. He and Amrita passed the finish markers—two small piles of stones with yellow spray paint on them—and staggered into line next to Jet. Four seconds later, Leon and his partner, Maddison from Round One in Australasia, huffed up on their other side. It was too cold to drop armor, but the exos stood attentively at parade rest, noisily recovering their breath and trying not to shiver too much as they cooled. Within minutes, the rest of the cadre arrived in pairs and fell into line.

Except for one. The last to arrive, big, sandy-haired Dmitri from Round Seven, sprinted into place two seconds before the timer went off in Commander Li's hand. Everyone down the line breathed a sigh of relief. It was the first time they'd all made it in under thirty minutes.

Commander Li, who was taking time out of his busy schedule to spend three days as a guest instructor at Camp Govi before returning east to Round Eleven, was quite a bit shorter than Commander Tate, but with his arms crossed, armor raised, and SecPac uniform immaculate, Donovan could tell that he was as towering a figure in Round Eleven as Tate was in Round Three. The commander stowed the stopwatch and surveyed the group of armored young men and women. His piercing eyes reached the end of the line and landed on Dmitri.

"Where is your partner?" he demanded. The portable translation machine Li carried picked up his words and transmitted them in English into the earbud in Donovan's left ear. Every trainee wore the same device to communicate with international cadre mates and instructors, as well as zhree supervisors, the staff Nurse, and occasional visitors. Donovan shifted his eyes and surreptiously counted down the line; he knew his cadre mates were doing the same. Thirty-five. One missing. Dmitri's partner today, Jong-Kyu from Round Eleven, was not there.

"He had to turn back, sir," Dmitri explained in hurried Russian. "He caught sick last night and had trouble breathing within the first few minutes. One of the nurses-in-erze took—"

"What were your orders for this task?" Li asked in a tone that made everyone flinch.

"To . . . to run the course in under thirty minutes, sir," Dmitri stammered.

"Wrong!" Li barked at him. "The orders were for the *cadre* to run the course in under thirty minutes. I do not see the entire cadre present, do you, trainee?"

"No, sir," Dmitri said, visibly paling. Donovan cringed in sympathy for him. Dmitri had unwittingly broken the first rule of being a soldier-in-erze: always, *always* stay with your erze mate.

During CRP, partner assignments changed every three days. It was disorienting the first few times, but one became accustomed to it. Everything was done in two-person teams. Each pair of exos was expected to arrive at training activities together and to complete tasks jointly. All grades and punishments applied to both trainees. The rule held outside of training exercises as well. You didn't leave the dining hall table until your assigned erze mate was done eating. If your partner needed to use the bathroom, you went too and stood outside the door.

It bordered on ludicrous, but there was a purpose. In cities around the world, SecPac officers patrolled in pairs, which scrambled at a moment's notice into strike teams of four, six, eight, ten, or more to conduct missions or react to terrorist threats. SecPac training and terminology was the same across the world; with a few words of shorthand speech, two teams from one Round and two from another could fall into an instant understanding of roles and function as if they'd been trained together. Under such circumstances, it was vital that they trust each other immediately.

"You have all failed this exercise," Commander Li declared. "And whose fault is that?"

"Mine, sir," Dmitri admitted miserably.

"Wrong!" Li barked again. "Pok Jong-Kyu failed to inform his erze mates that he could not run the course without assistance. The rest of the cadre failed to notice the problem. The fault lies with all of you. The failure belongs to all of you. Drop! Armor down!"

All thirty-five teenage exos dropped immediately into plank position on the rocky ground, armor completely lowered. Donovan gasped. Pulling his exocel down was like plunging into an icy lake: the freezing wind struck his bare skin like a full-body slap. Within seconds, his arms were shaking. Next to him, he could hear Amrita's teeth chattering violently.

"Soldiers-in-erze are always true to their oaths. They always obey orders. And they always stay with their erze mates." Commander Li's boots strode up and down the line through Donovan's field of view. "Each of you tested as having the physical qualities, intelligence, and character required to be a soldier-in-erze. But that is not enough. Every year our erze master spends weeks traveling the world to conduct erze selections. He looks for something *more*: a willingness to consider the erze above the individual, to place others ahead of yourself."

Donovan dug his bare fingers into the ground and bit the inside of his cheek, trying to distract himself with pain. The strain of not allowing his exocel to rise was unbearable, but if Commander Li saw any panotin on their backs, they'd be here even longer.

"You will run the course every day until you succeed. Together, or not at all. You will carry your erze mates on your backs if need be," Commander Li declared. His boots came to a halt not far from Donovan's head. The vast and harshly beautiful steppe stretched in every direction so that it seemed the exos were atop the world and alone in it, save for one another.

"The erze has existed since before we humans came to be, and now it connects all of us who carry these markings on our hands," Commander Li said. "It will always be there for you, and as long as you live, you will serve and obey the erze."

12

"Here's what we're looking at: high-alert patrol protocols, rotating double shifts, and mission-ready status at all times. Extra security around all Liaison Office locations, Hardening facilities, and erze-marked neighborhoods and businesses. Your comm stays on and attached to your body every minute of every day. Try to help out the non-Hardened reservists—we're bringing on every one we've got. As of this morning, Congress has declared a national state of emergency, so as soldiers-in-erze you have the right to overrule any civilian police who get in your way if it means upholding the Accord."

Commander Tate's announcements in the briefing hall were met with stoic acceptance. With last week's failure of the West America Future Summit, the country was threatening to descend into chaos. The rest of the world seemed not far behind. Everyone in the room expected their workloads and hours to shoot through the roof.

The shocking execution of an undercover SecPac agent in front of millions of viewers had done exactly what Kevin must've intended: completely derailed the transition talks. It had also emboldened True Sapience—in the following days, SecPac received hundreds of reports of violence against Hardened and erze-marked citizens. The public outcry had been fierce on all sides: some accused SecPac of encouraging violence with its aggressive tactics and brutal destruction of the Warren; others said it didn't go far enough to combat terrorism. The President, the Prime Liaison, numerous politicians, and even some leaders of the Human Action Party had been quick to condemn Jonathan's murder. Saul Strong Winter remained noticeably silent.

Donovan understood why: Too many of Saul's followers were also supporters of Kevin Warde. Saul couldn't afford to alienate his Sapience base. Cooperationists seized on the weakness at once, demanding the government refuse any further dealings with the HAP unless it took a public stand against violent extremism. Instead, the Human Action Party delegation had walked out of the Future Summit and left the Round. Saul's statement had been terse. "There's no point in attempting a discussion when we're being treated like criminals."

"They *are* criminals," Thad pointed out. They'd watched the departure of the three green SUVs from Gate 2 in helpless frustration. Commander Tate had argued ferociously to detain and question the entire HAP delegation regarding the whereabouts of Kevin Warde, but the Liaison Office had guaranteed the delegates political immunity for the duration of the summit and there was nothing SecPac could do. "I'll bet you anything someone in those vans knows where Warde is right now," Jet muttered. "And Nakada too. And they're driving right out of here."

Donovan hadn't managed to catch even a glimpse of Anya through the SUV's tinted windows as she'd exited his life. Again. This time, he couldn't bring himself to hope that there would be another meeting between them, and he realized with dull surprise that he wasn't sure he wanted one. Anya too must've watched Kevin murder the man they both knew as Brett. Had she felt the horror Donovan had felt, watching a stripe killed on screen by the man who'd nearly done the same to him? Or was Anya—ever loyal to that bloodthirsty psychopath—only concerned for Kevin's safety now, worried about him being caught?

Last night, one of Donovan's old nightmares had returned, but it was different this time. Usually, he was tied up and being tortured, but in the new version, Donovan was the one setting up the video camera, sweating under Kevin's watchful eye while Jonathan struggled, terrified, against the restraints that bound him to the chair in the concrete room. "Help me," Jonathan begged.

A hand went up in the front row of the briefing hall. "Commander," asked Claudius, "what's going to happen now that the Human Action Party's walked away from the talks?"

"Damned if anyone knows," Tate replied. "Before the withdrawal announcement, the HAP was gaining mainstream support as a legitimate political party. A lot of their members are moderates who want species equality and political change, but not for the zhree to be actually *gone,* and not violent revolution or anarchy. Now they're stuck between a rock and a hard place. Do they support the government they've opposed or join up with True Sapience?" Tate snorted. "While the armchair political analysts are mulling it over, *we* have to be prepared for the worst."

"The worst has been pretty solid about delivering lately," Leon muttered.

Tate took off her glasses and swept a slow gaze around the crowded briefing room. "All right. Let's address the burning question on every one of your minds. The evacuation plan."

The rest of the room went entirely silent. Tate said, "Here's what Soldier Werth has been able to tell me so far: The zhree will evacuate ninety thousand humans with them as part of the drawdown. It might be more than that, but ninety thousand is the initial goal, divided across three equally sized groups. Incidentally, that's how many people will comfortably fit on three Quasar-class transport ships, after accounting for zhree crew."

It seemed as if no one in the room was breathing. Donovan's stomach was in knots. Every eye was on Tate as she went on. "The time line isn't firmed up yet, but they're discussing one ship launch per year, over the next three years. The first ship will draw from the jurisdictions of Rounds One through Six, the second from Rounds Seven through Thirteen, the third from Rounds Fourteen through Twenty, to ensure a cross section of humanity in each group."

Ninety thousand people from eighteen Rounds (not counting the long-extinct Rounds Nine and Sixteen, destroyed in the War Era) across the entire world. Donovan did the quick math: five thousand people from each Round. In Round Three alone there were over *five hundred thousand* erze-marked people. The evacuation plan would apply to less than one percent of humans-in-erze, to say nothing of the five billion unmarked humans out there.

Commander Tate consulted her notes. "Evacuees will be selected by each erze, the goal being to form a well-balanced population of exos of reproductive age." That made the odds far better for those in the room. "There'll be a rolling process until the quota is filled; the first wave of selections from Round Three will be made by the end of July."

"What about family members?" Lucius called.

"If they're Hardened, you can submit a family petition. If one member of the family is selected for evacuation, the others will be bumped up to priority consideration for the next round. No allowances will be made for non-Hardened relatives."

Worried and despairing murmurs began rising. Donovan glanced at his partner. Jet's expression was grim. The two of them and most of their close friends were young, Hardened, and healthy—they stood a good chance of being selected. As for their families—Jet's mom was an exo, but his dad wasn't. Neither of Vic's parents were Hardened, and neither were Leon's.

"Some of us have spouses or kids who aren't exos," Emmanuel pointed out angrily. "If those are the rules we're being given, then we *can't* leave, even if we're selected."

"After the notices are sent, you'll have ten days to accept or decline," Tate said. "If you decline, you must explain your extenuating circumstances. Your spot will go to someone else."

Donovan's dread deepened, then sharpened into angry, burning conviction. The evacuation was wrong, all of it. It was going to divide the erze. It would tear families apart.

"We should turn down all the spots." He spoke louder than he'd intended to, and everyone in the room turned. Commander Tate peered at him over the tops of her glasses, her stare laser sharp. Donovan swallowed at the sudden attention.

"That would mean giving up all our spots to exos in other erze," Ariadne said.

"Once the zhree leave and Sapience takes over, it's going to be the Dark Ages around here," Tennyson exclaimed hotly. "We've already seen the beginning of that. Those who can leave ought to do it—they'll be safer on any planet besides this one."

Even after Donovan had woken sweating from his nightmare, Brett/Jonathan's face remained stuck in his mind, as did the man's final words to him: *Please catch him for me.* There was nothing Donovan could've done, yet he still felt as if he'd failed in the worst possible way. The undercover agent had given up everything, including his identity and maybe his sanity, for SecPac, and never been properly recognized for it. He'd saved Donovan's life, and Donovan had not been able to do the same in return. Instead, he'd suspected the agent of being a traitor.

The thought made him queasy with guilt. Jonathan had been a squishy; he would never have been offered evacuation under Soldier Gur's criteria, but he'd been as much a soldier-in-erze as any of them, if not more. He should've been better protected. He shouldn't have died that way.

Donovan stepped away from the wall he'd been leaning on. "If the zhree take away the younger, fitter exos in the Soldier erze, it'll gut SecPac. We're already running at full throttle with everyone we've got. If a bunch of us leave this year, what happens to those who stay?" Uncomfortable silence; he'd gotten their attention now. "And what about all the civilians we've sworn to protect—the ones who don't have any choice but to stay? If civilization falls and True Sapience unleashes a rampage of vengeance on marked people, it really *will* be the Dark Ages, like Tenny said. If we evacuate with the zhree, who's going to be here to stop it?"

He was gathering momentum now. His face was hot and his armor was crawling up his chest and neck, but the murmurs of agreement that had begun to rise in the room made him even more certain that this was something that needed to be said. "Soldier Gur and the homeworlders—they're covering their asses with this evacuation plan. So long as they save some humans, they don't care what happens to Earth after they're gone. But we're *stripes*. We hold true to oaths and we stay together. Isn't that what we've always been taught?"

"Are you quite done, Reyes?" Commander Tate asked. "Or would you like to come up here to the front of the room and finish the briefing for me?"

"No, ma'am," Donovan said, his face burning even hotter now.

Tate's face went through a number of small indecisive contortions before settling into a more typical scowl. "We can all appreciate those sentiments," she said, her tone relenting. "But this is too unusual a situation and too personal a decision. Some of you have relatives whom you can get to safety with the family petition if you take your spots. Some of you aren't going to want to leave Earth no matter what. Erze is everything, but with the Soldiers preparing to withdraw, it's not clear where the erze stands now." The twitch of Tate's cheek showed how much it pained her to make such an unprecedented admission. "I'm not going to tell any of you what you ought to do if you're selected for evacuation. If Soldier Werth has something more to say about it, we'll hear it from him soon enough."

Donovan slouched against the wall, trying to blend back into the periphery of the crowd. Challenging Commander Tate in this forum wasn't as cringeworthy as his outburst in front of the zhree zun, but still—no exo could easily stomach being at odds with erze authority. Donovan's fellow soldiers-in-erze were shooting quick glances in his direction, as if expecting more from him, but he had nothing else to say.

"That's all for now," Commander Tate said. "Back to work, stripes."

13

Two days later, Donovan received a message instructing him to report to Soldier Werth in the Towers after his patrol shift ended. "I think I'm in trouble," he told Jet.

"For what?" His partner frowned. "Soldier Werth wouldn't dress you down just for getting opinionated in that briefing, would he? Have you done something else to piss him off?"

"I'm not sure," Donovan admitted. "But every time someone wants to talk to me alone, it's never good news." He squinted at a blue car that had been parked for too long on the other side of the street across from the erze application center he and Jet had been guarding all morning. "I'm going to tell them to move along."

Jet nodded, moving to a position where he could see Donovan and the vehicle while still keeping an eye on the front of the building. Donovan crossed the street. The driver of the car was a skinny blond man in his early twenties. He didn't appear to be doing anything besides drinking a soda and looking at a screen. Donovan rapped on the window. The driver rolled it down a third of the way.

"You can't park here," Donovan said. "You need to move your car."

"Sure. Sure, Officer." The driver's voice was sugary with false respect. Donovan's eyes slid past him and landed on the man and woman sitting in the rear seat. A fumbled movement with a small object, a flash of apprehensive guilt on the woman's face, and Donovan's suspicion bloomed into instant certainty.

"Get out, all of you," he commanded.

Instead of obeying, the driver lunged forward and started the car. Donovan's left arm shot through the half-open window and his armored fingers locked around the man's chin in a vise grip, pinning his head back against the headrest of the seat. Donovan drew his sidearm with his right hand and pointed it through the window at the couple in the back. "*Out.*"

Jet was there in an instant, yanking the couple from the car and ordering them onto the asphalt. The driver's face turned red as he gurgled and struggled. Donovan tightened his armored grip. "Keep that up and you could really hurt yourself. Take your hands off the wheel and hold them up where I can see them." The man's eyes darted wildly with anger and fear, but he stopped flailing and did as he was told. Donovan had him open the front door and get out slowly, then lie down on his stomach next to the others.

"Where is it?" Donovan demanded. He turned off the vehicle's ignition and began searching the car while Jet patted down the three conspirators. "Get your hands off me!" the woman protested shrilly. "This is SecPac harassment."

"You know what's actual harassment?" Donovan slid his hands under the seats. "Taking photos of people going in and out of government buildings and posting them for Sapience to build a public hit list." He rummaged through the glove compartment. "Or should I say *True* Sapience? It's hard to keep track of what you sapes are calling yourselves from day to day now."

"Found it," Jet said. He pulled out a small black device from the woman's pocket and held it up, then tossed it to Donovan, who examined it.

"That's from my vacation," the woman insisted.

"How long have you been a sape?" Jet asked her. "I'm guessing not long, since you don't seem to know when it's better to keep your mouth shut."

"You do get some credit for having a proper camera," said Donovan, turning the object in his hands. "Stripped down to minimal functionality, disposable, untraceable, and tracking disabled. Nothing to link you to any photos you post or any crimes that might occur as a result of you posting them. Good job."

"You can't arrest us for taking photos on a public street," the blond man said.

That was true. An identity search did not turn up prior records, and they weren't carrying any weapons on them or in the car. There was nothing to connect them directly to Sapience. There was a solid chance they weren't bona fide sapes, just supporters or simple opportunists. A number of Sapience and Sapience-affiliated sites posted photographs and identifying information about people who were erze marked so they could be targeted. Some of the sites paid contributors. With the prospect of a reckoning day approaching, the demand for information ferreting out all the traitors had spiked dramatically.

The photographers earned themselves permanent profiles in the SecPac database. Donovan stood vigilant watch while his partner did the saliva swab and fingerprinting on each of the trio; Jet always got those honors because he was the more intimidating one

and better at ensuring cooperation when the need arose. They con-
fiscated all electronic devices in addition to the disposable camera,
just to be on the safe side, then sent the three squishies away with
the promise that a second encounter would land them in a SecPac
detention facility.

The line at the front of the building had grown to a dozen people, all waiting for the office to reopen after lunch break. The
Liaison Office operated three erze application centers in the area;
this one on the south side of the Ring Belt was the busiest one. A
couple of days ago, a truck full of Sapience sympathizers had driven
by and peppered the bulletproof windows with gunfire (Lucius and
Tennyson had tracked down the perpetrators later that night), but
the threat of violence apparently hadn't dissuaded the applicants.
Jet paced away to survey the block from the street corner at the far
end of the queue.

A man waiting in line with his wife and child had been watching the entire drama unfold across the street. "You're just letting
those people go?" he demanded. "They'll be up to something worse
tomorrow."

"There's nothing else we can do right now, sir," Donovan
explained. The man, an exo engineer-in-erze who seemed to be in
his thirties and in good shape if incongruously balding, opened his
mouth as if to berate the officers further, but his wife put a rebuk-
ing hand on his arm and smiled at Donovan apologetically. She
was Hardened as well, slightly pudgy, also with Engineer's markings. "Thank you for being here, Officer," she said. "My
brother-in-law is a stripe; I know you've all been working really
hard. I want to say that we appreciate what you do."

"Thank you, ma'am," Donovan said. The husband looked

appropriately chastised and busied himself opening a packet of animal crackers for their daughter, who appeared to be three or four years old.

"Do you know if there's a long delay in Hardening applications these days?" the woman asked Donovan, looking anxiously at the line of people still forming behind them. The office had reopened, so at least people were moving now.

"I don't know, ma'am," Donovan said. "You'll have to ask inside."

"I'm sure we'll have some sort of priority," her husband assured her, in a tone of voice that suggested he damn well expected that to be the case for a dual-exo family.

The mother bent to roll up her daughter's sleeves before the girl could get crumbs on them. "Alissandra just turned four this month. Barely made the age cutoff for this application submission window," she told Donovan. "I don't know what they're saying in any other erze, but in the Engineer erze there's talk of *evacuations*. It's frightening." She shook her head, her hair swinging from side to side. "I'll feel a lot better once the whole family's Hardened."

— — —

"How long's it take, normally, to schedule a Hardening?" Donovan wondered aloud to Jet as they drove back to the Round that evening. "Six months? I've got to think the Liaison Office is running behind, so even assuming everything goes well, that little girl won't be an exo until next spring. Those parents figure being Hardened means they'll all be protected, but won't it be too late?

The zhree will have already made all the evacuation decisions for Round Three by then, won't they?"

"Who knows." Jet was in an uncharacteristically gloomy temper. "What good is it for you to be worried about that? We're not in the Engineer erze and we don't know those people. You can hope they make it, but that's about all you can do."

"Ninety thousand people, Jet," Donovan said. "That's *nothing*. That's a fraction of the exos around the world, to say nothing of everyone else." Their patrol skimmercar navigated through heavy traffic to the Gate 5 checkpoint. Normally, the guard waved them straight through, but security was extra tight now. Even SecPac officers had to pull over and verify their exocellular body signatures. A crowd of people pressed against the checkpoint's metal barricades, arguing with the guards, demanding to be let in. Donovan overheard one man loudly insisting that he had a current worker pass that he'd simply misplaced, and someone else pleading that she just needed to get in for a few hours to visit her sister.

"Residents and permanent workers with erze markings and valid identification only," the guard shouted. "No exceptions. Read the notices!"

"They think it's safe in here," Donovan muttered, pulling his hand out from under the reader as the status light turned green. Jet nudged the skimmercar through the gate and they continued into the Round. "We can't protect everyone in the Ring Belt as it is, and the way things are going, it'll only get worse when the zhree leave." Soldier Gur's plan to evacuate a small population of exos was not yet public knowledge, but Donovan suspected it wouldn't take long for rumors to find their way out of the Round and spread into the general population. Once people learned of evacuations they would be excluded from, fears would skyrocket even further.

"You've got to wonder how many Sapience sympathizers are waking up to what 'Earth for humans' actually means." Jet pulled the skimmercar up to the house. "You don't really think you're in trouble with Soldier Werth, do you? I'll come with you to the Towers if you want. Just give me a minute to go to the bathroom and grab a granola bar or something from the kitchen."

Donovan shook his head. Maybe he was imagining it, but since the night he'd snuck out to see Anya, the night Jonathan had been murdered, Jet seemed to be staying a little closer. "You don't need to come," Donovan told him. "What can you do anyway?"

Jet shrugged. "Offer moral support while you get your ass handed to you. Look appropriately guilty for not being a better partner and keeping you out of trouble." He broke into a slow, sardonic smile, and Donovan snorted.

"This isn't CRP," he said. "You're not obligated to get chewed out with me." He added more quietly, "Or to stick around just for my sake."

Jet's smile faded. "I'm not moving out, D, if that's what you're talking about." He shifted his weight and looked down. "Vic was right, it's not a good time. Especially not now when no one knows what's going to happen with this whole drawdown and evacuation thing."

Donovan nodded slowly, unsure what to say to that. So many things were messed up, and he couldn't help but wonder if Jet resented him for being one additional source of worry when there was already enough to worry about. "I should get going," he said.

"It'd be better if you stayed home and knocked off our reports so we're not up late again finishing them."

Jet couldn't disagree. Donovan drove to the Towers and parked where he could find space, then walked quickly across the ground floor of the central tower, shortcutting over to the eastern barracks, where Werth and the main contingent of his Soldiers in Round Three resided. Donovan dodged zhree and humans alike hurrying to and fro. The Towers were bustling with nervous activity and the woven metal walls seemed to hum at a high pitch with the musical mingled speech of many anxious voices. Ever since Soldier Gur had arrived and the withdrawal edict had come down from the homeworld, the Mur colonists had been in a state of near frantic preparation. Even if the drawdown would take years to complete, it was no mean feat to organize an orderly departure from a planet after more than a hundred and thirty years of occupation.

"Donovan!" He'd almost reached the other side of the main tower when a familiar trilling exclamation caused him to turn. Nurse Therrid's fins fanned in greeting and he came over to clasp Donovan's hand. "I haven't seen you much lately. Although," hummed the Nurse in a more considered tone, "that's generally a good thing." Nurse Therrid specialized in treating exos, and Donovan had been under his medical care entirely too much last year. On top of that, Donovan had flagrantly disobeyed Therrid, punched him in the eye, and locked him in a room. It had taken nearly two months for the Nurse to forgive him, though Donovan figured it could've been much worse. Therrid could've reported him to Soldier Werth—but he hadn't.

"What are you doing here, hatchling?" Therrid asked.

"Soldier Werth called me over to the barracks. What about you, zun Therrid?"

Therrid held up a computing disc. "Delivering this to Soldier Gur." The Nurse's fins twitched in a slight wince as he said the name. Apparently, Gur had returned from his travels around the planet. "I was asked to provide a report containing the health status, medical history, and genetic profile of every single exo in Round Three's jurisdiction. *Every* exo in West America, Donovan. Do you have any idea how long it took to compile this?"

Therrid's body sagged slightly, then one of his yellow eyes gave a nervous blink as he noticed two of Gur's Soldiers walking past. He lowered his voice. "I had to assign every exo into a tier based on health and age. You and Vercingetorix and most of your close erze mates will be fine," Therrid assured Donovan. "You're Tier 1—healthy, with many reproductive years ahead of you, eighth-generation exocels, and high erze ratings, even accounting for a few blemishes here and there. Some of the other exos, though, older ones or those with health problems or injuries . . ." the Nurse trailed off, troubled. Donovan shifted uneasily, knowing that Therrid had been pulled into the selection process made the evacuations seem far more real and disturbing.

The gently bulging egg sac on the underside of the Nurse's torso suddenly caught Donavan's eye. "Zun Therrid," he exclaimed, "you didn't mention you were brooding."

Therrid was quiet for a moment, then he sighed in a low hum. "It's best if I don't become too optimistic. The first brood is always the most uncertain. It takes fourteen months to produce eggs and six more months for them to mature to hatch readiness in the Nursery. I don't know what the withdrawal schedule will be for my erze and when I'll be expected to leave Earth."

"You could hatch your clutch elsewhere, couldn't you? On Kreet."

"No," Therrid snapped, his fins jerking with an abruptness that Donovan had rarely seen in him. "Brooding and hatch rates are a finicky thing. They won't happen if the conditions aren't right. There needs to be a certain level of gravity, atmospheric oxygen, and nutrition. I wouldn't reach Kreet in time to brood there properly. I don't think I could anyway, since the homeworld would be foreign to me. If we leave Earth soon, my body will simply break down and reabsorb my unhatched offspring."

"I didn't know that," Donovan said, uncomfortable now and worried his ignorant questions had offended the Nurse. "I'm sorry, zun."

"You should continue on your way, Donovan. I don't want to hold you up from reporting to your erze master." Therrid tapped the computing disc against the edge of his hull as if reminding himself of his unpleasant task before he walked away with heavier steps than before, some of his eyes strategically closed to avoid looking at Donovan as he crossed the floor.

Guiltily, Donovan watched him go. In all his angry worries about what would happen to his erze mates and to humans in general, he hadn't thought much about how the zhree colonists themselves would be reacting to the homeworld's decision. Many of them, like Wiest, and Wiv, and Therrid, had never known any other home but Earth.

The barracks were low, honeycomb-like structures situated

along the eastern perimeter of the Towers and adjacent to the restricted military landing fields and shipyards. Donovan had been here before—all SecPac officers toured it during training so they would be knowledgeable about the layout of the Towers and its defenses. Donovan went up to the largest of the buildings but came to an uncertain stop when he saw one of Gur's Soldiers standing by the entrance.

The foreign Soldier stood battle-armored with all six eyes open, his fins still and flat in an unapologetically aggressive posture that reminded Donovan of a frowning, muscled bouncer outside the entrance of a bar. Staring at the homeworlder's thin, jagged markings, Donovan felt an immediate sense of dislike rising along with his exocel. Determinedly, he approached the Soldier, halted in front of him, and dropped his armor respectfully.

Before he could open his mouth to speak, the Soldier whipped out a limb and smacked Donovan in the chest. It wasn't a hard blow, but it startled Donovan so much that he jumped back. "What do you want, human?" the Soldier demanded.

Donovan's armor had sprung up in reflex but barely in time—the blow still stung. "I'm here to see Soldier Werth," he said, unable to contain the surprise and anger in his voice. The homeworlder didn't answer. It was obvious he didn't understand what Donovan was saying. The smack had been delivered in wary disdain, like a man aiming a kick at a stray dog.

Not for the first frustrating time, Donovan wished that human vocal cords were capable of making the sounds of the Mur language. He pointed at himself, then at the entrance to the building—any dimwit could understand *that*. The zhree looked skeptically at him, then called out to a couple of Werth's

Soldiers walking past. "You two—this human seems to want to get inside."

"Then let him in," called back one of the passing Soldiers, annoyed. "How many times do we have to tell you? The humans inside the Round aren't dangerous."

"It's not hard to requisition yourself a translation machine," muttered the other.

The foreign Soldier drew himself up. "You frontier dwellers are staggeringly lax at supervising the natives." His voice vibrated with sneering authority. "*You* will escort this human where it needs to go."

The two Soldiers bristled, their armor thickening over their hulls, but they held back from openly defying someone with Gur's markings. "As you say, zun," one of the Soldiers said curtly. He gestured for Donovan to follow him inside.

Donovan glanced back over his shoulder with narrowed eyes, rubbing the bruise that was forming on his chest as he followed his escort into the barracks. "Thank you, zun."

"Insufferable homeworlders, acting as if they run the place," the Soldier muttered in a hum. "All the while complaining about the texture of our algae and jumping at the sight of every human. Where are you supposed to be going?"

"Soldier Werth asked me to see him, zun."

The Soldier had eyes of a lighter yellow than most zhree; the nearest two fixed on Donovan more closely and his annoyance turned to interest. "I recognize you. I was at the algae farm stand-off last year. You're Donovan Reyes."

"Yes, zun," Donovan said, surprised. Not all zhree were good at telling humans apart.

The Soldier's fins riffled in satisfaction. "You saved those two Engineers and their humans-in-erze. I was skeptical when SecPac insisted on trying to send in a negotiator, but you convinced the hostiles to back down. You must have high social rank among humans to be so influential."

Donovan choked back a laugh. The unusual circumstances of his family life would be too complicated to explain to the Soldier. "I'm nothing special, zun."

They passed through several of the barracks' large communal living spaces. Soldiers on sleep shift were dozing in wall niches, one or two eyes remaining disconcertingly open. A group of other Soldiers bantered while performing weapons inspection and maintenance; a few of them paused to watch curiously as Donovan's escort led him toward the large chamber in the center of the building—Soldier Werth's quarters and briefing room. Both man and zhree stopped just inside the entrance of the room and dropped their armor. "Zun Werth, Donovan is here to see you," said the Soldier.

Werth was standing in the curve of a semicircular console that wrapped nearly two hundred and seventy degrees around him, with different screens displaying an overwhelming array of information. Werth's many eyes opened and closed as he shifted his attention between them. "You're late, Donovan."

"I'm sorry, zun," Donovan began.

His zhree escort beat him to the explanation. "He ran into one of Gur's Soldiers."

Soldier Werth's fins shifted in a slow grimace. "Thank you, Wylt," their erze master said. "You may go. And have Wiest scrounge up a few more translation machines for the benefit of our friends from the homeworld."

In the Mur language, the word *friend* as humans understood it was only used to refer to amicable relationships with zhree of other erze. Werth and Gur were the leaders of two different erze but since both were Soldiers, the polite and hospitable thing to do would've been to refer to the visiting homeworlders as erze mates (though they were not technically so) or erze comrades. Werth's use of the more distant word *friend* was a nuance not lost on Wylt or Donovan. They glanced at each other in surprise.

"Yes, zun." Soldier Wylt left.

"Come closer, Donovan," Werth ordered. He paused what he was doing, setting all six limbs onto the ground as he fixed his attention on the human. "Commander Tate tells me that you have some very strong opinions about the evacuation plan, which you shared with your erze mates at the most recent briefing."

Donovan remained standing at attention in front of Werth, his exocel still lowered. "It's not out of erze to express one's opinions among erze mates, is it, zun?"

He had a suspicion his response came across as cheeky, but Werth merely continued looking at him. "I value initiative in humans. Your commander has been arguing with me since she was practically a hatchling, and I appreciate that it has made the working partnership between zhree and humans stronger. Eventually, however, we must align on the best course of action for the erze."

"I don't see how selecting and evacuating the younger and fitter exos is the best thing for the erze." Donovan did his best to keep his voice calm. "You're asking some stripes to leave their erze mates behind to save themselves. That doesn't make any sense. It's the opposite of what these markings mean."

"Those markings," said Soldier Werth, "are *my* markings."

"With respect, zun," Donovan said, "you don't own what they mean."

There was a long beat of silence between them; Donovan could no longer keep his armor from layering nervously. Soldier Werth's fins were still, his expression grudging. "Sometimes I forget," he said at last, "how closely humans can resemble their biological progenitors in temperament. You are clearly the offspring of Dominick Reyes. It's time you heard the truth."

14

Soldier Werth tapped on a section of the console in front of him. His pincers manipulated the controls and an image sprang into three-dimensional form over the console's projection pad.

Was it . . . a space station? A ship? It was some sort of space-faring structure, but it was unlike anything Donovan had ever seen, even in pictures. The massive cruisers and transport ships he was familiar with were sleek and cylindrical. The bodies of fighter craft were spherical, rotating freely within diamond-shaped wing frames. This holographic monstrosity was irregularly shaped, with all sorts of pieces connected seemingly haphazardly, so it was impossible to tell if there was an intended front or back or top or bottom. Some sections looked to be ancient and battered, others appeared new and constructed from entirely different metals. The thing was clearly not meant to ever take off or land. It looked like something that had not been designed, but had grown, like an amoeba or a cancer.

"This is a Rii Galaxysweeper," said Soldier Werth. "It's the size of the largest asteroid in our solar system. Ironically, the Rii were the original colonizers; long before the advent of reliable light-plus travel and even longer before the modern eon of the Commonwealth, they were among the first zhree to leave Kreet for new star systems. Traveling in great generation ships, they founded a robust civilization, distant and independent of the homeworld.

"Then, some millennia ago, their star system became uninhabitable when the orbit of one of its planets destabilized. The Rii constructed five enormous ships, which they intended to use to travel to new habitable worlds—but they were not successful. They'd been isolated from other zhree civilizations for so long that their terraforming technology was primitive, and the planets they found that could support life were already populated by early Commonwealth forces that refused to harbor them. Over time, the Rii became a nomadic race, relying not on planetary bases but on raiding and stealing to build upon their growing Galaxysweepers."

Soldier Werth paused, fins laid out in a scowl as he stared at the image of the enemy vessel with cold hostility in every eye. "There are currently thirty-six known Galaxysweepers, descendants of the original five. Each one is defended by fleets of warships and carries tens of millions of inhabitants, along with an intense historical grudge against the Commonwealth."

Werth touched the display again and the Galaxysweeper disappeared, only to be replaced by a projected image of two strange zhree, side by side. Donovan stared, unnerved and fascinated. The zhree on the left looked not dissimilar from the colonists Donovan had grown up around, but it had smaller, much darker eyes—an orange that was nearly red—and a flatter torso with hashed markings he'd never seen before. The one on the right, however, made Donovan's armor crawl. It had fearsomely serrated battle armor like a Soldier, but it was a third larger—as tall as a human man. Instead of stripes, a mottled pattern covered its hull. It too had reddish eyes, and thick, bladed fins lay against its domed body. Donovan had always thought his own erze master was intimidating in appearance, but this creature dwarfed even Soldier Werth.

"The Rii have only two erze: Stewards and Hunters." Soldier Werth came around from the other side of the console and walked to where Donovan stood. "Stewards reside on and maintain the Galaxysweepers. Hunters travel on long-ranging warships that seek out populated worlds to conquer and occupy. Like us, the Rii require certain planetary conditions to brood and hatch their young. But it's not in their culture to stay and establish permanent colonies; they believe it makes them vulnerable.

"If they seize control of Earth, they'll use it as a base from which to disrupt Commonwealth shipping corridors while they strip out all the technology and materials they can from the planet—the Towers themselves will be broken down and incorporated into the Galaxysweeper. They'll hoard whatever they find valuable, including useful sentient creatures. A great many of them will brood here at the same time, and once the surge in hatchlings matures, they'll move on." Soldier Werth's large amber eyes remained on Donovan. "But first they'll make certain the Mur won't be able to reoccupy the planet for a very long time."

Soldier Werth returned to the console and tapped it once more. The Rii Steward and Hunter vanished. This time Werth brought up the image of a blue-and-white globe, slowly revolving in space. "This was the planet Bithis, roughly a thousand years ago," Soldier Werth said. "Icy and cold, but habitable, with temperate equatorial oceans and a Class Three native marine species. The Commonwealth maintained a small colony there as a scientific and military outpost. The Rii attacked it, occupied it for three hundred years, then abandoned it to press farther into Mur territory. When they left, they unleashed thermal neutrons over Bithis that destroyed the planet's atmosphere, extinguishing life and making the surface uninhabitable." The blue-and-white globe faded and was replaced with a cloudless, barren planet the color of chalk. "This is Bithis now."

Donovan's disbelieving voice crawled out of a tight throat. "You're saying that could happen to Earth?"

"Bithis could be re-terraformed over a long time, at great cost to the homeworld. The native species on that planet, however—they are gone for good." Soldier Werth shut off the projection. He came toward Donovan once more and stopped in front of him. "The High Speaker and Soldier Gur know full well that withdrawing Mur presence from Earth means abandoning it to possible conquest and destruction. But defending it would require more support from the overstretched Mur fleet, and the Homeworld Council is under too much political pressure to pull back from the frontier areas of the galaxy. They've made their decision."

Donovan searched for a place to sit down. Since the zhree didn't use chairs, there were none. "You're letting this happen." His horror took a sharp turn into anger. "You're going along with what Kreet tells you to do. You don't care that Earth could be destroyed, and that billions of humans would die."

Soldier Werth's reaction made Donovan understand that he'd never before seen his erze master truly angry. Werth's armor crested across his hull so that he seemed to grow before Donovan's eyes. His fins flattened with bladed fury, and his eyes lit into orbs of yellow fire.

Donovan shrank back, filled with instinctive, cowering fear.

"I was hatched on this planet. I have expended every effort to argue for its worth." Soldier Werth's musical voice was as cold as the ringing of glass chimes. "You attended the many discussions in which the erze zun explored every angle—including mandating the Hardening of humans—to convince Kreet to continue support-ing Earth."

"I know." Donovan's exocel was pulled down low in submis-sion. "I spoke without thinking. I'm sorry, zun."

Soldier Werth's formidable battle armor fell slightly, but his fin movements remained harsh and reproving. "Ultimately, every erze must answer to the Mur Erzen. Administrator Seir and I and the rest of the erze zun have made our strongest arguments, but the greater interests of the Commonwealth must prevail. Only the continued strength of the Mur Erzen can blunt the aggression of the Rii. You understand now why the human evacuation plan is so important: Because it will *save your species*. And perhaps you also understand why your father was so invested in the erze sys-tem and the exo program. He was one of the most intelligent humans I ever knew. I believe he foresaw that when Earth's exis-tence was inevitably threatened, your species would survive only if it could leave the planet as willing partners in erze."

Donovan gulped back a lump in his throat.

"Under normal circumstances," Soldier Werth said, his fins straightening, "I would approve of your argument for erze unity. But these are not normal circumstances. It's better to leave some erze mates than to lose them all. When the first wave of selections is announced, I will issue orders that all soldiers-in-erze offered evacuation must comply."

"Zun Werth," Donovan protested, recovering enough to pull his stunned wits back together. "You'll be forcing people to leave behind their family and friends."

Werth paced away but all of his eyes remained open so it seemed as if he was looking at Donovan over his shoulder. "I remember every exo I've chosen. I will have to abandon some whom I've known since they were hatchlings but who do not meet the criteria that Soldier Gur has imposed. It will be difficult, but I certainly do not intend to lose *all* the humans in this erze."

Werth stopped and came back to Donovan, who tensed in expectation of some further reprimand. Instead, Werth reached out two limbs and grasped Donovan's arms with outstretched pincers in a firm gesture that struck Donovan as oddly human. "You are astute for such a young human, Donovan. You're well-known and well-spoken within our erze, and have proven on more than one occasion that you can exert influence above your rank. You must help, not hinder, the evacuation process. It's the only way to save humankind. Do you understand?"

Donovan looked miserably into the alien eyes and nodded.

15

Everywhere Donovan looked, he saw the doomed. Men and women, old people and little kids, marked and unmarked. He imagined all of them gone, the streets empty, the buildings crumbling to dust, and the blue of the sky stripped away to nothing. Earth reduced to a barren wasteland devoid of life. In the six weeks following his conversation with Soldier Werth, he often awoke feeling as if a weight were sitting on his chest. Images of the Galaxysweeper and the Rii and ruined worlds danced in his mind.

At other times, such as now, he couldn't muster the energy to care about the fate of the world. All he wanted was to make it to the end of his shift and collapse. It was evening, but the half-light might as well have been dawn for all Donovan could tell anymore.

Jet said, "I wish I could sleep like one of the zhree."

Donovan blinked hard, then kept running checks on the passing cars. "I think I'm almost there. I swear I actually fell asleep with my eyes open for a few seconds the other day."

"Two days," said Jet. "We can make it two more days."

"That's what we said eight days ago." Their last scheduled break had been canceled.

"Don't burst my delusional bubble."

At a petroleum fueling station across the street, a teenage girl was filling up her car, glancing around nervously as she waited for the meter to climb. The predominantly erze-marked neighborhood Donovan and Jet were patrolling had suffered vandalism, drive-by shootings, break-ins, and attempted kidnappings. The residents had taken to posting their own block patrol of armed civilians, who were jumpy, untrained, and more often than not, just another thing for SecPac to be worried about. Not that Donovan could blame them for feeling as if they needed to take some initiative to protect themselves.

The girl at the gas station hung up the nozzle. She was thin, with shoulder-length brown hair, and she wore a tank top and combat boots. For a second, as she crossed to the driver side of her car, she looked enough like Anya that despite his weariness, Donovan's heart gave a painful lurch. He didn't yearn constantly and hopelessly for Anya in the same way he used to, but he still longed for . . . something he couldn't put his finger on. Something *else*. Regret lay heavy on him; their last parting had felt so *wrong* and it seemed unlikely he'd ever get a chance to set things right.

A group of several hundred people paraded past, heading toward the Round with signs that read TAKE US WITH YOU and OUT OF EARTH IS OUT OF ERZE. It was the third such demonstration Donovan had seen this week. News of the zhree plan to evacuate a small population of Hardened humans had gone public and sent millions of cooperationists into an angry terror at being left behind by their allies in what might soon be anarchy. "You've got to give credit to DeGarmo for sticking to her talking points about 'stable transition,'" Jet said, scanning the crowd as it passed. "But I think people aren't buying it anymore."

Donovan was sure that if his father was still Prime Liaison, he too would be doing everything in his power to calm people and keep order, even if it meant concealing the truth. "People can't live without any hope, Jet. Take that away and it'll be chaos and anarchy."

"As opposed to the polite garden party going on right now," Jet deadpanned.

He had a point. The two of them had been sent from one crisis to another. After True Sapience set off a triple bombing in Phoenix that killed one hundred and fifty-three people, they'd spent a week in the SecPac satellite office in Arizona with only one change of uniform, sleeping on the conference room floor where twenty stripes were camped out in shifts when not digging through rubble for survivors or hunting the bombers, who were tracked to a Sapience hideout, cornered, and killed after a ten-hour standoff. They were supposed to get two days off duty when they returned to the Round, but that same afternoon, a SecPac officer was killed and four were injured in a street ambush, so they were sent back out that very evening.

Donovan wasn't close to Leander, the exo who'd been killed, but Thad knew him well and had been heartbroken when he heard the news. The death of an exo cast a terrible pall over SecPac. In the officer's common room, voices were hushed and the bulletin board was covered with written tributes and photos. The sadness was tinged with foreboding. This was just the beginning. The violence would get worse, and they would get more tired and careless.

Donovan and Jet had barely seen their own beds in weeks. The last time they'd seen Cass and Leon was five days ago, and only because both teams had been called in to a bomb scare at a shopping mall. Their housemates had been awake for two straight days.

Cass was making inappropriate terrorism jokes to the mall staff and Leon had misplaced his sketchbook.

The situation was unsustainable. Exhausted stripes were more likely to get killed or injured, or to make mistakes and hurt innocent civilians. There was a scandal in Round Four at the moment involving accidental shootings. *Two more days*, Donovan told himself, and yanked another hair from his forearm, as he'd taken to doing in order to stay awake.

"Maybe working us into the ground is part of the plan to get us to accept evacuation." Jet's expression was obscured by the growing shadows. "Because this place is really starting to suck. This whole planet. If this is just a taste of what it's going to be like after the zhree are gone and there's no real government anymore, maybe it *is* better to get out while we can."

Donovan looked over at his partner. "So you're going to take your spot, then?"

Jet hesitated. "None of us has a spot yet, so it's a moot point until they announce selections. I mean, we all know they only want the finest physical specimens of humanity."

"Which would rule you out."

"Which would mean I'd have to decide whether to abandon you." Jet grinned at him, a badly missed sight these days. Then he returned his attention to the scans running on his screen and sighed. "I don't know what I'm going to do," he said, seriously this time. "We've been run so ragged that I haven't had a proper chance to talk to my folks. Or to Vic."

Donovan was silent for a minute. When he spoke again, he heard something in his voice that he didn't like at all: defeat. "You ever wonder if this is all hopeless? Trying to maintain order in what might be an apocalypse? Saving people who might not be able to be saved?"

He'd told Jet what Soldier Werth had told him, about the Rii and what might happen to Earth in the long run once the Mur colonists left. Now his partner stared into the dusk pensively before shaking his head. "Commander Tate must know the truth. But she's still bulling through it, setting an example and doing her duty. That's what she expects of us." He finished his scans and began walking back to the patrol skimmercar with long, determined strides. "We can't change the fate of the world, Lesser D. We can only do our jobs until we can't do them anymore."

— — —

They did get their break after all.

The message Donovan received the next morning was simple. It arrived with a document security lock that could only be overridden via verification of his exocellular body signature, and stated, in part, *You have been selected by your erze for planetary evacuation.*

Evacuation of humans whose safety is deemed a priority of the Mur Erzen Commonwealth will commence in concurrence with the planned drawdown of troops. Respond within ten days. All requests to be exempted from evacuation are subject to approval.

The next message that flashed on Donovan's screen was from Soldier Werth. It was brief. *Soldiers-in-erze selected for evacuation are ordered to comply.*

The third and final message was from Commander Tate. SecPac officers who'd received first-round evacuation notices were granted the day off duty to inform their family members and discuss their decision with loved ones.

Jet and Vic were trying to keep their voices down in the living room, but Donovan could still hear them from the kitchen. "Why is this a surprise to you?" Vic demanded. "You know my parents aren't Hardened. I told you, I'm not going to leave them."

"But they're *erze orders*." Jet's voice was tinged with desperation.

"I don't care," Vic blurted. When she spoke again, Donovan could barely hear her. "I can't go along with this, Jet, I *can't*. My parents already lost Skye. I lost my *twin brother*. My family's given up enough for me to be an exo and I'm not breaking us up."

"What about me?" Jet asked. "What about us?"

"You should do what you think is right. And I know you think that means staying in erze." Vic's voice was wavering badly. "You shouldn't be basing this decision on me. You can use the family petition to try to take your mom. It's what I would do if I were you."

Donovan could hear his erze mate's breathing and his heavy steps across the floor. "I can't believe you're using the end of the world as an excuse to break up with me."

"How can you say that?" Vic's voice rose to a shout.

Donovan had been mechanically rinsing dishes with as much noise as possible. He turned off the water and dried his hands, determined to leave the house and give his friends some more privacy, but at that moment, the front door opened and he heard Cass and Leon come in. Awkward greetings ensued in the living room, and then Jet and Vic took their argument outside.

Cass and Leon came into the kitchen. "Who the hell are you?" Cass made her eyes go wide with mock surprise and threw her hands up. "Hey, Leon, did you know we had another housemate?" She flashed Donovan a teasing grin and gave him a tight hug. When they drew apart, Donovan saw that although Cass was smiling, her eyes were tired and a little puffy. "Jet and Vic sound like they're having a hard time," she said as she opened the fridge. "Makes me glad I wasn't given the choice."

Donovan didn't understand at first. "What do you mean?"

"She didn't get an evacuation notice." Leon spoke up from where he'd slumped into a chair at the table. It was a jarring shock to hear him so angry; Leon rarely raised his voice even when bullets were flying and things were exploding. Now his normally mild expression was warped with distress.

Donovan turned to Cass with alarm. She held up her right arm. "I'm damaged goods, remember? Only perfectly fit and healthy exos are being evacuated."

Cass had been injured last year in a grenade explosion during the raid on the Warren. After a lot of surgery and physiotherapy, she'd regained use of her right shoulder and arm and had been cleared to return to duty, but her exocel was permanently damaged; she couldn't armor the limb at all and wore a protective sleeve over the scarred tissue and misaligned nodes.

"You can't be serious," Donovan exclaimed, his voice mirroring Leon's dismay. "They disqualified you because of your *arm*?"

Cass emerged from the fridge with three bottles of beer and sat down at the table across from Leon. Leaning back, she propped her booted feet noisily onto the seat of an empty chair. "Honestly," she said, opening a bottle and taking a generous swig, "it's okay."

"It's not okay," Leon insisted. "You're still combat-rated. There's no reason—"

"There's nothing else to talk about," Cass said with finality, opening another bottle and pushing it toward her partner. "Let's not make D listen to a depressing bitch fest about what we can't change." She nudged an empty chair in Donovan's direction, inviting him to sit with them. "They had to set the criteria somehow. And like D said, the world's going to need good stripes to stay behind and deal with the fallout. I might as well be one of them."

This pronouncement made Leon look more unhappy than ever. He downed half his bottle of beer in a couple of forceful swallows. "I *have* to evacuate," he explained to Donovan. "My little brother's an exo in the erze, in his second year of SecPac training. My parents would never forgive me if I didn't go and use the family allowance to take him with me."

Donovan sat down, his heart aching. It was happening just as he'd imagined. Families were being torn apart. Close erze mates were being separated. It was all wrong. Jet and Vic were supposed to have a future together. Leon and Cass had started out as a bit of an odd pairing, but over the past year they'd grown nearly as close as Jet and Donovan. For Leon to be forced to leave his partner behind . . .

Donovan took the bottle Cass offered him, but his throat felt too closed up to drink it. The front door opened again. Donovan thought that perhaps Jet and Vic were coming back inside, but it turned out to be a whole group of people: Thad, Tennyson, Lucius, Ariadne, and Katerina. All of them crowded into the kitchen. "Are Vic and Jet still out there?" Cass asked Thad.

Thad nodded. He looked sad; Thad and Vic worked well together, but they'd never been particularly close as partners when not on duty. "I knew Vic would go out of erze on this."

The five new arrivals had been given evacuation notices, but they all had friends or family members whom they would have to leave behind as a result. Everyone felt even worse when they learned that Cass had not been selected. "This whole thing sucks," Katerina said.

"I think Donovan was onto something." Lucius nodded in Donovan's direction. "What if none of us agree to go? If the shrooms won't evacuate all of us, then we tell 'em to scorch off."

"If we go out of erze," Thad said, "we endanger the entire evacuation plan. There're a lot of other civilian exos who are relying on it." The lieutenant's expression was troubled, and when he spoke again, he sounded much older than his twenty-two years. "When there are no good choices, you need to put your faith *somewhere*. I have to believe Soldier Werth and Commander Tate have considered all the options and wouldn't issue erze orders unless it was the right decision. I'll keep doing what I know how to do, and that's trust in the erze."

Lucius looked back to Donovan. "What about you, D? You weren't this quiet at Commander Tate's briefing."

Donovan avoided the gazes of his erze mates. The Rii Galaxysweeper and the barren world of Bithis revolved in his mind as he tried to moisten his throat. "Erze orders are erze orders," he said, and from across the kitchen, Thad nodded.

— — —

"What am I going to do?" Jet moaned, pacing the living room while Donovan sat on the bottom step of the stairs and watched helplessly. "I told her what you told me—that Earth and everyone on it might end up scorched. She said she'd made her choice already and nothing would change her mind."

It was the evening before the deadline and Jet seemed no closer to a decision. He groaned and fell onto the sofa. "My mom and dad had a big fight. They *never* fight. My dad pretty much told me to save myself and petition to take my mom with me. He trotted out a bunch of examples from history where people who stayed behind when things started going south ended up dead, but those who left went on to shape the world in new ways. My mom said she wasn't going to leave him, but he argued that since we're both exos, we'd need each other more than him in the long run. They both ended up crying. It was the worst thing ever."

A long silence followed, during which Donovan picked at a frayed edge of carpet, unable to think of what to say. He'd lived in Jet's house for nearly two months after his father's death. As a kid, he'd probably spent as much time in Jet's place as he had in his own house, and lacking his own mother while growing up, Jet's mom had been the next best thing to him. The thought of the Mathews family in such distress was awful, and he was sure it was only one case in thousands.

Jet suddenly turned to Donovan. "You've accepted already, right?"

"Um. Not yet."

Jet sat up. "But you have to. Soldier Werth ordered you to help make sure people cooperate with the evacuation."

"You're under erze orders too," Donovan reminded him.

"And if I go against them and stay?"

Donovan tried to force a smile. "You're not going to get rid of me that easily."

Jet's expression crumpled further; he dropped his head in his hands. "This is unreal. I can't believe any of this is happening," he muttered at the ground. A long silence followed before he spoke again. "I must really love her."

Donovan ached for him. "We shouldn't have to choose between erze duty and the people we love," he said quietly. He understood that better than anyone.

Jet did nothing but breathe harshly for a minute. When he spoke again, his voice was a dull whisper. "I don't know what's the right thing to do. All I know is that it's wrong to put my own feelings ahead of everything else. That's not what being a stripe is about." His shoulders rose and fell. "I can't stand the idea of leaving Vic. It makes me feel sick to my stomach, D. Like I'm going to throw up." Jet raised his face at last, his expression utterly wretched but resolute. "But if I go against erze, I won't even know who I am anymore."

With the leadenness of a man condemned to the atomizer, Jet picked up his screen, already displaying the evacuation notice. He stared down at it in reluctant anguish for two final seconds, then pressed his thumb to the sensor to confirm his acceptance.

Jet sagged. He got up slowly, picked up Donovan's screen, and offered it to him without speaking. Donovan raised his eyes to his partner's face. Jet's expression was stoic and expectant and pleading, maybe even just a touch threatening. *Stay with me on this.*

Seven years ago, Donovan had told Soldier Werth that he wanted to be a soldier-in-erze because of his best friend. That fact had not, he realized now, changed all that much. Donovan took the proffered screen and thought, for an instant, of the business card in his pocket, of Anya's lips, her fingers on his neck—then he pressed his thumb down. The screen flashed a confirmation—oddly simple for something so momentous—and Donovan thought, *We're really going to do this. We're going to leave Earth.*

What have we done?

A loud booming began thudding overhead. Fast, deep, and vibratory, a frantic drumbeat. He and Jet stared upward in confusion and disbelief. They'd never heard this particular zhree emergency siren deployed except in military drills, but they understood the meaning in an instant.

The Round was under attack.

16

For a second, Donovan entertained the possibility that this might be some drill he hadn't known about. But then Jet looked at him, his face mirroring Donovan's alarm, and they sprang into motion. Neither of them was in uniform; Donovan was in jeans and an old shirt, Jet in cargo shorts and a tee. Donovan shoved on his boots; Jet grabbed their holstered duty guns. He passed Donovan's sidearm to him as they bolted from the house, running for the parked skimmercar. Once they were in their seats, Jet grabbed the controls and spun the vehicle out into the street as Donovan punched open the dashboard comm. "Command, what's going on?" he demanded.

"The Towers are under attack. M-multiple locations—the upper landing fields, th-the eastern and western entrances, the central—" The SecPac dispatcher, Liz, sounded uncharacteristically flustered and they could barely make out her words over the continued rapid booming of the emergency alarms, but it hardly mattered. Jet took the turn onto the first spoke road at a speed that made Donovan brace himself against the side of the skimmercar, digging armored fingers into the seat. Several other SecPac vehicles were already racing toward the shadowy spires of the Towers. Jet sped up and fell in behind them. As they neared the vast complex of alien skyscrapers, Donovan's gaze was pulled upward. "What in all erze is *that*?"

There was something *attached* to the Towers—a strange, blood-colored bulbous structure that marred the familiar outline of the tallest spire. It looked like a large fungal growth that had ballooned without warning, or a sticky ball of goo that had been thrown at the side of the structure and stuck, deforming and wrapping around the metal.

Jet said in a disbelieving voice, "I think it's a *ship*."

As Donovan stared, he saw movement pouring around, on, and inside the Towers. In the dark, it was hard to see exactly what was happening. The flexible, deformed red glob that had stuck to the side of the spire appeared to be opening—not from a single door but from numerous dilating pores, like a piece of rotten fruit developing worm-eaten tunnels through time-lapse footage. Dark shapes with many legs were clambering out of the alien structure, dropping to the ground or onto the Towers' causeways or open landings. So horribly mesmerizing was the sight that Donovan wasn't paying attention to where the skimmercar was going and was roughly thrown against the safety restraints when Jet spun the vehicle to a stop behind three other SecPac cruisers clustered at the foot of the Towers near one of the entrances.

Donovan knew the Towers as well as he knew anything in the Round. He'd been here countless times in his life. Now the incongruity of the deeply familiar with the utterly unbelievable stalled his mind for a moment as panotin erupted from every node in his body, bringing him instantly to full armor.

Jet sucked in a sharp breath. "Erze almighty."

Two Soldiers were lying on the ground beside the entrance. Donovan had never actually seen a zhree corpse before, but he was certain that these two zhree were dead. One was rolled over on his domed body, the six limbs sprawled limply; the other was in a half-upright, kneeling position, two legs bent as if still trying to push himself up, but he was motionless. The most vulnerable parts of a zhree were the eyes and the orifices on the underside of the torso; both the Soldiers had more than one eye shattered. Viscous liquid seeped out of the gaping holes of their fractured amber lenses.

Scrambling past the bodies and into the Towers were human-sized, six-limbed figures that Donovan recognized, after a second of confusion, from that day he'd been summoned to Soldier Werth's quarters. A cold rush of fear bathed him. Mottled hulls, reddish eyes, thick fins.

Rii Hunters.

Most of the Hunters continued rushing into the Towers, but at the sudden arrival of the SecPac vehicles, a handful of them paused, their many dusky, gleaming eyes taking in the appearance of the humans who advanced, weapons drawn, bristling with armor but silent with astonishment. Donovan threw open the skimmercar door. He and Jet ran toward the scene. Cass and Leon were already ahead of them, along with Tennyson, Lucius, and several others; Donovan didn't get the chance to see who else, because at that moment, everything around him erupted in a frenzy of violence.

There was no way to tell who fired first; it might have been one of the humans, it might have been the Hunters. It didn't matter; in an instant, the blast of electripulse weapons rent the air. Donovan and Jet had nothing more powerful on them than their handguns. As the night exploded with noise, Donovan threw himself behind the nearest skimmercar, tabbed the coil charger, and swung his weapon up toward the first alien figure he could see, trying frantically to aim for one of its eyes. It was near impossible—like shooting a spinning, leaping bull's-eye in the dark. The intruders were coming at them so fast that their many limbs blurred. Adrenaline flooded into Donovan's body and he opened fire. He got off two, perhaps three shots before his exocel fell—from full armor to nothing but soft, bare skin, pricked with sudden cold.

No. Understanding and panic rose together in a wave. *Sweet erze, no.*

Donovan grasped desperately for his armor, like a man feeling around a stump for his missing limb, knowing even as he kept trying that it would be in vain. The trip wire in his brain, present in every Hardened human, was triggered by aggression toward any zhree. And though they were different from the Mur colonists, the Rii Hunters—with their six limbs, domed and patterned torsos, flashing fins, and many eyes—were still zhree. By attacking them, he'd rendered himself defenseless.

The horrible truth hit him: He was facing death as a squishy.

As were all of his erze mates. Less than twenty feet in front of him, he glimpsed Tennyson stumbling back in alarm, staring down in shock at his unarmored hands. Donovan watched in horror as one of the Hunters leapt onto the roof of the first parked skimmercar, rocking it with its weight, a stocky weapon cradled in two of its limbs. It fired a blast that blew a hole in Tennyson's chest the size of a baseball. The exo's blood sprayed across Lucius's arms and face. Lucius stared uncomprehendingly at his partner's body as Tennyson collapsed. Donovan screamed, *"Get away from there!"* as another Hunter leapt over the first one, cleared the skimmercar, and drove an armored, serrated limb straight into Lucius's midsection, piercing it clean through.

The first Hunter swung his weapon around and Donovan threw himself on Jet, tackling his partner to the ground as the blast went through one side of their skimmercar and out the other with a metallic bang. Donovan's knees and hands struck the concrete; his breath left him in a whoosh as he and Jet landed hard. From somewhere, he heard a human scream—whose, he could not tell—and then a couple of the Rii Hunters began shouting to each other in a language that Donovan had never heard. Not Mur, with its lilting, musical trilling, but a rapid chirping, clicking language that sounded at once sinister and gleeful. They were exclaiming with delight, Donovan suspected, at the ease with which these Earth creatures died.

Donovan pushed up and grabbed his partner by the shoulders, bare fingers digging against bone, not so much as a thread of panotin to protect either of them. Jet lay still and staring, seemingly paralyzed, and Donovan remembered what it had been like when it had happened to him the first time—the feeling of complete and utter helplessness, the humiliation, the terror of losing control of one's body. It had paralyzed him too, at the time, but that had not been a life-or-death situation. "Jet!" Donovan shook his erze mate roughly, forcing him to focus. "We can still fight without our armor. We *have to* or we're all dead. Don't freeze up on me!"

Jet blinked, his gaze focusing, understanding registering behind the shock. He nodded, resolute, but with more fear in his eyes than Donovan had ever seen in any combat situation they had been in together. This was not something they'd trained for; they had never been taught how to fight zhree—why would they?—and though they had drilled to perform through hunger, thirst, pain, and fatigue, they had never, ever imagined having to go into battle without their exocels. They might as well have attempted to learn how to fight without arms.

Donovan rolled off Jet, grabbing the handgun that he'd dropped and scrambling back onto his feet in a crouch. The 9mm electripulse pistol in his hands seemed a weak, feeble toy, woefully inadequate against these monsters. On the other side of the skimmercar he could hear more gunfire, tearing metal, thuds, shouting. Over the commotion, he heard Cass's voice clearly over the others, yelling, "Don't just stand there, *move, dammit*! And aim for the eyes! You don't need your armor to spray some lead into these things!" and someone else howling—Ariadne, he thought—"They killed Tenny and Lucius! Those scorching shrooms killed them!" Mingled with the voices of the desperate humans rang the menacing chirping speech of the Hunters, like some birdsong from hell. Blood thundered in Donovan's ears. He had one thing on his mind now: survive. Drive these Hunters back long enough to allow him, Jet, and their erze mates to get away alive and warn the rest of the Round.

Tennyson and Lucius lay not far away from him, their torn bodies in the center of an expanding pool of blood. Donovan choked down fear and fury and focused on the two E201 electripulse rifles that had fallen to the ground from the men's hands as they had died. He grabbed Jet's arm and pointed, and they ran, hunched over between the skimmercars, toward the weapons. A loud chirrup, another metallic crunch, and then two blasts gouged the ground next to them like miniature asteroid impacts. Donovan dived for the E201 as he saw the shadow coming for him. Rolling onto his back in a puddle of Tennyson's blood, he slammed the rifle to full auto and blasted the Hunter on top of the car with a noisy volley of bullets. The Hunter gave a loud whistle of pain and anger and toppled off the roof of the vehicle, its damaged armor rippling as it disappeared from sight. Donovan kicked the other rifle toward Jet, who grabbed it and brought it up just as the other Hunter, its serrated limbs gleaming and slicked with bits of Lucius's flesh, spun toward Donovan and stabbed its deadly limbs down at him.

Donovan saw his own death—the Hunter would slice him to ribbons—and so strong was his terror in that one moment as he rolled away in a desperate last-ditch effort to escape, that the involuntary reflex to armor seemed to overcome every other. His exocel flickered; he felt it trying to shield him, to save him, as one of the Hunter's legs plunged down, missing him by inches, and another struck him in the space between the ball of his shoulder joint and his clavicle, pinning him to the ground. Donovan screamed as pain exploded at the place of impact. He glanced down to see the point of the Hunter's armored leg driven into his flesh, *through* the feeble layer of panotin that had sprung up at the last second. He'd never seen his own armor pierced, and he'd never seen his own blood in such dizzying quantity, pooling up around the wound, over the torn weave of his armor, mingling with the blood of fellow stripes already slicking the Hunter's gleaming, razored limb.

And then the Hunter was blasted back by a hurricane of shrill gunfire; Jet, Leon, Cass—all of them unloading their electripulse rifles, none of them armored, but all of them standing up and advancing, murderous. The Hunter jerked and Donovan felt the puncture wound tear even larger as it pulled its leg free from his body, releasing him as bullets rained down on its armored hull. The alien spun toward the cluster of attacking humans, but in the wall of flying ammunition, several shots finally found their mark—the Hunter gave a piercing whistle, covering a shattered eye, and then dual bullet holes burst in another of the orange-red lenses. Fluid gushed out and the Hunter staggered and tipped sideways, twitching.

The remaining Hunters moved faster than anything Donovan had ever seen. The scene became a chaotic mess of movement, gunfire, and armored limbs, his erze mates running, shouting, diving out of the way. Donovan tried to get to his feet, tried to hoist the E201 with what felt like a nerveless meat arm attached to his torso with pure fire. He expected at any moment for something lethal to strike his soft body; it was a sickeningly incongruous feeling to be fighting for his life so naked.

"Jet." Frantically, Donovan tried to make sense of the mayhem; he glimpsed his partner rolling behind the cover of a skimmercar only to see the entire vehicle violently shoved out of the way by alien legs. All of Donovan's pain vanished in a blaze of panic; he leveled the rifle and pumped bullets at the Hunter, only half-aware that he was screaming unintelligibly. Leon joined him, both of them firing, Leon's face pale and bloodied but his expression made of steel, until the Hunter fell under the hailstorm of their combined lead.

Donovan saw the indicator on the E201 turn red and heard the snap of electric coils on an empty chamber. He fumbled for the extra ammunition he usually kept in his uniform pocket before he realized with plummeting despair that he was in civilian clothes and had no spare magazine. Leon turned toward him, took a step, and from behind him two of the remaining Hunters appeared. Donovan tried to yell a warning, but it barely left his mouth before two sets of razored limbs slashed at Leon in a cross-cutting motion, cleaving the unarmored exo in half at the waist.

From seemingly very far away, Donovan heard Cass scream. The world seemed to fall out from under him as one of the aliens scrambled over the two parts of Leon's body and came at Donovan where he stood, the useless, empty E201 in his blood-slicked bare hands.

Something flew out of the darkness and struck the Hunter less than ten feet in front of him; the alien was lifted off its feet and for a second, Donovan, astonished to still be alive, stared mutely at the spot where the monster had been. Then movement surrounded him and he realized that Soldiers had arrived. A dozen of them descended on the pack of Hunters, striped hulls and patterned fins flashing in the light of discharging weapons as they flowed around the stunned humans. Three Soldiers leapt onto one Hunter, and in mesmerized, revolted relief, Donovan saw a massive tangle of flailing limbs as they pulled the Hunter's legs out from under it and flipped it onto its hull. A fourth Soldier fired directly into the Hunter's underbelly and a horrible sizzling sound and acidic burning smell pervaded the Hunter's dying whistling screams.

The Soldiers raced on; Donovan heard snatches of musical shouting in Mur, not at all unlike the short, clipped battle communication of human soldiers: "Erzeless Rii filth." "Get these humans out of here!" "Go, go, go!" The shadowed entry into the Towers lit up with weapons fire, blurred movement, and high-pitched screaming as Werth's Soldiers were met by additional Hunters, some of them dropping from the sides of the building as they continued to pour forth nightmarishly from the globular vessel still stuck high above.

And then over the tumult, other zhree voices began shouting, in that peculiar homeworld accent, "Fall back!" One of Gur's

Soldiers bounded past Donovan into the melee, ignoring him completely. "Erze orders! Fall back!"

The call seemed to travel like magic from Soldier to Soldier, Werth's and Gur's alike. They began to retreat, still firing shots at the Hunters, pairs of them lifting injured erze mates, covering one another as they yielded to the invaders. Loud clicks and whistles ran through the packs of Hunters, who held their ground at the base of the Towers, chirruping and stabbing the air with their limbs in triumph. The gunfire fell silent.

The Towers were lost.

Donovan fell to his knees, the empty rifle clattering to the ground. His arms and shoulders began to shake uncontrollably as the battle mania drained out of him. Sensation started to return to his exocel in the form of tingling pain that stabbed from node to node up his spine, sharp pinpricks like the thawing of a frozen limb. His armor crawled weakly over his wounds, large and small; it packed around the tattered flesh where the Hunter's leg had punctured him, staunching the blood.

The bodies of his fellow exos were scattered on the ground around him. Tennyson, Lucius, and Leon, and others he had not seen until now: Nicodemus, shot in the head, Katerina's leg torn off. Donovan's mind faltered, unable to take in all the horror at once. Cass was rocking back and forth, cradling the top half of Leon's body in her lap. Donovan heard a noise several feet away that he did not recognize and turned his head toward it: Jet, storming back and forth, shrieking with grief.

Soldiers swept through efficiently. "This one's still alive," called one, lifting an unconscious Ariadne in two limbs and carrying her off. A couple of others examined the human bodies with curiosity and distaste. "So this is what they look like inside," one of them said, bending to peer at Leon's remains, oblivious to Cass, still bent double under the weight of wracking sobs. The world seemed to tilt dangerously. Donovan felt himself sag and someone caught him up under the arms.

"Can you stand? You need medical attention." The zhree voice was vaguely familiar. Donovan stared into two of the pale yellow eyes. It was Soldier Wylt, who'd recognized him in the barracks. Donovan had no wherewithal to reply, and Wylt ordered, a little impatiently, "Get up, Donovan." The tone of command from a zhree of his own erze moved him where his own will seemed to have abandoned him. He got to his feet and swayed against one of the nearly destroyed skimmercars. Wylt took a firm hold of his arm with vise-like pincers and kept him upright. "Come along," he said, a touch more gently, and supporting him, led Donovan away.

17

They were taken to the hospital in the Round. It was not designed to treat exos—there was a medical wing in the Towers for that, but the Towers were currently occupied by the enemy. Donovan and Jet, whose injuries were not life-threatening, sat slumped against the wall in the starkly lit emergency room lobby. All the other patients had been moved elsewhere to accommodate dozens of injured stripes. The group Jet and Donovan had been in was not the only one to have responded to the alarms; from all over the Round, soldiers-in-erze had rushed to defend the Towers and the result had been the same everywhere: Exocels had failed. People had died.

Donovan's eyes drifted over faces strained with pain or blank with shock, but each one that he recognized brought a small flutter of relief—at least those of them in here were alive.

Vic wasn't in the hospital. Neither was Thad. Jet checked his comm again, for the thousandth time—still no answer to any of his frantic messages. "Maybe they can't get through." The note of hope in his taut voice strained against the agony of worry. "Too many crises going on. The system must be overloaded."

"Have you heard?" The woman sitting on the other side of Jet was named Anastasia. She'd suffered three broken ribs, a broken leg, and lacerations all down the left side of her body when she'd been pinned and dragged under an overturned skimmercar during the fighting. Her exocel bulged extensively over the wounds, the strands of panotin glistening as they knit over raw abrasions. "There were attacks all over the planet," she told them. "We weren't the only Round invaded. Cities got hit too, some of the biggest ones: Los Angeles, Shanghai, Mumbai . . . They all got hit. I heard half of Mexico City is gone."

That *had* to be an exaggeration. There was always a lot of confusion and wildly overstated rumors during disasters. What Anastasia was saying seemed too huge to be real. But yesterday the idea of so many stripes dead and injured and the Towers being taken over by the Rii would've also seemed impossible. If she was right, there'd been, how many?—*millions*?—of civilian casualties all over the world. Donovan couldn't process that. Distant tragedies couldn't penetrate the numbness of others that were so close and fresh.

The Hunters had apparently allowed Nurses and other nonmilitary Mur colonists to flee the Towers unharmed. Therrid had been brought over here by Soldiers to do what he could for the injured exos. Donovan caught the incongruous sight of the Nurse hurrying about the hospital lobby, his nurse-in-erze, Sanjay, trying his best to keep up. Two other nurses-in-erze and a couple of emergency room doctors were helping to triage the patients, bringing the worst cases to Therrid's attention and making the less severely injured more comfortable where possible. Donovan overheard Therrid telling one of the doctors: "No, don't worry about severed limbs! As long as the exocel is undamaged, it'll seal off the stump and they'll be fine. But anyone who's unable to armor needs to be seen immediately, and broken or bleeding cerebrospinal nodes are an *emergency*."

By the time Therrid made it around to their corner of the room, his fins were fluttering in distress and he was mumbling to himself in a constant low susurrus. "Vercingetorix," he exclaimed, bending toward Jet. "And Donovan . . . thank the Highest State of Erze. I've lost so many of the hatchlings already. If you two had been . . ." He didn't finish but began examining Jet quickly, feeling the nodes along the back of his neck and head and peering into his eyes.

"I'm fine, zun Therrid." Jet had suffered some nasty cuts and bruises, including a deep laceration on the thigh, all of them now sealed under his exocel. "Have you seen or heard from Vic? Or Thad?" Donovan knew the answer was likely to be no; they'd been looking through the room themselves every few minutes, and Jet's mounting desperation was plain in his voice.

Therrid's fins swept across in a negative. "I haven't," he said sadly, moving on to look at Donovan, whose exocel was bulged so thickly around the stab wound that it looked as if he'd developed a frighteningly large tumor where his arm met his body. The pain there had become a dull, throbbing ache and he could barely move his right arm. Therrid probed the lump and Donovan winced.

"You ought to be in a therapy tank, but we don't have any here," Therrid said. "Without access to the medical facilities in the Towers, I don't have much to work with. This human medical center has a limited supply of emergency packs of panotin replenishment gel but not much else." Therrid's voice and fins vibrated with frustration. He thrust clear containers of milky liquid at them. "Drink this. It'll bring down the inflammation and alleviate the pain. Both of you need to stay hydrated and get enough hydrocarbons and minerals. Your wounds aren't serious, but if your exocels are too depleted, you'll end up with scarring and mobility issues."

After Therrid moved on, they slumped back against the wall, drinking what seemed to Donovan to be a gritty, oily smoothie that tasted like raw eggs and sand. Anastasia had been moved elsewhere by one of the nurses-in-erze, so they were somewhat alone. "I just got through to my mom," Jet said a few minutes later, looking at his comm yet again. "At least we know the network's up."

Donovan looked down at his own comm display. Dozens of message notifications were lighting up on his cadre channel. With an increasingly sick feeling in his stomach, he began skimming through them. Anastasia had been right; the Rii attack had hit Rounds and cities elsewhere in the world and the consequences had been just as devastating.

Maddison Chu had sent: *Are you all okay, C-mates?! We fought them off, but it's really bad here in Round One. Lots of stripes dead. Don't know how many yet.*

Dmitri replied: *We're fine in Seven. No attack here. Moscow bombed but missiles shot down, not too much damage.*

Kamo/R17: *I'm alive but what in all erze happened? Did everyone else's exocel crap out?*

Maddison/R1: *Yeah. This is a scorching nightmare.*

Pauliina/R6: *I heard Round Ten is occupied. Anyone hear from Amrita??*

Bartholomew/R4: *How about the guys in Rounds Three and Twelve?*

Fernando/R12: *Matias is dead.*

The last was a gut punch. Donovan closed his eyes and dropped his head against the wall. Matias had been a hell of a guy to have around during CRP; he always had funny stories to tell, and a smile or a joke to lighten the mood no matter what sort of grueling torment they were being put through. He and Fernando had been like Donovan and Jet, as close as brothers.

Donovan composed a reply of his own: *They took the Towers in Round Three. Jet and I are okay.* His hands were unsteady for the last bit: *We lost Leon.* Donovan stared at the three words, but seeing them did not make them any more real.

He'd barely sent out the message when a priority alert came through on all local SecPac frequencies, causing every conscious stripe in the room to sit up and take notice.

"This is Command One." The grave voice in Donovan's earbud was barely recognizable as Commander Tate's. "Those of you who are able, make your way to Central Command by oh six hundred." There was a long pause on the line. "Go in erze. Command out."

About a third of the soldiers-in-erze in the room began to get up. Donovan struggled to his feet, stifling a groan. His aching body protested vehemently, but he wanted to hear what Commander Tate would say and find out what was going on. He turned to give Jet a hand up, but his partner was already on his feet, staring toward the lobby entrance.

SecPac lights were pulsing in the early morning dark outside the hospital doors as stretchers were wheeled into the emergency room. This scene had already happened several times while Jet and Donovan had been here, but this time, the motionless figure on the stretcher was Thaddeus Lowell. Even with an oxygen mask over his face, there was no mistaking him; one of Thad's large, striped hands dangled limply off the side of the moving stretcher. Half of his dark hair was singed off, his complexion waxen.

Jet was running toward the second gurney that was being wheeled in. Donovan rushed after him, getting a glimpse over his partner's shoulder as Jet pushed his way to the side of the stretcher. Vic's pale hair was matted with blood. Her exocel crawled feebly over her scalp and face. She seemed to be half-conscious because at Jet's wordless moan, her eyelids fluttered and her fingers twitched on top of the sheets.

"Vic. *Vic.*" Jet's whisper was choked.

Nurse Therrid had to push Jet back so he could get through to examine her. "Get them into operating rooms and start them on surgical exocel suppressant," Therrid ordered. The stretchers began moving again.

Jet began to follow, then half-turned toward Donovan. He seemed unable to talk but Donovan understood; he put a hand on his erze mate's arm. "I'll go," he said. "I'll find out what's going on and come back here. You stay with her." Jet nodded gratefully, then ran after Therrid and the stretchers.

Something clenched violently inside Donovan's chest like a poked clam—a visceral reflex to the expectation of more grief. *Please not Vic and Thad too.* He cringed with the desire to fold his head under his arms and sink back down to the floor of the emergency room lobby.

Instead, he followed the small crowd of stripes heeding Commander Tate's call and left the hospital.

— — —

He was surprised to see that the sun wasn't even up yet. It seemed to him as if days must've passed when in truth it had been only ten hours since the Rii attack. He was even more surprised when he arrived at SecPac Central Command to discover that the campus had become a zhree military encampment. From a distance, in the faint haze of predawn light mingled with distant street illumination, the largest training field behind the Comm Hub building looked like a pool of identically striped torsos, moving around like a repeating floor-tile pattern come to life. Even as a soldier-in-erze, Donovan had rarely seen so many Soldiers in one place at the same time. The fact that they had taken over SecPac's property was utterly disconcerting.

As he got closer, Donovan saw Soldiers standing and talking in clusters, some of them injured and being tended to by Nurses, others walking around and checking in on the status of comrades, accounting for weapons and ammunition, setting rotating guards, and doing the sorts of tasks one did when holed up in a position after a battle. Here and there, different markings stood out—Gur's Soldiers, standing alone or in pairs, but a circle of space always seeming to separate them from the others, who did not approach.

Donovan started for the Comm Hub building, but a couple of other officers waved to get his attention and pointed him toward a far corner of the field where a sizable crowd of humans was gathering. Donovan saw the unmistakeable figure of Commander Tate among them. In the dim light, Tate looked haggard almost beyond recognition. She was not striding about or shouting orders as usual but standing quietly with those gathered around her. Donovan had seen his commander in victory and in defeat but never had he seen her battered by such terrible loss to the officer corps that she'd led for so many years. She gave a single nod at the approach of each person, a fractional amount of tension easing with each face she recognized, as if to say: *Good, he's alive. And he's alive. And she's alive as well.*

Donovan had not imagined that a group of soldiers-in-erze

could look so ruined. Men and women were openly weeping. Some fell on one another in relief to find their friends alive. Many wore blank expressions, their shock and bewilderment still too fresh, compounded by the guilt of being here when equally deserving erze mates were not. Donovan searched frantically until he saw Cass, sitting in the grass at the edge of the crowd, hugging herself, her gaze distant and downcast.

He hurried to her and touched her on the shoulder. She looked up at him slowly, her eyes dry but swollen and Leon's blood still on her hands and clothes. When Donovan knelt beside her, a flicker of renewed alarm crossed her face. "Where's Jet?" Cass's voice was raw, hoarse.

"He's fine." Donovan spoke quietly. "He's with Vic. She and Thad were brought to the hospital just as we were leaving. They're pretty badly hurt."

Cass's throat moved in a dry swallow. "They made me leave him," she whispered angrily. "A Soldier picked me up and carried me away."

At that moment, Commander Tate cleared her throat for their attention. It was an unusually subdued sound, but in the near silence, they all heard it and turned toward her. Donovan put an arm around Cass and together they got to their feet. Tate surveyed the gathered officers with a leaden gaze. "The zhree zun have taken over the Comm Hub building as a base of operations in order to communicate with the other Rounds and discuss what's to be done next. So I'm afraid this is the best we can do for now." Tate's hands shook as she unfolded her glasses and put them on. For a long moment, the commander stared down at the screen in her hands; she didn't seem to be seeing the words. Tate pulled her glasses off again and looked up. "First, a moment of silence for the erze mates who aren't with us anymore."

Silence fell over bowed heads. Donovan could hear the footsteps and background musical burble of conversation from the Soldiers walking about in the field, accompanied by the usual machine sounds of weapons checks and the hum of vehicles in the streets. Standing out here, mere feet away from a bustling camp full of Soldiers, only highlighted the wrongness of the moment, the inescapable truth that the erze had been severely maimed. Beside him, Cass took a shuddering breath. *Leon.* Donovan recited the names of the erze mates he knew had been lost. *Tennyson. Lucius. Matias. Nicodemus. Leander.* So many others he didn't know about yet.

Commander Tate cleared her throat again and, consulting her notes, began to speak. "Earth was attacked last night by an advance force of Rii Hunters. The source of the attack came from a stealth vessel that transferred into the solar system in the signal shadow of a civilian cargo ship scheduled to dock in orbit for trade and refueling. Upon entering Earth's orbit, the Rii vessel broke away and released five occupied surface-landing spores that separated and proceeded to Rounds One, Three, Ten, Twelve, and Seventeen.

"At the same time, the Rii ship launched targeted warheads at many of Earth's largest human cities including Los Angeles, Mexico City, Jakarta, Karachi, Moscow, Shanghai, Mumbai, and New Cairo, among others. Orbital defenses destroyed the Rii ship and most of the missiles were shot down before they reached their destinations, but some made it through. We're still receiving damage and casualty reports from around the world. It might be a while before we get the full picture.

"It appears the missile bombardment was intended as cover for the five spore vessels to reach their destinations. At Round Twelve, the spore missed its coordinates and landed outside the wall. The invading party was destroyed in heavy fighting. Round One also repelled the attack. But the Towers of Rounds Three, Ten, and Seventeen are now under Rii occupation."

Shocked and angry murmurs ran through the assembled soldiers-in-erze. "It's because we couldn't fight them," Sebastian exclaimed, loudly enough for everyone to hear him. "Our exocels stopped working the second we needed them the most!"

Shouts of agreement rose at once. "No one warned us!"

"It was a slaughter. We were no better than squishies out there."

"How many exos died last night *for no reason*?"

A day ago, Donovan couldn't have imagined soldiers-in-erze shouting at Commander Tate in such a disorderly manner, nor Tate ever allowing such a breakdown of discipline. Yet now she let the raw emotion of the officers run loud, and after a minute, Donovan realized that she was staring steadily past them to a spot beyond the crowd. When Donovan turned to follow her gaze, he saw Soldier Werth standing motionless behind them.

How long he'd been there, Donovan had no idea. Certainly long enough to have heard the uproar. The commotion had even reached the notice of the Soldiers sharing the field; several of them had paused behind Werth and were watching the humans as well. Instinctively, Donovan stiffened and dropped his armor, causing Cass to look over her shoulder, and a couple of seconds later, everyone else had turned, and an abrupt, uncomfortable silence descended like a curtain.

Soldier Werth stepped forward into the cluster of humans, which parted for him. A wave of receding armor followed, but the sudden quiet did not dispel the tension that seemed to stretch from person to person, through tense jaws and clenched fists and angry expressions, like a taut, invisible web with Commander Tate anchoring one end and Soldier Werth the other. Werth's alien expression was unreadable as his eyes swept over the diminished ranks of exos. Donovan wondered if the erze master was noticing who was here and who was missing.

"Speaking to your commander with such disrespect is not in erze behavior for soldiers." The translation machine behind Soldier Werth repeated the words in a cold, flat rebuke that made more than a few stripes wince. "Particularly as she is not to blame for the losses you've suffered." Werth stopped in place. Commander Tate still said nothing, and Donovan, looking between them, understood that Tate had not put a halt to the turmoil because she'd wanted Werth to hear it all—the despair and fury of the humans who wore his markings on their hands.

"I am the one to blame," Werth said matter-of-factly. "We are—the Mur colonists who first brought humans-in-erze and granted you exocellular technology but let you remain in ignorance of its limitations. Last night, you saw the tragic consequences. Exos were never meant to fight zhree—Mur or Rii."

"You can change that." The words left Donovan's mouth before he really knew what he was doing. Everyone stared at him. With a pang of chagrin, he realized that his months of being an adviser to the zhree zun had accustomed him to speaking above his rank, directly to Soldier Werth. He'd forgotten how rude and unusual it appeared under other circumstances. Swallowing his discomfort,

Donovan kept his armor respectfully lowered as he stepped forward.

He was remembering suddenly the memory discs sitting in a small envelope in his desk drawer at home, posthumously sent to his father by the assassinated scientist-in-erze, Dr. Ghosh. He'd all but forgotten about them in the tumultuous months since Gur's arrival. They hadn't seemed that important—until now. Only now did it seem obvious that his father *must* have considered the possibility of an eventual Rii attack—and secretly set about to prepare for it.

"Zun Werth," Donovan said, his excitement rising, "the exocel inhibition reflex is just a neural connection in the part of the brain tied to aggression." If a human scientist-in-erze had discovered how the reflex arc worked, and could even suggest a possible way to jam it, then surely the Nurses in charge of human Hardening would know as well. "You could remove the trip wire. Without it, we could fight the Rii. There are at least as many soldiers-in-erze as there are Soldiers. We could help take back the Towers."

Donovan glanced at Commander Tate. Tate's eyes were narrowed in warning, and Donovan could feel her unspoken question raking over him: *How do you know this? Since when did you become a neuroscientist, Reyes?*

A palpable change had come over the assembled exos, who shifted in closer, nodding and murmuring agreement. Their grief was not diminished, but they were soldiers. They wanted to *act*, to take revenge against the Hunters who had invaded their home and killed their erze mates.

"*No.*" The word was as curt and final in Mur as it was in English, and it cut down the rising eagerness of the crowd like a scythe. Soldier Werth's multiple eyes held Donovan in a stare as hard as iron. "What you suggest is not possible."

"But . . ." Blood rushed into Donovan's face. Werth was wrong, or lying. Or worse, simply *refusing*. "Zun, you've always said that you personally chose each one of us for the erze. This thing in our brains—maybe it made sense to the colonists a hundred years ago, but it doesn't anymore. If you really do have faith in us, you'd let us fight. You'd treat us the way you treat your Soldiers."

"This is not a matter of my confidence in your abilities." Soldier Werth's voice was low, bordering on threat. "The inhibition reflex can't be removed."

"Can't?" Donovan said through gritted teeth. "Or *won't*?"

"Reyes, that's *enough*," Commander Tate said. "This isn't the—"

"Soldier Werth!" Soldier Gur's accented voice rang out as he crossed the field, Administrator Seir following a few paces behind.

Slowly, Werth shifted his gaze. "Zun," he said, dropping armor.

Gur surveyed the gathered humans, pausing curiously on Donovan, who was still standing in front of the others. Trying not to look too hasty, Donovan kept his armor down and took a step back into the crowd. He suspected Gur had heard the last few seconds of angry conversation and was wondering why an exo would be arguing so heatedly with his erze master.

Gur's attention returned to Werth. "You've had a chance to check over your humans, then? It appears as if most of them survived?"

"At least those you see here, zun," Werth said.

"Good," Gur said. The translation machine began to repeat him in English; Gur turned it off. "Administrator Seir and I were discussing to what extent human casualties would affect the evacuation plans, but fortunately, you have enough exos that there is a sizable pool to draw from even with losses to the first selection round." Gur paused thoughtfully. "We will have to completely redo the selection from Round One, however, given the particularly high number of fatalities there."

"Rounds One and Twelve suffered heavy casualties because they fought until every invading Hunter was killed," Soldier Werth said. "Your Soldiers were not stationed there to give the order to retreat and surrender their Towers to the enemy."

It was suddenly apparent that nearly all the background noise had vanished. Every zhree on the field was watching the exchange between the two Soldiers. Donovan thought he glimpsed those with Werth's markings shifting forward discreetly, fins flattening. Thinking back more clearly on the confusion and madness of the battle, Donovan remembered that Werth's troops had seemed to be winning. They'd been charging forward into the Towers when Gur's Soldiers had given the order to fall back. They had not looked happy about it then and they did not look happy about it now.

Soldier Gur's smallish eyes were flinty. A few of his own Soldiers drew nearer to him. "I do not approve of your tone, Soldier Werth," Gur said. "It suggests you are questioning my mandate from the Homeworld Council to secure the safety of Mur colonists on this planet and to wield erze authority in the best interests of the Commonwealth."

"Soldier Gur," Administrator Seir interjected, "that is the shared goal of all erze zun, regardless of whether we were hatched on the homeworld or not." Seir's fins seemed to be moving too quickly. Donovan had never seen the highest Administrator on Earth appear nervous before. The tension was affecting the Soldiers, and even though not all the humans could understand what was being said, they could feel it as well—panotin was rising quickly across skin and armored hulls alike.

One of Soldier Werth's fins gave a small twitch. Then he spread them and dropped his armor. "I apologize if I gave the wrong impression," he said. "I would not presume to question a more senior Soldier's judgment as to the best interests of the Commonwealth."

The strain slackened. Armor came down and fins relaxed, though not entirely. Soldier Gur seemed cautiously appeased. "No Soldier likes to yield to the enemy. However, in this case, there was nothing to be gained from battle. We were planning to phase out our presence from this planet as it was. Indeed, this turn of events may have provided us with the opportunity to negotiate for a more favorable outcome. Rii representatives should be arriving at any minute."

"Rii representatives," Soldier Werth repeated slowly, "are coming here?"

"Werth, have you asked yourself why the Rii would attack *now*, so soon after the Homeworld Council's decision to begin withdrawing from Earth? Why risk a battle with us instead of simply waiting to seize the planet without contest? There is only one logical possibility. I am certain the Hunters here are from *Chi'tok*." Soldier Gur made a *chirp-click* noise that Donovan could not think of how to translate into any comparable sound in Mur much less into English. "It is the smallest but fastest-growing and most aggressive Galaxysweeper in the sector. The Rii are not unified; they compete among themselves for territory and *Chi'tok* has the most to gain from taking Earth. They must have learned of our intention to withdraw from this planet and decided to take a chance on sending an advance invasion party to claim the prestige of conquering a Mur colony ahead of any larger, rival Galaxysweepers."

Soldier Gur paced away, fins snapping briskly. "A rather daring gamble on their part. One sacrificial ship, bombarding multiple human cities as a distraction for orbital defenses, while Hunters landed spore vessels in hopes of occupying at least one Round and thus securing conquest rights for *Chi'tok*." Gur gave a thoughtful hum. "While successful, they are now in a precarious position until their main force arrives. They will be willing to discuss terms."

"Discuss terms?" Administrator Seir echoed. "The Commonwealth did not discuss terms when Ortem 4 was attacked. And when Rygur was threatened, the Homeworld Council sent the Mur fleet in force to defend it, crippling a much larger Galaxysweeper than *Chi'tok*. Only three of the Towers on Earth have been lost. If Kreet were to send even a relatively small force—"

Soldier Gur cut Seir off with a sharp slash of his fin. "Ortem 4 and Rygur were completely different situations, Administrator. I have every reason to believe that attempting a negotiation is the proper course of action in this case. The High Speaker has given me the authority to proceed."

Donovan was having a hard time keeping up with what was happening. He still couldn't get past how bluntly Soldier Werth had shot him down earlier. With the zhree leaders going on about interplanetary politics and military tactics, confusing things were happening too fast. Donovan looked toward Commander Tate, hoping for direction, but her expression was stony.

"Soldier Gur," said Administrator Seir, "perhaps we ought to delay until after we have consulted with the rest of the Rounds and with Kreet. There is—"

Seir didn't finish because at that moment, Soldiers burst into movement, running to form a defensive semicircle, armor springing up, raised weapons pointed down the road. "What's happening?" Cass asked in alarm. At the edge of the field, rounding the entrance to SecPac's campus, came a vehicle such as Donovan had never seen before—an open, ovoid mobile platform with mounted artillery and articulated legs not unlike a SecPac assault scrambler, but with six Hunters riding on the uppermost tier of the carrier. At the sight of them, musical muttering and low whistles of profanity ran through the ranks of Werth's Soldiers and the effect it had on the humans wasn't much better—the exos backed away hastily, hands reaching for weapons.

"Hold!" Soldier Gur commanded.

The vehicle stopped. An amplified voice let out a string of chirping, chittering, clicking noises that sounded like a monstrous bird's mating call. A second later, a scratchy-sounding translation machine sang out in badly rendered Mur: "Who of erze zun on this planet with authority to parlay?"

Administrator Seir began to respond, but Soldier Gur stepped forward and called out, "I am Soldier erze zun Gur, senior military adviser to the Homeworld Council of Kreet, acting with full authority on behalf of the High Speaker of the Mur Erzen Commonwealth." He walked in his deliberate, limping way toward the Rii Hunters. Half a dozen of his Soldiers fell immediately into a flanking curve behind him.

There was a pause before the Rii replied, "We bring you to Towers to speak with Chief Hunter *Shrii'meep*."

"Very good," said Gur.

Werth followed. "I ought to accompany you, zun Gur," he insisted in a low strum. "The High Speaker may have given you authority here, but any negotiation with the enemy will require someone more knowledgeable when it comes to the specifics of Earth."

"The presence of one Soldier erze zun is sufficient for this meeting, Soldier Werth," Gur said curtly, continuing ahead. "Let's not confuse the situation."

Werth stopped, his exocel thickening around his yellow eyes. "The bodies of my Soldiers and humans-in-erze," he called after Gur, loud enough for the Rii Hunters up in the platform to hear. "I want them returned for proper atomization."

Soldier Gur paused and dipped his fins. "That is a reasonable demand."

After a moment of consideration, the Rii Hunter's voice blared out again from the platform. "Soldiers and Earth creatures able to collect dead."

Cass spoke up as soon as the translation ended. "Zun Werth, I'll go."

Donovan gaped at her, then quickly stepped up beside his erze mate. "I'll go too, zun."

18

As the sun rose, they traveled in three skimmercars behind the scrambling Rii vehicle as it led them back toward the center of the Round. The familiar silhouette of the Towers was marred by the deflated shape of the alien spore vessel clinging like a gooey, sagging bubble to the side of the tallest spire.

"They're designed to conform to whatever surface they land on," Soldier Wylt said, noticing Donovan, Cass, and the third human in the car, Zachariah, staring out the window at the remains of the thing. "Spores spread the invading footprint as wide as possible. Makes it difficult to intercept all the exiting troops. They only have basic navigation and transmission—no engines, no life support—and once they land, they disintegrate. The Hunters inside know they're on a one-way trip."

"Leave the humans alone, Wylt." Soldier Wiest held the skimmercar to a crawl behind the scrambler. "I doubt they want to hear you blather any more than we do, but they can't tell you to break your fins."

"We don't mind," Donovan said. He, Cass, and Zach were sitting on the floor at the back of the skimmercar. There were no seats; unlike SecPac's vehicles, this one wasn't designed for humans. Donovan glanced back out the window. The spore looked as if it had melted further in just a few minutes.

"Hunters taking the Towers." Wiv, the third Soldier in the car, whistled and made a profane fin movement.

The skimmercar stopped. In the light of morning, the scene of carnage in the streets around the Towers was even worse to behold than it had been in the dark. Donovan saw human and zhree bloodstains, chunks of debris, twisted metal remains of skimmercars, and scattered corpses and body parts of both species. The Soldiers and the soldiers-in-erze fell silent in the car. Donovan was struck by the overwhelming desire not to open the door. Cass gripped his hand in mutual support.

Wiest opened the skimmercar and began unrolling wide body bags on the street. "These should fit humans as well."

Still holding Cass's hand, Donovan made himself get out of the car. As the three Soldiers moved off, Donovan glanced toward the Rii scrambler parked by the entrance of the Towers. The Hunters were disembarking, jumping fifteen feet from the carrier platform and landing as if it were nothing. Amid the mottled hulls, Donovan caught a glimpse of several striped ones. The Hunters escorted Soldier Gur and his retinue inside the Towers and they disappeared from view.

What was going to happen in there? What would Soldier Gur and the leader of the Rii Hunters talk about? Donovan turned away; it seemed pointless to speculate. He had always thought of his father as a powerful man who wielded a position of global influence. That seemed almost laughable now; Prime Liaison Angela DeGarmo was nowhere to be seen. The other individuals who had always held highest authority in Donovan's world—Administrator Seir, Soldier Werth, Commander Tate—they were not here either. The fate of the planet was being decided by outside forces far beyond anything he'd ever known.

We've lost Earth.

Oddly, that dark realization made it a little easier to get on with the task of finding and collecting the bodies of dead comrades. At least *they* had died quickly and suddenly, as soldiers who'd lived their lives in erze and given them in battle. They wouldn't be around to see whatever madness came next. It was a tiny comfort to Donovan, but it was something.

When they found Leon, it was less horrific than Donovan had expected. Cass had already closed his eyes, and so long as Donovan kept his gaze fixed firmly on his friend's peaceful face, he could almost handle it. It was only when he had to lift the severed lower half of Leon's body into the black bag that his gorge rose. Donovan knelt by the side of the street and retched into the grass, then wiped his watering eyes.

"Sorry," he said to Cass. When he turned back around, she'd already sealed the body bag up to Leon's chest. She tucked the corner of his protruding coil-bound sketchbook under his uniform jacket and crossed her partner's arms over his chest, placing one of his hands over the square bulge.

Cass pressed her lips to Leon's brow, tears running off her chin onto her erze mate's pale face. "Wherever you've gone, partner, make some glorious art." She closed the bag over his head.

— — —

Donovan was numb by the time they were finished. After Leon, his stomach and his mind seemed to take a trip away from the rest of his body, and he'd been able to gather Tennyson, Lucius, and about ten others in a kind of purposeful haze, executing his task as a respectful duty without thinking about the loss of each person. Zach, who'd been close to Lucius, broke down at one point and had to step away but came back after a short while. Cass had no grief left to give and was the most efficient of them all, arranging the bodies carefully in the open trailer that had been hitched to the skimmercar. Zhree bodies on one side, humans on the other.

At first, the Soldiers and the soldiers-in-erze handled their own, but after a while, the distinction vanished under the unspoken but shared desire to get the job over with. Donovan helped bundle and carry the legs of a dead Soldier while Wylt hefted the torso end.

"We can't even send them off properly," Wylt said sadly. The zhree usually atomized their dead from the sacred sanctuary in the highest part of the Towers.

"Rest well until the coming of the Highest State of Erze," Soldier Wiv murmured, touching each enclosed body that was delivered to the trailer.

They received word from the second skimmercar on the other side of the Round that it too was finally done. The sun had climbed high into a cloudless sky. Whatever medicine Therrid had given Donovan in the hospital had taken away the pain in his swollen shoulder for several hours, but now it returned, repaying him for his overexertion with a vengeance that made him want to whimper. He, Cass, and Zach sat on the ground against the shaded side of the skimmercar, exhausted and sharing a canteen of water. The Soldiers stood together some distance away, conversing in low voices. The Round was eerily quiet.

Finally, Soldier Gur and his Soldiers emerged from the Towers, escorted by six Hunters. The group paused; words were exchanged. Donovan could hear the scratchy translation machine but could not make out anything that was being said. The Hunter addressing Gur was huge, the largest zhree Donovan had ever seen—taller than a man, with eyes the size of tennis balls and strikingly contrasted light and dark mottled patterning on his hull. Soldier Gur looked small next to him. The Hunter spoke in rapid clicks, then dipped his fins to Gur. The Soldier dipped his own fins in reply and brought his armor partway down—a wary but respectful handshake, as far as zhree niceties were concerned. It seemed an agreement of some sort had been reached.

"I don't like the look of this," Soldier Wylt muttered.

— — —

Once they were back at the field camp at SecPac Central Command, Soldier Gur crossed the lawn and was met by Administrator Seir. Donovan jogged after them at a distance, trying to keep them in sight and wanting to listen to whatever Gur was going to say, but he needn't have bothered. The old Soldier declared, "Administrator Seir, gather the rest of the zhree zun at once and prepare a transmission back to Kreet. I have important news to share."

Within minutes, Gur was ringed by all the erze leaders, who'd been summoned from inside the Comm Hub building. Administrator Seir and Soldier Werth seemed to suspect what was coming, but the others—Merchant Hess, Nurse Thet, Builder Dor, and the rest—were shifting their fins and murmuring nervously. Beyond them, Werth's Soldiers and some Nurses pressed in as close as decorum permitted to hear what would be said. Donovan and Cass slipped in behind the tall figure of Commander Tate. Most of the other SecPac officers appeared to have left; Tate, Donovan, and Cass were among the few humans still present.

Soldier Gur raised one limb and tapped it on the ground for attention. "An agreement has been reached with the Rii. There will be no further hostilities over Earth. All Mur colonists will be permitted to leave the planet unharmed, beginning with an immediate withdrawal of Soldiers and followed by an orderly evacuation of all civilian erze and their selected humans, within half an orbital cycle."

"Half a year?" trilled Scientist Laah. "We thought we'd have more—"

"In exchange for peacefully surrendering this star system on an accelerated schedule," Soldier Gur went on, ignoring him, "the Rii of *Chi'tok* have agreed to lift their blockade of light-plus transfer points in the Siryean corridor, as well as recognize Mur sovereignty and uncontested mining rights in the Danushian sector." Soldier Gur's normally stiff fins riffled in satisfaction. "A more than fair trade, considering the commercial and military value of both those concessions."

Gur's announcement was met with initial silence. Builder Dor spoke first. "We won't be reclaiming the Towers, then. The lives of those who died defending them last night were wasted."

"Not true, Builder," Soldier Gur scolded. "Only a narrow frontier mentality would suggest the lost lives did not ultimately benefit the Mur Erzen. The resistance demonstrated the strength of the Commonwealth, even so far from Kreet, and placed us in a far better negotiating position."

Donovan's mind stumbled and stuck on Builder Dor's words. *We won't be reclaiming the Towers.* The Towers were the only place with the medical facilities to treat injured exos, and Soldier Gur had just surrendered them for good.

"Given only six months," Administrator Seir said slowly, "we will have to leave behind many of our planetary assets and take only what is needed. We will also not have time to oversee transition of key responsibilities to Earth's human governments."

"We're nowhere near done collecting and preserving genetic samples of all the native plant and animal species," Scientist Laah exclaimed.

"Nor have we secured off-world warehousing for algae crops that—"

"Naturally, we must make trade-offs." Soldier Gur interrupted Merchant Hess with a sharp fin flick of impatience. "The withdrawal will not be as thorough as we intended, however, with rigorous prioritization, we can accomplish all that is necessary. For example, the total human population taken from Earth will be less than our original plan—closer to fifty or sixty thousand humans instead of the original ninety thousand—but certainly still robust enough for long-term genetic viability."

Cass gave Donovan a pale, wide-eyed look. There was a roaring sound building in Donovan's ears; he found he could barely form words in his own mind. The evacuation plan had been piddling at ninety thousand humans. Fifty thousand was . . . *all that is necessary.*

"I must deliver this news to Kreet immediately," Soldier Gur finished. "There's much to be done to prepare for the busy and disruptive times ahead, but I'm confident your famous frontier work ethic will shine through under any form of pressure. I'll communicate further instructions from the homeworld once I receive them." Gur gazed out stiffly at the ring of colonists as if daring them to make further comments, but none did. "Go in erze."

The zhree dispersed immediately in all directions. Donovan saw a lot of grimly flattened fins, but once a decision was made for the erze, there was no more debate. Soldier Werth strode into the midst of his troops, gathering his subordinates around him. The erze master's limbs rose and gestured and his fins flashed as he conveyed orders—no doubt handling all the practical considerations of large interstellar troop movements called on short notice. Donovan felt left behind already.

Commander Tate was exiting the field. Donovan and Cass hurried to catch up with her. "Commander?" Donovan asked. "What do we do now?"

Tate stopped and glanced at the two young officers with a strangely empty expression. She looked like someone who'd recently spent time sitting in the darkness, reevaluating every moment of her life. "Ma'am?" Donovan realized he was almost begging for Tate to yell orders at him. "What do you want us to do?"

"Go spend time with loved ones." Tate turned and began to walk back toward the Comm Hub building, a tall, proud figure cutting a slow, straight line through the field of armored hulls.

Cass looked bleakly at Donovan. Together, they ran for the garage.

19

Jet looked up blearily from Vic's bedside when Donovan and Cass got back to the hospital and came into the room. The space around Jet's eyes seemed hollowed out. "She's not doing too well," he said hoarsely. "Therrid says the next couple of days are key."

Cass squeezed Jet's shoulder, then sat down on the other side of Vic's bed. "Hey, Vic, you were going to stay on Earth and be my apocalypse buddy. You can't ditch, okay?" Cass enfolded Vic's motionless hand. "I'm not even jealous of your good looks anymore, not with how banged up you are now."

Vic's chest rose and fell in shallow breaths. Her face was as bloodless as chalk. Donovan swallowed thickly. "Has she woken up at all?"

"For a little while, about a couple of hours ago," Jet said. "She was pretty out of it. She told me what happened, though."

Two SecPac stealthcopters had been deployed to attack the Rii spore vessel. Thad and Vic had been in one of them along with two other soldiers-in-erze and the pilot. Like everyone else, they lost the use of their exocels once they began shooting at the emerging Hunters. The Hunters returned fire; one of them leapt clear across a gap of forty feet and boarded the moving aircraft. The pilot, one of the other exos, and the Hunter itself were killed in the subsequent fighting. Vic grabbed the controls and crash-landed the stealthcopter in one of the Round's shipyards, barely missing an apartment building on the way down. They lost another man in the crash.

"Thad's got a punctured lung," Jet said. "He might not make it."

Nurse Therrid came into the room. "You ought to be getting some sleep," he admonished. "Donovan, you only have two prehensile limbs and that one won't heal if you don't rest it." Therrid touched Vic on the forehead and positioned a medical scanning arm over her. The Nurse looked exhausted—his fins sagged and he couldn't keep more than two eyes open at a time. One of his limbs crept up and encircled his bulging egg sac.

"Is there anything else you can do, Nurse Therrid?" Jet pleaded.

"I wish there was, Vercingetorix," the Nurse strummed softly. "Some injuries are too severe for even an eighth-generation exocel to handle. If only I had access to the therapy tanks and the nanosurgical tools in the Towers . . ." He trailed off, then forced his fins more upright. "Tamaravick and Thaddeus are young and strong; we will have to hope for the best."

Cass went down the hall to see Thad. Donovan followed Nurse Therrid out of the room. "Zun Therrid," he said, catching up to the zhree, "Soldier Gur went and negotiated with the leader of the Rii Hunters." Sickly disbelief rose again in Donovan's throat. "He *gave* them Earth. In exchange for some transfer points or mining rights or something. There's not going to be any counterattack. We're not going to get back into the Towers." When Therrid stared steadily at him without responding, Donovan wanted to grab the Nurse and shake him. "All these injured people—you won't be able to save some of them now, will you?"

"I'm still going to do the best I can, Donovan. I've requested that supplies and equipment be brought in from satellite clinics and other Rounds, but I don't know how long that will take. As I said, we will have to hope for the best." Therrid took Donovan by the arm and led him to a bench, easing him down onto it so they were eye to eye. "You need to rest and regain your strength, hatchling. Nurse Thet already informed me of the news and ... I ... " Therrid's fins stuttered. "I've been told to provide an updated account of which Hardened soldiers-in-erze are still fit for evacuation. You're not badly wounded. You'll still be—"

"You think I care about being on Soldier Gur's list anymore?" Donovan yanked his arm out of Therrid's grip. "Leon's *dead*. So's Tennyson, and Lucius, and erze knows how many other people who were on the roster. Cass wasn't included to begin with because her exocel doesn't cover her *arm*. If Vic and Thad pull through, they probably won't be in any sort of shape to be deemed worth saving. Scorch erze orders to hell, I'm *not* evacuating. Not anymore."

"Donovan," Therrid protested in a weakly vibrating voice, "you don't understand. You can't stay here with the Rii in control. They'll ... they'll ... "

"Destroy Earth," Donovan finished for him. "I know. Soldier Werth told me. He showed me what happened to other planets that the Rii conquered. He wanted me to cooperate, to help convince others in the erze to accept evacuation."

"But then you know you can't possibly affect the outcome! All the humans that stay will be lost." Therrid began turning on the spot in agitation. "Please don't be foolish, hatchling. You'll do far more good for your species by listening to your erze master. You and Vercingetorix—you were two of the first humans I ever met. You're the reason I came to care for exos. I've lost so many already . . . You *have* to survive, Donovan. You and the other exos, you're the best of your kind . . ."

"No," Donovan interjected. "Only on a planet where the zhree decide what makes a better human are we more worthy of saving than other people. And soon, when all of you leave and follow Soldier Gur back to your homeworld, that won't be the case anymore."

"Do you think I want to go?" Therrid trilled in an angry outburst. One of his limbs moved protectively to his egg sac. "But we're one remote outpost colony. We can't fight the Rii without military support from Kreet. The decision's been made. There's nothing more we can do."

"There *is*." Donovan glanced down the hall to make sure it was empty but lowered his voice anyway. He really was taking a risk now, but Therrid was the only one who might help him. "So many exos died or were injured yesterday because our exocels stop working if we try to attack zhree. There's a connection in the brain that controls that reflex. When my father was Prime Liaison, he asked a scientist-in-erze named Vincent Ghosh to investigate it. Dr. Ghosh thought that the connection could be cut or jammed. Soldier Werth said it's not possible, but it *is*, isn't it? The fail-safe can be taken out."

All six of Therrid's opaque yellow eyes had gone wide. "No one," he said in a slow, adamant voice, "has ever attempted such a thing."

"But theoretically, it could be done, right?" Donovan pressed. "If I showed you Dr. Ghosh's research, could you—"

"No!" Therrid whistled so that the sound echoed down the hospital corridor. The Nurse stepped closer and brought his voice down to a humming whisper. "You're asking too much now, Donovan. Suggesting I help you deliberately sabotage zhree biotechnology—"

"Zun Therrid." Donovan grasped the sides of the Nurse's hull with pleading urgency. "You've spent your life caring for exos. Saving fifty or sixty thousand is all that Soldier Gur figures he needs to do. There'll be so many of us left on Earth and we *might* have a fighting chance against the Rii if we didn't have this hobble in our brains. If you could help me figure this thing out—"

"Your own erze master refused to entertain the idea. Why do you think that is, Donovan?" Therrid demanded, his voice hitting high notes. Therrid wrapped two sets of pincers around Donovan's forearms. "The inhibition reflex has been a mandatory feature of human exocels for as long as human Hardening has been in place. It was designed by the early colonists a hundred years ago to ensure that humans couldn't use the abilities granted to them to turn against the zhree. *That* is the reason why Kreet tolerates the existence of exos at all. You saw that for yourself last year, when the High Speaker visited. Removing what the homeworld sees as a necessary restraint on human capability could turn Kreet's opinion against exos completely. It would put the entire evacuation plan at risk, for exos of every erze."

"Right. We can't have that." Donovan's voice was flat and cold. He dropped his hands to his sides. "Better to save a small, subservient population of humans than do something that might help all of us."

"Donovan . . ." Nurse Therrid said weakly. "The human exocel is a complicated thing. Even if Dr. Ghosh's research is sound, there's no guarantee that . . ."

"I understand, zun." Donovan stood up, no longer able to bear the pitying yellow eyes. "I should never have asked you to go out of erze like that. I'm sorry." He'd known the Nurse since he was five years old; if there was any zhree he considered a friend, it was Therrid. Soldier Werth's blunt refusal hadn't felt as bad as this. Donovan turned and walked away, leaving Nurse Therrid standing in the middle of the hospital corridor, staring after him.

— — —

He thought he might suffocate or lose his mind if he stayed in the hospital another minute. Donovan walked out to get some air and found the streets unnaturally empty. The Round was in a state of siege. People were barricaded inside their homes, frightened by the sight of the disintegrating spore vessel, the presence of Soldiers in the streets, and the news that numerous cities on Earth were burning. The late afternoon sky seemed gray and hazy; smoke was rising from somewhere in the Ring Belt. Donovan walked for thirty minutes before he found an open sandwich shop, where he ordered the first meal he'd had in over a day and devoured it in seconds. He bought sandwiches for Jet and Cass and began walking back.

With his hunger abated, his steps began to drag with fatigue. His shoulder ached badly and he thought about asking for more painkillers once he got back to the hospital, but he didn't want to talk to Therrid again. Donovan kicked angrily at a loose rock by the side of the road, sending it sailing into some bushes. He punched a fence post with his uninjured arm, leaving gouge marks in the wood. All these months, he'd done *everything* that had been asked of him. He'd acted as an adviser to the zhree zun, he'd supported the failed transition talks, he'd been a good stripe. Commander Tate and Soldier Werth and Therrid were all telling him there was nothing more he could do, that the enormous events happening now were beyond even their control, much less his. So why did he feel like such a *failure*?

Because his father—farsighted, pragmatic, shrewd Prime Liaison Dominick Reyes—*must've* considered the possibility of this disaster unfolding. If he were alive, he would be able to see all the political angles, he would have some idea of what to do. What had he planned to accomplish with Dr. Ghosh's secret research? Donovan rubbed his knuckles against his forehead as if he could wring some elusive insight from his exhausted brain. All his life, he'd felt as if his father expected something *more* from him. *The future depends on people like you.* What his father had always said to him wasn't just the annoying parental rhetoric he'd always assumed it to be. It was the literal truth. Fifty thousand exos were destined to be the only human survivors.

What am I supposed to do about it?

Donovan reached the hospital and once again saw all the SecPac skimmercars parked outside. Doubt and despair swept back in like a cold tide. He was wrong. His father wouldn't have been able to change any of this. He'd been merely one human, foolishly committed to the idea of interspecies partnership. Perhaps Donovan's mother and her Sapience comrades had been right all along: the zhree were and always had been the enemy—Mur or Rii, it didn't matter. The voice of Hannah Maxine Russell started speaking in his mind: *Exos are a terrible thing, Donovan. Designed to serve an alien race, to divide and oppress other humans. They shouldn't exist.*

Donovan's guts clenched like a fist. *That's not true.*

Reluctantly, he went back inside the hospital. There were fewer people in the waiting room now, but an oppressive sense of post-disaster disorder still pervaded the sterile air. He helped a couple of Nurses (here to lend Therrid a few extra sets of pincers, presumably) who were having difficulty figuring out how to use the elevator, and eventually found his way to the room where Cass was sitting and talking with Thad, who was conscious but unable to answer her, on account of being hooked up to a breathing machine and having a tube in his chest. When he saw Donovan, Thad smiled from behind the oxygen mask and wrote on a pad of paper Cass had placed under his right hand: *Glad you're alive.* Seeing Cass dig gratefully into the takeout bag Donovan handed her, he added, *Didn't get anything for me?*

"Hospital mush for you, busted-lungs lieutenant," Cass said, unwrapping her sandwich and waving it in front of Thad's face. "Mmm, meatballs." Thad gave Cass the middle finger and scratched out: *Vic okay?* Donovan exchanged a glance with Cass and said, "We don't know yet. Jet's with her right now." Thad wrote: *Leon?* Donovan hesitated, then shook his head. Cass's momentary sense of cheer vanished. She put her sandwich down, uneaten.

Donovan found Jet asleep, one arm pillowed under his head on Vic's bed, his other hand holding hers, exhaustion having finally gotten the better of him. Donovan placed the remaining sandwich in its bag under his friend's chair and sank into the empty chair on the other side of the bed, too bone weary to take another step. Sleep began sucking him down as well when he heard Vic's voice. "No. Please, no," she whispered urgently. "Not him too."

Donovan opened his eyes. "Vic?" He scooted closer to her. Vic's eyes were glassy and bloodshot but open. She seemed to be staring past Donovan into midair. "They're all dead," Vic wailed. She thrashed her head back and forth on the pillow. "All dead. All my friends are dead. Jet, poor Jet . . ."

"Vic." Donovan gently grabbed her head and held it still. "It's not real." Wounded soldiers sometimes hallucinated the most horrible things. Vic's delirious utterances made Donovan want to cry. Under his fingers, her exocel nodes were feverishly hot, and her armor was patchy across her neck and face, no longer doing even the basic job of protecting her wounds. "You're in a hospital, and you're going to be all right." Donovan did his best to sound reassuring, but his voice shook. "I'm here, and Jet's here. Jet's right here, see?"

Jet stirred, his dark-ringed eyes blinking open in alarm. Sitting up quickly, he leaned over his girlfriend's terrified face, kissing her cheeks and brushing a trembling thumb over her brow. "Vic, I'm right here."

Slowly, Vic's gaze pulled back and found them. Her eyes focused and the skin around them slackened in relief and dawning lucidity.

Jet's face was cracked with worry. "I'll get Nurse Therrid." He started to get up, but Vic clutched his hand and wouldn't relinquish it.

"Don't go. Stay with me, both of you."

"I'll be back in a minute," Jet promised.

"No," Vic whispered. "You're leaving. You're going far away and not coming back."

Jet sat back down and stared straight into Vic's eyes, his mouth a firm anchor trying hard to keep the rest of his face together. "I'm not going anywhere. I was wrong, and I'm sorry we argued. I'm going to stay with you. Just get better, okay? I promise I'll stay."

Tears began leaking out of Vic's eyes. "You have to go. I want you to live. I was never a good reason for you to stay, Jet. I was never the right person for you, I always knew that. I just wanted to keep pretending that I was."

"What are you talking about?" Jet drew back, his voice full of hurt. "Why would you say that?"

Vic closed her eyes for a second, then opened them again. "I have to tell you something," she said quietly. "Just listen and try not to interrupt."

"Maybe you should rest instead," Donovan suggested, increasingly alarmed by the sweaty pallor of Vic's skin. "When you're feeling better . . ."

"You're already interrupting, D," Vic said. "You should hear it too." She drew in a wheezing breath, ignoring both of their expressions of concern. "After we were Hardened, after Skye died, I tried to kill myself. I was only six years old and didn't know what I was doing. All I knew was that if my twin was dead, I ought to be dead too, because we did everything together. I jumped off a balcony. I tried to cut myself with a knife. At first my parents thought I was just testing my armor, like all new exos do. When they realized it wasn't that, we started going to a therapy group."

Vic licked her lips and tried to reach for the glass of water on the side table. Donovan propped her up a little as Jet picked up the glass and helped her to sip from it. "The group was for families who'd lost children," Vic continued. "There was another couple there who'd lost their daughter in Hardening. After a while, the woman stopped showing up, but the man still came every week. Sometimes he talked about his daughter like she was still alive. Most of the time he just seemed sad, but sometimes he was angry. He said his daughter had been murdered by human ignorance and complacency. Those were the words he used. He didn't blame the zhree. He blamed himself, I guess. He was a scientist-in-erze and he blamed people for making the wrong choices."

A slow sinking feeling had begun pulling at Donovan. Jet had gone entirely still. Vic said, "That man ended up going out of erze and leaving the Round. The next I heard of Eugene Nakada was last year, when I learned he was a fugitive affiliated with Sapience. I couldn't believe it. We'd been in that support group together for so long and he was one of the few people who ever really understood how I felt about losing Skye." Vic swallowed with difficulty. "I hadn't been to the group in years, but I still went onto the forum boards once in a while. When I saw Eugene's face on the screen at that mission briefing, I sent him a message. I told him to get out of Denver."

Jet's voice was a whisper of denial. "Vic, you're delirious . . ."

Vic began to sob quietly. "I tipped off the sapes that night, Jet. I caused the mission to fail. I knew Eugene was studying exocels, but I didn't know he was dissecting murder victims. He used to say that if exocels weren't this powerful, mysterious thing, then people wouldn't want them so badly. And I always thought, maybe that would actually be a good thing." She turned pleading eyes to Donovan. "I'm so sorry. You were almost killed by a basement bomb because of me. It's been eating at me every day for months. I didn't mean to betray any of you. I've tried for so long to be in erze, to be a good stripe, a good exo . . . but I've never been okay with what we are."

Vic's lovely features seemed to break in a dozen tiny ways as she gazed into Jet's stunned, disbelieving face. "I love you, but I'm looking forward to finally catching up with Skye." She closed her eyes. "Don't miss me too much; I don't deserve it."

Vic's heart stopped sometime after midnight. Donovan left Jet alone with her in the end. Just before he slipped out of the room, Donovan heard his partner whispering, "Vic, if you're trying to make me angry with you so I'll let you go, it's not working. It's not working at all."

Donovan went around a bend in the hall and curled up on a hard bench, his heart aching and his vision blurred. Therrid woke him with a touch on the arm some hours later, and Donovan, in that moment of sunken grief, couldn't remember to still be angry with the Nurse. Therrid's many eyes were dull and his limp fins trembled with sorrow. "I couldn't do anything more for her, besides take away the pain at the end," the zhree said. "She was just a hatchling. She should've lived for another hundred and fifty years."

Jet was gone. Donovan searched the corridors. He hailed his erze mate on the comm. Nothing. Donovan took the first free electricycle he could find and went back to their house.

"Jet?" He walked up the stairs and pushed opened the door to his partner's room. Jet was sitting on the floor in the corner, his shoulders hunched, his eyes red. He didn't look up at Donovan's entry.

Slowly, as if approaching a wounded animal, Donovan stepped into the room and sat down silently on the floor opposite him. After several minutes, Jet said, "When Vic let Nakada off the hook that night, it tipped off Warde as well. She put the whole mission team at risk." Jet's voice was as flat as if he were reading from a script in his head. "She was a traitor."

Donovan said nothing. He recognized what Jet was doing—he'd done it to himself after his mother had been executed. *She was a terrorist. She hated exos. She wanted to be a martyr.* And he'd done it when he missed Anya: *She's a sape. A squishy who prefers sadists.* Donovan was intimately familiar with the mental gymnastics of trying to convince himself that he shouldn't be as crushed as he was. He also knew it didn't actually work.

"I *knew* Nakada had a personal connection in the Round," Jet went on. "I even knew from interviewing his ex-wife that he'd been in a support group. I'd started digging into it, before the world went to hell. But I never connected the dots to Vic. I had no reason to. She was in erze. She was one of us." Jet's voice broke on the last words.

Donovan squeezed his eyes shut for a second. "Don't remember her unkindly, Jet. Trust me, it won't help."

After several long minutes, Jet said, "It doesn't matter anymore. Nakada, Sapience, SecPac—none of it matters now." He looked down at his striped hands and clenched them. "We're all scorched anyway. Nothing to do but wait for this sick joke to end."

Donovan found it hard to speak for a moment. He had never heard Jet talk like this. "Maybe it doesn't have to be like that," he said hesitantly. "There *has* to be a way we can fight the Hunters. If the zhree are determined to give up on Earth, then it's going to be up to humans—exos *and* squishies—to defend it once they're gone."

Jet raised sunken eyes. "Don't be ridiculous. A planet full of squishies won't stand a chance against an invading army of those monsters. And we're only different from squishies because of *this*."

Jet raised his hands, armoring fully in a burst of frustration. "And this is useless against the Rii. All it's good for now is a ticket off the planet." Jet thudded his head back against the wall. His armor receded and his voice fell. "If we stay, our fellow humans will get us before the Hunters do. That's what we'll get for putting our lives on the line every day, for keeping the peace, for fighting Sapience all these years. The rest of humankind doesn't give a damn about us."

Donovan stared at the carpet, jaw clenched. "It doesn't matter if they give a damn or not. If they hate us or not. We swore oaths to protect people."

"We can't even protect ourselves," Jet whispered. "Or those we love."

"There's a way to take out the trip wire that causes our exocels to fail. That's what was in those memory discs. My dad was the world's number one cooperationist but he hedged his bets. He went behind the zhree zun and asked Dr. Ghosh to research exocels. He must've known that someday we'd have to fight the Rii on our own."

Jet didn't open his eyes. "Did you tell this to Soldier Werth?"

Donovan exhaled in frustration. "He won't consider removing the fail-safe. It'd be going against Kreet."

"I guess you're just going to have to learn brain surgery on your own, then." Jet put his head between his hands, a gesture at once both achingly vulnerable and entirely exasperated. "Oath and erze, what do you expect me to say? Maybe you're right. Maybe your dad had some brilliant plan. But you're not your dad, Lesser D. And I can't help anyone."

A pressure was building in Donovan's chest. "You're saying we should give up. Follow Soldier Gur's orders and leave everyone else behind to die. After seeing the Hunters and what they can do . . ."

Donovan's fingers curled in the carpet. *I need you with me on this, Jet. I know you're hurting, but I need you to be my partner right now.* "We shouldn't have accepted the evacuation spots. You said so yourself that we were wrong; you promised Vic we'd stay."

Jet's eyes snapped open, blazing. "I said that before I knew what she'd done. We were nearly blown up in Denver. Warde escaped and publicly murdered a SecPac agent, rallying True Sapience and sinking the transition talks. All because Vic didn't follow orders. She went out of erze for someone who didn't deserve it, and she didn't think about the consequences. You want to be worse than her?"

The words tumbled from Donovan's mouth before he knew why he was letting them. "I already *am* worse, Jet." Vic had been his friend, and the way Jet was trying to paint over who she was with stubborn, grief-stricken scorn—it was as if a hand had reached inside Donovan and yanked the top off a kettle, and suddenly he couldn't stop the guilt he'd carried for months from boiling over. "I'm more of a traitor than Vic was. Last year, when my mom was going to be executed, I tried to stop it, I tried to get Sapience to rescue her. I gave information to—"

"Stop," Jet said, staggering to his feet. "I don't want to hear this."

"—to the Guerras." Donovan got to his feet as well, words still spilling from him in an agonizing burst of shame and relief. "That day I convinced you to take off early from shift, I tried to send word to Saul Strong Winter."

"Stop it!" Jet howled at him, his armor visibly rippling over his knuckles.

"The Guerras killed my dad. They used the information I gave them to do it. I'm the reason my dad's dead, Jet, and I hate myself for it, but I couldn't tell you. I couldn't stand the idea of you thinking of me the way you're thinking of Vic now, trying to convince yourself that you shouldn't have ever loved her." Donovan was breathing hard. "We made mistakes, but who's to say we haven't made mistakes in other ways—arrested the wrong people, kicked in the wrong doors, hurt someone who went on to hate us and become a sape?"

Jet's battle armor was raised. His face was twisted with hurt and disbelief and a mess of painful, indecipherable emotion. "*Get out*," he whispered.

"Maybe I *am* a traitor, but being in erze isn't what makes someone a good person, Jet." Part of him wanted to die with shame, but he refused to look away from his partner's bloodshot eyes. "Trying to do the right thing is what keeps us in erze, whether that means following orders or not."

"I said *get out*." Jet's hoarse voice trembled. "You squishy-brained head case, I don't even know who you are anymore, and I don't care. Just get out and *leave me alone!*"

Donovan opened his mouth again, but Jet took a single, menacing step forward and whatever else Donovan had hoped to say dissolved in his mouth. Wordlessly, he backed out into the hall. Jet stalked after him, put a hand on the door, and shut it firmly in Donovan's face.

Donovan stood for a long minute, staring at the closed door, even more forbidding to him now than the one he'd faced when hoping to find Anya in the TransHabs.

Remorse washed in. Donovan let out a shuddering breath and dropped his forehead against the wood. Jet hadn't needed that, not now—to be burdened with further evidence that everything and everyone he'd trusted was unreliable. Donovan put a hand on the doorknob. He would beg for his erze mate's forgiveness and understanding, the way Jonathan had once pleaded before him. He would implore Jet for his help no matter what contempt his partner held him in. Because now, standing alone in the hall, Donovan had an idea, one that Jet himself had given him—a horribly insane, out-of-erze idea.

Donovan hesitated, then took his hand off the doorknob. He remembered all the times he'd been too sunken into darkness and grief and self-pity to be of much use, and Jet had gone on alone and done his job and held up Donovan's end for him wherever he could. Because that was what the erze was about in the end, wasn't it? Putting others ahead of yourself. Soldier Werth scrutinized eleven-year-old boys and girls around the world and chose the ones who understood that. Because armor didn't protect anyone from suffering. People had to do that for each other.

He went into his own room and changed out of his torn and bloodstained shirt and jeans, rummaging in his laundry basket for his least offensively stale set of civilian clothes: rumpled pants, a shirt, a light hooded jacket that concealed the nodes on his arms and neck. From his desk drawer, he removed the envelope with Ghosh's research and tucked it into his jacket pocket.

Jet was right. Donovan wasn't his father. He had to stop guessing at what Prime Liaison Dominick Reyes would have done, and do only what he could do. And he could do something.

He grabbed an apple and a cereal bar from the kitchen. In the bathroom, he dug around in the medicine cabinet and swallowed the maximum daily recommended dose of over-the-counter painkillers. With a final glance back at Jet's closed door, Donovan left the house.

21

It was not easy to leave the Round now. It would be even harder, he knew, to get back in. Every one of the six gates was guarded by Soldiers, many of them bearing Gur's stripes. Fortunately, there were two unofficial passages, intended for emergencies but more commonly used by SecPac to discreetly transport important individuals or high-value prisoners in and out of the Round without garnering any public attention. One of them ran underground directly to SecPac Central Command, emerging from underneath the squat administrative building adjoining the Pen, the campus's on-site detention facility. The problem was that the SecPac campus had been commandeered as a zhree military camp and Donovan had no idea if he could still move around freely and access the tunnel without being questioned.

He decided he had to chance it. Sending up a mental apology to his friend, he took Leon's electricycle from the garage and drove it back to Central Command, this time avoiding the main approach and circling around to one of the side entrances. The first building on his left was the officers' common hall. Donovan parked and went in the back door.

It was like walking into a wake. The common hall was one of the few places on campus that hadn't been appropriated for zhree use, and it appeared as if a large percentage of last night's surviving soldiers-in-erze had congregated in the corridors, some standing

223

and talking in subdued voices, others sitting on the floor, staring into space or staring desperately at their comm unit displays for news about distant friends and loved ones. The large bulletin board that normally held notices and announcements was completely covered over with photographs and written tributes to slain erze mates. A screen was being updated every few minutes with SecPac's confirmed casualties. Donovan slowed, his eyes drawn to searching for familiar faces and names, but he pulled his gaze away and didn't let himself stop—there wasn't time for that now.

When he was alone in the locker room, he allowed himself to check the latest messages from his cadre mates. Soldier Gur's negotiated agreement with the Rii had become erze-wide news.

Maddison/R1: *Is this for real?!! We're being told to stand down and prepare to evacuate.*

Fernando/R12: *Same here. 242 stripes dead and they want us to open the gates and let in the monsters that killed them.*

Jong-Kyu/R11: *We had a force mustered to take back Ten but new orders are not to interfere. Commander Li is bursting his nodes furious.*

Antonio/R5: *Speaking of Ten, still no one's heard from Amrita?!*

Sariyah/R15: *Managed to pull her last recorded comm audio from the global network. All I could find.*

Donovan listened to the transmission clip. Amrita's voice, louder and more urgent that he'd ever heard it, but still oddly, eminently sensible: *"Command, we're outnumbered. Our exocels are failing. We're dying here. Send reinforcements, please."* In the background, there was a great deal of noise—gunfire, shouting, and some garbled reply from Round Ten's SecPac dispatch, and then Amrita's voice again. *"Yes, sir. Please hurry. Thank you."* That was all there was. Polite to the end.

Donovan stowed his comm unit and closed his eyes for a long moment. There was nothing he could do for Amrita, or for Vic, or Leon, or the others whose names were scrolling on the screen in the hallway. But maybe, just *maybe*, there was still something he could do for those who remained. Palming open his locker door, Donovan grabbed a spare compact electripulse from the shelf, which he tucked into a concealed waistband holster. Then he rummaged around inside the plastic box where he threw random items—pens, empty ammunition clips, sunglasses, spare comm unit earbuds. He fished out a data storage stick and pocketed it.

In the common office area, he chose the workstation that was the farthest away from anyone else and pulled out the envelope with Dr. Ghosh's research. It took several minutes to copy over everything on the memory discs one by one, compact the files, and send them electronically to the Prime Liaison's Office. Not to the public mailbox, where he knew it might sit for weeks before being looked at, but to the Prime Liaison's personal account, which he could only hope and assume had been retained and transferred from Dominick Reyes to Angela DeGarmo. Just to be on the safe side, he sent them to himself and to Jet as well. He returned all of Ghosh's discs to the envelope and tucked them back into his jacket pocket.

Donovan glanced around the office area. He was alone, but if anyone came over and asked Donovan what he was doing, he was going to have a hard time explaining. He tilted the workstation screen away from any inadvertently prying eyes and called up SecPac's video security feeds. SecPac had numerous cameras situated throughout the Round—the fences around the Pen, the checkpoints at Gates 1 through 6, the airport, the interplanetary shipyards and landing fields of the Towers. At the system's prompting, Donovan provided his security clearance information, then searched specifically for footage taken as close as possible to the Towers on the night of the Rii attack.

What he found wasn't perfect—much of it was dark, confusing, grainy—but there was enough. A few seconds here and there that captured clear images of Rii Hunters as they swarmed the Towers. Donovan snipped clips of video and transferred them to the data storage stick. If he had an uninterrupted day or two to work on this, he was sure he could piece together much better footage, but he didn't have that kind of time. As it was, he'd probably spent a couple of hours here already. Too long. He needed to get going. He copied one final snippet of video that made him wince—a Rii Hunter appearing in the corner of the screen, firing into a line of SecPac officers, killing three or four of them before being attacked in turn by two Soldiers. Donovan pulled out the data stick, closed everything he'd been working on, and shut down the workstation.

Running back out to the electricycle, he felt laden down with the weight of all the confidential information he was carrying in his pockets. Stealing SecPac data and taking it into the Ring Belt without authorization was egregiously out of erze—and to think, it was probably the least out-of-erze part of his whole scheme. He hissed out a breath from between clenched teeth. What did it matter anymore? The erze he'd sworn to serve and obey was falling apart before his eyes.

Feeling vaguely sick, Donovan drove past the stone sculpture of the Scroll and slowed for a squad of armed Soldiers crossing the road; they glanced over but otherwise ignored him. Taking a sharp right turn after the security gate to the Pen led Donovan to an administrative building attached to what looked like a garage with a thick steel door. To his immense relief, he saw that the guard box next to it was occupied by a single human—an older, non-Hardened reservist.

Donovan placed his hand under the reader; it verified his markings and exocellular body signature, and flashed a picture of his face and his SecPac identification onto the screen in the guard box. The guard looked between it and Donovan, in his civilian clothes on an unmarked electricycle, and frowned. "The tunnel is only supposed to be used for emergencies and priority missions, Officer."

"Yes, ma'am," said Donovan, "but Gate 5 has been shut down for at least an hour due to civilian unrest and I need to speak personally with Officer Sebastian Thurber as soon as possible—he's dealing with the riots in the TransHabs right now." As far as he knew, there were still SecPac teams in the Ring Belt, guarding government buildings and erze-marked neighborhoods and dealing with the worst of the turmoil. He didn't know if Sebastian was among them, but he was betting this guard didn't either. When she still hesitated, Donovan shaped his expression into one of concern and urgency. "It's about his wife, ma'am."

Sebastian is married, isn't he? Donovan asked himself. Yes, he was sure of it. Donovan crossed his fingers that the guard didn't know the Thurbers personally and wouldn't start any alarming rumors. "Oh dear." She looked worried now. "Well, under the circumstances . . ." The guard touched the controls to open the door. It slid open to reveal a descending concrete ramp.

Donovan nodded his thanks, then gunned the e-cycle and shot down into the tunnel underneath the Round.

———

A mile and half later, the tunnel emerged on the other side of the wall, onto SecPac property consisting of warehouse space, concrete yards, and garages behind a high barbed wire fence with severe red signs warning against trespassing. Donovan had been here once or twice before. This overflow space was used for staging missions and raids, conducting training simulations, and temporarily holding larger groups of detainees. It was quiet right now, but the guards on duty were skittish. Donovan raised a striped hand and one of them said, "Be careful out there, Officer. It's a scorching mess, like something out of the first days of the War Era, I imagine. No one knows what's happening. Panicked people are ransacking and shooting."

Donovan turned on the e-cycle's navigation and drove through the Ring Belt. It felt strange to be doing so by himself, out of uniform, especially since every few minutes he noticed something that would warrant a stop if he and Jet were out on regular patrol: broken windows on houses, popping noises that might be firecrackers or gunfire, an overturned car, the smell of smoke coming from not too far away. He gritted his teeth and told himself to focus. He would only be wasting time if he tried to investigate all the incidents of chaos he came across—like trying to plug tiny holes in a sieve one by one while a geyser of water shot through.

The address he was looking for was located in a dense commercial district full of sand-colored brick buildings dating back to the first post–War Era boom, when humans from around the country had migrated here by the hundreds of thousands in search of zhree-sponsored work and housing. Driving slowly now, Donovan could make out a familiar but eroded blocky patterning carved over the entrances of many buildings: Builder Dor's markings. Though of course it had not been Builder Dor but one of his predecessors who'd been erze zun way back then. The Builder erze had been one of the first to employ humans in large numbers. These old structures had once formed the center of a burgeoning town of postwar workers who'd helped the colonists to construct everything from the refugee TransHabs to new freeways and vast algae farms.

Today's builders-in-erze lived in better neighborhoods in the Round, or in the newer parts of the Ring Belt. Now, even on the best of days, the Buildertown district had a slightly run-down and neglected quality to it. It wasn't anywhere near as bad as the TransHabs, but the walls and sidewalks displayed a perpetually dirty and stained appearance. The cars gave off the smell of burning petroleum, and it seemed as if 90 percent of the people on the streets were unmarked squishies. Donovan's long sleeves and fingerless leather gloves hid his nodes and stripes, but given that he was riding Leon's gleaming electricycle, that only made it even more glaringly obvious to people here that he was marked. Even though they couldn't immediately tell that he was an exo and a SecPac officer, they eyed him with naked suspicion nevertheless.

Donovan pulled up across the street from his destination and parked the e-cycle. He removed the slightly bent business card from his back pocket and held it up, double-checking the address. *Is two months too long to call a girl back?* he asked himself wryly. Then he took a deep breath and crossed the street to the office building of the Human Action Party.

The front door was locked. Donovan rapped on it. When there was no answer, he knocked again, louder, and tried to peer into the nearest window, which had thick metal bars in front of it. There was an intercom panel on the wall next to the door. He pressed the button and waited. No answer. He tried again and, frustrated, banged loudly on the door at the same time. At last a voice came through the small speaker in the intercom panel. "We're closed," it snapped.

"It's the middle of the afternoon," Donovan exclaimed.

"We're closed to *you*," the woman on the other end clarified. "Leave before we call the police. Or friends of ours who aren't as nice as the police."

"Wait," Donovan blurted at the speaker. "I need to talk to Anya."

There was a moment's hesitation from the other end. "There's no one here by that name. And we don't collect or give out any member contact information."

"Yeah, she told me that," Donovan said quickly, "but she also said that unofficially, you'll pass on messages. I need to pass a message to Anne Leah Dodson, but she goes by Anya. It's important." He was afraid the person on the other end had hung up on him. He pressed the intercom button again. "Hello?"

"Who are you?" The words were slow with suspicion now.

"I'm . . ." He had to risk it. "Donovan Reyes. I'm a friend. She might not believe it, but I still am. And I need her help. I have something important, something that could make a big difference in the war that's coming. I need to show her—"

The person on the other end hung up on him.

Donovan swore and kicked the brick wall. He jabbed the intercom button again and held it down. "If you can still hear me, tell Anya that even if she hates me, what I have to say is really important." He paused, tempted to tear the black panel from the wall and try to force his way into the building. "Look, I'm not your enemy. Just let me in these doors and hear me out." He rattled the locked doors once more, then backed up on the sidewalk until he could shout up at the second-story windows. "I'm going to stand out here until someone answers me!"

"I wouldn't do that if I were you."

Donovan turned to see three men spacing apart defensively as they approached him. All three were armed. The one in the center who had spoken held a compact semiautomatic rifle at low ready. Another carried a pump-action shotgun and the third had his hand resting on the grip of a holstered pistol. They eyed him the way hunters eye a moose.

"We don't like disturbances," said the one with the rifle.

"I'm not here to cause trouble." Donovan faced them, arms slightly spread in a nonthreatening posture. *Stay down*, he ordered his own exocel. *Stay the hell down.* His nodes prickled from the effort of restraint. Were these guys from Sapience? True Sapience? Neighborhood militia? The distinctions were blurry and overlapping these days. Donovan supposed it didn't really matter, since any one of those groups would likely not hesitate to inflict serious bodily harm upon him.

"Not here to cause trouble?" The rifle holder was lanky, with a stubbled face and a black beanie on his pill-shaped head. "You *are* trouble. Take off your gloves, boy. No sudden moves or they'll be your last ones."

Slowly, Donovan reached his open left hand over to his right and peeled off his gloves, dropping them to the ground. He turned his hands so the backs were visible. "Yeah, I'm a stripe. It's not a good idea to shoot stripes. It puts you on lists that you don't want to be on."

"That used to be true," said the barrel-chested man on the right, the one with the shotgun. "The rules are changing now and the way we see it, your sort isn't faring so well. Where're your pals? Stripes don't travel alone."

"They're around," Donovan said with feigned unconcern. He jerked his head back toward the locked building behind him. "Are you friends with the people in there? You look like you keep a close eye on the neighborhood."

"I'm going to be a lot more generous than I need to be and give you ten seconds to get back on your fancy bike and clear out," said the gangly leader.

"And that's only because we'd rather save our ammo for the shrooms," added the one with the pistol, an acne-pocked teenager younger than Donovan.

Donovan looked among the three men. "I came to talk to the people inside that office, and I'm not leaving until I get that chance. I'm not going to fight you, but I'm not leaving either. So take me to someone who'll listen."

It was not the response the trio wanted to hear. Donovan stood his ground, barely breathing as the man in the center walked forward, his squinty eyes narrowed to slits below the rim of his beanie.

"Get on your knees," he ordered. "Keep your hands up."

Slowly, Donovan knelt. He was suddenly aware of all the people watching. There were perhaps a dozen bystanders with their eyes on the scene, some wisely placing themselves behind cars or corners in case gunfire broke out, others pulling away children or peering from behind windows.

The men came closer, so close that Donovan wondered if he was cooperating with his own public execution. His exocel wasn't going to endure triple bursts of gunfire at near point-blank range. Still, he kept it lowered, though his back trembled from the strain of doing so. There was a chance these men were affiliated with the Human Action Party, and that after roughing him up somewhat, they would drag him in front of Saul or one of their other superiors.

Donovan kept his eyes on the man in front of him. "Before you decide whether to kill me," he said in as even a voice as he could manage, "there's a data storage stick in my right-hand jacket pocket. If you let me take it out and—"

The teenager drew a knife and slashed it across Donovan's cheek.

Donovan jerked in reflex, his exocel breaking free of his control; the blade scraped harmlessly across panotin. "Like I thought—an exo," spat the leader. He slammed the butt of his rifle into Donovan's face.

A white explosion of pain erupted in Donovan's head. He clutched his face, momentarily blinded, and felt blood running from his nose into his mouth and down his chin. Bleeding was such an infrequent experience for exos that it triggered gut panic— his armor rose instantaneously and the sight of it encasing every inch of his exposed skin sent the three men into a fury.

"Stop that *right now* or you're dead!" bellowed the man with the shotgun. All three weapons were inches from Donovan's head. "I can't," he tried to say. The center man hit him with the rifle again, planted a boot in his chest, and kicked him backward. Donovan landed hard and found himself blinking upward dizzily, the barrel of the rifle pointed down into his face.

"Why did you come here?" snarled the gangly leader. "Your kind are in league with the shrooms. Why are there new ones arriving? Before I kill you, I want you to tell me *why*. Why now? Why the bombings? They've finally Hardened enough people that they can do away with the rest of us, is that it?"

Donovan could feel the hard shape of his electripulse pistol sandwiched between the pavement and the small of his back; all this time, he hadn't made a single move for it and now it was pinned underneath him. He could try to roll to his feet and grab for it, but he would get shot. He supposed there was a chance he could kill all three men before his armor was fatally overwhelmed, but nothing would be solved by it. He'd end up dying from his injuries, though most likely not before other sapes arrived and lynched him.

With every shred of willpower he possessed, Donovan lay still and tried to breathe, to pull his armor back down, to speak calmly around his profusely bleeding nose. "I came here to explain," he managed to gurgle. "The new shrooms who've arrived, the ones who bombed the cities—they're enemies of the colonists. If they take over, they'll kill us all—exos included. We're *not* working with them, but maybe we can fight them."

The man's trigger finger flexed. "I don't believe you."

"I do." The voice made Donovan unwisely jerk his head up. Anya stood framed in the flung-open doorway of the previously locked building behind them. In her haste, she balanced on the balls of her feet, one hand clutching the doorframe, a scowling older woman poised just behind her shoulder.

"Let him up, Carter," Anya said. "And bring him inside."

"You *stupid* stripe." Anya gave him a handful of ice cubes wrapped in a thin towel. "I'm starting to think you really do have a death wish."

"I can see why." Donovan pressed the cold cloth to his face. The bleeding had stopped, and after a good yank, his nose was mostly straight again. His exocel had thickened up around his nose and eyes, so he appeared to be wearing a faint raccoon's mask. He looked up from the metal folding chair he was sitting in and, despite everything, couldn't help grinning at Anya. She was wearing cutoff shorts and a frayed yellow T-shirt, and she'd changed her hair color yet again—it was sandy blond now, roughly cropped past her chin. He was surprised and grateful to find that he was glad to see her again after all. The insanity of the past two months had dulled the memory of their awkward parting in the Round, and being in a Sapience hideout with his face bleeding seemed to put them back on more familiar ground.

"I'm serious," Anya hissed, not smiling back. "A few nights ago, there were two bodies found in the park three blocks from here. A Hardened couple drowned in the pond and no one came forward to say they saw anything. It's open season on your kind."

"Well," Donovan said, sobering at the thought, "you could've just let me in the door to begin with." He looked over at Minh, the owner of the voice he'd heard through the intercom, a leathery-faced woman standing a short distance away with her arms crossed.

Minh glared at him. "These days you keep the doors locked and you don't open them for anyone you don't know. Survival 101. We look out for ourselves first. Marked people have been coming here, pounding on the door and asking for help, hoping we've got food and supplies and will keep them safe from True Sapience." Minh snorted. "That's what I call ironic."

Ironic? Donovan thought it was horrifying. People with erze markings should always be able to depend on their erze. But the zhree were busy planning their hasty evacuation. Did they even know how many of their humans-in-erze had been locked out of the Round after the Rii attack?

Donovan looked around the large basement-level room. It was, indeed, filled with boxes of emergency supplies—dried and canned food, water, first aid gear, blankets, ammunition, canisters of propane. The Human Action Party's roots in Sapience were never more abundantly clear. These headquarters weren't so much a political office as a survivalist depot.

Donovan returned his attention to Anya. "So, what are you all doing in here?"

She glanced at the others in the room: a half dozen curious and wary faces including an elderly man, a little girl, and a grimy couple who looked as if they'd just arrived from spending a month in the wilderness, in addition to the three men—Carter, Myles, and Harrison—who'd given Donovan the welcome reception outside. "We're waiting for word from Saul. When the bombings started, we went to our nearest SRPs. Secure Refuge Points," she explained.

"Here we've got supplies and secure communication with Sapience cells, and can send news out to the rest of the HAP membership."

Carter was still staring at Donovan as if he might take him back outside and shoot him. "Word is that Saul's been asked to meet privately with the Prime Liaison in a secret bunker somewhere. If he makes it back, he'll tell us what's what."

"*When* he makes it back," Anya insisted.

"What if they Harden him and control his brain?" asked the little girl, who was perhaps eight years old. "Then he'll turn into one of the bad people and bomb us."

Donovan couldn't help staring askance at the little girl, who grabbed the elderly man's hand and hid behind him, peering at Donovan with wide, fearful eyes. Anya said, "Who told you that nonsense, Chloe?"

The elderly man raised a bony finger indignantly. "Now, you don't know what is and isn't true. A lot of people are saying that—"

"A lot of people believe whatever crazy thing they hear first, Julian." Anya pointed at Donovan. "Look, he's an exo. Let's ask him. Can you transform into a shroom?"

"No," Donovan said.

"Did the shrooms activate a computer chip in people's brains that made sleeper agents in the government set off bombs against the cities?"

Donovan shook his head. "That doesn't even make sense . . ."

"Have the shrooms been waiting for a hundred years to harvest our bodies for food?"

"The zhree don't even eat meat." Donovan could no longer keep the contemptuous incredulity out of his voice. He knew that

Sapience spread wild disinformation about the enemy, but it was still astounding to meet people who believed such things and were using it to interpret the current chaos. What sort of wild conspiracy theories and rumors had taken root since the Rii attack?

Donovan stood up and walked slowly toward the little girl, stopping and crouching down before he got too close, so as not to frighten her. Carter and his friends put their hands on their weapons in warning, but Donovan ignored them. "Chloe," he said gently, "I've been Hardened, and I promise I'm telling you the truth: You can't Harden a grown-up. You can't even Harden a big kid, like you. Your friend Saul is safe, and so are you. And even Hardened people don't turn into bad guys. No one controls our brains." *Well, not in the way you're thinking, at least.*

The girl stared at Donovan, mouth slightly agape in a nervous but tentatively relieved expression. She clung tighter to the gnarled hand in her grip and looked up at the old man, hoping for his confirmation.

"As if *he* would tell us the truth," sniffed Julian.

Donovan raised his eyes and stood up. "I risked my life to come here and tell you the truth. We're all hiding in a basement together right now. I've no reason to lie to you."

Julian's flabby lips came together tightly around his teeth as he averted his eyes, pulling Chloe closer to him. Donovan turned around to face the rest of the people in the room. He removed the data storage stick from his pocket and handed it to Carter, who accepted it cautiously, as if it might be a live grenade. "That's raw SecPac security camera footage from inside the Round," Donovan said. "That's what we're up against."

Minh found a screen to play the files. The sapes gathered

around to watch. The concentrated silence that followed was broken only by the occasional gasp or murmur.

"Those shrooms," Myles muttered, "they're killing *each other*."

"Those huge ones are Rii Hunters," said Donovan.

"The Rii are real?" muttered Harrison. "They're not a myth?"

"All the crazy things you sapes believe in, and you think the Rii are a myth." Donovan would've laughed out loud if the images on the screen were any less terrible a reminder of what he and his erze mates had been through. "I've seen Hunters up close—closer than I'm standing to you right now. I've seen them kill my friends. At the same time as they bombed the cities, they attacked five of the Rounds on Earth. They're occupying the Towers of Round Three now. The zhree *you* know, the Mur colonists—they tried to fight at first, but they've been ordered by their homeworld to retreat from Earth and hand the planet over to the Rii."

Anya looked up from the screen and met his gaze. Wariness stretched between them, held rigid in the presence of all these other people, but in her straight expression he saw that she believed him. That was all he could ask for right now. Anya had been to the Towers, had learned that not all zhree were the same, and aliens that, to her, looked nearly identical might have differing motives. Donovan pointed to the Hunter on the screen. "Soon Earth will belong to these monsters. And if you have no lost love for the shrooms you're already familiar with, just know that these new ones don't Harden people and they don't colonize planets. They destroy them."

There was a collective silence. Feet shifted as uncertain glances were exchanged. "How can we be sure this is real? That you're telling the truth?" Carter still sounded suspicious and accusing, but he replayed the clips again, his eyes fixed on the screen.

"We can't be sure," argued Julian.

"No, you can't," Donovan said. "You're inclined to distrust me and anyone with armor and markings. But my mom was a sape. She gave her life for the cause. I never lied to her, and I never lied to Saul. We're at the start of a new War Era, so you could make the argument that everyone left on Earth is part of the cause now." He pulled the data stick from the screen and held it back up to Carter. "Show this to Saul and tell him it's from me. Let him decide whether to believe it or not."

Carter eyed Donovan for a long moment. Then he took the device, firmly this time, and closed his hand around it in a fist. "God help us all if you're right," he said grudgingly. "Welcome to the cause, zebrahands."

— — —

Minh and the grungy-looking couple, Sam and Tara, made a large pot of bean soup and corn bread that served as dinner for everyone who wished to stay. After quietly eating their meals, Carter, Myles, and Harrison left. Anya explained that they were one of a few Sapience-trained militia teams that patrolled the Buildertown district, distributing emergency supplies, discouraging looting and violence, and maintaining some semblance of order.

Donovan mulled this over as he helped clear away disposable bowls and spoons from the main floor conference room table that now doubled as a cook station and dinner line. The idea of openly armed gangs of Sapience members walking around the neighborhoods of the Ring Belt made him deeply uncomfortable. It was SecPac's role (and to a lesser extent that of the civilian police) to maintain order and security. Things were truly out of hand if people were relying on terrorists to keep the peace in the streets. But SecPac was overwhelmed. It couldn't be everywhere at once, not with so many exos dead, injured, or confined to the Round, and those in the Ring Belt dealing with major crises and prioritizing protection of the government and the erze-marked.

Tonight, however, the three men would be doing something other than patrolling. Anya had copied the video files for safekeeping, and Carter had taken the data stick with him. "We'll take this where it needs to go," he said. Donovan suspected that by the end of the night, Sapience cells across the country would be able to access and view the footage, in the same way they had once been able to read Max Russell's latest propaganda or watch Kevin Warde torture exos to death on camera.

All the furniture upstairs was cleared to the sides of the room so everyone had a place to sleep. Donovan's instinct was to join in and help with the unrolling of mats and the distribution of blankets, but he was well aware that everyone except Anya was visibly uncomfortable around him. No one spoke to him or met his eyes, except for the girl, Chloe, who, like most kids, was curious about armor and could be drawn into watching Donovan show off rock-paper-scissors with his exocel. Julian took the girl by the arm and pulled her away, squinting at Donovan with hostility.

Two more people showed up later in the evening, a pair of travel-worn women who apparently knew whatever Sapience password or signs were required to gain entry because they were admitted by Minh without trouble. They were initially horrified by Donovan's presence, but Anya calmed them down, gave them some leftover soup and bread, and showed them to two mats on the floor where they would sleep. After that, Donovan sat off to the side, observing the goings-on quietly and staying out of the way. As his eyes followed Anya around the room, he felt a growing sense of melancholy—a sort of odd pride mingled with sadness.

"You can stay as long as you need, but no longer than you need," Anya said to the two women. "If you're heading west to join one of the armies, I can give you a list of the other SRPs along the way." She bit her bottom lip, considering what else she might have neglected to mention. "I think that's it. We've got network access and hot water, but keep your use of either of them down to ten minutes." The two women thanked her and dropped their bags before stumbling off to wash up and collapse on their mats.

Donovan realized he was finally seeing Anya clearly for what she had become: a young lieutenant of the cause. Their one evening together in the Round had been spent on his turf and his terms, not hers, and he'd been so stunned and excited to reunite with her that he hadn't really noticed that she'd changed in more ways than the color of her hair. Now he saw that she spoke and held herself more confidently, that people who were older than her seemed to look to her and listen to what she had to say. She'd survived for more than a year as a terrorist operative, learning from the best, first as an apprentice to Kevin and then to Saul. By Sapience standards, she was a veteran.

Some unnameable, bittersweet emotion jogged through Donovan. It was like that tearing sensation he'd felt in the hotel room months ago—the undeniable connection and yet the impossible distance—but this time it didn't cause him pain or distress.

It was what it was. A lingering echo of his old longing and desire stirred, subdued behind a wall of urgent pragmatism. He needed to speak to Anya—alone, and soon.

At last she seemed to not be occupied in some immediate task, and he went to her and whispered, "Can we talk? There's something else I have to tell you." Anya didn't get a chance to reply because at that moment Julian grumbled loudly to the two newcomers, "Ridiculous, I say. We shouldn't be expected to sleep under the same roof as a *shroom pet*."

Anya turned and raised her voice. "I agree. You shouldn't have to put up with that. You can take your things and clear out because you'd obviously be more comfortable elsewhere."

Julian's bristly eyebrows shot into his mop of gray hair. "Young lady, you'd turn Chloe and me out onto the street with the way things are out there? You wouldn't do that." The old man sounded incensed, but there was a tremor of uncertainty in his voice.

"No, Chloe can stay," Anya said, "but if you feel strongly enough to turn down a safe place to sleep, or you have a problem with Minh and me being the SRP keepers, you can leave knowing we'll take care of her." At this, Chloe began to whimper, and Julian, alarmed, began to mutter a recantation and busily fix her blankets.

Donovan put a hand on Anya's arm. "It's okay." He spoke loudly enough for everyone else to hear. "I'm not staying the night. I'll be gone as soon as I can."

Anya's eyebrows rose as she turned to him. Then her back stiffened. "You're right. No reason for you to sleep in this dump. You've got a house and a bed in the Round waiting for you."

There it was again, the inescapable friction between them:

Anya always pointing out their differences, reading arrogance and privilege into everything he said. "I'm not going back to the Round," he said, keeping his voice level and lowered. "That's what I need to talk to you about."

The coolness of Anya's glare betrayed more than a few unkind thoughts toward him, but she said, "Minh, can you finish helping everyone get settled?" The older woman gave Donovan yet another distrustful glower before nodding and taking the remaining stack of blankets.

"Come on." Anya didn't sound any less annoyed, but she took Donovan by the hand and walked him across the floor to a fire escape door, which she pushed open onto a dark stairwell. She flicked a wall switch and a buzzing fluorescent light shone greenish on the bare concrete stairs. Together, they climbed the two flights of steps and emerged through another door onto the roof of the building. Anya propped the door open with a piece of wood, walked a few feet away, and turned to face Donovan, hugging her bare arms, her face in shadow, backlit by the streetlights of the Ring Belt and the distant otherworldly glow of the Towers.

Donovan walked toward her, strangely grateful that she seemed as awkward facing him as he did facing her. He stopped in front of her. "I'm sorry. For the way things ended last time. I was expecting something from you that I shouldn't have." Tentatively, he reached out and placed a hand under her elbow. "I was trying to change your mind about the Round, about the zhree, and about exos, even just a little bit, because..." He hesitated, swallowing thickly before continuing. "Because meeting you last year changed *my* mind about some things. I guess I hoped that maybe... maybe you'd see more of who I am, where I live, and what I do... and still like me anyway." Donovan dropped his hand back to his side. "I know it was too much to ask. We both have our reasons for believing what we do. But I got hurt and angry, and I didn't listen to what you were saying that night."

Anya's eyes rose briefly to his, then dropped to a spot somewhere between his feet. "Well. It's not like I've been very nice to you either." She hunched her shoulders and her voice fell. "Whenever you try to get closer, I put up a wall. I say mean things to keep you away. I don't know why. Maybe because of Kevin; he always told me not to trust anyone, especially outside of Sapience. He used to say trust is a weapon, and when you give it to someone, they might turn around and shoot you."

Anya sighed and walked a few paces away. She sat down cross-legged but still spoke to Donovan as she gazed out over the rooftops. "But maybe it's because I'm afraid," she admitted quietly. "I joined the cause to fight against what's wrong in the world and try to make things better." She looked over at him with a faintly aching resentment. "You made me start thinking of exos and shrooms as people and . . . maybe I didn't really want that. Because that would just make things harder. It's hard enough, sometimes, to be okay with the things we do for the cause."

Donovan sat down next to her. From up here, the Ring Belt seemed almost peaceful—except that parts of it were lit with electricity and other sections were dark, the faint stench of smoke hung in the air, and every few minutes they heard the nearby wail of sirens or the crack and boom of gunfire. Donovan remained silent; Anya had never spoken about her decision to join Sapience nor expressed doubt in the cause before. "It'll only get worse, won't it?" she whispered after a spell. "And there's not much we can do about it."

Donovan wasn't sure if she was talking about their relationship or the disintegrating state of the world in general. "Probably. But apparently we're both too dumb to stop trying."

A wry smile lifted the corner of Anya's mouth and Donovan felt a little better. He figured it was safe to ask a question. "When you were talking to those two women, you mentioned them heading west to join one of the armies. What did you mean? What armies?"

Anya leaned back on straight arms. "The Sapience cells around the world are combining to create regional defense forces. There're a few different ones that have already gathered and are putting out the call for people to join. There'll be more that get off the ground soon." When Donovan tilted his head questioningly, she shrugged and smiled. "Being Saul's main communications person is a good way to keep up with what's going on."

"So, Sapience is building an army?" Donovan found the idea more than a little disturbing.

"It's not one army exactly because there's not one person in charge. Some of the groups call themselves Sapience, but others don't. Some answer to Saul, but some do their own thing. And there are some that've declared they're True Sapience only."

"How're they organizing so quickly?" Donovan wondered. "It's only been a few days since the attack."

Anya looked over at him, eyebrows raised. "You called this the start of the next War Era, didn't you? Sapience has been planning for the next War Era ever since the last one ended."

Anya was right. Sapience and its more extreme offshoot, True Sapience, existed to oppose anything they saw as alien. Their military forces might be comprised of autonomous guerrilla squads who weren't able to understand a word of Mur or tell two zhree apart to save their lives, but they were eager and prepared to fight.

They wouldn't win, though, not in the long run, not against a raiding civilization with far more advanced technology and the eventual goal of scouring the planet of life.

"Anya," he said, "I'm going to ask you to do something for me that I didn't do for you."

She leaned slightly away from him. "What's that?"

"To listen carefully to everything I say. And to trust me." He took out the padded envelope with Dr. Ghosh's research files. "I need to deliver this to Dr. Eugene Nakada."

Donovan told her everything. He explained that the Mur colonists were being ordered by their homeworld to relinquish Earth, and that they planned to evacuate a small population of exos to preserve the human species in the face of the planet's likely eventual destruction. He told her about the exocel inhibition reflex, the research his father had commissioned, and the awful casualties the exos had suffered when the Hunters had attacked. With difficulty, he even told her about Vic, about the twin brother she'd lost in Hardening and why she'd betrayed her erze to help Nakada, and how she'd died needlessly because they weren't able to get back into the Towers.

Anya did as he asked. She listened, with that watchful, childlike stare he knew so well, the one that betrayed her unselfconscious fascination with the alien world she so opposed.

"There'll be a lot of exos left on Earth," Donovan said at the end. "Including an awful lot of soldiers-in-erze with weapons and training, but who can't use their armor against zhree. I told you before that I'm not special, and it's true. There are hundreds of thousands of stripes like me who would fight the Rii if we could, with Sapience if we had to." He opened the envelope and shook the memory discs into his hand. "No one on the inside of the Round will use this research to give exos that freedom. But there's one person here on the outside who knows a lot more about exocels than most humans."

Anya took the small discs and turned them over in her hand. Donovan tried to read her expression, but her face was hidden by the darkness and the curtain of her hair. She did not speak. Softly, Donovan said, "I know you have plenty of reasons not to like me— or my kind, as you call us. But have I ever lied to you, Anya?"

Slowly, Anya shook her head.

"Then, please . . . will you tell me where to find Dr. Nakada?"

"No." Anya stood up. "But I'll take you to him."

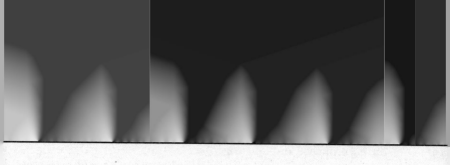

Minh disapproved vehemently of the idea of Anya leaving the Secure Refuge Point with Donovan, late at night no less. "You're supposed to stay here," she insisted, dragging Anya aside. "What're people going to think if one of the keepers leaves?"

"That's why there are always two keepers, right? If I'm not back in three days, then follow the rules and appoint a new co-keeper."

Minh's wrinkled face contracted like the skin of a prune.

"This is important," Anya told her. "It'll help the cause."

"Wait until morning, at least. It's dangerous out there."

"I can't wait," Donovan said. "Someone is bound to notice I'm missing soon. When they discover I'm not in the Round, they might come looking. You don't want more stripes showing up here, do you?"

The look Minh gave him could've frozen salt water.

Anya hugged the older woman. "I'll be fine."

Leon's electricycle was where Donovan had left it. He hadn't been worried about it being stolen—it wouldn't start for anyone without an approved exocellular body signature—but vandals had already attacked it with heavy implements and there were scratches on the paint and dents on the surface that would've made Leon unhappy. Guiltily, Donovan swung a leg over the seat and gripped the handlebars.

Anya remained standing on the sidewalk. "We can't take that."

Donovan felt stupid. She was right. No unmarked squishy would own a vehicle like this. They wouldn't get anywhere near a Sapience hideout without being shot at. "How're we going to get there, then?"

They moved the e-cycle to the alley behind the building where it would attract less attention. After disabling the tracking system, Donovan parked the vehicle out of sight behind a dumpster. Anya jangled a set of car keys and led him down the street to an ancient brown pickup truck.

It was exactly the sort of cheap petroleum burner Kevin always seemed to have on hand. Anya climbed into the driver's seat. Donovan opened the rusty passenger-side door and got in. "Where're we going?"

"Laramie." The truck coughed and started on the third try.

"That's where Nakada is?"

"That's where he checked in from a couple of days ago." Anya turned on the headlights and pulled the grumbling vehicle into the street. "After something happens, like a major operation or a SecPac raid, people get on the Sapience network to let others know that they're okay. That's what happened after the bombs started falling. As long as Eugene hasn't moved, that's where we'll find him. Sapience has a lot of folks around there and there's an old university with medical lab space."

In a skimmercar, the drive to Laramie might take an hour. An hour and a half, tops. In this old thing, it would take twice as long. It would be past midnight by the time they arrived. Donovan glanced at Anya nervously. The truck seemed too big for her. None of these stripped-down petroleum burners had computer navigation, automatic collision safeguards, or shielding. Death traps for squishies, when he thought about it. He knew Anya would be annoyed or scornful if she knew of his concerns, or worse, if he offered to drive. Donovan bit his tongue. Anya was a Sapience operative; driving a truck at night was the least dangerous of her activities.

Instead, he stared intently out the window, falling into the SecPac officer's habit of scanning every street, building, and vehicle they passed. His armor came down and he breathed a little easier once they were out of the Ring Belt and the countryside began expanding in front of them as a flat indigo vista. "You could sleep," Anya suggested.

"I'll stay up." He hadn't had a proper night's rest in days but was determined not to drift off right now. "I'd rather keep you company."

Anya turned toward him, a smile curving her lips in the dark. She faced forward again and rolled down the windows. The summer night's air whistled into the cab of the truck, drowning out the steady hum of the highway. Donovan wished he could make himself temporarily forget the circumstances of why they were out here, because the open prairie at night was beautiful. He leaned out slightly to better see the brilliantly clear sky, vast and dusted with stars. From this unimaginable distance, the stars all looked the same to the naked eye. But some of them, he knew, belonged to other systems in the Mur Erzen Commonwealth. Some warmed planets that were home to zhree or other species. But not humans. Humans were nowhere else.

His comm unit flashed a priority message. Donovan pulled it up on the display and felt his brief moment of contemplative peace vanish. All able-bodied exo soldiers-in-erze slated for first-round evacuation were ordered to report to Soldier Werth at SecPac Central Command at zero eight hundred hours for inspection and instructions. The military withdrawal had already begun; ships full of Soldiers were already leaving Earth. The first wave of human evacuation would occur within the week. In about ten hours, Donovan's absence would be apparent.

Anya rolled the windows back up. "Are they looking for you?"

"Not yet." Donovan silenced his comm unit's alerts and stowed the device.

Anya's mouth turned down. "I thought exos were compulsive about being with their own kind and following orders. What you're doing could get you into a lot of trouble, couldn't it?"

"You mean smuggling secrets about zhree biotechnology to a Sapience scientist? Yeah, I'd say so." He hadn't stopped to think too much about the possible personal consequences of his actions and decided he didn't want to do so now. At least he hadn't dragged Jet into this. Remembering the look on Jet's face as he'd closed the door, imagining him now grieving alone in his room—the pang it brought to Donovan's chest made him grimace.

He changed the subject. "Is Saul really meeting with the Prime Liaison? Even after the disastrous way the transition talks ended?"

Anya hunched forward over the wheel as they passed a road sign indicating Laramie was ninety miles away. "A lot has happened since then. Wanting change and wanting the shrooms gone was something everyone in Sapience used to be able to agree on. But with everything happening so quickly, and now with the bombings and fighting . . . People are scared out of their minds. They don't know what to think and they're losing faith in the cause." Anya's hands tightened on the wheel. "Saul will find a way to keep the cause together. He always has."

Donovan remembered what Commander Tate had said in the briefing several weeks ago, about the dilemma facing the Human Action Party: *Support the government they've opposed or join True Sapience.* Was that what Saul was deciding right now? "I hope something comes out of the meeting this time," Donovan said. "We all deserve a second chance, I think."

Anya put one hand on the seat between them. "Personally, I just hope we don't all die."

A seemingly incongruous statement coming from a girl committed to an illegal terrorist organization, but then Donovan remembered that the Rii attack had killed more people outside the Round than inside it. He'd been so consumed by the losses close to him that it was easy to forget that cities containing millions of people had also been bombarded in the attack. How many people had died as "distraction" so that the Hunters could take the Rounds?

Donovan reached over and placed his hand on top of Anya's. She turned her palm up and laced her fingers into his, and they sat silently with hands joined as the rumbling pickup ate mile after mile of dark highway. Not long ago, he would've wanted and hoped for more, but now, holding Anya's hand didn't overwhelm him with lustful yearning. Instead, he felt comforted and resolute. For the first time, they were going somewhere together of their own free will. As allies.

"Can I ask you a question?" Donovan asked.

"You just did," she pointed out.

"Can I ask you another question?"

Anya snorted softly. "Is it some sort of deep meaning-of-life question?"

"Maybe." He smiled. "What color is your hair, really?"

Anya gave a short, incredulous laugh. "*That's* what you want to know?" When he kept looking at her expectantly, she shook her head and said, in a more melancholy tone than he'd anticipated, "I don't really know, to be honest. I've changed it so many times, I've kind of lost track."

"Is that a Sapience thing? To make yourself less recognizable?"

"It helps, I suppose, but . . . it's more of a me thing." She glanced at him with a touch of self-consciousness, then faced forward again and said thoughtfully, "It's not easy to change most things, but it's easy to change hair. If it turns out badly, it's okay, it won't last long. It can be fixed. If you make yourself look different, sometimes you *feel* different too—like a better person." She was pensive for a moment before deliberately lightening her voice. "Or maybe I just haven't figured out my look. I don't know . . . What color do you like?"

Donovan studied her profile. "It doesn't matter to me. I was only curious." Quietly, he said, "Thank you. For trusting me, again. You've never needed to stick your neck out for me, but you keep doing it. I don't think you need to change who you are at all. You're . . ." *Amazing. Beautiful. Perfect the way you are.* He wanted to say the truth, not something that might come across as superficial flattery. "You're one of the most decent people I've ever met."

Anya didn't reply at first. Then she squeezed his hand in gratitude. "Everyone's got something decent about them, deep down."

Watching the passing landscape with Anya's hand in his, the drive did not seem as long as Donovan had feared. City streetlights began appearing and a short while later they were driving onto a university campus, past wide lawns and large, historic-looking brick buildings. "I've only been here once. I think we need to go a little farther down this road." Anya drove slowly, looking from side to side. "All of this was built before the War Era. Kind of amazing, isn't it?"

"Yeah," Donovan agreed. The buildings looming out of the darkness, their facades illuminated by streetlight, seemed stoic and dependable, as if they'd emerged from the earth and rock of this area. They were square and solid. Brick and metal and glass. There were no zhree architectural features, no imported materials or construction methods, no sign of alien influence at all. The place seemed to be a reminder that humans had been studying and building things long before the zhree had arrived. Anya stopped the truck on the side of the road.

"What do we do now?" Donovan asked.

Ahead of them was a road closed off by a simple swinging metal barricade. Anya flashed the pickup's headlights: once, twice. Then she turned them off and the cab of the truck went dark. "We wait. Outside."

Anya got out of the pickup truck and walked to stand in front of it. Donovan threw open his own door and followed. "Are you sure about this?" There didn't seem to be anyone in sight.

Anya sat down patiently on the truck's front bumper, seemingly unconcerned. "This is why you needed me along. Just trust me."

No sooner had Anya finished speaking than Donovan spotted a lone figure approaching from the other side of the waist-high metal arm barring the road. Anya got back to her feet. "Stay back here and don't let him get a look at you."

Donovan did as she suggested, pulling the hood of his jacket over his head and stuffing his hands in his pockets. He leaned against the front of the truck in a posture of sullen indifference, but his fingers curled, tense, and he breathed steadily to keep his armor down.

Anya walked to meet the stranger at the gate. Donovan heard only the first few seconds of their exchange. A man's young but cold voice called, "Did you take a wrong turn, miss? Because you look lost."

Anya's response was strange. "We are lost to time. Strangers who look upon where we once dwelled exclaim upon a bright burning spark in the black void, the fuel of the flame long gone but the light it gave traveling forever."

A recitation from *The Last Salute,* a classic if fatalistic War Era work of literature much admired in Sapience circles. The man at the gate said more warmly, "You're arriving late. Come a long way?"

Their voices hushed as they conversed. The sentry raised one arm, fingers moving in a hand gesture to someone unseen in the darkness. Donovan glanced around surreptitiously, noting the ample cover of trees and the vantage points afforded by the surrounding buildings. Panotin prickled up his neck. He strained to hear what Anya and the man were saying without looking as if he was doing so. He caught the words *Ring Belt, Kevin, Saul, SRP,* and *Eugene Nakada.*

The sentry's eyes slid past Anya and settled on Donovan. Donovan kept his gaze neutral and wandering somewhere off to the left, as if he were staring into the trees, bored and impatient. He could feel the man's suspicion raking over him. Anya half-turned, shooting a pointedly concerned and irritated look at

Donovan, then sighed and turned back to the man in front of her. "Sorry about my brother," Donovan heard her say, and then she lowered her voice in a long, intensely whispered explanation.

To Donovan's surprise, the man nodded. He glanced over at Donovan again, but this time his face showed signs of worry and sympathy. He and Anya talked animatedly for a little longer. Now and again the man paused to point to nearby buildings. Then he unlocked the metal barricade and swung it open. Anya walked back to the truck.

"Come on, let's go." She climbed back into the cab.

Donovan didn't ask questions. He jumped back into the truck and slumped down into the seat as Anya started the pickup again (after only two tries this time) and rolled through the gate, thanking the sentry with a wave as they passed through. Donovan let out a breath he hadn't realized he'd been holding. "We're okay, then? What did you tell him?"

"That you have a social anxiety disorder. Every time we move SRPs, you freak out and sometimes you get violent. After the bombings, the drugstores were looted and you haven't had your meds for two days."

Donovan blinked. "That's . . . a good story."

"A cover story ought to be believable, thorough, and specific," Anya said, as if sardonically quoting a well-known Sapience maxim.

An ironic smile climbed Donovan's face. The one other time he and Anya had gone through a road closure together, he'd been the one forced to think quickly on his feet to get past a Builder and his work crew before Kevin resorted to murdering them. "So, what about Nakada?" Donovan asked. "Is he here?"

"He's here." Anya took a turn down a smaller road, pulled the truck into a parking lot, and stopped it. She pointed into the distance at what looked like an old mansion. "The official SRP is in one of the residence houses. That's where people can get food and supplies and a place to sleep." She pointed at a much larger building across the street. "When I mentioned to Darren back there that I'd worked with Kevin and was hoping to see Eugene again, he told me that the doctor spends almost all his time in the basement of the Biological Sciences Building."

"That's where we'll try first, then."

They got out of the truck, crossed the street, and hurried down paths across expansive lawns. Donovan had to admit he was impressed. He'd known there were a lot of Sapience camps and militias in this area, but clearly they had powerful sympathizers in the university administration. A Sapience cell hidden in plain sight on a college campus . . . *Commander Tate needs to be told about this.* He kicked himself for the thought. He couldn't report this. Anya had snuck him in here; she was trusting him not to turn around and betray her.

The main entrance of the Biological Sciences Building was locked. They circled the outside and tried other doors. None of them opened, even though there were lights on in the corridors. Donovan tugged at the front entrance in frustration. He considered shooting out the lock but gunfire wouldn't go unnoticed, especially if Sapience had any sort of active security scanning net that could pick up electripulse discharges. He moved to a ground-level window and began feeling around its perimeter. He bladed his hand and pried at the window frame.

"We can go to the SRP residence house," Anya suggested.

"Maybe Eugene is there and if he's not, they might have a way to call him."

Donovan shook his head. Any interaction with Sapience members was further risk they'd be found out. He'd come too far to be thwarted, and with time ticking down, he wasn't going to leave and hope for better luck later. Donovan armored his left fist, encasing his knuckles, wrist, and forearm in layers of panotin, and slammed it into the window with all his strength. The impact reverberated through his upper body and into his injured right shoulder, making him bite down hard from the sudden pain. The window shook; a spiderweb of cracks appeared in the glass. Donovan waited for an alarm to go off or a guard to appear, but none did.

Anya jumped back as he punched the window again. The cracks multiplied and spread. Donovan shifted back and kicked the window in. The lower pane gave way, the shatterproof glass buckling into chunks. Donovan cleared the pieces away and climbed through the hole. Anya gaped at him, then followed.

They were inside a classroom. Out in the corridor, they followed the partially lit hallway to a set of stairs and took them down into the basement. Doors led into laboratories on both sides. Most of the rooms were dark, but one of them was not. His pulse rising steadily, Donovan followed the light, paused just for a second to hope for the best, then pushed the door open.

Dr. Eugene Nakada was working at a lab bench in the corner of the room, hunched over a microscope and tray of slides. He looked up at the sound of the door opening and froze, the blood draining from his face for one almost comical instant. Then he scrambled back as violently as if a demon had materialized in his lab. Diving for a drawer, he yanked it open, pulled out a revolver, and pointed it at Donovan's chest. "Don't come any closer!" he shouted shrilly.

Donovan stepped into the room with his arms outstretched, keeping Anya behind him. "Dr. Nakada, do you remember me?"

Nakada stared at him, the gun in his two-handed grip shaking. Donovan was quite sure that if the man fired it, he would miss even at this close a range. "You're . . . you're Max Russell's son." Nakada's eyes darted past Donovan as if expecting to see more SecPac officers storming down the hallway. Instead, they landed on Anya in bewilderment.

Anya stepped forward. "It's okay. I brought him here."

Donovan said, "Put the gun down, Doctor. We came alone. There aren't any other stripes with me." When Nakada still didn't move, Donovan raised his voice and spoke more firmly. "You know that I have an eighth-generation exocel. If I wanted to hurt or arrest you, that revolver wouldn't stop me. I'm sorry if I scared you, but we need to talk. Please. Put the gun down and I'll explain everything."

— — —

An hour later, Donovan and Anya stood hovering over Nakada's shoulder as he studied Dr. Ghosh's research files on his screen.

"Vincent was an extremely thorough man," Nakada said with grudging admiration. "Of course, I was aware of the exocel inhibition reflex, but lacking live subjects and advanced imaging equipment, I wasn't able to pinpoint the neural cluster with such precision." The doctor sounded a little jealous.

"So is he right?" Donovan asked. "In the letter that he wrote to my father, Ghosh said he thought the reflex could be jammed. You're looking at his work. Do you think that it could be done?"

"I don't see why not." Dr. Nakada tapped two fingers on his chin, a slightly distant but eager expression on his face. He seemed to have recovered completely from his scare. Indeed, after Donovan had shown him the memory discs, Nakada had begun scrutinizing Ghosh's data with the keen interest of a child immediately distracted from upset by the appearance of candy.

"The procedure is straightforward enough in theory," the former scientist-in-erze said. "However, as Vincent pointed out, no one has ever attempted it before. To operate on a Hardened patient, one would need exocel suppressing medication, the proper neurosurgical tools, and an advanced knowledge of exo neurophysiology so as not to damage any of the cerebrospinal node connections. In other words, only zhree Nurses would be able to do it, and as you've said, they wouldn't."

Donovan took a nervous breath and let it out slowly. "But you could do it. You've replicated the exocel suppressing drug. You've operated on . . . cadavers. And you've spent years studying how Hardening and exocels work. You probably know as much as any human."

Dr. Nakada gave a modest shrug. "Yes, well, I suppose I would be one of the few capable of accomplishing what Vincent suggests." The doctor said it casually, but there was a definite hint of self-aggrandizement in his voice. "Assuming his conclusions are correct."

Donovan nodded. His hands tightened around the edge of a lab bench. "Could you do it on me?"

For the first time in several minutes, Nakada looked up from his screen. He swiveled in his chair and regarded Donovan full on, as if suddenly remembering that he was there: a real, live, Hardened subject with an eighth-generation exoçel. "On you," the doctor said incredulously. "You're volunteering yourself as a test subject?"

Anya stared at Donovan, her lips parted in a circle of astonishment.

Donovan felt a sudden leap of fear in his stomach. He couldn't believe what he was doing but words kept coming. "You said it would work in theory, but no one's tried it yet. Someone has to, right? If the zhree won't remove the neural override so that exos can fight the Rii, then we have to do it ourselves. Someone has to be the first to prove that Ghosh's idea works."

"It might not," Nakada pointed out.

Donovan swallowed. "Then we have to know that too."

Nakada pursed his lips thoughtfully, scrutinizing Donovan with far too much scientific curiosity for comfort. "I admit I'm intrigued. This is certainly beyond what any human scientist has ever attempted, and to be able to test it on a live patient . . ." Dr. Nakada trailed off; then he shook his head and his eyes seemed to clear of their dreaminess. "Ah, but there's the personal risk to think of. Anything that could aid soldiers-in-erze wouldn't sit well with my Sapience sponsors. And if something goes wrong, your SecPac friends will be after me as well. I'm afraid I'd be placing myself in a very precarious position."

Donovan goggled at the man. *You think* you're *in a precarious position? I'm the one offering to let you muck about in my brain!* When he opened his mouth, instead of speaking the retort that was on his mind, he heard himself say, "Tamaravick Kohl is dead."

"Wh-what . . . ?" Dr. Nakada drew back.

"She fought the Rii Hunters when they attacked but, like the rest of us, her exocel wasn't of any help. The Hunters occupied the Towers, including the medical facilities that treat exos. Vic died from her injuries last night." Just saying the truth out loud was hard; the words made it real all over again. Donovan had to lower his voice to steady it. "I know Vic was your friend, once. I know she went out of erze and betrayed her fellow SecPac officers because she didn't want to see you hurt or killed. She knew better than anyone what you'd been through and why you left the Round, and I think in a way she even believed in the research you were doing. Vic was . . ." He swallowed. "She was my friend and one of the most caring people I ever knew, and she's dead when she shouldn't be, because of this exocel hobble in our brains."

"Tamaravick?" Nakada's chin trembled. "She was just a little girl . . ."

Donovan shook his head. "She was an exo soldier-in-erze. One of many."

Nakada's face sagged and he turned it aside. For the first time, Donovan glimpsed the old and deep chasm of grief hidden below the protective shield of impassive scientific obsession.

He waited until the man brought a wavering gaze back around to him, then said, "The world needs exos that will be able to fight for all of us. I don't think you left the Round because you wanted to join the Sapience cause. You left because you wanted to do research that the zhree wouldn't let you do. You wanted knowledge that Hardened humans ought to have but don't."

Donovan picked up the screen and thrust it into Nakada's hands. "Here's your chance to do what no other scientist has done. I've made copies of these files and sent them to the Prime Liaison.

If you try the procedure on me and it works, then others will be able to replicate it. Other exos won't die needlessly, the way Vic did. You'll be giving all of humankind a chance."

Donovan was keenly aware of Anya's eyes on him. When he'd been a captive in the Warren, Anya used to stare at him steadily the way she was staring now—eyes wide, mouth slightly parted—fascinated and perplexed and subtly accusing.

Dr. Nakada looked down at the screen in his hand and back up at Donovan. His Adam's apple bobbed under the thin skin of his neck. "I'll need a few hours to get set up."

A few hours was exactly what Donovan didn't need. It gave him ample time to regret his decision and contemplate the fact that he might have volunteered himself for a fate worse than death. Dr. Nakada's matter-of-fact explanation of the procedure did not reassure him.

"The neural cluster is located in the amygdala, the part of the brain that controls fear, aggression, and emotions tied to survival instincts." Dr. Nakada held up a metal frame. "Once you're sedated and your exocel has been suppressed, this frame will keep your head immobilized while I drill a one-centimeter hole here." He tapped a spot on Donovan's temple. "I'll insert an electrode deep into the brain and use a radio-frequency pulse to hopefully disable the neural connection."

"Basically, you're going to drill into my skull and fry my brain with electricity," Donovan said. "Great. Sounds simple enough."

"In a non-Hardened human, yes," Nakada replied, ignoring Donovan's sarcasm. "But an exo's brain is different. There are additional cerebral functions that control the exocellular system. And as with any untested medical procedure, the risks are greater." Nakada cleared his work table and wiped it down with disinfectant. Donovan refused to think upon the fact that the doctor's operating surface had previously accommodated the corpses of murder victims. "Death or brain damage are possible. Long term, you might suffer memory or emotional problems."

Donovan imagined himself as a brain-dead vegetable, or a drooling, limping, half-armored ruin of a man. *If this goes horribly wrong, just let me die on the operating table,* he prayed.

Though it was larger and better equipped, the doctor's lab reminded Donovan unpleasantly of the basement that he and his erze mates had raided in Denver. Sapience had obviously gone to some effort to help Nakada rebuild. Instruments Donovan couldn't make sense of sat next to shelves laden with containers of preserved samples. An orderly array of petri dishes was lined up on one counter. Each held a piece of what looked like pale pink tissue overlaid with panotin, floating on top of a film of some sort of nutrient gel that kept the whole thing alive. As Donovan watched, a machine with a small robotic arm lowered a needle into each dish and took some mysterious measurement as each fragment of panotin responded, knitting layers to protect the bit of flesh underneath. It was as morbid as seeing a row of dis-embodied fingers twitching on the table. Donovan backed off hastily.

"Please don't touch any of the experiment setups," Dr. Nakada said sternly.

Donovan turned away and gripped the back of Nakada's empty chair, his knuckles thickening with armor. He felt a sudden urge to spin around and sweep his arm across the counter, to destroy the equipment and the grisly petri dishes. What was he doing here? This was a terrible idea. His worst one ever. He ought to leave this butcher's shop right now. No one was stopping him. Go back to the

Round, apologize to Jet, rejoin his erze mates. Follow orders and abandon Earth. Survive.

Anya's hand on his arm nearly made him jump. She eyed him, possibly noticing his slightly wild expression. "Let's get out of this room," she said, leading him to the door.

Out in the greenish hallway, Anya spun to face him and spoke in a loud whisper. "You don't have to do this." Her voice echoed a little in the empty corridor. "You said the shrooms would save some of the exos. You would be one of them, wouldn't you?" When Donovan didn't answer, she stepped close and curled one hand around his forearm, her grip surprisingly strong as she tilted her face up to his. "Why take such a big risk when you don't have to? Why not save yourself?"

Hearing Anya echo his thoughts as if she'd read his mind and seeing the frustrated look on her face somehow dissipated Donovan's sense of panic. His pulse came back down. "Would you leave if you could?" he asked.

"Yes," Anya said. "You do whatever you have to do to look after yourself. You can't count on anyone else to do it. Sometimes that means you have to leave." Her fingers tightened urgently on his arm. "I'd even get on a spaceship with shrooms. I'd do it."

He wasn't sure how to reply. Anya had had a much harder childhood than he'd had. Donovan didn't imagine she'd have made it to where she was today if she didn't have an instinct for survival. She'd attached herself to Kevin, she'd joined Sapience, she'd made herself useful to Saul. Donovan believed her when she said she would leave Earth if it came down to it.

Donovan lowered his eyes. "My mom didn't save herself even

though she could have. She believed there were things worth dying for. My dad was the Prime Liaison for sixteen years; he always knew he might be assassinated. If I take the easy way out, if I save myself, what does that say about me?"

"It would say that you're smart," Anya insisted. "Smarter than them. If they were alive, I'm sure they would both want you to live." She put a hand under his chin and lifted his face back up so she could meet his eyes. Donovan's heart gave a little stutter of surprise to see her eyes glistening, beseechingly, in the dim fluorescent light. "*I* want you to live."

"You're sounding awfully fatalistic," Donovan said, smiling weakly and trying to leaven his voice. "Trust me, I want to live too. Don't you have faith in Dr. Nakada?"

Anya hesitated. "Yeah." Her tone did not suggest overwhelming optimism.

"There are some things you can't leave behind. Including who you are. The way I was raised . . ." *Duty. Responsibility. Sacrifice. The greater good.* Ideas that had been drilled into him by his father and his erze for as long as he could remember. He unwrapped Anya's hand from his arm and held on to it tightly. "I might be the only person who has Ghosh's information and can do anything about it right now. If that's true, then it means I *have* to do this."

Anya blinked hard and lowered her eyes, dropping the crown of her head so it rested gently on Donovan's chest. He put an arm around her, as much to comfort himself as to reassure her. The grumble of the old building's ventilation system filled the grudging silence. In a small voice, Anya said, "We should try to get some sleep."

They found two benches in the hallway. Anya wadded her jacket up into a pillow and curled up onto one of them. Donovan lay down on the other. He was so exhausted that even on the hard, narrow surface, he dropped off quickly.

Some unguessable time later, he was awakened by Anya's hand on his shoulder. She didn't draw her touch away even when he opened his eyes and sat up. Donovan reached up and placed his own hand over hers. "What time is it?" he croaked, his voice thick with sleep.

"It's seven thirty in the morning," Anya said. "I went over to the SRP house and talked to a few folks so no one gets too suspicious. I told them we came in late after a long drive and were sleeping in the truck because you felt more comfortable there." Anya glanced over at the door to Nakada's lab. "The doctor says he's ready and that if you're still going to do this, we probably shouldn't wait. People will leave us alone for a while, but then they'll start to wonder."

Donovan nodded. He still felt weary but more clearheaded. As he got up from the bench, he was struck more acutely than ever by how sore he was. The pain in his shoulder was less sharp now, more nagging, but the joint remained swollen and difficult to move. And his stomach would be rumbling if it wasn't so tightly knotted with anxiety and fear. What he was about to do seemed even more insane now than it had last night.

Dr. Nakada's lab had been transformed into a makeshift operating room. The table had been covered with a pad and plastic sheeting. A surgical arm was mounted at the head of the table and a nearby mobile cart contained trays of instruments. The scientist was moving about in a decidedly purposeful manner now, alternately reviewing his screen and making mysterious adjustments to equipment. Donovan doubted the doctor had slept at all, but Nakada didn't seem any the worse for wear; perhaps he was used to working through the night.

Donovan stood in the doorway of the lab and suddenly found it hard to take another step forward. He thought of body parts in jars and corpses with exposed brains, and his mouth went dry. The sense of panic he'd quelled earlier began rising again. There had to be another way. Some solution he'd overlooked that didn't involve putting his own life at risk.

Whose life, then? Some exo had to be the test case. The Rii were here *now*. The Mur colonists were leaving *now* and taking their chosen young exos with them. There wasn't time to hope that the Prime Liaison or someone in the government would read Ghosh's files and gather together real doctors who could run proper tests in real hospitals. Donovan's father had been the one to go behind everyone's back to obtain this vital information. If he'd intended for it to be used, Donovan couldn't ask or hope for some other exo to be the first to risk his life.

At that moment, his comm unit vibrated insistently and he nearly jumped. He looked down it. Jet. Donovan's stomach contorted sharply. He'd forgotten that he was supposed to be with his erze mates right now, receiving evacuation instructions. Donovan's hand froze just over his transmitter toggle. If he answered his partner's call, what would he say? How could he explain where he was and what he was doing? Several long seconds of paralyzed indecision passed. The comm unit fell silent and a new message flashed alongside a list of other missed calls. Jet had been trying to reach him for hours. It was a testament to his exhaustion that Donovan had slept so deeply he'd missed his partner's increasingly frantic attempts.

WE'RE SUPPOSED TO REPORT TO CENTRAL AT 0800. ERZE ORDERS.

IT'S 0400. WHERE ARE YOU??

I'M SORRY I KICKED YOU OUT. JUST TELL ME WHERE YOU ARE.

DAMMIT ANSWER ME.

When Donovan raised his eyes, he saw that Dr. Nakada and Anya were watching him. "They've noticed you're gone," Anya said.

Donovan nodded. "I've shut off location tracking on my comm. They can still trace me eventually, but it won't be for a while."

Dr. Nakada bent over a sink and washed his hands, then turned back to Donovan as he dried them on a clean towel. Donovan hadn't moved. "Are you still prepared to go through with this?" Nakada asked.

Donovan's hands and feet had gone quite cold. "Yes," he said.

Nakada turned to Anya. "An operation like this usually requires assistants. I realize you have no training, but I've labeled everything on the trays. If you'd be so kind as to hand me tools when I ask for them?"

Anya nodded and went to wash her hands.

Donovan set his comm unit aside. He removed his holstered sidearm and set it down as well, then shrugged out of his jacket and slung it over Nakada's chair. Clinging tight to his delicate sense of resolve, he hopped up onto the table. It wasn't a particularly comfortable surface, but it wasn't any worse than the bench he'd slept on out in the hallway.

"You have to record everything," he told Nakada. "Whatever happens, you have to make notes and get them out there."

The doctor nodded. Donovan lay down and stared up at the bank of ceiling lights. *Don't think.* He tried to take a deep breath, but it came out shaky; his armor was up and his heart was racing.

This was worse than going into a firefight. At least a soldier-in-erze with a weapon in his hands would have some control over his situation.

Dr. Nakada held a plastic mask up to Donovan's nose and mouth. "Exocel suppressant," he explained. "Just breathe normally."

"Why does this thing smell funny?" Donovan asked.

"It's been mostly used on primate test subjects. Don't worry, I've completely sterilized it, but the smell doesn't quite come out."

An image of grotesquely Hardened monkeys flashed into Donovan's mind and it was all he could do to not jerk away. He picked out a water stain on the ceiling and focused on it, trying to use the breathing patterns he'd learned in combat training.

Anya's face appeared over his. She gazed down at him, then bent over and pressed her lips to his brow. Her touch on his skin fortified him and his hands unclenched. "You're brave," she whispered. "Crazy, but brave."

The suppressant worked fast. In less than a minute, his exocel dropped away and he couldn't feel it anymore. "I'm administering the sedative." Dr. Nakada's voice was unexpectedly soothing, as if he were talking his way through a demonstration video. Donovan heard the soft hiss of gas from the tube connected to the face mask. A sense of calm began to settle over him. His muscles relaxed; his limbs grew heavy. The lights above turned fuzzy.

Suddenly, Dr. Nakada and Anya jerked their heads up at some sound in the hallway. Alarm swept across both their faces, and then the door of the laboratory slammed open.

Kevin Warde barged in and stopped. His eyes went wide and his cruel mouth fell agape at the scene before him. "Well, I'll be damned."

25

Donovan tore the mask off. Regular air flooded into his lungs and awareness shot back into his brain, but when he tried to roll off the table and lunge for his gun on the desk, his rubbery, unresponsive limbs folded and he collapsed to the floor. Kevin crossed the distance between them in a few strides and kicked Donovan hard in the side with his steel-toed boot.

Donovan felt the impact, but not the pain. He could thank the drugs in his system for that mercy at least, though they had rendered him helpless. He tried to leverage himself forward, to tackle Kevin around the knees, but he felt as if he were moving through molasses. His coordination was gone, his sense of distance distorted. Kevin stepped away from Donovan's clumsy grab and kicked him again. Donovan's body curled around the blow. He grabbed Kevin's leg, pulling across with both hands to slice through the calf, but nothing happened. He still had no use of his exocel. He couldn't even armor himself, much less form blades.

Kevin kicked him square in the chest. All the breath left Donovan's body. His grip fell away and he gasped noisily, like a fish suddenly thrown onto the deck of a ship. In the background, he heard noisy commotion and Anya screaming. "Kevin, stop! *Stop it!*"

As he flopped on the floor, Donovan caught a glimpse of Anya twisting and struggling, her arms pinned to her sides from behind by another man, dark-skinned with pale eyes—Kevin's friend Javid.

In desperation, Donovan grabbed the first thing he could get his hands on: the mask and tube now hanging discarded from Nakada's surgical setup. His nearly dead weight dragged the whole mobile cart of equipment over. Clattering metal instruments hit the concrete floor in a shower of noise. Kevin stumbled back from the tipping equipment and into the surgical arm; it swung around and barely missed striking Dr. Nakada, who jumped back, cowering against the wall, his shaking hands over his head.

Donovan snatched the nearest thing on the ground—a metal tool that looked like a drill bit—then pushed himself to his feet and lunged at Kevin with all the willpower left at his command. Two seconds faster and six inches over to the left and he would've planted the object in Kevin's throat. Instead, he missed and went staggering forward. Almost casually, Kevin smashed him in the temple with the butt of his pistol.

This time he felt the pain.

The next thing Donovan knew he was being dragged across the floor. He must've passed out for several seconds when he hit the ground. The world was oddly muted and blurred and his body seemed disconnected.

"Don't kill him," Anya pleaded. "Just leave him and let's get out of here. I'll go with you, Kevin. We'll go wherever you want."

"Jesus, Anya," Kevin grunted. "After all the years we've known each other, do you take me for an idiot? You think this is about *you*?" Kevin heaved Donovan another few feet and dropped him. "As if I'd want you back after you've been with a shroom pet." Kevin patted his cargo-vest pockets and took out a pair of handcuffs. He pulled Donovan's limp arms over his head and locked them around a metal table leg.

"Don't kill him," Anya begged again, quietly.

Kevin straightened up. He took off his ball cap, wiped his brow with the back of his sleeve, and jammed it back on. "Eugene," he said to the cringing Dr. Nakada, "you want to tell me what's going on?"

Dr. Nakada gulped, looking around his wrecked laboratory. "Kevin," he said, wringing his hands, "I wasn't expecting you."

"Javid and I came to move you to a safer spot. I don't trust the folks here anymore. They've been slipping. Lax security, for one thing. We've got an army going in Nevada now, with good, smart people—one-hundred-percent True Sapience. But when we arrived, we saw the smashed window and got worried about you, Doc. Real worried."

"I . . . well . . ." Dr. Nakada looked almost apologetic for having caused Kevin any concern.

Donovan felt as if the nerves in his torso and limbs were slowly reconnecting to his brain, but he found he didn't want this. Pain was interfering conspicuously with his body's desire that he return to unconsciousness. He couldn't think clearly beyond knowing that he was, once again, at the mercy of the man he loathed most in the world. His cheek was pressed to the cold ground and there was a wetness under him that he realized from the smell was blood. Without the protection of his exocel, his shoulder wound had opened and was leaking.

"Are you working with the shroom pets now, Doc?" Javid's voice from the other side of the room, with that unpredictable, manic edge to it that Donovan remembered so well. "Why's this stripe here? Are you a turncoat for the government?"

"No, no," Dr. Nakada reassured the two men hastily, sweat beading on his forehead. "It's nothing like that."

"What's it like, then?" Javid demanded.

Stay with it, Donovan commanded himself. *Don't pass out again. Think. Think, dammit. You're handcuffed to a table. Kevin has a gun. Javid has Anya. What can you do?*

Anya broke in. "The Rii are real, Kevin. I saw a video of them. They're the ones who dropped the bombs on the cities. They're kicking the other shrooms off Earth and taking over."

Kevin shrugged, kicking some scattered surgical tools out of the way. "Shrooms are shrooms. If it takes new ones arriving to finally bring about the war, so be it. All's the same to me."

"It's not the same," Donovan slurred, managing to crawl to his knees so that he was hugging the table leg. "The Rii don't care about humans."

Kevin squatted back down to Donovan's level. "Shrooms have *never* cared about humans. Sure, maybe they value their *pets*. But not humans."

"Still, no one is explaining what the hell is going on here." Javid's voice was becoming menacingly impatient.

"I agreed to test some research he brought to me, that's all." Dr. Nakada dabbed nervously at his upper lip with the back of his wrist. "Hardened individuals have a neural reflex that prevents them from armoring in aggression toward zhree. He was . . . We were . . . interested in whether the reflex could be eliminated with a surgical procedure."

Kevin cocked his head for a moment. Then a broad smirk spread across his face. He didn't take his eyes off Donovan. "You want to fight the shrooms now, zebrahands? Is that it? Just woke up to the fact that your masters have been keeping you shackled all this time, and now you want to join the cause?" Kevin looked over his shoulder and exchanged a look of vicious amusement with Javid. "How about that, Javid? A feral shroom pet. Never seen one before."

Javid chuckled to satisfy Kevin, but he was staring down at Donovan with pure malice. Donovan recalled all too clearly that Javid had tried to kill him on two occasions before, and now his expression suggested that he believed a third attempt would be the charm. "We ought to put it down," he said.

Anya twisted over her shoulder to fix Javid with a look of furious scorn. "Let go of me, Javid. You're hurting my wrists." She turned back around. "Kevin, tell him to get his hands off me."

"Let her go," Kevin said in an offhanded tone.

Javid released Anya's arms and steered her roughly into Nakada's desk chair. "Be a pain, and I'll tie you into it," he warned.

Surreptitiously, Donovan tried to armor again, just around his bleeding shoulder. The effort brought tingling pain, like trying to move a frozen limb. How long would it take for the exocel suppressant to wear off? *Keep playing helpless. Once you can armor again, all you need is for Kevin to get careless, to get too close for just a few seconds . . .*

Kevin put a hand on Dr. Nakada's shoulder and leaned in to speak with the sympathetic but firm voice of someone advising a wayward friend as to what's good for him. "You're a smart guy, Eugene, but easily distracted. You're losing focus on what's important here. I've helped you out a lot, haven't I? Kept you safe, helped you get lab space and equipment and samples—whatever you needed. Set you up again after we got raided by SecPac—*twice*. Isn't that right?"

"Ah, well, yes," Dr. Nakada said, blinking rapidly.

"Why do you think I've gone to the trouble for you all these years?" Kevin squeezed the doctor's shoulder and his voice hardened. "Out of the kindness of my heart? For the good of science?"

"No, I don't suppose so," admitted Nakada.

"So where is it, then? I've been awfully patient, Doc. What've you got for me?" He glanced meaningfully at Donovan, then back to the scientist. "Unless you're lying and really have gone to the stripes."

Dr. Nakada's swallow was audible. "Well, it's only a prototype but . . ." He picked his way through the clutter-strewn lab and unlocked a cabinet underneath the counter where his eerie petri dishes were arranged. Kevin followed him; Javid and Anya craned slightly forward as well. From his place on the floor, Donovan had to twist around awkwardly to see what was going on. His vision was still wobbly, but he saw Dr. Nakada bend and retrieve a tray of vials from the cabinet and set them on the counter. The vials were full of a cloudy orange liquid, like apricot juice.

Kevin picked up one of the vials and turned it over. "What does it do?"

"You asked for something more lethal and with greater range than the suppressant spray," Dr. Nakada said. "So I developed a more potent compound that evaporates quickly upon release. Instead of suppressing the exocel, it does the precise opposite: It attacks the enzyme that acts as the 'off switch' for the exocellular system. With this enzyme blocked, the exocel would be instantly overstimulated, leading to spasms, paralysis, oxygen depletion, and death." Nakada tugged the collar of his shirt uncomfortably. "Non-Hardened humans don't produce the enzyme in question, of course, so it should have no effect on them, but on a Hardened population it would . . . theoretically . . . be an effective chemical weapon."

Kevin held the vial up to the light. A wolfish grin stretched across his face. "Doc, you're a genius."

"Now, as I said, this is just a prototype." Dr. Nakada tugged the tray of vials closer toward himself, as if intending to return it to the cabinet under the counter. "It hasn't been tested, and I can't say for certain that it's safe to use around non-Hardened civilians. I'll need additional time to conduct animal studies before . . ." He tried to retrieve the vial from Kevin's hand, but the man held it out of reach and, smiling, tucked it into a pocket of his vest. He plucked another vial from the tray and handed it to Javid, who palmed it eagerly.

"Javid and I will keep some on hand for field testing," Kevin said, patting his pocket. "As for animal studies . . ." Kevin looked back down at Donovan. "Seems we've got the perfect opportunity, right now."

Anya stood, fists balled. "You said you wouldn't kill him."

"Did I say that?" Kevin looked to Javid.

Javid smiled broadly. "You never said that."

Kevin clapped Nakada on the back. "Start packing up your stuff, Doctor. You know the drill." Kevin was all efficiency now. "Javid, run on over to the SRP's main house and get us resupplied. Let them know we're taking Eugene with us. I want to be back on the road before noon."

Javid nodded and turned to go, then hesitated. "Maybe we should go over to the house together." He jerked his head toward Donovan. "I don't like the idea of leaving you here with a stripe, tied up or not. There's something about *that* one in particular. He's always got some trick up his sleeve."

Kevin glanced at Donovan. His lips twitched. "This shroom

pet and I have a history. I'm not taking my eyes off him for a second. Don't worry about one drugged, handcuffed stripe, Javid. Worry about the twenty of them that might show up if we don't get our asses out of here right quick. Get over to the main house and get us sorted."

"What about her?" Javid asked.

Kevin walked over to Anya and gently but firmly pushed her back into the chair. "Anya's not going to cause any trouble. Are you?"

Anya glared, her mouth set in a defiant scowl, but she crossed her arms and stayed in the seat. Kevin smirked and turned away.

Javid left. Dr. Nakada set the tray of remaining test tube vials inside a metal box and latched it. He opened a closet door and began rolling out large plastic crates on wheels. The doctor was clearly no stranger to sudden Sapience-mandated relocations. His shoulders were slouched forward in resignation, and he didn't look at anyone as he packed up the items in his lab with methodical efficiency.

Donovan tried to think past the pain, the grogginess, his mounting sense of horror and helplessness. He couldn't let Kevin Warde escape yet *again*, with Anya and Dr. Nakada and a box of deadly chemical weapons. Once more, he tried to armor. This time he felt his exocel respond, a little slow and achy. *Wait. Wait until you're ready.*

"You're not being smart about this, Kevin," Anya insisted. "Killing exos has never done us any good, and now it's plain dumb. The exos would fight the Rii if they could. They could actually help us."

Kevin helped to unstack the doctor's crates and open them up. "You're such a *kid*, Anya." He didn't sound angry, simply disappointed. "Getting a schoolgirl crush on a stripe, being star-struck by Saul's speeches—it's embarrassing, you know that? I'm so used to looking out for you that I've been making excuses for your bad choices, but I'm done with that now. You've got to stop screwing around and *grow up*."

Kevin swept the contents of Nakada's desk into a box. He turned, put his hands on the armrests of the chair, and loomed over Anya. "We don't need exos. We *never* have. In fact, I thank these new shrooms for finally bringing the war we've needed for a long time. The marked people who chose to side with the aliens over their own kind—they've spent the last hundred years counting on peace, on the shrooms taking care of them, all while enjoying the perks that come from keeping the rest of us in line. They're going to be the first ones to go. They made their bed and now they've got to lie in it. It's *justice*, long overdue."

Anya lifted her chin. "I don't believe it has to be that way."

"It does." Kevin touched the vial in his pocket. "After the shroom pets are gone, we'll still be here, those of us who know how to hide and fight and survive. We've been doing it all this time, and we'll only get better at it. People are *flocking* to the cause, Anya. We'll train and organize them, and we'll take back our planet from the aliens—doesn't matter which ones."

"You're insane," Donovan said.

Kevin ignored him. "You know that when things go south, you've got a better chance with me than with anyone else. A better chance than with Saul. Who taught you to drive? To shoot? Who got the meds your mom needed when no one else could? Who got us through those three weeks in Boise?" Kevin put his hands on the sides of Anya's arms and gave her a slight shake. "This week was just the beginning; things are going to get worse. Anyone who plans to survive had better be with people they can count on." Kevin leaned in closer to Anya; his harsh voice softened. "We're practically family, Anya. Deep down, you know that, don't you?"

Anya dropped her gaze and slowly nodded, her eyes swimming. Donovan's heart seemed to seize. "You're *not* her family." Rage made it difficult for him to speak coherently. "You're a predator. A psychopath." But even as he flung the words, he could tell Anya wasn't listening. *Everyone's got something decent about them, deep down.* That's what Anya believed. It was why she'd trusted Donovan—but it was also why, no matter what, she stuck by Kevin Warde.

You do whatever you have to do to look after yourself. She'd said that too.

At the lab bench, Dr. Nakada's hands shook as he covered each of his petri dish samples and placed them, one by one, inside an insulated container. Donovan had lost all hope of trying to catch the doctor's eye or sway his sympathies. Nakada latched the first two crates and wheeled them hurriedly out the door, as if he couldn't leave the room fast enough.

Kevin brushed Anya's hair back and put his mouth near her ear, whispering things Donovan couldn't hear. Donovan jerked against the handcuffs, rattling them against the metal table leg. "Anya, don't listen to him." The fury coursing hard through his veins cleared his head completely. "Kevin! You and your trigger-happy gang of thugs, you've *no* idea how deluded you are."

Kevin turned around, his eyes slitted. He walked toward Donovan and crouched in front of him, well out of reach. "You're one of my biggest regrets from last year, stripe. You were the one that got away from me." Kevin pulled out the vial of orange liquid and wagged it with anticipation. "Life rarely gives us second chances. You were about to make yourself useful to science earlier. No reason why that can't still be the case."

Donovan stared the man down. "Killing me won't change a thing. It'll make you feel smug for a few days, but that's it. Even if your weapon works, the Rii will conquer Earth, and you don't have a clue what you're up against." Donovan shifted as if trying to alleviate the pressure of the handcuffs on his wrists, while sliding himself into a more mobile position. *Get him angry. Get him closer.* "That's the problem with you, Kevin. You confuse killing your enemies with actual victory. Brett scored a *real* victory. He fooled you and led SecPac to destroy the Warren. All you could do was torture and kill him, but he'd already beaten you."

That hit a nerve. Kevin's expression turned venomous.

Donovan plowed into the opportunity. "Go ahead, break open that test tube. Be sure to get the whole thing on video and play it to yourself at night to get off on what a big-time exo-killing patriot you are." He was on a roll now. "Maybe you'll even convince yourself that you're half the Sapience leader that Saul is. At least *he's* an opponent I can respect."

Kevin started up, murder dancing in his eyes. Donovan readied himself. This was some surreal replay of a nightmare he'd been in before: He was a captive about to die. But this time he felt no terror, only determined hatred. If he could wrap his legs around the man and pull him forward . . .

Kevin didn't come a step closer. "Soon." The word was a promise. "I'll have the others wait outside and we'll have our time together. Not as much time as I'd like, but believe me, I'm going to enjoy every second of it."

"Don't move, Kevin," Anya said. "Or I'll shoot."

Kevin turned around. Surprise and fear leapt into Donovan's chest in a double beat. Anya had opened the desk drawer and taken out Dr. Nakada's revolver. She stood pointing it at Kevin's chest. "I'm not going to let you kill him." Her voice wavered, but her thumb pressed down firmly on the hammer, cocking it. "Put that vial on the desk, and your gun too."

"Don't be ridiculous." Kevin's voice was calm but furious. "Put the gun down, Anya. Does this stripe really mean that much to you?"

Anya was breathing hard. "Just do what I said, Kevin."

Kevin's mouth twisted. He walked toward Anya, his hands open and at his sides. "Do it, then. Me or him. Make your choice."

"Anya, shoot him!" Donovan cried. He lunged but the fixed table didn't move an inch. "Don't let him take the gun from you. *Shoot him.*"

"Is he worth it? Worth betraying me, and the cause, and all of humankind? Worth ruining your own chances?" Kevin advanced until he was within six feet of Anya's outstretched gun hand. "You think he cares about you more than I do?"

"I do." Donovan's voice was a helpless whisper. "Anya."

Anya's gun hand trembled. The barrel drifted downward, and Anya's eyes overflowed with tears of frustration. Kevin reached out and put his hand on the gun. Gently, he lifted it from Anya's unresisting hands. Putting a thumb between the hammer and the frame, he carefully de-cocked the revolver, then opened the cylinder and removed the ammunition. Donovan felt the sense of momentary hope die, whimpering in his chest, as Kevin tucked the empty weapon into his waistband. Anya hugged herself, her downcast eyes full of shame.

Kevin's hand shot out and grabbed her around the throat, pulling her forward. Anya gasped. "If you ever do that again," Kevin snarled, "I'll kill you." He released Anya roughly and turned his back on her.

The next second, Kevin jerked. His eyes and mouth flew open, and a sharp yell of surprise and pain escaped him as he rose onto his toes and then toppled forward like a statue, twitching and spasming as he went. His forehead smashed hard into the edge of the metal table that Donovan was handcuffed to, dislodging his ball cap, and he collapsed to the ground. Anya stepped over him and jabbed him in the back again with the short black object in her hand, and Kevin's body jumped on the floor, limbs beating against the ground as electric current poured through him. Kevin's eyes rolled back in their sockets. His legs gave a few last involuntary jerks before he fell limp.

Anya dropped to her knees and began rummaging frantically in the front pocket of Kevin's pants. She pulled out a set of keys and hurried over to Donovan, her fingers fumbling as she found the thin handcuff key and fitted it to his restraints.

Donovan stared, speechless at what she'd done.

"What?" She paused just long enough to look down into his bruised face. A quick, scoffing expression puckered her mouth. "It's funny how no one ever sees that coming."

The key turned in the handcuffs and they opened. Donovan yanked the metal from his wrists and without wasting a second, scrambled over to Kevin's prone form. He pulled the man's hands together behind his back. "You have no idea how long I've been wanting to do this." Donovan slapped the handcuffs over Kevin's wrists, ratcheting them tight. "By authority of the Global Security and Pacification Forces, I charge you with being Earth's biggest asshole."

He rolled Kevin over onto his back and patted him down, taking the handgun from his waistband, the empty revolver, the smaller, second gun from his shoulder holster, and the sheathed knife clipped to the man's belt. Carefully, he removed the vial of nerve agent from Kevin's vest pocket, breathing a sigh of relief that the tube hadn't broken in Kevin's fall.

Anya touched him on the arm and he looked up. Dr. Nakada stood in the doorway, looking down at them, his thin face frozen in surprise.

Donovan got to his feet. "Javid will be back soon, possibly with more members from the Sapience cell," he said. "We have to leave. Now."

26

Anya ran outside and pulled the truck as close as possible to the entrance of the Biological Sciences Building. Donovan found a roll of duct tape, bound Kevin's ankles and knees together tightly, slapped a strip of tape over his mouth, and dragged the man down the hall to the elevator.

"Maybe we should just leave him," Dr. Nakada suggested.

"No way," Donovan panted, hauling Kevin along by the arm-pits and wincing from all the wounds that made physical exertion difficult. Nakada was right; leaving Warde behind would speed their escape, but Donovan would be damned if he was going to let the man ever roam free again. "It's hard enough for me to not kill him right now. I'm not taking any chances."

He maneuvered Kevin into the elevator and rested against the wall as the slow contraption climbed up to the ground floor and let them out. Dr. Nakada went out first and stacked the two crates he was carrying next to the ones he'd brought out earlier and left by the door in preparation for departing with Kevin and Javid. Donovan side-eyed the doctor with disgust. A few hours ago, Nakada had been willing to help him try to save exo lives. Then Kevin had shown up, and the scientist had submissively handed over a weapon to take those same lives. He operated on the bodies of people he knew Kevin had murdered, and he would've stood by and let Donovan become the next of those victims. Nakada was a coward.

Anya was already waiting by the pickup. Donovan hefted the bound and gagged Kevin into the truck bed, taking pains not to be gentle about it. Kevin was already stirring, his forehead a swollen shade of purple where it had struck the lab table. Donovan dropped the truck bed cover and latched it.

They loaded Nakada's crates into the rear of the cab. There was barely enough room for the three of them on the front bench. "You'd better drive," Anya said, handing Donovan the keys. "I can squeeze into the middle between the two of you."

Donovan climbed into the driver's seat. He studied the steering wheel and dashboard uncertainly. Anya gave him an incredulous look. "Don't tell me you don't know how to drive a regular car."

"I've driven petroleum burners before." It was the sort of thing everyone learned in training, then filed away as a skill unlikely to ever be needed. Donovan put the truck's key into the ignition and turned it. To his surprise, it came to life on the first try with a deep grumble.

"Hey, it likes you," Anya said.

Donovan took the truck out of park and touched his foot to the gas. It didn't move at first; then it jerked like a whipped ox, throwing them all forward. Anya gripped the dash. "It's a little temperamental."

"No kidding." Donovan relaxed his grip on the wheel and eased the vehicle forward. Erze almighty, he'd handled SecPac skimmercars in high-speed chases before. This rusty machine only moved in two directions, and not very quickly; how hard could it be in comparison?

"Where are we going?" Dr. Nakada asked, sounding as nervous as a hitchhiker who wasn't sure he'd made the right decision.

"Let's get off this campus and away from the sapes first." Donovan glanced over at Nakada. The metal box containing the vials of deadly chemicals was braced between the doctor's feet on the floor of the passenger-side front seat. There was nowhere more secure to put them. Donovan was eager to leave quickly but decided he would drive as slowly and smoothly as possible. The nerve agent might be harmless to Anya and the doctor, but if a vial of the stuff broke while Donovan was at the wheel, they were all dead.

"Oh no." Anya grabbed Donovan's arm and pointed out the window. A white SUV had just pulled into the parking lot. Behind the wheel of the SUV, Javid spotted them going in the opposite direction and slammed on his brakes. His face contorted in near-comical disbelief. For a second, Donovan felt an almost near irresistible urge to grin at him.

Then the door of the vehicle flew open and Javid jumped out, drawing his gun and opening fire. A bullet cracked the upper left-hand corner of the truck's windshield. Donovan's resolution to drive with extreme caution flew out the window. He floored the gas, clutched the wheel, and roared the truck through the lot toward the street. "Get down!"

Anya covered her head with her arms as she ducked below the dashboard. Dr. Nakada moaned and clutched the door handle. Gritting his teeth, Donovan barreled the truck toward Javid. The man's eyes widened, but he stood his ground and fired again. Another shot punched through the driver's side of the windshield. Donovan flinched as the bullet passed inches from his head. Hurling curses, Javid leapt out of the way, firing once more into the side of the truck as it careened past him.

Donovan took a sharp turn onto the main road, concentrating

on driving the rickety contraption while glancing behind them. Javid was on his feet and running, but in another second he was out of sight.

"Oh God," Anya cried. "Stop, *stop*. He's been *shot*."

Donovan glanced over and sucked in a breath. Dr. Nakada was slumped against the far door, clutching his stomach, his face sallow with pain and surprise. Blood soaked through his shirt and coated his hands and lap. Anya was wedged near the floor of the truck, trying frantically to scrabble for something under the seat. *"Pull over!* He needs help."

"We need to get off this road first." Otherwise, Javid and the Sapience cell members would spot them easily. Donovan sped away from the campus, down a commercial street, turned behind what looked like a warehouse, and rattled the truck to a stop. He slammed the gear shift into park and jumped out, then ran around to the other side of the vehicle and pulled the passenger door open, catching Nakada as the man slid partway out.

Anya, her hair mussed, her shirt and hands red with the doctor's blood, pulled an emergency first aid kit from beneath the seat. She pressed gauze padding to Nakada's stomach, applying pressure to the wound. The pads were soaked through almost at once. The cracked leather seat of the truck was slick. Nakada moaned in pain and fixed Donovan with the most pitiful expression. "I'm sorry," he whimpered. "I've caused nothing but harm."

Donovan held the man's frightened gaze and spoke with convincing insistency. "There'll be time to change that." With bladed fingers, Donovan tore the sleeves off his own shirt. He wadded one piece of fabric into a tight square and tied it over the bullet wound, securing the makeshift bandage in place by wrapping around

Nakada's waist with additional strips of fabric ripped from his other sleeve.

"We need to get him to a hospital." Anya continued applying pressure as Donovan yanked the final knot tight, eliciting another moan.

"The local hospital is one of the first places Javid will look." By now, Javid would've run back into the basement lab to search for Kevin, and finding him missing, he would've gone to the Sapience cell to sound the alarm. People would be searching for them all over town and the call would be spreading nationwide through the network of Sapience sympathizers. Every second of delay was one they couldn't afford.

Anya opened her mouth as if to argue, then closed it and nodded. "You're right. Every hospital's overloaded and there'll be sympathizers on staff who'd tip off Javid." She gnawed on her bottom lip, her voice strained. "Where, then?"

Donovan eased Nakada back into the passenger seat, making up his mind. "The Round. We have the best hospital anywhere in the country." More important, the Round was the one place Sapience could not follow. Eugene Nakada, bleeding out from the gut in an old pickup truck, held knowledge of the exocel inhibition reflex as well as the recipe for Sapience's chemical weapons. His life was a planetary security issue.

Muffled sounds and banging issued from the truck bed. Kevin was conscious again and very angry. Donovan opened the drop gate and lifted the cover. Kevin was lying on his side, dirty and bruised from being tossed around by the rough ride. At the sight of Donovan, his eyes lit with a hatred that promised every form of slow and horrible torment if their positions were ever reversed.

Donovan hopped up next to him. "This is for Jonathan Resnick," he said, and punched Kevin straight in the jaw, knocking him out cold again.

Donovan slammed the drop gate, locked the flat cover, and jumped back into the driver's seat. His comm unit vibrated again and he glanced down at it long enough to see the priority message from Commander Tate: *YOU ARE AWOL. REPORT IMMEDIATELY.*

With Anya still wedged between him and the half-conscious Dr. Nakada, Donovan turned onto I-80 and gunned it for the Ring Belt.

"The Round is over two hours away," Anya said.

"Stomach wounds don't kill quickly. We'll make it." If this petroleum burner didn't fail on them and if Sapience didn't find them before they got there. The ride was silent and anxious. The sound of wind whistling through the bullet holes in the windshield overlaid the rattling of the truck and the frequent whimpers of pain from Dr. Nakada.

When they were about halfway there, Anya said, "Javid might have people watching for us already. It'll take longer, but we should circle the Belt. Come in from the south end instead of the west."

Donovan nodded. He'd already been mentally mapping a non-intuitive way through the Belt that would take them to the SecPac underground entrance. "Anya, you can't come into the Round."

"I know. You'll have to let me out once we're in the Belt. It'll be too dangerous for you to go back to the SRP in Buildertown. Just let me out anywhere. I'll find my way back. You have to save Eugene."

"What if Javid or other True Sapience come after you?"

Anya's eyebrows drew together pensively as she rubbed at the dried blood on her hands. "Minh will keep me safe. So will Saul." She raised her head and stared out the window. "Kevin had a lot of friends, but . . . there're also a lot of people who'll be glad to see him gone."

The buildings of the Ring Belt started to come into view long before the Round did. Donovan did as Anya had suggested, veering onto a secondary highway that took them on a route that added another twenty minutes to their already long drive before they entered the industrial area near SecPac's unmarked compound. "Anywhere here," Anya said.

Donovan pulled up to a bus stop. As he let Anya out of the truck, he retrieved the envelope of Dr. Ghosh's memory discs and put it in her hands. "Give this to Saul. Explain everything. If the doctor doesn't make it, or if anything happens to me, it won't be lost. Some other scientist and some other exo will do what we couldn't."

Anya nodded and tucked the envelope into the pocket of her shorts. Donovan glanced around the gray cement surroundings. It seemed beyond wrong to simply leave Anya here alone and possibly in danger. She placed a hand on his cheek and turned his face back toward hers. Her gaze was firm, reminding him without words that she'd been staying alive in the bad parts of the Ring Belt for a long time. "Trust me."

Donovan met her eyes and felt his heart clench. "I'm glad I did." He pulled Anya forward and kissed her. He felt as if he were stealing something, one last bite from an undeserved meal, one last look at something he could not have, and even as their lips met with fierce urgency, he felt with an inexplicable and sad certainty that it would be for the last time. He let her go.

Anya swallowed and dropped her eyes to the concrete. She glanced over at the rear of the truck and her mouth tightened into a pale line of guilt and regret.

"I'll turn him in," Donovan said. "But I won't hurt him."

"What will happen to him?"

Donovan hesitated. "Do you feel like you need to know?"

Anya considered. "No," she said finally. "I made my choice." Without looking back, she turned and walked away, swiftly and purposefully, rounding the corner and disappearing from sight. Donovan held on to the door of the truck, nearly overcome by the urge to go after her, to make sure she got to safety. Again, he remembered wretchedly what she'd said to him the previous night: *You do whatever you have to do. Sometimes that means you have to leave.*

He got back into the truck. The interior stank of blood. "We're almost there, Doctor," Donovan said. "We'll get you patched up."

At first, he thought that Nakada had fallen unconscious, but then the scientist replied, in a weak and tremulous voice, "When you take me into the Round, whether I live or not, I'm not coming out again."

Donovan glanced at the man and kept driving. "No," he agreed.

Nakada nodded, resigned. "You must think I'm a horrible person. You're wondering how Tamaravick could've ever befriended someone like me." Donovan didn't answer. Nakada gave a painful cough and said, "I used to be a different person. A scientist-in-erze. I'm not that person anymore, but I never wanted to kill or hurt anyone. Not even exos."

"Don't talk. You should save your energy."

"I had no choice." Nakada sounded truly plaintive now. "When I left the erze, I had nothing anymore. I depended on Sapience for everything—safety, shelter, supplies, the ability to pursue my research. Kevin kept insisting that I focus on weapons development. I couldn't keep putting him off. You know what he does to people who betray him . . ." Nakada's eyes closed. For several minutes, the cab of the truck was silent save for the man's ragged breathing. "It will be good . . ." he wheezed, "to stop running."

— — —

The guards stationed at the SecPac compound nearly shot them. Seeing an unfamiliar pickup truck heading straight for the barbed wire fence, they raised their rifles and screamed warnings until Donovan stopped the vehicle and got out with his striped hands over his head, shouting back at them that he was a soldier-in-erze.

Then they recognized him from the day before but were understandably bewildered by what had happened to him in such a short period of time. His face was bruised and patchy with thickened panotin, his shirt was torn and bloodstained, and his electricycle had been replaced with a petroleum-burning junker with bullet holes in the windshield, a man trussed up in the back, and another one bleeding all over the front seat.

"The man in the back is Kevin Warde, one of the most wanted terrorists in the country," Donovan told them. "Look him up if you don't believe me. And that's Eugene Nakada, another high-value Sapience fugitive. He's been shot and he's going to die if I don't get him to a secure hospital immediately. I need to get into the Round. Now."

The guards were non-Hardened SecPac reservists whose erze status was only good for five years at a time; Donovan outranked them on account of being both an officer and an exo. They scanned the pickup truck, verified Donovan's identification, then let him into the compound and through the metal doors that led down into the tunnel under the wall.

Donovan's mind was racing as they reached the end of the dim underground passageway. How was he going to get through the Round unnoticed in this exhaust-spewing piece of scrap metal? The fuel gauge on the truck was red and he swore any minute the engine would die. Before he could formulate any good solution, the gate opened, exactly where he'd entered next to the Pen on the SecPac campus the day before.

The truck chugged heroically past the guard box. Donovan's heart skipped a beat. The woman who'd waved him through on the way out was not there. The guard box was empty. Instead, standing at the corner of the road was a zhree with thin, jagged stripes. One of Gur's Soldiers.

The Soldier waved Donovan to a stop. He walked up to the strange machine, tapped the hood curiously, and motioned Donovan out of the vehicle. Donovan got out, an explanation forming on his lips.

"Humans are no longer allowed in this area," the Soldier said brusquely. "They're to remain in designated areas in the Round."

"I . . . didn't know that, zun. I just returned from the Ring Belt, and need to . . ." *I need to speak with someone who understands what I'm saying.* It was obvious the Soldier did not understand a word of English, and he didn't have a translation machine with him. He eyed the human with wary distaste, as if Donovan were an animal making unusual noises.

Humans confined to designated areas? What in all erze was

going on? There had never been any restrictions on human move-ment within the Round. Everyone here was marked; that was the whole point. "Zun, let me through. It's important." Donovan pointed to himself, to the truck, and then in the direction of the main road beyond SecPac campus.

The Soldier slashed a negative with his fins. "By Kreet, I'm tired of seeing Werth's creatures prowling around with no restraint." The Soldier banged the side of the truck with one of his limbs. "Leave the way you came."

Donovan shook his head vehemently. He had *not* come this far to be foiled by an ignorant homeworlder. He couldn't turn around and go back into the Ring Belt or Nakada would die. If he dis-obeyed and tried to fight, the Soldier would overpower him in seconds. As he stood, fists clenched, trying to think of a way out of his predicament, the Soldier made an impatient noise, clamped his pincers around the back of Donovan's neck, and steered him toward the cab of the truck like a puppy.

Donovan braced both his hands on the sides of the truck door and refused to get in. "Scorching idiot shroom," he exclaimed. "Get your damn pincers off me. Why won't you even bother to try and *listen*?" His armor gave an uncertain shudder. "Wylt," Donovan blurted.

Gur's Soldier gave him a hard shove that nearly banged his head against the doorframe. "Wylt," Donovan shouted again in inspired desperation, then whistled a short, high note with a trembling, ris-ing finish—as close as he could manage to pronouncing Wylt's name in Mur. The Soldier hesitated. "Are you trying to say something?"

Donovan took one hand off the truck and made a short down-ward stroke with his fingers held flat together as he repeated himself. Words only made sense in Mur with their associated fin movements and pattern, and he wasn't optimistic he was getting through with his unavoidably human butchering of the name. Nevertheless, the Soldier was puzzled. He released Donovan. "Bag? Crater? What?" Donovan spun around, shook his head in frustration, and tried again. This time, he moved both his hands, then pointed to the stripes on the back of them.

"A Soldier of your erze," the zhree deduced. "Wiln? Wylt?"

Donovan nodded vigorously and dipped his hands in a gesture of fins indicating assent. The Soldier's fins perked up in self-satisfaction at the success of their arduous attempt at communication. Then they flattened again in skepticism. "You belong to Soldier Wylt?"

Donovan hesitated, offended, then dipped his hands again. "Sure, yeah, fine. Whatever you need to believe, you dumbass homeworlder. Just call Wylt."

The zhree seemed to wage an internal debate. He still looked as if he would like to forcibly eject Donovan from the Round, but perhaps he was under orders to make nice with the colonial Soldiers. Reluctantly, he lifted one of his limbs to eye height and tapped the communication device strapped just above his foot plate. "Soldier Wylt, are you missing any humans? I found one near the encampment and it appears to be asking for you."

"I don't know what you're—" Wylt's voice came through the device as a string of musical notes and flashing light and dark patterns on a small display screen. Before it could finish, Donovan shouted in a rush, "Zun Wylt, it's me, Donovan. Please, I need your help. I'm on the SecPac campus. This homeworlder won't let me go and doesn't understand a thing I'm saying."

There was silence from the other end. "Wylt?" Gur's Soldier prodded.

"Stay there," Wylt said. "I'll come retrieve him."

The next several minutes passed in an agony of delay for Donovan. The Soldier detaining him stood patient and unmoving, as the zhree were wont to do, but Donovan paced near the truck like a captive animal. It seemed Gur's Soldier had been correct; all humans had been moved elsewhere because Donovan could see none of his fellow stripes, only Soldiers. The Round was more disconcertingly quiet than ever, but when Donovan looked up he saw an odd sight: more than a dozen ships—construction paverships, he guessed from the shape of them—taking off from the landing fields near the Towers and speeding across the sky in different directions.

Dr. Nakada lay stretched, apparently unconscious, on the front seat of the vehicle, his breathing growing more and more labored with each second.

Wylt arrived on foot in a rotating, multi-limbed lope, his fins fanning slightly from exertion. He stopped rather abruptly at the sight of Donovan, the truck, and Gur's subordinate, who accosted him at once.

"All humans ought to be appropriately confined by now." The foreign Soldier's tone made it clear he resented being inconvenienced.

"They . . . yes . . ." Wylt fixed two yellow eyes on Donovan, bewildered. "Clearly, there are a few stragglers coming in from outside the Round. Not to worry; I'll take care of it from here, zun Grier."

"Do so," rebuked the other Soldier with a fin flick of disdain.

Once the other zhree had departed down the road and was out of earshot, Wylt said, "Donovan, what in the Highest State of Erze are you doing here? Why aren't you with the other soldiers-in-erze?"

"I was in the Ring Belt, zun." Donovan hurried over to the back of the truck and opened it. Wylt's fins shot up in surprise at the sight of Kevin, tied up and just beginning to stir again. "He's a criminal, zun Wylt, one of the world's most dangerous humans. He's killed dozens of people, and this"—he took the metal box from the floor of the cab and handed it carefully to Wylt—"contains a chemical weapon he was planning to use to kill countless more."

"How did you—" Wylt's gaze fell on Dr. Nakada. "Who's that other human you have with you? He appears to be gravely injured."

"He's a former scientist-in-erze with an awful lot of valuable information. It's hard to explain. And yes, he's going to die unless he gets medical help right away." Donovan took off his comm unit, enabled location tracking, and sent a single message to Commander Tate: *I HAVE SOMETHING FOR YOU.* Then he tossed the comm unit onto the front seat of the truck.

Donovan turned to Wylt and dropped his armor in entreating obeisance. "Zun, I need to get this man to the hospital. Commander Tate and SecPac officers will be here soon. Can you make sure that this man and those vials get safely into their hands? Please."

Wylt regarded him suspiciously. "You're up to something." The certainty in the Soldier's voice made Donovan go completely still. He'd asked for Wylt in order to get free of Grier, but this might end the same way. If a zhree of his own erze decided to detain him, there was nothing he could do.

Wylt said flatly, "Do you know what you're doing?"

300

"About as much as I did when I walked into that algae farm."

Wylt didn't move at first. Then he dipped one fin in a curt nod. "Take a skimmercar from the garage, but stay off the spoke roads and don't let any more of Gur's Soldiers catch you out of bounds."

— — —

Donovan sprinted across the SecPac campus. He was sweaty and breathing hard by the time he got to the Comm Hub building, but thankfully, he wasn't accosted by anyone else along the way. Several skimmercars were parked in the building's hangar-sized garage. There was no human or zhree in sight. As relieved as he was, the sight struck Donovan as unusual; where *was* everyone? SecPac's campus was weirdly empty, even of Soldiers. The large field had been a crowded zhree military camp just a few days ago; now it looked as if it had been partially taken down and held less than a quarter of the troops that it did before.

Donovan took one of SecPac's unmarked skimmercars and drove it back to where Wylt waited with the pickup truck. "Come on, Doctor." Panting, Donovan heaved the unconscious man from the truck. To his surprise, Wylt came to his aid, picking Nakada up easily and placing him inside the skimmercar. Donovan was reminded that it had been only two days ago that he and Wylt had worked side by side, collecting the dead from around the Towers. Perhaps the Soldier felt as if he'd seen enough dead humans lately because his fins moved in a grimace as he looked down at Nakada's unresponsive form. "It appears as if you'd better hurry."

Donovan dropped his armor again in thanks, then got into the car and sped away from SecPac property. He did as Wylt had instructed, veering away from the main roads and taking a circuitous route through the Round to reach the hospital that had recently become far too familiar. When he reached it, he pulled up to the emergency room entrance and leapt out.

Hospital staff hurried over when he staggered into the lobby with Dr. Nakada in his arms. Nakada was taken from him and placed on a stretcher. Medics surrounded them and called out vital signs: the scientist was breathing, but his pulse was weak and his blood pressure was dangerously low. A minute later, the stretcher was rushed down the hall and Donovan was alone.

Everything caught up to him at once. He moved numbly to the nearest chair and fell into it, dropping his head into his hands. Whether Nakada lived or died now was out of his control. He'd done what he could. But it wasn't what he'd hoped for at all. His plan had gone completely, disastrously awry. With a heaviness in his gut, he knew he'd changed nothing.

A hand fell hard on his shoulder, pulling him upright in the chair and turning him around roughly. Donovan looked up and flinched at the sight of Jet's angry face. His partner's voice was a snarl of disbelief.

"Have you *completely* lost your mind?"

27

"You didn't answer me when I comm'ed you about a hundred times. You didn't show up as ordered this morning. Tate declared you AWOL. *Where have you been*? And what the hell happened to you?"

Donovan got to his feet. He could only imagine how he must look—battered, bloodstained, disheveled, his clothing a ragged mess. Jet appeared far from well himself: his face was stubbled and his eyes were so darkly ringed they looked bruised. Donovan winced with shame, though after their hurtful parting yesterday he was almost relieved his partner even cared enough to look so murderous.

All he could manage to say was, "How did you know I was here?"

"I didn't. You sent me Ghosh's research files without any explanation, so I came to show them to Therrid. He told me what you asked him to do."

"He *refused*. Just like Soldier Werth."

"So you left the Round." Jet's lips were pulled back. "You went to *her*, didn't you? To the sapes."

"I found Eugene Nakada."

"Of course you did." Jet's tone was acidic. "We've been hunting the traitor for nearly a year and you suddenly manage to find him in one day."

"I did it by getting beaten up and nearly shot in the face outside a Sapience hideout, Jet. The only way I could get their cooperation was to explain everything—Soldier Gur, the Rii, the evacuation, *everything*." Donovan gripped his partner's arm insistently. "Nakada says he can do it. He can use Ghosh's research to disable the trip wire on human exocels. *That's* what we need—not a zhree plan to evacuate one percent of humans, but something that'll even the odds for the ninety-nine percent left on Earth."

Jet stared at him. "So where's Nakada?"

Donovan let go of Jet's arm. "In an operating room. He got shot in the stomach. Kevin Warde and one of his pals showed up, and . . . it's a long story."

Jet ran an agitated hand through his hair. "You have to stop this. What you're doing will screw up everything and get you killed." Jet seized Donovan by the elbow. "You have to come with me, right now. I'll explain along the—"

The distinctive sound of zhree footsteps on hard flooring made Jet stop in mid-motion. Nurse Therrid came hurrying across the lobby and skidded to a sudden halt, fins fanning. "*Donovan*? What are you doing here?"

Jet took a step back from Donovan but didn't take his eyes off him. "Zun Therrid, my partner is out of erze. He disobeyed orders and left the Round to reveal sensitive information to Sapience terrorists. I'm under orders from Commander Tate to detain him and inform her as soon as he's found—for the security of the erze as well as his own safety."

Donovan's stomach plummeted. He stared at Jet in betrayal.

Nurse Therrid's yellow eyes were wide. He clamped a set of pincers firmly around Donovan's arm. In as stern and commanding a voice as Donovan had ever heard from him, he said, "Come with me. Both of you."

Jet followed behind as Therrid steered Donovan across the lobby of the emergency room. The place no longer looked like a military infirmary. The injured soldiers-in-erze were gone, the chairs back in their usual place. A few non-Hardened patients watched as they passed. Therrid led them down a hallway.

"Where are you taking me?" Donovan demanded.

The Nurse opened a door into an extremely plain room, with a simple bed and a small window. Donovan suspected it was used to house psychiatric patients. "Vercingetorix," Therrid said, "do you have a set of restraints?"

Jet's dark eyes were apologetic but unflinching as he pulled a pair of handcuffs from his duty belt and handed them over to Nurse Therrid without a word.

"Zun Therrid," Donovan pleaded. "Wait—"

"I'm sorry to have to do this." Therrid fastened one of the cuffs to the railing of the bed, then seized Jet's arm and slapped the other over his wrist.

Jet was too stunned to react at first. In an instant, another two of Therrid's limbs snatched Jet's comm unit, gun, and keys from his belt. The Nurse stepped away at once, pushing Donovan back toward the door.

Jet yanked on the handcuffs, ringing metal against metal. "What the—" Understanding and fury lit across his face as armor raced over his arms. "Therrid, what are you doing?" Jet tried to follow them, wrenching against the restraints so violently that on a non-Hardened person the force would've broken the wrist. Donovan was so taken aback he jerked and nearly went to Jet's aid. Nurse Therrid tugged him from the room.

"Your commitment to duty is admirable, Vercingetorix. I couldn't ask you to disobey orders, but I'm afraid I can't have you interfering or informing anyone," Therrid strummed regretfully. "Please don't hurt yourself, hatchling."

"You double-crossing shroom," Jet shouted. "Donovan! Don't do this!" His voice cracked in rising desperation. "I can't . . . not *both* of them . . ."

Therrid shut the door behind them. It locked with a click, muffling Jet's howl of frustration. Donovan's heart was hammering. He stared at Therrid in disbelief. "Hurry," the Nurse said, and took off down the hall. Donovan cast a final look at the room with his now-imprisoned partner, then raced after Therrid.

There was a trainee nurse-in-erze, no older than fourteen or fifteen, tidying up the operating room when they burst in. "Find Sanjay and send him here," Therrid ordered, and the girl dropped her armor and obeyed at once, running out of the room. With two limbs, the Nurse began positioning a machine that looked like a laser beam emitter while a third limb tapped the controls on the table's medical scanning arm. "Thank all erze the equipment and supplies I requested arrived this morning," Therrid muttered in a hum. "Too late for poor Tamaravick and so many others, but at least I now have a proper, if limited, medical facility to work with. Lie back, Donovan."

Still speechless, Donovan lay down on the table. Therrid grasped his left arm and pressed a small device to one of the nodes just above his elbow. A stinging sensation spread down Donovan's limb and his exocel fell away from the joint down. "With your injuries, any amount of exocel suppressant is inadvisable right now, but local suppression shouldn't be too risky." Therrid slid a needle into the vein on the inside of Donovan's left unarmored elbow, then reached across the table with another limb and took Donovan's right hand.

"Armor your fingers and squeeze," Therrid said. "Do your best to hurt me. Once the exocel inhibition reflex is triggered, the nanotracer I injected will pinpoint the neuronal circuit so the radiosurgical beams can triangulate on it."

Donovan said, "You can cut the connection with radiation beams?"

"It's a crude approach, but it's the best I can do without access to the full suite of nanosurgical equipment in the Towers. I believe it'll still work."

"Dr. Nakada was going to insert an electrode into my brain."

"A *what*?" Nurse Therrid looked aghast; he let out a soft, mortified whistle, his fins shuddering and seeming to shrink into his body. "Highest State of Erze, you were going to let a *human* open your *skull*?"

Sanjay came into the room, and Donovan was saved from answering. Therrid directed his nurse-in-erze to lock the door and start monitoring the medical scanner over Donovan's head, which was beginning to blink images on the screen. At Therrid's prompting, Donovan serrated the fingers of his right hand and imagined ripping off Soldier Gur's fins.

Nurse Therrid gave a stifled trill of discomfort as Donovan's grip crushed down, armor on armor. Donovan's exocel wavered and began to fall. "That's sufficient," Therrid said, wincing. He looked at the scans, then consulted a computing disc held up to one eye by another limb. "The scientist-in-erze Vincent Ghosh was remarkably accurate in his conclusions."

Sanjay injected him with a sedative and in seconds Donovan felt it kicking in, putting him pleasantly at ease. He held on to the Nurse's pincers. "You wouldn't help me before, zun Therrid. Why are you helping me now?"

Nurse Therrid paused. Two of his eyes focused on Donovan for a long moment. Then he hummed a sigh, his fins sinking slightly. "The last time I refused to listen to you and tried to keep you safe from the algae farm standoff, you circumvented me and acted anyway. I should have reported you, but . . . what you did was heroic, Donovan. You were disobedient, but you saved zhree and human lives. I've been reminded lately that humans have social values and dynamics that are different from ours. It's what makes you such a fascinating species, and perhaps I . . . should have paid attention to what you were saying."

Therrid shut the eyes facing Donovan and focused his gaze elsewhere, his voice shifting as his fin movements turned stiff. "I've been grieving every exo whom I couldn't save these past several days, but what you said is true: that number is tiny compared to the millions more who will be left behind to face the Rii after we evacuate. I can't change Homeworld Council decisions, but if you're so determined to do what you believe is right that you would go against all your erze instincts and act alone in the most reckless manner imaginable, then . . . I can do the same. I can give the exos who remain a better chance."

Donovan felt the Nurse's cool touch on his brow, turning his head slightly to the side, and then pressure was applied first to the node at the crown of his head, and then several more in a row down to the nape of his neck. The same stinging sensation spread across his scalp, over the muscles of his face and jaw, dropping all the panotin from his skin. "Lie still. It'll be over soon."

———

Donovan wasn't sure how long the procedure took, but he drifted into a state of half-conscious slumber while the machine over his head whirred and repositioned itself. His eyes grew heavy and fell shut. When he opened them again, the machine was still and silent. Jet was there, staring down at him with an unreadable expression on his face. Donovan blinked. "Jet."

"It's been hard to stand here and not throttle you." Jet's voice was low and without warmth, but the corners of his eyes squeezed down, betraying his relief.

"How did you—" Donovan began.

The fins and domed torso of Nurse Therrid appeared in the periphery of Donovan's vision. "I thought it best to release your erze mate from his confinement before he destroyed the room." Therrid seemed to be keeping a wary distance from Jet. "Considering how angry he was at me, I can now appreciate why the early colonists designed the exocel inhibition reflex to begin with."

"That was a low trick, zun Therrid," Jet growled.

"Having pranks played on me over the years by a pair of mischievous human hatchlings taught me a few useful things," Nurse Therrid replied.

Donovan sat up slowly. He didn't feel particularly different, which was to say, he still felt like crap—bruised and exhausted. He put a hand to the back of his head. His nodes were still numb. "Well? Did it work?"

"The scans look fine, but we won't know for sure until the exocel suppressant wears off, which shouldn't take long." Therrid helped Donovan to his feet. Jet hopped onto the table Donovan had vacated.

"Vercingetorix . . . we ought to wait to be certain."

Jet shook his head, his mouth set. "We don't have time for that. I'll take the same chance D did. Just get it done so I can get him out of here."

"Jet, what are you *doing*?" Donovan felt as if his thoughts were moving sluggishly through soup. "I made the decision to go out of erze on this, but there's no reason for you to do the same. You'd lose your evacuation spot."

"We're not evacuating," Jet said.

"Vic wanted you to go. You can use the family allowance to try to save your mom. I took this risk on my own because I didn't want to drag you—"

"You're not listening." Jet jumped back off the table and seized Donovan by the front of the shirt. "*We're not evacuating.* I was trying to tell you that earlier." Jet released him roughly. "Yesterday, while you were running around on your lunatic scheme instead of being where you belonged, the rest of us reported to Central Command. We were supposed to receive further evacuation instructions, but Commander Tate refused them. She announced that she's countermanding Soldier Gur's orders. We took a stand together, just like you said we ought to. None of the soldiers-in-erze are leaving. Tate's been in secret communication with the

SecPac commanders in all the other Rounds and they're standing together on this. We're *all* out of erze now."

Donovan stared at Jet. "What changed Commander Tate's mind?"

"What changed all of our minds, I suppose. The Hunters attacking and occupying the Towers, losing our people because of this handicap in our brains, Gur ordering the healthy exos to abandon the injured ones." Jet let out a tight breath. "Commander Tate said it straight up yesterday: for the first time, our erze duty is different—and more important—than erze orders."

Donovan strived to process this. "So . . . what happened?"

"Soldier Gur's scorching mad. Soldiers-in-erze make up over a third of the exos he was planning to have on that ship by the end of the week and we messed up his plans completely. There isn't time for him to redo the whole selection process, and if he delays, he's going to have to explain it to the High Speaker."

Donovan glanced at Therrid; no wonder the Nurse had had a change of heart about tampering with the neural fail-safe. Gur's evacuation plan was falling apart. *Every* exo was now at risk. "Is that why I didn't see anyone on the SecPac campus? Why humans are restricted to certain parts of the Round?"

"Yeah." Jet grimaced. "Gur's blaming Soldier Werth for this. He says the erze hasn't conditioned and disciplined us properly. We're being confined to three human neighborhoods so Gur's Soldiers can keep tabs on us. The zhree zun are meeting right now, deciding what to do."

Nurse Therrid handed Donovan a screen with an inserted data storage stick. "That contains Ghosh's original research, appended with all the details of the procedure I performed on you. I've converted it off my computing disc into formats that can be translated into human text, including instructions that any competent human medical expert should be able to follow." The Nurse's opaque eyes were somber. He clasped Donovan's hand in his pincers tightly. "I've sent Sanjay to gather some supplies for you both. Vercingetorix is right—you need to leave the Round right away, and for good. Take refuge with other humans and keep this information safe until all the Soldiers have left."

Perhaps the sedatives were lingering in Donovan's blood, or he simply hadn't given enough thought as to what would happen after he accomplished his goal, because he felt as if he was struggling to catch up to Jet and Therrid. "Leave the Round? Why?"

Jet was pacing, but he stopped to stare at Donovan in disbelief. "Did you hear anything I just said? Gur is already furious that humans are defying the homeworld's agenda and he's holding Soldier Werth accountable. You just broke the pact that the Mur colonists have had with Kreet for a hundred years. How do you think that'll go over right now?" A muscle twitched in Jet's cheek. "What do you think is going to happen if they catch you?"

Donovan put a hand out to steady himself against a wall. Oath and erze, Jet was right. His actions were going to bring down consequences on many others besides himself. "What about you, zun Therrid?" he asked in alarm. "What will happen to you, once they find out what you've done?"

Therrid was repositioning the scanner and checking the calibrations on the radiosurgery machine. "Don't worry about me, hatchling," he said, but his voice sounded forced and his armor thickened heavily over the swirling markings on his hull.

A sound out in the hallway: the rapid beat of zhree footsteps.

Therrid's fins shot up and he froze in mid-motion. "You have to get out of here, now." He grabbed Jet's arm with one limb and Donovan with another, pulling them both toward the door and throwing it open. Therrid skidded to a halt and backpedaled with a whistled profanity. From the hall, three Soldiers with Gur's markings advanced into the room.

Commander Tate strode up between them, her expression deeply pained. "Reyes, what have you done?"

The sight of the armed and battle-armored foreign Soldiers woke Donovan's exocel like a shock. Panotin sprang over his body with almost painful abruptness. Jet too went to full armor, hand twitching for his sidearm.

"Stay where you are!" Commander Tate barked.

"Disarm them," one of the Soldiers said to the others. In seconds, Donovan and Jet were relieved of their duty guns. The Soldiers also took the screen Donovan held in his hand. The lead Soldier had wide fins and one slightly milky eye. He focused his attention on Therrid. "Nurse, explain this," he demanded. "Are you not aware that humans are no longer permitted outside of designated areas?"

All six of Therrid's eyes were fearfully wide, but his fins snapped as he spoke. "These humans needed medical care. Isn't there an exception for that?"

The Soldier on the left—the largest of the three—crossed the room, seized Therrid by his fins, and twisted. The Nurse let out a shrill whistle of pain and his limbs buckled. The Soldier's voice vibrated derisively as he forced the smaller zhree toward the ground. "We didn't travel erze knows how many light-years to this worthless ball of dirt in the middle of nowhere to be condescended to by a *Nurse* from the *colonies*."

Donovan and Jet moved in unison before either of them could

think properly, grabbing the Soldier by the torso and shoving him back violently. The homeworlder let go of Therrid and stumbled backward with a whistle of surprise.

The distinctive *click-buzz* of primed electripulse coils sounded as Gur's Soldiers swung up their weapons. "*NO!*" Commander Tate placed herself between the zhree and their targets, arms held wide, her face livid. "You *dare* fire on soldiers of another erze?"

"You're not Soldiers." The third zhree, a youngster judging from the unblemished smoothness of his hull, had his weapon pointed at Tate's chest.

"We have Soldier's markings. *Another* Soldier's markings." Tate's voice was edged with suppressed fury. The portable translation machine strapped to one of the lead Soldier's limbs relayed her words in Mur.

A moment of considered stalemate; then the wide-finned Soldier in charge grudgingly lowered his weapon and spoke to the others. "It's true; these humans aren't ours to dispense with." Matters of discipline and punishment were always handled within an erze. "We'll bring all of them, including the Nurse, to the zun master. He'll sort it out with the colonials."

"They *attacked* me," protested the large one who'd grabbed Therrid. "So much for the colonials insisting that their creatures aren't dangerous."

"You provoked them! They were only defending me." The stuttering movement of Therrid's injured fins made his voice seem slurred.

"Gorm, look at that one." The youngest Soldier pointed. Only then did Donovan realize that he was the sole human still fully armored. Jet was half-crouched, his hands clenched, but his exocel completely down. Commander Tate's armor wavered precariously as she continued to face down the Soldiers. But Donovan remained in full battle armor, the bladed ridges along his arms continuing to rise warily even as he stood frozen, one arm held extended in front of Therrid, his heart pounding like a fist against the inside of his rib cage.

"Donovan," Nurse Therrid whispered. "It worked."

"Reyes." Tate did not turn her head, but her voice was an icy warning. "Armor down."

Forcing a deep, shaky breath, Donovan lowered his armor. As soon as he did, he felt light-headed. With a burst of adrenaline, he'd pushed his weakened and drugged exocel too quickly and too far and now the skin of his back shivered with cold sweat. But that didn't matter. What mattered was that he'd done it—he'd armored against Soldiers. Despite everything, he shot a look of triumph at Jet. His partner stared back, looking ill with dread.

Soldier Gorm circled around Donovan, fins held flat in suspicion. Then, slowly, Gorm walked around the operating room, examining the machinery and tapping a set of pincers together thoughtfully, his milky eye remaining fixed on the humans.

"How did they find us?" Jet hissed.

"You can thank your partner for that, Mathews," Tate replied over her shoulder, moving her lips very slightly. "I seem to recall that I ordered you to alert me on a secure line as soon as you found him."

"I was prevented from doing so, ma'am."

Tate's eyes followed Gorm around the room as she continued to speak quietly. "Reyes, I'm not even going to begin to guess how you ended up with Kevin Warde and a tray of chemical weapons in a pickup truck, but the 'present' you left for me couldn't hate you more. As soon as we took the tape off his mouth, he was quick to tell us where you were headed. Unfortunately, as you can see, Gur's Soldiers now monitor all my communications and accompany my every move. They knew the second that I did."

Donovan winced. Leave it to Kevin to be the bane of his existence even while bound hand and foot. Soldier Gorm was peering at the screen displaying Donovan's recent brain scans. He picked up Therrid's computing disc and examined its contents, his eyes and fins perfectly still. The slightly milky eye continued staring at Donovan with unsettling interest.

Gorm lowered the computing disc but hung onto it as he strode forward decisively and raised his voice. "Keep your armor down, humans, and move slowly where we tell you. That goes for you as well, Nurse. It's up to Soldier Gur to decide your fate, but if you offer any further resistance along the way, we won't hesitate to harm you."

The large Soldier asked, "What is it, Gorm? What did you find?"

Gorm's pincers jabbed Donovan in the back. "Treason."

29

The inside of the Comm Hub building was barely recognizable. All the furniture was gone. The translucent flex screens newly mounted on the walls displayed star charts and ship rosters and lists too complicated for Donovan to make any sense of. The lobby echoed with the mingling of musical voices and the sound of many armored feet on the hard floor. Gur's Soldiers escorted Commander Tate, Donovan, Jet, and Nurse Therrid inside and the noise fell as dozens of nearby yellow eyes paused to watch them. There didn't seem to be any other humans present. Donovan had been in this building countless times since he'd put on the SecPac uniform, but now he felt like an intruder. He could only imagine what it must be like for Commander Tate, to be led like a prisoner into her own seat of command.

The hall where Tate had presided over hundreds of briefings had been turned into Soldier Gur's chambers. Donovan's guards prodded the group inside, where they stood waiting at the periphery of the room. The chairs that used to be lined up in rows were gone, as was Tate's podium, the wall screen, the water dispenser—all the human things. Now a mobile, semicircular standing workstation, not unlike the one Soldier Werth had in his quarters in the barracks, stood in the corner. More flex screens displaying shifting information covered the walls.

In the center of the room, Soldier Gur was holding a

conference. Half a dozen of his top Soldiers surrounded him. Wedged between two large striped bodies was Administrator Seir, the only zhree from Earth still standing in a position of status. In a ring behind the inner circle stood the rest of the zhree zun, including Soldier Werth, who appeared so motionless he might have been carved from stone. In the third, outermost ring, stood the remaining colonial zhree who'd been allowed to attend—two dozen of Werth's Soldiers, Seir's Administrators, a few Scientists and Engineers. All in all, there were perhaps fifty zhree present. Donovan wondered where the rest of Werth's Soldiers were, until he caught the tail end of the conversation Gur was having with one of his subordinates.

"The majority of the colonial troops have now been transferred to orbital staging areas, zun," said the Soldier. "We're ready to initiate light-plus transfers at your command. The sooner we begin, the better. Morale among the colonial Soldiers is worsening by the day. It would be best to reintegrate their erze with the homeworld fleet as soon as possible."

"Of course their morale is low," Soldier Gur said matter-of-factly. "An erze relies on the leadership of the zun. With their erze master still on Earth and apparently unwilling to cooperate, they are understandably adrift."

Admistrator Seir and several other colonial zhree shifted their fins uncomfortably. In the outer ring, Werth's Soldiers bristled, but Werth remained unmoving. Soldier Gur went on as if he hadn't noticed anything. "How quickly we can begin the transfers will depend on when we can complete the first stage of human evacuations." Soldier Gur's gaze slid over the domed bodies around him, over to the entrance where Commander Tate could not help but tower over the room full of zhree. "Perhaps we will find out now whether that will be a smooth process or a difficult one." Gur raised one limb and motioned.

Immediately, the rings parted to open a wedge for Donovan's guards to escort their captives forward. Commander Tate went first. When she stood before Gur, she dropped her armor, but only briefly. A nod, nothing more.

Gur tilted back slightly so that he could better regard the tall human in front of him. "Have you reconsidered your position, then?"

"No," Tate said. "We still refuse any evacuation from Earth."

Gur's fins flattened in severe displeasure as the translation machine relayed Tate's words. "Then why are you here, disrupting these discussions?"

Soldier Gorm pulled Nurse Therrid forward. "Zun, we apprehended these three humans along with this Nurse in violation of restrictions at a human medical facility. They appeared to be conspiring in tampering with human exocels. We found this in the room." Gorm handed over Therrid's computing disc.

Soldier Gur held the disc up to one eye and scrolled the display skeptically. When he lowered the device, Gur turned his gaze on Nurse Therrid, whose fins trembled under the Soldier's weighty attention. "Nurse, what sort of medical procedure were you performing on these humans?"

Donovan couldn't bear it. Therrid was going to be punished, maybe even exiled or executed, because of him. "I forced him to do it," Donovan blurted. "I made him cut the reflex that cripples our exocels against zhree."

Jet's armored fingers dug into Donovan's left shoulder. "*Shut up.*"

"Donovan—" Therrid protested.

"It's true." The large Soldier who'd twisted Therrid's fins clamped his pincers around the back of Donovan's neck and dragged him forward roughly. Donovan gritted his teeth as he was forced to his knees before Gur. "This human battle-armored and attacked me. The colonials are lying about these creatures."

Shocked and angry musical murmuring broke out in the room. "That's not true! You—you're—" Therrid could barely speak from helpless anger.

"Enough." Soldier Gur banged one foot on the floor. "Am I to understand," he said with incredulity, staring at Donovan, "that this human has been altered to enable it to commit acts of violence against zhree?"

Silence fell hard. Then Gur's fins slashed through the air as he erupted in a string of musical fury. "I believed I'd seen the height of colonial conceit and lunacy, but I was wrong. Administrator Seir! How do you explain this?"

"I don't have an explanation, zun Gur." Administrator Seir stepped forward uncertainly. "It appears as if humans have unraveled one of the aspects of their exocellular technology and some have taken it upon themselves to act on that knowledge."

"Do you expect me to believe that?" Gur whistled in scorn. "You're suggesting that humans took the initiative of disabling a feature of their exocels, all on their own? That they didn't have help from colonials intent on undermining the authority of the Homeworld Council?" Gur's fins vibrated with blustering indignation. "The evidence is here: This Nurse performed the procedure. These humans answer to an erze master. Werth!"

Soldier Werth stepped forward from the second ring back. The other zhree shifted away, opening a column of space between him and Gur.

"Do you know *why* the Homeworld Council rejected your plan to further support the colony with more Hardened humans? Why they sent *me* here to oversee the withdrawal from this planet?" Gur's short, thick fins snapped and his voice rose in heated accusation, but Werth stood silently, his expression betraying nothing as the other Soldier raged. "The High Speaker was deeply concerned that the Earth-born erze zun had become too separated from Kreet, that your armor had grown soft, your perspective warped. If we granted you permission to create millions more Hardened humans, exos under your control who would answer to you and no other authority, what was to prevent you from one day removing your lauded fail-safe and turning these humans into an army?" Gur straightened to his full height and his Soldiers flanked him. "Now I see that the Council was right to be suspicious all along."

Soldier Werth spoke at last. "I can assure you of one thing, Soldier Gur. The humans in my erze are hardly acting with my interests in mind right now."

An odd guilt gripped Donovan's insides. "I didn't act for or against anyone in this room," he insisted. "This was for *us*. For humans." For the exos who were too old or young or injured or who simply didn't make the cutoff, the marked people with nowhere to turn, the billions of squishies like Anya who didn't even figure as a shadow of a thought in Gur's calculations.

"Listen to him!" Jet exclaimed. "Don't you understand? This isn't a conspiracy; all we want is the chance to defend ourselves against the Rii and you won't give it to us. You're the ones *forcing* us out of erze."

Their words seemed to go unnoticed. All of the zhree in the room were now muttering in a tense, undulating hum. Werth's Soldiers and Gur's Soldiers were shifting, eyeing each other, fins stiff and armor thick on their hulls. The other zhree around them were shuffling nervously. Donovan had never seen a perfectly orderly zhree speaking circle come apart in such a way.

"I will have to report to the High Speaker that matters on this planet are even more fundamentally out of erze than I'd feared," Gur intoned.

"Soldier Gur." Administrator Seir's tone was forcefully reasonable, but an edge of anger made his melodic voice tinny. "We have cooperated fully with all of the Homeworld Council's decisions. Out of the supposed best interests of the Commonwealth, we are abandoning this colony we so laboriously developed, a planet where many of us were hatched. For you to now accuse us of gross treachery based on the isolated actions of a few humans—"

Gur cut him off. "This was *not* done by humans. Nurse Thet!"

Therrid's erze master came forward reluctantly. Gur declared, "A member of your erze has broken the long-standing agreement between Earth and Kreet regarding the use of exocellular biotechnology on other species."

Nurse Thet said, "That particular Nurse has always been a little strange, zun. Socially awkward and overly interested in humans ever since he was a hatchling." Nurse Therrid's fins drooped in humiliation at his erze master's words, and Donovan very much wanted to punch Nurse Thet in all six eyes.

"Such criminally out-of-erze behavior indicates a deviant personality that cannot be rehabilitated," Gur said. "I expect you to act as a proper zun and remove him from your erze."

Therrid let out a barely audible humming moan.

Thet's fins stiffened in insult. "Yes, zun. As you say."

"*No . . .*" Donovan breathed, but there was nothing he could say or do. Jet turned on the spot, wide-eyed, as if searching for a way out of the room. He cast desperate glances at Werth and Tate, whose expressions were like granite.

Soldier Gur fanned his fins and raised his voice. "I see that the Commonwealth can no longer rely on the loyalty or sound judgment of the colonial erze on this planet. The evacuation plans have already been disrupted; the defiance of the soldiers-in-erze is already spreading to other Hardened humans and these developments will only cause further problems." Soldier Gur's eyes opened and closed as he spun his gaze around to search out two of his senior Soldiers. "Grier, Gye, see to it that the human evacuation proceeds as planned and on schedule. Use whatever force you deem necessary. Don't damage the ones that have been selected, but you may make it clear that other humans in the Round will be harmed if they do not fully cooperate."

Commander Tate's face went rigid with horror. "You can't . . ."

"How many humans have had the neural fail-safe removed?" Gur stabbed a limb at Therrid, demanding an answer. "Any others besides this one?"

"No." Donovan managed to call out from his place on the floor with the Soldier's pincers still clamped around the back of the neck. "Not yet."

Something in Donovan's voice made Soldier Gur pause. Slowly, he approached Donovan, until they were eye to eye. The alien's gaze gave a wary flicker. He gestured to the other Soldier to release the hold on Donovan's neck. "You're only a human." Soldier Gur's hum was quiet, almost kindly. "Not even a scientist or an administrator, just a soldier. You didn't engineer this little act of defiance on your own. You had help from within the Towers. Who helped you?"

Donovan rose to his feet, his gaze steady. "I did have help from within the Towers. My father was the Prime Liaison for sixteen years. No one believed more strongly in the partnership of humans and zhree than he did. But he suspected that one day that partnership would end, that you would betray us and we'd need to be able to fight on our own."

Soldier Gur stepped back, dissatisfied. The yellow gaze he laid on Donovan was curious and pitying. "There was never a partnership. You're a Class Two species. You owe your continued existence to the Homeworld Council and the generous regard we zhree extend to other sentients." Soldier Gur stepped back and gestured to his subordinates. "Take this aberrant human outside at once and destroy it."

Jet lunged. He nearly pulled off the unthinkable—getting a hold of a Soldier's weapon—but zhree reflexes were too fast. Two Soldiers seized Jet and pinned him to the ground in seconds. Therrid gave a helpless, whistling cry as armored limbs clamped around Donovan's arms from both sides and began to pull him away.

For an instant, Donovan's mind went white; armor sprang instantly from his nodes and began to furrow into rows of bladed edges. The Soldiers tightened their grip and Donovan felt the barrel of a weapon press against the base of his spine. "Don't fight, human." Gorm's whispered suggestion was calm but indifferent, as if he didn't care whether Donovan took it or not. "Consider what's best for your erze mates."

Jet was struggling wildly on the ground, as bare-skinned as a squishy and bleeding where he'd cut himself against battle armor. *"Do something!"*

It was unclear who Jet was screaming at, but suddenly, his partner's panic calmed Donovan. He breathed again. Gorm was right; he couldn't win an unarmed battle against half a dozen of Gur's Soldiers. If he put on a dramatic show of human aggression, he'd only make things go worse for Jet and Commander Tate and his friends.

Donovan lowered his armor and stopped resisting. Mechanically, he let himself be led toward the entrance of the briefing hall. Jet's curses rose into frantic howls. The sound tore at Donovan. He looked over his shoulder and caught Commander Tate's eye. Tate's expression was unutterably bleak, but their exchange held something else: an understanding.

He'd gotten the truth of the Rii threat out into the world. He'd set an example and proven Dr. Ghosh's research. He'd passed vital information on to the human leaders of the country. It was all he could do, surely all that either of his parents could've ever expected of him. Tate would see to it that the exos who remained fought on, for Earth and for all humans.

The Soldiers would make it quick.

"No."

A single note in Mur, delivered in a familiar tone of command that carried clearly across the room. Soldier Werth's eyes were piercing in their intensity. "That human is a member of my erze. If he's to be destroyed, it will be on my orders. Not yours."

Two of Werth's Soldiers near the door moved instantly to block it. Gur's Soldiers battle-armored, fins flattening into blades, bodies bristling, and suddenly Donovan found himself in the center of a zhree standoff. Everyone in the room fell silent, even Jet, who lay on the ground, heaving for breath.

Soldier Gur was taken aback, but only for a second. "You've lost the right to give orders here, Werth. If you directed the actions of these humans, then you're a traitor to the Commonwealth. If you did not, then you've clearly lost control of them. Either way, you can no longer be trusted to make decisions as an erze zun."

"I didn't lose control of the humans," Soldier Werth said. "They lost confidence in me. Soldiers expect the erze zun to make decisions for the good of the erze. The *entire* erze." Soldier Werth raised his voice and it rang out in the hall. "There will be no military withdrawal from Earth."

Soldier Gur's fins flattened against his body in a furious glower. "You are speaking nonsense. The decision has been made. Most of your Soldiers have been removed to orbit and are awaiting interstellar transfer."

"I will recall them to Earth," Soldier Werth said, "as soon as I have you and your Soldiers removed from command." There was an immediate and dramatic convulsion of motion in the room. All of Werth's Soldiers, who'd been standing subservient and resentful at the outer edges of the room, battle-armored at the same time and moved in unison, drawing weapons and encircling the smaller knot of homeworlders, who closed ranks at once around Gur.

Soldier Gur's eyes seemed to bulge from six directions on his body. "You've lost your mental faculties. This is the most out-of-erze behavior imaginable . . ." His voice vibrated without any of its usual composure. "You're committing treason against the Commonwealth."

"You accused me of such before it was even true," Soldier

Werth replied. "It must be gratifying to have your assessment further confirmed."

"Administrator Seir!" Gur trilled, his infuriated voice hitting high notes. "Contact the High Speaker at once. Inform him that I am exercising my authority as a senior military adviser to the Homeworld Council in declaring Soldier Werth an exile of the Mur Erzen. Henceforth his markings connote no status or authority, no planet will harbor any member of his erze, his broods will find no sanctuary and have no place in the civilized galaxy."

Seir's eyes opened and closed as his gaze swung between the two Soldiers, then swept decisively around the room. "They will have a place here on Earth." Seir straightened his fins with an audible snap, appearing, for the first time in months, like the erze leader that Donovan's father had answered to for years. "I will contact the High Speaker, but it will be to inform him that we are sending you and your Soldiers back to Kreet. Regrettably, the colonists of this planet cannot abide by the decision of the Homeworld Council to surrender Earth to the Rii. As a result, we can no longer be part of the Mur Erzen Commonwealth."

For the first time since his arrival on the planet, Soldier Gur seemed beyond speech. His armor kept thickening until his torso seemed swollen with compressed rage. All of his Soldiers had drawn their weapons and raised battle armor. Donovan found himself suddenly roughly shoved aside and ignored as the two contingents of zhree faced each other down.

Gur's multi-directional gaze took in the situation: Werth's Soldiers outnumbered his by more than two to one. For a minute, the old Soldier's fins twitched and stuttered in indecisive outrage. Then his calculating pragmatism seemed to reassert itself and get the better of him. He wasn't about to risk losing his most senior Soldiers to a bunch of unhinged colonials.

Gur gestured for his retinue to lower their weapons and stand down. "I will return to Kreet," he said, his voice slow and firm with reestablished control, "along with any from this planet who wish to join me. Consider it your last chance to remain in erze. After that, this planet will be cut off from the Commonwealth and you will have only yourselves to blame for your fate."

"Escort Soldier Gur and his erze members to the chambers belowground and see that they are comfortably confined there." Werth's Soldiers seemed all too enthusiastic to fall in around the homeworlders and nudge them toward the exit.

Gur strode past Werth in his lopsided but firmly dignified manner, then paused and focused his gaze on the other Soldier. "You've made a terrible mistake. You know full well that you cannot win against the full might of a Rii Galaxysweeper. You've doomed your entire erze and many others." He stabbed a limb in Donovan's direction. "All this madness over a human?"

"If you think this is about one human, then you haven't been paying attention." Soldier Werth gestured for his Soldiers to continue out the door. "Humans are strange creatures, Gur. Sometimes, *they* remind *us* what erze duty means."

Donovan, Jet, and Tate found themselves suddenly unhanded. They were too stunned to move from where they were in the room of remaining zhree. Jet climbed to his feet unsteadily with the disoriented look of someone waking from a nightmare. Donovan looked down to see that his hands were shaking.

Administrator Seir stepped into the center of the room recently vacated by Gur. "How long will it take to recall the Soldiers from the orbital stations?" he asked Werth, as if this were a routine meeting of the zhree zun in an assembly room in the Towers, just like the ones Donovan had once attended.

"Two to three days," said Soldier Werth, "but as soon as we make any attempt to do so, the Rii will know that the withdrawal is not occurring as Gur negotiated. We'll lose any advantage of surprise if we intend to retake the Towers before the Hunters reinforce their position."

"They're not wasting time," Builder Dor put in. "They've already appropriated our paverships to begin clearing land for expanded algae farms and sent drones to strip the human cities of refined hydrothermal ores." The paverships Donovan had seen in the sky—that must be what Builder Dor was referring to. The Rii starting to make themselves at home.

"What's our best estimate as to how many Hunters are in the Towers?" Seir asked.

"A typical Rii spore vessel has a capacity of approximately seven hundred and twenty," Engineer Phee volunteered. "After accounting for casualties incurred during the invasion, we can estimate that a third of their remaining number have been transferred to Rounds One and Seventeen to begin the planetary takeover process, leaving roughly four hundred and ten Hunters in the Towers."

"How many Soldiers are there remaining in Round Three now?"

"Three hundred," Soldier Werth said. "As for the other occupied Rounds, there are another three hundred Soldiers in Round Twelve, four hundred and twenty each in Rounds Ten and Seventeen, and two hundred and ten in Round One. Taken together, not enough to mount a coordinated assault, even with the advantages of surprise and familiar terrain." Soldier Werth paused, and for the first time, turned two of his yellow eyes on Commander Tate. "Commander, how many uninjured and combat-rated exo soldiers-in-erze are currently in Round Three?"

Commander Tate met the erze master's gaze. A tentative exchange seemed to occur between the Soldier and his most senior human-in-erze. "Twenty-six hundred, zun."

"And in the other Rounds?" Administrator Seir asked.

"Not counting regional satellite offices, SecPac has between two and four thousand Hardened officers based in each Round, zun," Tate said.

For a few seconds, despite everything unprecedented that had transpired in the last five minutes, Donovan could feel the beat of hesitation stilling every fin in the reformed circle of zhree colonists—a shared sense of fear and danger, of solidarity and irrevocability in what they were about to do.

"Nurse Therrid," Administrator Seir said, "how long and difficult is the procedure to remove the exocel inhibition reflex in Hardened humans?"

Nurse Therrid seemed dazed and bewildered by the fact that he was being addressed by the Administrator. "It's a . . . precise sort of operation, but a fairly quick one, zun."

Administrator Seir considered this. "Nurse Thet," he said. "I must ask that you forgo punishing this member of your erze so he can help to save the colony."

Nurse Thet regarded Therrid with some disdain, then dipped his fins. "Indeed."

"The High Speaker will be expecting an update from Gur prior to when the ships in orbit are scheduled to begin interstellar transfers." Seir spoke again to Soldier Werth. "We can't declare Earth independent of either the Commonwealth or the Rii until we regain control of all the Rounds. Five, perhaps six, days is as long as I dare delay contacting Kreet."

"Understood. My erze knows what's at stake." One of Werth's fins swiveled slowly toward the humans in the room. In a low hum, "Some knew before I did."

Two Soldiers escorted Commander Tate and Jet back to the common hall, where a third of SecPac's officers were currently confined under Gur's orders. Soldier Wiest drove Donovan and Nurse Therrid back to the hospital. Donovan was so physically and emotionally drained that he fell asleep in the skimmercar ride and half-woke with the vague awareness of Therrid carrying him inside like a child.

The next two days passed in a haze, mostly because he spent at least half the time sedated and in a therapy tank, one of the handful that had arrived from satellite offices and other Rounds. It seemed surreal and unaccountable to Donovan that he was even alive. Sanjay and other nurses-in-erze came and went, checking up on him and bringing him food, but for a while, he didn't see Therrid or anyone else he knew. On the third day, he woke feeling considerably better and more clearheaded, and saw his partner sitting in a chair beside him, studying something on a screen.

"Jet," he croaked.

"I'm starting to really hate this," Jet said.

"What?"

"Sitting next to sickbeds in this damn hospital." Jet put the screen down on a side table. "I've had enough of it to last the rest of my life."

Donovan lifted his head and pushed up onto his elbows. The

pain and swelling in his shoulder that had been constant over the past several days was gone. The other injuries to his face and body remained only as patches of slightly thickened panotin under the shallow bath of curative liquid covering his body. His surroundings were weirdly incongruous: a typical rectangular hospital room but with the ovoid, faintly humming therapy tank in place of where a bed would be. "Am I dreaming?" he muttered, mostly to himself. "The world's been turned upside down so many times already I can't even tell anymore."

Jet averted his eyes. "I know what you mean. Every time I wake up, I think that maybe I hallucinated the worst parts." He faced Donovan again, and because he knew Jet better than anyone, Donovan glimpsed the toll of the last several days—sorrow and anger and worry, and the still-fresh hurt and betrayal that he was responsible for—flashing into Jet's eyes and straining his jawline.

Donovan's hand tightened around the lip of the therapy tank. "Jet," he began. "I . . ."

Jet grabbed the towel from the side table and handed it to Donovan. "Therrid needs that tank freed up. He wants everyone who comes out of the operation to spend an hour in one."

Donovan took the towel without meeting his erze mate's gaze. Now was not the time, then. He ran the towel through his damp hair. "So they're really doing it."

"Therrid's trained about twelve other Nurses and they've been working nonstop. They've shared the procedure across the Nurse erze, and the ones in the other occupied Rounds are working as fast as they can too." Jet held up the screen he'd been looking at, the corner of his mouth quirking up in a way that seemed almost like himself. "I told the cadre that you were the very first one to have it done, the original guinea pig. They were impressed; said that must've taken serious balls." Jet shook his head in disbelief. "To think they don't know the half of it."

"Have any of them been through the operation already?"

"Fernando's injured and has to wait. Maddie and Kamo went through it yesterday. Jong-Kyu's scheduled for today. The Nurses have got it down cold. You're in and out in less than an hour. Another hour of downtime in a tank, and you're good to go. You know what the zhree are like when it comes to getting things done."

The door opened. Donovan broke into the first grin he'd worn in what felt like ages. Thad, still looking a little pale, but on his feet and in SecPac uniform, cast them his slow, familiar laid-back smile. "About time. There's a line of people waiting for that tank." He tossed a clean uniform in Donovan's direction. "Briefing in three hours."

Donovan got out and dressed, grateful for clean clothes. He had no idea what had happened to his torn shirt and jeans, and he didn't care. "What's going on?" he asked as he, Thad, and Jet left the room. Thad hadn't been kidding; there was a long line of chairs against the wall in the hospital corridor. The dozen or so exo soldiers-in-erze sitting in them looked impatient and nervous. A Nurse was walking down the row with a scanner and computing disc, checking each exo in turn, taking their temperature and vital signs and having them armor up and down. In a strange, ironic way, Donovan was reminded of the check-in process he'd gone through as a five-year-old, prior to being Hardened. That procedure had endowed them with armor; this one would allow them to use it in war.

"We're taking back the Towers," Thad said. "Tomorrow."

The briefing was held in the hospital's largest meeting room. Donovan realized how famished he was when he saw the tables along the wall laden with plates of sandwiches, bowls of chips, and flats of armor juice. Having his mouth full of food prevented him from needing to make much conversation with the other stripes who nodded to him and clapped him on the back. Once everyone's hunger was sated, the remaining food and empty plates were cleared away.

Soldier Werth and Commander Tate arrived and walked them through the plan, rotating and zooming in on projections displaying cut-in views of the Towers. The room was so crowded Donovan could barely move but people were silent. Utilizing the full capacity of available Nurses, hospital space, and equipment, Therrid and his peers were removing the exocel hobble on three hundred and twenty combat-rated soldiers-in-erze in Round Three. Nurses in the other four occupied Rounds had gotten a slightly later start and were aiming for at least two hundred and seventy battle-ready stripes in each location. With more time, they could have more people, or move officers around to optimize the numbers across the Rounds, but further delay was too great a risk. The Hunters would notice if the evacuation plans of the Mur colonists were not moving apace.

The counterattack would be coordinated among all five Rii-occupied locations. In Round Three, the mission would launch from the hospital parking lot. An unusual staging area, but "the Rii have no reason to pay attention to a large gathering of humans around this building," Tate explained. "No doubt they've already figured out it's a medical facility and they don't consider us a serious threat."

"They'll be far more interested in the three hundred Soldiers that will leave the field encampment and veer off course from the shipyards to launch an eastern assault on the Towers." Soldier Werth mapped out the approach the Soldiers would take. "Once the Hunters scramble to defend their position, a disguised human attack through the western sector will meet with reduced resistance."

"Work your way in and up," Commander Tate explained, drawing lines through the projected image of the Towers. "The Hunters will do their best to keep us contained to lower levels. Once they realize we've broken the negotiated agreement, they'll have nothing to lose. We need to seize control of the main communications centers before they can take control of our orbital weaponry and set off retaliatory attacks on the Rounds and other human cities."

Tate and Werth gave the appearance of working in tandem as always, but Donovan noticed they stood at a distance from each other in the room and some of their usual nonverbal signals— a questioning glance from Tate, a subtle fin movement from Werth—were missing. As committed as they both were to this joint mission, the friction of lost faith lingered between them. Theirs was as long a partnership as had ever existed between zhree and human; Donovan wondered whether, after the events of the past several months, it could be repaired.

At a gesture of permission from Werth, two other Soldiers who'd been hovering in the background stepped forward. One of them Donovan recognized from his distinctively notched fins as Wiv, the other he didn't know. "This is what the Hunters will be carrying: a Myx/Yovian-assembled compact Grade 7 Er combat pulse weapon with armor-corroding ammunition," said Wiv, hefting the enemy firearm with enthusiasm. Donovan smiled; Wiv reminded him of a typical gun nerd. "If the rounds fail to tear through your exocel, they fragment, dispelling damaging chemicals that burn and weaken panotin."

"In short, these are a lot worse than what the sapes shoot at us," Commander Tate said. "Don't go in thinking you can take half a dozen of these and come out just fine after a few days in the tank. Our best guess is that a seventh- or eighth-generation human exocel can handle three, maybe four, shots before further impact starts being fatal."

"That's if you attend to wounds right away," Wiv added.

Cass muttered behind Donovan, "Bottom line, don't get shot."

In the translation delay of Wiv's words, Donovan overheard someone else whispering in amazement, "This is really going to happen. Scorch me, we're actually going to fight those monsters."

The Soldier that Donovan didn't recognize pulled up an image of a Rii Hunter. "Spore team Hunters don't retreat or surrender. The only way to take the Towers back is to eliminate them. It's unfortunate that we don't have time for more preparation, but here's what you need to know: Shots to the eyes and the center of the underbelly are the most lethal. Fin injuries aren't fatal, but they're extremely painful and disorienting."

"All this information and the full use of our exocels would've been awfully handy last week, wouldn't it?" Sebastian grumbled darkly under his breath.

Several people around him muttered agreement. The Rii invasion had cost SecPac a lot of lives. The survivors wouldn't soon forget that their zhree allies—the ones they would be going into battle alongside tomorrow—still shared the blame for the deaths of their fellow stripes.

After the large group briefing, Thad called together Donovan, Jet, Cass, and Zach, as well as three other exos: Angelina Tucker, MacAllister Pierce, and Sergio Martinez. SecPac had always operated on the basis of small, flexible teams and it had seemed best to preserve that, even in a large assault like this one. Their eight-person squad would be among the first into the Towers. Thad walked through every detail of the planned attack in his typical straightforward manner, but there was a darkness now, a grim set to his face that Donovan had not seen before.

Afterward, there was no point in hanging around the hospital, so they went home. Donovan felt as if he hadn't been back to the house in ages. He, Jet, and Cass threw cushions and blankets onto the floor and spent the night camped out together in the living room. There wasn't much talking. They just didn't want to be alone, nor to go upstairs and pass Leon's room.

Cass fell asleep eventually. Donovan couldn't do the same. He knew he ought to get as much rest as possible, but now that all there was to do was wait, he couldn't shut his brain down. He checked his comm unit surreptitiously. Coded well wishes and nervous dread and excitement stretched from Round to Round through the small screen in his hand: *Good luck all. Kick some shroom ass. 198 Alpha forever.* Donovan wrote: *Matias, Amrita, and Leon—wish you were here.*

Donovan heard Jet turn restlessly. "I can't sleep," Jet whispered.

"Me neither." It was two o'clock in the morning.

Silence from the shadowy lump on the sofa that was his

partner. "I just want it to happen already. I want to scorch those red-eyed shrooms." Jet rolled over to stare at the ceiling. "I'm not afraid. I don't care what happens to me anymore."

The pain in his partner's voice made Donovan's stomach clench. *I care.* He'd done everything in his power to give exos the chance to fight for their planet, but now that it was actually about to happen, he was terrified. Not for his own life—he'd come close to death enough times lately that he couldn't muster up much more fear for himself—but his friends were going into battle when they could've been safely aboard a Quasar-class transport ship.

On top of everything else, the possibility of losing Jet made Donovan's mind want to shut down. He couldn't face what might come the next day knowing there were open wounds between them. Lying in the dark, he tried to think of what to say, but before he could find the right words, Jet spoke.

"You were right," Jet said. "About how being in erze doesn't make you a good person." A long exhalation. Quietly, "I've tried to live my whole life in erze and I haven't figured it out."

Donovan was so startled and confused by this admission that he had no immediate reply. Not a good person? Donovan could think of many times he'd wished he was more like Jet. His partner was one of the best soldiers-in-erze there was, and a better friend than Donovan knew he deserved.

Jet kept talking. "Last winter, I knew there were things eating at you—things you weren't telling me." Jet glanced in Donovan's direction but kept speaking to the ceiling in a voice just above a whisper. "I'm not going to lie; it was pretty frustrating. I thought I was doing everything I could to help you, but you still didn't trust me enough to tell me what was going on. I figured there was nothing else I could do; you just needed time, the same way Vic said she needed time when we talked about moving in together. But that wasn't really it, with either of you."

"Jet."

"You knew I'd judge you. The way I judged you for falling for a squishy. Or got mad that Vic refused her evacuation spot. You knew I'd take it badly, and I did. I called you a squishy-brained nutjob."

"Head case," Donovan corrected.

"Right. Well, sometimes it takes a crazy person to hold up the truth." Jet shifted onto his side, though his face was barely visible in the dark. "You were right about the evacuation, about taking a stand, about what erze duty really is."

On the other side of Donovan, Cass moved, then settled. The sudden silence seemed deafening before Jet spoke again. "I said that if I went out of erze I wouldn't know who I was anymore. But you aren't like that—you went so far out of erze you fell off the erze map and did a full slingshot in orbit and landed back here, somehow miraculously not dead."

Donovan swallowed. "I admit I don't quite believe it myself."

Jet rolled onto his back again, and his voice turned rough and accusing. "I think being your partner is going to kill me. I feel like it already nearly has, about half a dozen times."

"Hey," Donovan protested, "you were the one threatening to throttle me." He tried to sound light, but Jet's words cut him badly.

"An act of self-preservation." Jet flung an arm over his face so his voice was slightly muffled. "God, if you knew how—"

"Oath and erze," Donovan broke in. "I'm sorry. I know that doesn't cut it, but I am." He'd lied to Jet, had taken him for granted, had broken the cardinal rule drilled into them since they were trainees—*never, ever leave your erze mate*. All for reasons that had made sense at the time but were terrible when he considered what he'd put his partner through; no one took erze oaths more seriously than Jet.

"I never told you this," Donovan said, "but when we were kids I wanted to be a stripe because of you. The times I've gone out of erze, I felt like I had no choice—but I thought I might be stripped of my marks or worse. I never wanted to go behind your back, but I didn't want to pull you down with me either." Donovan rubbed at his eyes and was glad he couldn't see Jet's face. "I know it made me a bad partner and a terrible friend. I can't blame you if you don't trust me anymore. I just wish I could . . . earn it back somehow." He stopped. "I don't know what else to say."

"Say that these markings still mean something," Jet said hoarsely. "Everything I ever believed in has been flipped upside down and I don't know what to think anymore. Say that we're still erze. You and me, even if nothing else in the world is the same."

Donovan propped himself up onto his elbows, enough so that his eyes were level with his partner's. "You're my brother, Jet. You could take away my uniform, my stripes, even the erze, and that wouldn't change." He slumped back to the floor and closed his eyes, letting the pillow muffle his words. "Heck, before everything fell apart, I would've left Earth with you."

Jet did not reply for some time. Donovan heard an ambulance siren off in the distance, and the clunking sound of the ice maker in their fridge. At last, Jet said, in a thick voice that he tried to make sound normal, "It's kind of a bummer, come to think of it. I always thought it would be fun to go into space."

Donovan smiled to himself in the dark. "Yeah. We used to collect those model ships, remember? I wanted to pilot a low-orbit fighter. I remember I was so disappointed when my dad said humans couldn't fly them."

"Your old man sure didn't believe in encouraging childhood ambitions."

"Crusher of dreams, my dad. I think I was about seven years old at the time too."

Jet said quietly, "You know what, I lied. I *am* afraid of what'll happen tomorrow."

"Me too. I'm scared out of my gourd." Then he snorted. "Wouldn't it be funny if Cass were awake this whole time, listening to us have this manly heart-to-heart?"

"Nah, if she was awake, she'd tell us to pull ourselves together and stop being such wet blankets." Jet raised his whisper by an octave in a passable imitation of Cass's voice: "Shut up and go to sleep, you two! We've got shrooms to send to hell tomorrow!"

They chuckled quietly so as not to disturb Cass. Jet rolled over and a few minutes later, Donovan heard his friend's breathing even out into soft snores. Donovan stayed awake, listening and taking comfort in the sound for a while longer.

31

At precisely sixteen hundred hours the following day, convoys of unmarked transport vehicles sped through the Round toward the Towers. Crouched inside one of them, Donovan patted the pockets of his tactical vest, checking that everything was in place. Four magazines for his E81 electripulse carbine, two flash grenades, flares, panotin replenishment gel pack, chemical burn spray, secured comm unit and earbud tuned to the mission-team frequency.

There was no talking inside the vehicle; so far this was the quietest mission Donovan had ever been on. Everyone understood the significance of what they were being sent to do. This was unlike any task SecPac had ever been called upon to perform.

"Soldiers have begun the assault at the eastern entrance of the Towers. Enemy has been engaged." Commander Tate's voice in their earbuds. "SecPac red group, two minutes out."

Donovan counted the long seconds in his head, pacing out his breaths. Cass caught his eye and winked. For the first time since Leon's death, she looked like herself. Her cropped hair was tied back under a green bandana. On the black protective sleeve she wore over her right arm, she'd written in curly script with silver marker: *Hunt the Hunters.*

The truck came to a stop. The back of it flung open. Donovan gave Jet a smack on the shoulder. *Go! I'm behind you.* And then their boots were on the ground and they were running.

The Hunters guarding the western side of the Towers must've been bewildered by the sudden appearance of so many humans. At first they reacted with more surprise and curiosity than alarm, chittering to one another and pointing. The exos at the very front of the line came to a smooth halt a hundred meters from the entrance and opened fire.

Directly in front of him, Donovan saw Jet and Thad standing shoulder to shoulder as they aimed and fired in unison. The air whined with electripulse rifle blasts. Well-placed bullets tore through orange-red eyes and a handful of Hunters went down in the initial attack. Several more let out whistles of pain and surprise, retreating into the entryway of the Towers as gunfire peppered their armored bodies and limbs.

The advancing exos flowed immediately into the opening. Donovan ran past on Jet's left, his heart thundering in his ears, Cass and Sergio on his heels. He didn't expect to get far before the Hunters recovered from their initial surprise. With less than fifteen yards between him and the Towers, a dozen Hunters swarmed out of the entryway like a scene from a nightmare, a wave of bristling armor and mottled hulls, innumerable fiery eyes blazing. With an eruption of chirping rage, they spun out in a blur, pointed their weapons into the onrush of attacking humans, and let fly with a deafening onslaught of return fire.

From a dead sprint, Donovan threw himself stomach-down as the volley tore up asphalt, nearby parked vehicles, the sides of buildings, trees and shrubbery. He heard human screams go up behind him, but all he could see were the serrated, armored legs of the Hunters nearby as they went sailing over and around the spot where he lay. Donovan rolled onto his back, braced his E81 awkwardly, and pulled on the trigger, violently rattling his own ribs but sending several rounds of ammunition into the vulnerable undersides of the two Hunters nearest him. One of them collapsed at once; the other jerked and twisted like a marionette, glistening liquid spattering the ground below it. It staggered about with its fins taut in a silent scream before its limbs folded and Angelina ran up and placed a shot directly through one of its eyes.

Donovan scrambled to his feet and kept moving. Adrenaline poured into his veins, but in terrified elation instead of the helpless panic he'd felt when they'd first faced the Hunters. This time *they* were the attackers. This was their Round, their home, and even though Donovan still expected he might die at any moment, his mind was clear and focused. His exocel rebalanced itself, stabilizing his calves and ankles and strengthening his gait as he rushed inside.

His teammates ran with him and broke right and left, covering their neighbors and keeping clear of one another's fields of fire with the automaticity instilled from years of drilling in searches and raids. What met them inside was not anything like a Sapience ambush, however. Donovan had almost no time to put his back against a wall before Hunters flew at them like armored whirling dervishes. As uncommonly large as they were, they moved as fast—*faster*—than any zhree Donovan had ever seen. A Hunter appeared in his rifle sights. He unleashed a spurt of gunfire and felt a jolt of satisfaction as the alien was flung back under the hail of metal.

Pain exploded in Donovan's stomach.

He'd been shot before. This was different. The impact slammed him into the wall as if he'd been hit by a truck. Donovan's weapon slid from his grip as he struck the ground, torso on fire. The smell of his own burning panotin pervaded his nostrils and he nearly gagged. Sucking air as if through a straw, he tried to claw back his scattered wits. *You're okay, you're okay, you're okay.* The mantra cleared his head. As much as it hurt, this wasn't going to kill him. An abdominal shot distributed impact through the exocel evenly and none of his bones were broken.

All around him, the blast of weapons fire was still going on, punctuated by human and alien shouting. Cass stood over him, emptying her weapon, screaming. *"Not. Anyone. Else!"*

The pain receded under the realization that every second he spent on the ground was one in which he wasn't returning fire and helping his erze mates. Donovan grabbed his rifle, got to his feet, and kept firing.

Following some unseen command, the Hunters retreated into the curving corridors of the Towers. Two fresh SecPac teams hurried past, weapons up and eyes forward as they pursued the enemy down the passageway. There was sudden silence save for the rapid clacking of reloading ammunition and the muted but urgent calls of people checking up on erze mates. "Who's hit?" Thad's voice demanded, sounding strangely normal after all the madness.

A hand grabbed Donovan by the shoulder. To his inexpressible relief, Jet was beside him. He pointed at Donovan's stomach. Donovan looked down at himself for the first time. With bladed fingers, he tore away the bottom of his vest and winced at the sight of his own damaged and chemically burned armor, knitting frantically, trying to protect the site of injury and eject the crushed projectile fragments.

Donovan laughed weakly. When his partner looked at him oddly, he said, "TGINS." Jet broke into a pained, slightly mad grin.

Thank Goodness I'm Not Squishy. "I'll say," he agreed. As incomprehensible as this firefight was, there was a bizarre sense of rightness to it as well.

Thad came over to them. "Get some of that burn stuff on it, stat." Donovan reached for the small container in his vest pocket. Jet took the canister from him; it dispensed a white medical foam that felt tacky but cooling as Jet sprayed it over the wound. Donovan had no idea how it worked, other than it counteracted whatever corrosive residue was eating at his panotin. He ejected his nearly spent magazine and slammed a full one into the breech.

"Tucker, your armor's scorched, you're staying put. You too, Martinez," Thad ordered. "The rest of you form up; let's go."

They pressed forward toward the sounds of battle.

The center of the main Tower, a tall open space that stretched past the upper levels, had become a vaulted echo chamber of gunfire and chaos. It was immediately apparent that the Rii had retreated deeper inside to gain the advantage of ground where they could fire down on the humans from above. Following close behind Cass and Mac, Donovan hugged the curving wall, rifle aimed upward, firing at the mottled figures on the level above them. A dozen stripes already lay on the ground, some of them unmoving, others trying to crawl away from the barrage, or still determinedly returning fire even as they were dragged to safety by teammates. The battle had begun as an orderly and disciplined assault, but it was fast becoming a melee. The open layout of the Towers provided little cover and the fast, animalistic attacks of the Hunters quickly broke apart human formations; it was getting hard for both sides to shoot without hitting their own erze mates.

Scores of Hunters were dropping fifteen, twenty, or thirty feet from the causeways above, landing on six legs as lightly as spiders and attacking the exos armor on armor. Donovan saw one Hunter grab a man by the leg; another grabbed him by an arm, and like dogs with a rag, they yanked their victim violently side to side until his spine snapped.

Three stripes rushed one of the Hunters and as Donovan had once seen Soldiers do, two of them bore it down with their superior weight, forcing it sideways onto its hull while the third fired several rounds into the underside of its torso, slamming the Hunter's body into the ground.

In the deafening noise, Thad was shouting, but only after Donovan focused on the lieutenant's face did he hear the words. "Up! Up! Go up!" Cass took point, leading the way up one of the winding ramps to the chambers above. Mac, Donovan, Jet, and Zach fell in behind her. They advanced together, Thad covering the rear.

Cass slowed before the next landing and threw a flash grenade. A bang was followed by a shrill, whistling exclamation as a concealed Hunter leapt from the vantage point where it had been sniping the humans below. Cass and Mac rushed forward and opened fire.

Bullets tore into the Hunter's exocel and shattered an eye, but the Hunter leapt forward and seized Mac around the neck and torso with its long limbs. Before anyone could come to his aid, the Hunter had thrown itself from the third floor, its legs wrapped around the human as they both plummeted to the ground below.

The other exos rushed to the spot where their teammate had gone over, but there was nothing they could do. Far below, the

Hunter lay motionless, but any hope that Mac had survived the fall vanished when two other Hunters rushed to the spot and fired down on his body.

Jet roared in denial and trained his aim below, but it was too difficult to place a shot with the number of mingled humans on the first floor and the Hunters already on the move again.

Thad banged a fist against the wall, his face grim. "We keep going."

They continued upward. Sweat wicked up through Donovan's armor and trickled under his vest. The battle continued to rage, but the sound of it changed. Donovan understood why: Werth's Soldiers had arrived. They'd fought their way through the other side of the Towers, and now both humans and zhree of the same erze were converging in the main chamber. They poured in from the ground floor and from walkways connected to the secondary spires.

"Thank erze. About time," Zach said. Donovan agreed; he'd never been happier to see Soldiers. He could sense the tide of the battle turning. Striped hulls clashed with mottled ones. Soldiers boosted one another, leaping off the domed bodies of their erze mates and pulling themselves onto higher floors, their musical shouting mixing with human voices and the rapid clicking and chirruping of the Hunters.

The five exos fired and climbed, paused to reload, and continued. It was like fighting their way up a well. Close-quarters combat inside the Towers was not something Donovan could've ever imagined a few months ago. There were no corners around which to take cover. Bullets didn't pass through the unearthly walls but instead lodged in the metallic weave or ricocheted dangerously off support frames. Soldiers, Hunters, and humans fought up and down the height of the spires. "Should have . . . taken . . . the elevators," Cass joked, catching her breath. She held out a hand. "Flash grenade. I'm out."

Donovan handed her one of his. They'd learned a hard lesson after what happened to Mac and now always moved forward along the interior wall. Cass threw the grenade into the open archway ahead on their right. A Hunter burst through a cloud of smoke and charged them. They mowed it down with electripulse rifle fire, but not before it hurtled through them, plowing into Jet and Thad with razored limbs extended, sending all three careening several feet down the passage.

Donovan ran up. Thad had been knocked clear and was pushing himself to his feet. The Hunter lay dying, two sets of pincers wrapped around Jet's throat. Jet's bladed hand was sunk into one of the reddish eyes, the opaque lens shattered and leaking pale fluid. Donovan and Zach blew out two more eyes and the alien let out a final sigh like gas escaping a tire.

Donovan dropped to his knees and pried the sharp pincers away from his partner's throat. "I'm okay," Jet said hoarsely. He grimaced as he disentangled himself from the zhree corpse and got to his feet, a hand on his neck where the weave of his armor showed dark laceration marks.

Donovan felt weak in the legs for a second as he stood. He forced a steadying breath as he picked up his E81, but when he opened his mouth to speak, Zach hollered, "Look out!"

Two of Werth's Soldiers barreled into their midst, one of them limping badly on three limbs, both of them firing behind at pursuers. A Hunter ran and leapt from a causeway above, clearing at least thirty-five feet of open air and landing on four legs. With its other two limbs it shifted its grip on its heavy weapon with the nimbleness of a baton twirler and fired a blast that took one of the limping Soldier's fins clean off his torso. The Soldier staggered back, stunned; his companion let out a shrill whistle.

Donovan and his teammates opened fire, triangulating a hailstorm of lead on the Hunter's mottled hull. It fell back with a warbling cry. Two other Hunters appeared in its place. Almost faster than Donovan's eye could track, one of them tore Cass's rifle from her grip and sent it spinning off the edge of the ramp. A whipping limb connected with Cass's midsection, hurling her against the wall. Cass tumbled to the ground.

The two Soldiers threw themselves onto one of the Hunters and together they pulled the much larger zhree off balance. All three of them fell, stabbing and slashing at one another in a frenzy of limbs. Jet and Donovan ran up and emptied their magazines into the Hunter's body at close range. "For Vic," Jet snarled as he held down the trigger. "For Leon." The mottled armor rippled and spasmed and tore in several dozen places at once, spurting whitish liquid.

Gunfire choked the air. Donovan hit the ground in time to see Zach go down, his leg obviously broken. Before anyone could get to him, the second Hunter fired again and shot him in the back of the head. Donovan's stomach dropped out of his body. Zach was dead; even an eighth-generation exocel couldn't withstand skull impact at that range.

Thad let loose a guttural howl and got off two shots before a sniper on an upper ramp nailed him in the chest. The lieutenant staggered and collapsed. Time turned to sludge. Donovan saw everything; Jet returning fire across the tower, blasting at the enemy across the way, Cass trying to get to Thad, the remaining Hunter bringing its weapon around toward them.

Donovan launched himself at the alien's legs. It was stronger than him, but he was heavier. His momentum knocked it aside and its next shots went up into the ceiling. That was enough time for the two Soldiers to act. Like a pair of wolves, they took the Hunter down, rolling it to the ground, stabbing it again and again in the eyes and underside. Zhree blood spurted, mixed with the expanding pool from Zach's body.

Donovan stumbled away. "Cass!" he yelled. "Thad!"

"Still here." Cass was yanking open their squad leader's tactical vest and fumbling for the burn spray. Thad reeked of charred panotin, but he pushed himself to a sitting position, clutching a hand to his chest. His breath came out shallow and labored; the lieutenant's punctured lung had barely healed enough for him to even fight today. "The three of you keep going." His voice was wheezy but utterly calm. "You're almost there. We've almost got this squared away."

Cass spread medical foam across Thad's frayed armor. "Don't go anywhere, Lieutenant, and I'll give you a better chest massage later." She stood. "Where's my rifle? Someone see where my rifle went?"

"Take this one, human." One of the Soldiers extricated himself from the tangle of the dead Hunter's limbs. He picked up his weapon and limped toward them on three good legs. There was a ragged scrap of tissue and panotin where one of his fins had been. The other Soldier lay unmoving, an alarming amount of whitish zhree blood pooling around him, one of the dead Hunter's limbs embedded in his underside.

"It's not designed for humans, but you can still fire it," slurred the Soldier. "Set the tips of your armored digits into these holes and pinch the two contact plates together. It's simple." He handed the weapon to Cass. "Get to the uppermost communications center and shut it down."

They went on: Donovan, Jet, and Cass. It seemed incomprehensible to Donovan that just a few months ago, he'd passed this very spot with Anya's hand in his own, eager to show her the alien magnificence of the Towers and the impressive view of the Round, hoping to convince just one person that the world he knew was worth saving.

Just a few more yards. They paused to reload their rifles. Donovan was drenched in sweat and down to his last magazine. The communications center lay ahead—a chamber full of consoles and screens and complex machinery for controlling orbital equipment and weapons as well as encrypting and transmitting messages through space-time.

They approached the room cautiously, weapons at the ready. Standing at the chamber's central wraparound console was the Hunter that Donovan had seen speaking to Soldier Gur—the huge one with striking light and dark mottling. The Hunter was clicking and whistling in rapid speech as it manipulated various controls. It seemed to be having difficulty dealing with the unfamiliar Mur technology because its broad fins snapped with frustration, and as Donovan watched, it banged a limb on the top of the console.

The massive, agitated Hunter was not, however, the most shocking sight in the room. Standing behind the Hunter, flanking it like bodyguards, were two men. At least, Donovan thought they must be men. They were each easily seven feet tall, broad shouldered and slightly hunched. Their faces were not quite human: longer jaws and hairless sloping heads, eyes that were large and round and solid black. Ridged, exocellular armor covered their bare, muscled bodies.

"What in all erze are *those*?" Cass exclaimed.

The Chief Hunter caught sight of them and for a moment, paused. Then it flicked a fin and gave some sort of sharp, chirping command. Without a moment's hesitation, the two armored man-creatures charged at the exos like linebackers from hell.

Donovan was so shocked that he lost half a second of reaction time. He pulled the trigger on his E81 and got off two rounds that struck one of the men in the chest at near point-blank range at the same time as Jet shot him in the head. The man—if it was a man—staggered, armor shuddering as he collapsed, but the second attacker grabbed the hot barrel of Donovan's carbine, ripping it from his hands and swinging it like a crude cudgel into the side of Jet's face.

Jet fell sideways onto his hands and knees. Donovan began to move, but the man on the floor, the one they'd shot, was still alive and lurched upward like a monster, tackling him around the waist, dragging Donovan to the ground. Cass had been trying to open fire but lack of familiarity with the zhree weapon in her hands had cost her precious seconds. She got off only one round that struck the shoulder of Jet's attacker before the armored man knocked her weapon aside and swung both armored fists down on Cass as if to smash her like a piece of fruit.

Cass raised her arms in defense. One of the brute's blows sheared across her heavily armored left forearm, but the other smashed into her right elbow. It broke with an audible snap.

Cass let out a cry of pain. "Oh, you ape-faced *bastard*!" Cass dove for Donovan's weapon on the floor and tried to bring it into position with her left arm.

Donovan could not help her; he struggled against the unbreakable grip of the attacker who was pinning him. The man was so much larger and heavier; he'd immobilized Donovan's legs and was crawling up his body like a boa constrictor. Jet's shot had deformed part of the vaguely human face. The cheek was grotesquely caved in and one black marble of an eye was destroyed and bleeding— bright red blood, like any human—but he was still, horribly, very much alive and staring at Donovan fixedly with his one good eye. Donovan shoved at the massive armored shoulders. He slashed at the awful face and neck with the serrated ridges of his armored forearms. The impact of panotin on panotin vibrated across both of their heaving bodies. The man had no nodes, Donovan realized. Whatever he was, he wasn't an exo. He hadn't been Hardened by any method Donovan knew of, and while his armor seemed astonishingly strong, it remained fixed in place, like an animal's.

"What *are* you?" Donovan screamed.

One huge palm closed over Donovan's face. The man-creature lifted up slightly and made an incongruously soft clicking sound, and in that instant Donovan surged his exocel for all he was worth and thrust the point of his bladed fingers into the open mouth. He shoved as hard as he could, feeling, with a shudder that ran through his body, the wet thunk of his hand sinking in up to the wrist, slicing through tissue and hitting bone. Blood gushed down Donovan's trembling arm. The light in the remaining black eye died and the grip around Donovan's throat fell slack.

With a moan of horror, Donovan pulled his arm free of gore

and struggled out from underneath the dead weight in time to see the remaining armored man lift Cass and throw her bodily out of the room, where she rolled several times and came to a limp stop. Jet drove himself up and forward, ramming his shoulder hard into the man's abdomen and sending them both crashing into a bank of screens. For a moment, Jet held the advantage as he rained down slashing body blows that opened gashes in the enemy's exocel. They knit up again.

Donovan struggled to his feet. The large mottled Hunter was still manipulating console controls in the center of the room with barely a glance spared at the battling humans. Donovan knew his priority ought to be stopping the Rii leader. Whatever he was doing, it couldn't be good. But the horrible armored man-creature was pinning his best friend to the wall by the throat and pounding him relentlessly, armor on armor. Jet's mouth bled freely. His battle armor collapsed as he weakened.

Donovan spotted his assault rifle on the ground, the barrel hopelessly bent. Jet's was nowhere in sight. Lying a few feet away was the zhree weapon that the Soldier had given to Cass. Donovan picked it up, walked over, set the business end of the Soldier's weapon against the base of the elongated head, and muttered a fervent prayer. He pinched the trigger points hard with armored forefinger and thumb. The weapon discharged, tearing through armor, blasting apart the sloping skull.

Jet fell to the ground, dazed and gasping.

And the Chief Hunter shot Donovan in the back.

Donovan blacked out for two or three seconds when he hit the floor. When he came to, he couldn't move; his shoulder blades felt as if they'd been smashed into powder. He could only lift his head enough to see the Rii leader tap the console two more times with satisfied finality. Only then did the huge Hunter step out from behind the communications station, chirping and clicking something unpleasantly triumphant as he almost lazily leveled his Grade 7 Er combat pulse weapon.

Jet lurched over Donovan, simultaneously shielding him and trying to reach the zhree firearm that had fallen from his hands.

Half a dozen Soldiers burst into the room. "Highest State," one of them exclaimed, taking in the bewildering sight of the armored humans on the ground and the splatters of carnage. The Chief Hunter shifted the barrel of his weapon toward the newcomers, whistling hateful defiance.

All the Soldiers opened fire at the same time. The Hunter was thrown back into the console, jerking and convulsing, mottled armor spasming as it was torn apart under the onslaught of weapons fire. Two eyes cracked like breaking mirrors. Limbs collapsed like noodles beneath the torso. The gunfire fell silent.

Two Soldiers sprang over the sprawled humans, the monstrous corpses, and the body of the Rii Hunter to reach the central console. One of them tapped and manipulated controls with rapid ease, then let out a whistling sigh of relief. "Standing down orbital weapons."

Donovan crawled to his knees. He hurt like hell, but he could move after all. Jet collapsed next to him, his face streaked with blood. Their stunned gazes met. The Soldiers were moving around the room purposefully now, dragging the bodies away, examining the displays and reestablishing communications control. One of them came over.

"Humans, if you can, either help or get out of the way."

"Is it over?" Donovan's voice sounded numb. "Did we win?"

The Soldier was not one that Donovan recognized. He studied the two exos for a moment, then his fins moved in a slight frown. He seemed to only now be realizing that it had not been Soldiers but humans who had reached and stormed the top of the Towers first.

"Yes, human." The Soldier's musical voice softened a fraction. "Earth is ours again."

32

Donovan opened his eyes. It took several seconds for him to remember where he was. He was lying on a thin mat on the floor in the Towers. The battle—all of it—came back to him. Afterward, he and Jet had stayed on their feet for several hours past advisable, helping to clear the dead and wounded and to search the entire Towers for any remaining enemy.

At last the pain, adrenaline fallout, and sheer exhaustion had forced Donovan to stagger into this room. Thad and Cass had been evacuated to the medical wing, where the Nurses were already busily restoring operations, but exos who were less severely injured were being directed to temporary first aid rooms. A nurse-in-erze had given him fluids and applied packs of panotin replenishment gel to the damaged sections of his armor, and Donovan had fallen unconscious.

It was dark now. A faint amount of moonlight was coming from somewhere, but whatever power source normally illuminated the Towers was not working. Muffled noises rose distantly from elsewhere. The smell of burned explosives and scorched panotin still lingered unpleasantly in the air. Donovan lifted his head slightly and saw Jet lying on his side, fast asleep, a few feet away. He turned his head in the other direction and found himself staring up at Soldier Werth.

"I have been standing here trying to decide," Soldier Werth

said quietly, "whether to have you stripped of your markings and executed."

It was not the sort of thing one wanted to hear from one's erze master after fighting a pitched battle and surviving several near-death experiences. Weakly, Donovan pushed up onto his elbows. "You could've let Soldier Gur take care of it for you earlier, zun," he said.

"No," Werth said. "You know I could not have."

Donovan looked around the room of sleeping exos. Some of them moaned or stirred restlessly. "What happens now, zun?" Donovan asked.

"With all the captured Rounds back in our control, Administrator Seir has declared Earth an independent planet. The troops that were moved into orbit to await transfer are being recalled to Earth. Tomorrow, Soldier Gur and all those from his erze will board their ship and be escorted out of the solar system to return to the homeworld."

"What will Kreet do once they find out?"

"Under other circumstances, they would send warships to reclaim the colony. But I suspect the High Speaker will do nothing. According to the agreement that Soldier Gur negotiated with the Hunters, the Mur Commonwealth already ceded all rights over Earth to the Rii Galaxysweeper *Chi'tok*. There's nothing more for the Homeworld Council to do about us."

Donovan tried to swallow the dryness in his throat, then he sat up fully, and too quickly. "Zun Werth, who were—*what* were those people, those creatures that were guarding the communications center and the Chief Hunter? In the briefing you gave us, you never warned us to expect anything like that. Are they . . . *human*?"

Soldier Werth's fins leveled in a scowl. "I didn't warn you because until today I didn't know they existed. The Rii are raiders; it's common for them to steal biological resources. They alter and engineer life forms to serve their purposes. They've created several augmented servant species, which differ by Galaxysweeper, but this is the first augmented form I've seen that bears resemblance to humans."

Donovan fought a shudder. "How's that possible?"

"At some point in the past, the Rii must have managed to obtain human genetic material. It might have been from a stolen Mur ship with humans-in-erze on board, or a hijacked science vessel with samples from Earth. It's even possible that some Hunters scouted this planet hundreds or thousands of years ago and took some specimens of interest with them. I suspect those fabricated creatures you saw are prototypes, brought here in the spore vessels for testing. They are no doubt distantly related to the human species, but they exist nowhere else except in service to the Rii."

"But why would the Rii make them?"

"Humans are the most successful native species on this planet. When the Rii turned their attention to Earth more recently, they must've consulted their available biological stores and designed something they knew would survive well here, that would be useful to them during the period of occupation they expected to enjoy."

Donovan fell silent. He searched within himself; in the aftermath of the battle he felt no great sense of triumph or joy, only deeply weary relief, and a hollow, nagging dread that wasn't sharp or specific enough to put into words, but that clung like a film over the weave of his armor.

"So have you decided yet, zun?" he asked. "What you'll do with me?"

Soldier Werth did not answer at first. Then, with a strain in his strumming voice, he said, "The early colonists took a great but visionary risk. It succeeded beyond their expectations. On no other planet that I know of has a second species become so integrated into the erze."

Werth's next words fell hard. "You placed me in a terrible position, Donovan. You, and your commander, and your fellow soldiers-in-erze."

Donovan said nothing. The terrible position was mutual.

"We've gone down a strange and dangerous path. Few colonies in the Commonwealth have ever rebelled against the homeworld. Fewer have ever stood alone against the Rii. I have no regrets about betraying the Hunters, nor sending away Gur and those arrogant homeworlders, but I did far worse than that. Today I enabled and sent humans to kill zhree." Werth's fins fell motionless for a long beat before moving with great heaviness. "History, I fear, will judge me harshly."

Soldier Werth walked away, the solemn gaze of two of his yellow eyes lingering behind. "Rest a little longer, Donovan. We are at war, and I need every good soldier I have."

— — —

The Joint Planetary Defense Agreement was signed six weeks later between the erze zun of the former Mur colonists, human government leaders, and key representatives of Sapience. Commander Tate traveled to Perth to attend as a senior representative of the

Global Security and Pacification Forces, and to his surprise, Donovan was granted a special invitation to accompany her to witness the historic event, which was already being referred to unofficially as the Second Accord.

"I didn't have anything to do with it. You can thank the Prime Liaison for the invite," Tate told him on the long flight over. Grudgingly, "It's the least you deserve."

Donovan hadn't been sure he wanted to attend. He'd caught the highlights of everything thus far from the news: all over the world, zhree and human leaders were scrambling to deal with the damage to Rounds and human cities, adjusting to the idea of an Earth no longer protected by the Commonwealth, and coming together to strike new bargains. In West America, three months after the first failed negotiations in Round Three, Prime Liaison DeGarmo announced that the government had reached an agreement with the Human Action Party and its paramilitary affiliates in Sapience to cease hostilities and work together for the defense of the country and humankind.

Within SecPac, the news caused some stir of derision and skepticism, but there was less surprise than might be expected toward something that would've been unthinkable merely a year ago. "They had to do it," Cass concluded.

Jet agreed. "Sapience has always promised people freedom if they kicked the colonists off Earth and overthrew the government. They can't promise that anymore. They have to shift gears to maintain support from people, but it's not as if they've changed their views about the zhree or exos. It's just survival politics."

The gathering in Perth would be the first global attempt to codify the new rules of the world. It was probably the most historic event

Donovan would see in his lifetime. Truth be told, he'd rather watch it on the screen at home with Jet and Cass. The thought of getting on a plane and being separated from his erze mates again, even for a few days, caused Donovan's chest to tighten with anxiety that made it hard to breathe. A lot of horrible things could happen without warning in a short time. He had a feeling the visceral knowledge of that fact would continue waking him at night for some time to come.

But when the day came, he went. It was where both of his parents would surely be if they'd still been alive, and it seemed important that he honor them in that small way.

He shifted in the airplane seat, trying to stretch his stiff back. "What will happen to Dr. Nakada?" he asked.

Commander Tate turned away from the window, swirling the ice in her glass. "He's still recovering in the hospital, but he'll be moved to a medium-security facility next week. We're arranging to convert some space into a dedicated lab so he can begin the work he's agreed to as a condition of his sentence. Starting with developing defenses against the weapons he made for Sapience."

Donovan thought about the vial of experimental nerve agent in Javid's possession. "And what about Warde?" he asked.

Tate's expression soured. "Sadly, the execution he deserves won't happen for a while, not with the political situation as it is right now. The Prime Liaison doesn't want to risk antagonizing the True Sapience faction just when things are starting to settle down." Tate turned back to the window, staring out at the clouds, her wiry hair a metallic silver in the sunlight, a preoccupied expression on her lined face.

"Ma'am?" Donovan said tentatively.

Tate turned back from the window. "What is it, Reyes?"

"You told me before that you didn't think these sorts of talks would ever succeed. That we couldn't reach a common under-standing between humans on Earth." How long ago that conversation seemed now. "Do you still believe that?"

Tate regarded him with eyes that had aged even beyond her many years. "Common ground isn't found through talk. It's what people realize they're standing on together when it starts to give way under them." One of Tate's hands curled around the armrest, the lump of a vein visible under the pattern of stripes. "That's what you did that day, Reyes. You shook the Earth."

If he had, few people seemed to know about it. Commander Tate and Jet had been the only human witnesses, and they weren't spreading the word, which was for the best. Donovan didn't want or need any more notoriety. The news that he'd captured Kevin Warde was crazy enough.

As for the rest of it: The general story was that after the soldiers-in-erze made a united show of refusing evacuation, other humans-in-erze around the world began to follow suit. Given the emergency situation on Earth, the Mur colonists were forced to reconsider their plans to withdraw military forces. Facing severe pressure for assistance from human governments and growing ten-sion with Kreet, the zhree zun broke from the Mur Commonwealth and sent a joint force of Soldiers and exos to expel the remaining Rii from where they were holding out under seige in the Rounds, thus precipitating the beginning of Earth's new era of independence.

It was as complete and true a version as it needed to be, the sort of narrative that would make it into the history books. And to be honest, Donovan liked it as well as any other. His father would've approved.

— — —

Perth was the capital of Australasia and the nearest major human city to Round One, which was located three hundred miles inland to the northeast. Round One had repelled the initial attack by the Rii but had been reoccupied as a condition of Gur's agreement with the Chief Hunter. A few days later, Soldiers and exos had fought and triumphed again as part of the coordinated counter-attack against the invaders. The cost in casualties for all this had been terrible: nearly a thousand Soldiers, soldiers-in-erze, and civilian zhree and humans of various erze had been killed in Round One in one week. Roughly fifteen hundred people in Perth itself had died in the initial Rii missile attack. It was a sad and symbolic honor for all the leaders of the world to be congregating here, near the first established Round. For Donovan, it was strange and sobering to be reminded that others had suffered losses as great as his. Other exos had lost erze mates. Other people had lost family. Other soldiers had lost friends.

The final presentation and ratifying of the agreement took place in a large convention center auditorium. There was not much to do but sit and watch and clap. Donovan sat in a section of the theater with other SecPac representatives from other countries. They were all grim senior soldiers-in-erze who conversed with one another in low, serious voices. Donovan saw Commander Tate standing with Commander Li, engrossed in a long, intense discussion. The President of West America, as well as Prime Liaison DeGarmo, mingled among world leaders at the front of the vast room. Earlier, Donovan had spotted Saul in the hallway, wearing better clothes but still looking like a grizzled revolutionary general as he moved around with a contingent of suspicious-looking followers and bodyguards, greeting people that Donovan suspected had SecPac files to rival Saul's own.

Strangest of all, though, were all the zhree in the building—more than he'd ever seen in one place outside of the Round. The many ring-patterned hulls of the Administrators blended together in Donovan's eye so that he couldn't even pick out Administrator Seir until he spotted Soldier Wylt's pale eyes and Soldier Wiv's distinctively notched fins hovering nearby. Translation machines were everywhere, burbling conversations from Mur into a dozen different human languages and vice versa and among the human languages themselves. Over a hundred years ago, the signatories of the Accord of Peace and Governance had hoped that Earth could become a peaceful home planet for both species. Looking around today, seeing humans of all races and nationalities and zhree of all erze, Donovan could almost believe it. Almost.

It was near the end of the day when he saw her. Sitting in a crowd always made Donovan restless and nervous, so he'd slipped out of the auditorium to go to the bathroom and stretch his legs. On his way back, he passed one of the many entrances propped open onto the aisle, and there she was. Standing just outside the door, arms crossed, leaning one shoulder against the wall. Everyone around her was in a suit, but she was in jeans, boots, and a loose gray shirt that draped open partway down her back. Donovan smiled; the dyed blond of her untidy hair was fading, growing out darker at the roots.

For a whole minute, he stood and looked and wondered whether to call out to her, and then, as if sensing him, she turned around. Her expression didn't change at first. She straightened away from the wall and walked toward him, her steps slowly squeezing the space between them until, like a plastic bubble pressed between hands, it popped. Anya ran the rest of the way and Donovan caught her, and they were hugging each other so tightly they could barely breathe.

When they came apart, neither of them spoke at first. There didn't seem to be any right way to begin a conversation. Anya said, "Let's go outside. Get away from here for a while."

They walked along the road to a green park by the river. It was springtime in this part of the world and the air was pleasantly warm, the sky a uniform pale blue marred only by the distant vapor trails of zhree fighter craft and the haze that lingered over the parts of the city skyline destroyed in the Rii bombardment.

Anya scoffed, "Look at us. Big-time international diplomats."

"We've come a long way, that's for sure," Donovan admitted.

Anya gazed out across the park to the glint of water. "This is supposed to be a nice city. It's kind of dirty, if you ask me. But that might just be from all the bombs and fires and stuff." She kicked at a chunk of rubble. "Still, this is the first time I've been out of West America. I wish I could stay longer."

"Saul's leaving right afterward, then?" Historic agreements or no, Donovan imagined that Saul Strong Winter would never feel comfortable with anything less than a hundred miles between him and the government, SecPac, and any shrooms. "Where will you go, after this?"

"I don't know yet." Anya chewed her bottom lip. "Maybe Colorado or Arizona. Somewhere the armies are gathering and organizing. There are lots of refugees fleeing from the bombed cities. I could help out there."

Donovan nodded. "You're good at that. Helping people, that is."

"I'm sure Saul will want me to keep up the communications support too. It's going to be even more important from now on."

It wasn't yet clear what would actually happen on the ground, but Sapience, as part of its agreement to cease hostilities against the government and the zhree colonists, had committed its immediate attention to civilian aid and organizing defense plans in case of further attacks on Earth. In exchange, thousands of moderate- and low-risk Sapience prisoners would be released from SecPac's detention facilities and penal camps, and hundreds of thousands of names removed from SecPac's target lists. Commander Tate wouldn't like it one bit, but the move was as much in SecPac's interests as Sapience's. They had other problems to focus on.

True Sapience had already denounced the agreement as a betrayal of their principles and had made public promises to continue to wage war on all zhree and exos. According to them, the Rii were a fabrication, and the bombing of the cities and supposed attacks on the Towers were a conspiracy designed and executed by the Mur colonists and the puppet human government.

"How about you?" Anya stopped and crouched at the water's edge. She picked up a stick, idly cracking it into pieces. "What will you be doing?"

"Training. Preparing. We don't know if, or when, the Rii will be back." Or if Kreet might change its mind and choose to send warships against the rebellious colonists after all. At that very moment, thousands of Nurses were still at work, removing the exocel inhibition reflex in exo soldiers-in-erze all over the world. Werth was building an army of Hardened humans or, more accurately, repurposing the one he already had. SecPac officers who'd been trained to patrol cities and combat human terrorists would now also be taught how to fight alongside Soldiers.

Meanwhile, Soldier Werth's ambitous plan to accelerate the rates of human Hardening would proceed. If Earth survived as an independent planet, it would need more exos than ever to form a planetary defense force, to work in space, to travel and trade with other planets. However, there were restrictions: Conscripted Hardening could not occur without an amendment to the Second Accord, and future exos would never again be Hardened with the neural fail-safe. Human scientists and doctors would be allowed to observe and participate in the process and gradually trained in how to perform it. In the long run, humans would gain access to exocel technology, light-plus travel, and fission energy.

There was even more to the agreement than that—Donovan had only paid close attention to the parts that most affected him and his fellow stripes. The shift in Earth's future felt too big to wrap one's head around, even for someone who'd grown up as the son of a state leader.

Anya tossed the remnants of the stick into the water and stood up. She tilted her chin up to look Donovan in the face. "You did change my mind, you know." A storm seemed to swirl behind the greenish flecks in her eyes. "On the rooftop, you said you took me through the Round hoping I'd see more of who you are and still like you. But I think you showed me who you are from the start. Even when I was trying *not* to like you, I still saw it." Her subdued voice carried something that it took Donovan a moment to place: respect. "Everything you've done—sneaking information out to the world, saving the doctor, fighting the Rii—was because of who and what you are. Armor and markings included." Anya stepped close and wrapped her arms around his waist, laying her head against his chest. "I never thought I'd say this," she whispered, "but I'm glad you're an exo."

Donovan closed his eyes and kissed her brow. "I couldn't have done it without you. You're the most out-of-erze thing that ever happened to me, and I . . . I'm glad for it." He held her in his arms for a long minute, savoring the shape and warmth of her against his body, trying to draw some of her fearlessness and strength into himself, to hold in reserve for all that might be to come. He did not want to ruin the moment with more words, by asking her for anything, or by promising anything himself. As much as he felt that surely by now he must be numbed to the pain of loss, he knew that wasn't true.

Hand in hand, they walked back toward the convention center. The historic gathering was over; people were spilling out of the building as journalists crowded up the steps to meet them. Human and zhree figures were lingering in conversation or being escorted toward waiting skimmercars.

A familiar bulky figure approached. "We're out of here," Saul said to Anya gruffly. "After I have a smoke." His weighty gaze traveled from Anya to Donovan. "I'd like a word with you, stripe." The Sapience commander turned and walked down the street, jamming a cigarette between his lips.

Donovan slipped his hand from Anya's and took long strides to catch up. Saul reached into the inside breast pocket of his brown jacket and drew out a badly wrinkled notebook.

Donovan recognized it at once. It had belonged to his mother, and he had given it to Saul a year ago. Saul held it out to him.

"Take it back. After today, I don't want to be reminded of what she'd think of me if she were still alive."

"And what would that be?"

Saul made a gravelly noise in his throat, his thick lips twisting. "I betrayed the cause. I laid down arms and made peace with the government that killed her and the shrooms that took her son from her." Saul's rough face shifted like rock in a slow landslide. "I did what had to be done. And she would've hated me for it."

Donovan looked at the notebook Saul was offering him. It was the only remaining memento of his mother and it had been hard for him to give it up. His hand twitched at his side. Then he shook his head. "I'm an exo and a soldier-in-erze and still she never hated me," Donovan said. "You didn't betray the cause. The cause changed. For all of us."

Saul studied Donovan for a long moment, his unlit cigarette hanging from the corner of a mouth that trembled slightly before firming with resignation and grudging respect. Slowly, almost reluctantly, the Sapience commander stowed the notebook back in his pocket. "All my life I've fought your kind and everything you stand for," he said.

"And now you need us. And we need you."

"Today is a truce," Saul said. "Not a solution. Not an end."

"I don't suppose so," Donovan agreed.

Saul grunted. He walked away, and Anya joined him and walked alongside. Donovan watched them go. Only when they were lost from sight in the crowd did he realize that neither of them had spoken the name of Kevin Warde, and he let a grim bit of satisfaction settle on his face.

"Reyes? Donovan Reyes, is that you?"

Donovan turned to see a young woman in a SecPac uniform. Her black hair was pulled back in a clasp, and telltale patches of healing panotin burns marred her otherwise pretty face. "Maddison?"

"As the only member of 198 Alpha from Round One, I've been telling you blokes to come visit for years, and this is finally what it takes?" She poked him in the chest, then gave him a fierce hug. "It's good to see you, mate. You got time to grab a bevvy and call up the rest of the cadre?"

"Yeah," Donovan said, breaking out in a true smile. "That sounds great."

— — —

When he returned to Round Three, Donovan searched for his partner and found Jet at the erze cemetery. The memorial site on the SecPac campus lay tucked away on a low, sparsely treed hill that was normally quiet save for the groups of trainees that jogged past on the running trail at regular drill times. These days, there was no shortage of visitors leaving flowers and cards that brightened the beige of the frost-burned yellow grass and the slate gray of the new plaques honoring all the SecPac officers slain in the Rii invasion and the retaking of the Towers.

Jet was sitting on the cold ground in front of Vic's name, his arms resting on his knees, his unmoving gaze a million miles away. He didn't turn when Donovan walked up and sat down beside him, but slowly his focus seemed to draw in and his shoulders relaxed a little. At last he asked, "So how was it?"

"It was the most significant political event in a hundred years," Donovan said. "Historians like your dad will discuss it for ages."

"In other words, boring."

"You didn't miss a thing." After a minute, "It was good to see Madds, though."

Jet nodded. More quietly, "Did you see her too? Anya?" It was the first time he'd ever used her name.

"Yeah. Only for a few minutes. Neither of us could stay long." Donovan closed his eyes. A few brief, warm moments—even that was something Jet would never be able to share with Vic again.

His erze mate let out a long breath. "After the hard time I gave you, it's tough for me to admit that you were right to trust her. You saw past things like armor and markings." Jet's hands fisted in the grass and his voice fell. "I can't help thinking that I never really understood Vic the way I should've. That I didn't try hard enough . . . and now I'll never get the chance."

Donovan put a hand on the back of his friend's neck. "She loved you," he said. "I think you know that."

"Here we are." Cass came up on Donovan's other side and crouched down next to him, a little gingerly, as her right arm was back in a sling. She'd told them that she had metal pins and rods stabilizing the bones now, making her, in her own words, "the first woman to be both an exo *and* a cyborg."

A dark-haired boy of about fourteen came up next to Cass and stood looking at the memorial plaques with them. He held a folded piece of sketch-pad paper, slightly bent around the edges from being carried in his back pocket. The boy unfolded the paper and looked at it with sudden trepidation, as if discovering that it was more meager than he'd feared. Then, seeming to resolve himself, he bent and carefully placed the paper on the plaque below the name of Leonides Hsu and held it in place with two rocks. He stepped back, straightened, and dropped his armor sharply, the way SecPac trainees were taught.

"Jet, D, this is Aristides," Cass said.

The teen nodded a little shyly at the older exos. "It's not very good," he said, looking apologetically at the offering he'd left on his brother's grave marker: a passable sketch of a warrior angel with eagle wings unfurled and an E201 pulse rifle in his hands.

Cass put her good arm around Ari's shoulders. "He would've loved it."

The four erze mates remained for some time in consoling, comfortable silence. The handfuls of dry yellow grass that Donovan and Jet had pulled from in front of their feet were lifted and scattered by the stiff autumn wind that rose and snapped the cemetery's flags. The flag of West America and the seal of the Global Security and Pacification Forces flew at half mast. The third and central flagpole was empty; the icons of the Mur Erzen Commonwealth had been taken down. They would be replaced by something new, some as-yet-unknown symbol of an independent Earth, threatened, friendless, and alone in the galaxy. When Donovan looked past the flagpoles, down the hill toward the road, he realized that while he'd been away, wreathes and doves had gone up in windows and on street posts throughout the Round. It was, inconceivably, almost Peace Day again.

He hoped there would be more.

ACKNOWLEDGMENTS

In February of 2016, I attended the Rainforest Writers Retreat, where over the course of four days, I wrote the outline and first three chapters of the sequel to *Exo*. A year later, having written two full drafts of *Cross Fire* already, I returned to Rainforest in a state of near panic over my manuscript, and, in that magical writing place, I broke the back on a hefty round of revision and shaped this story into its largely final form. I'm consequently grateful to organizer Patrick Swenson and my fellow retreat attendees for the special creative space that helped me so immensely with this book.

It turns out that writing a sequel is more difficult than one would initially suspect. Fortunately for readers, my editor, Jody Corbett, is not one to settle for anything less than the maximum extent of my abilities. Thank you, Jody, for so wholeheartedly partnering with me to continue Donovan's story and for constantly pushing me to make this book as strong as it could be.

I'm grateful to the entire team at Scholastic: Rachel Gluckstern for paying attention to every production detail; Bonnie Cutler for working her copyediting magic; Lizette Serrano and Emily Heddleson for championing my books with librarians; Rachel Feld, Mindy Stockfield, and Isa Caban in marketing; and Alan Smagler,

Elizabeth Whiting, Alexis Lunsford, Sue Flynn, Jackie Rubin, Jody Stigliano, Chris Satterlund, Nikki Mutch, and the rest of the team for the fantastic sales energy. Thank you to Phil Falco for designing another stunning cover. My thanks to Scholastic Canada for enthusiastically supporting *Exo* north of the border.

Jim McCarthy keeps selling my books and guiding my writing career, proving time and again that there's simply no substitute for a kick-ass agent. Four books in four years together—and hopefully many more to come. Thanks, Jim.

Thank you to S. J. Kincaid, Kass Morgan, and Sabaa Tahir for saying such nice things about *Exo*.

Dr. Raymund Yong patiently answered all my questions about neurosurgery, and David Two Hawks deserves belated thanks for giving me Saul's name. While I have yet to write a book that takes full advantage of the wealth of knowledge I gained at the Launch Pad Astronomy Workshop, I was inspired while I was there to set part of this book in Laramie, Wyoming.

I do not often enough express appreciation for the understanding and support of my family, especially my husband and first reader, Nathan, and our two children, who are proud to have an author mom even though it means she spends an awful lot of time in front of the computer.

To the YA librarians and teachers who've emailed me; book-talked my novels to students; invited me to speak at schools, conferences, or festivals; nominated my books for awards; gotten me on state reading lists; and placed my books in the hands of teens: thank you endlessly for the vital work that you do in creating the next generation of curious and thoughtful readers.

Finally and always, to my readers: thank you for being here.